GRAVE DOUBTS

ALSO BY ELIZABETH CORLEY

Requiem Mass

Fatal Legacy

GRAVE DOUBTS

ELIZABETH CORLEY

MINOTAUR BOOKS
A THOMAS DUNNE BOOK
NEW YORK

This is a work of fiction. All of the characters, organizations, and events portrayed in this novel are either products of the author's imagination or are used fictitiously.

A THOMAS DUNNE BOOK FOR MINOTAUR BOOKS.
An imprint of St. Martin's Publishing Group.

GRAVE DOUBTS. Copyright © 2006 by Elizabeth Corley. All rights reserved. Printed in the United States of America. For information, address St. Martin's Press, 175 Fifth Avenue, New York, N.Y. 10010.

www.thomasdunnebooks.com
www.minotaurbooks.com

Design by Omar Chapa

Library of Congress Cataloging-in-Publication Data

Corley, Elizabeth.
Grave doubts : a DCI Andrew Fenwick mystery / Elizabeth Corley.
p. cm. — (; 3)
ISBN 978-1-250-02486-2 (hardcover)
ISBN 978-1-250-02485-5 (e-book)
1. Murder—Investigation—Fiction. 2. Police—Fiction. 3. Serial murderers—Fiction. I. Title.
PR6053.O713G83 2014
823'.914—dc23

2014009404

Minotaur books may be purchased for educational, business, or promotional use. For information on bulk purchases, please contact Macmillan Corporate and Premium Sales Department at 1-800-221-7945 extension 5442 or write specialmarkets@macmillan.com.

First published in Great Britain in 2006 by Allison & Busby Limited

First U.S. Edition: July 2014

10 9 8 7 6 5 4 3 2 1

For Kathleen and Robert. With love.

FEBRUARY

He watched the woman from his hiding place deep in the bushes. It would be dark soon and the remaining occupants of the park would leave. The chill evening and threat of rain had driven most away already but he knew that she would wait because she had an appointment, with him.

It pleased him that he had this power over her. The first time he'd suggested that they meet she'd been eager. She had lingered in the rain for nearly an hour while he waited in the warmth of his car. When she finally gave up he'd followed her home, delighting in the glimpse of her long calves as they flashed from the confines of her winter coat. He should have taken her soon afterward, that had been the dare. Instead he'd hesitated. Hours of delay had turned into days, days into a week. He let opportunities pass, happy enough with his fantasies and the pleasure of anonymous proximity. He had brushed by her in the street, smelt her perfume and pondered over her solitary, idle existence. She never went to work.

After a week his points were forfeit. He should have abandoned her and moved on to someone else. Instead he'd asked her out for a second time, something he had never done before but she was special. He knew that she'd be better than all the rest, worth the danger, and the punishment he was risking because of his disobedience. It was forbidden to go back for the same woman twice, completely against the rules.

He glanced at his watch, pulling down the cuff of new leather gloves to study its luminous dial. Not long now. Slowly color drained from the sky, leaving it ashy and featureless, like the underbelly of a great bird of prey that was circling the earth, waiting. The woman was pacing now, stamping her feet to keep warm in the chill winter evening. He studied her clothes: the long black coat concealed her figure but he knew what she looked like. With the aid of binoculars he had penetrated the privacy of her bedroom. Stupid woman, to imagine that because she lived on the top floor it was all right to leave her curtains askew. He'd seen glimpses of pale skin, the pink of a nipple and once perhaps the dark suspicion of pubic hair. In her rubbish he'd found discarded underwear and kept it, breaking another rule. *"No traces."* If his souvenir were discovered he would be in serious trouble.

He was only a pupil, learning from a master who was uncompromising about the rules of the game he had invented. Normally he obeyed them but with her the temptation had been too strong. Otherwise he was an adept pupil, becoming more skilled every time. This one would be his best, he was certain. Perhaps tonight he might . . . even . . . kill her.

Just thinking the words made him shake. He knew that it was what was expected of him and that, until he had proved himself, there would be secrets unshared. He wanted those secrets badly. Once he had them he would truly belong.

The young man shuddered in anticipatory pleasure. His breathing grew faster, the excitement bringing an uncontrollable flutter to his throat. He imagined closing his hands about her neck and heat spread through him.

"No!" It was a hiss through clenched teeth. He despised his lack of self-control. It was always over too quickly, not like . . .

He stopped the thought. Once he began making comparisons his confidence would evaporate, like before.

At last. The courting couple on the bench at the far side of the rose garden stood up to go, glancing at the solitary woman as they passed. She was worth a second look. Pale, perfect skin, full lips that would burst in his mouth like ripe fruit as he bit into them, and hair so black it would bury his darkest thoughts.

He started to flex, stretching to ease his muscles so that he would be fast and strong. Streetlights came on beyond the stone wall, spilling deeper shadows in pools across the gardens and into the park. His hiding place in the leaves grew darker. When she finally gave up she would have to walk along the flagstones toward him and his ready hands. He stepped a few inches closer to the path and waited.

She looked at her watch again. He wasn't coming. Relief and disappointment battled within her and relief won. Accepting this blind date had not been her idea. Others had put her up to it and she'd fallen victim to their persuasion. When he stood her up the previous week she'd hoped that it would mark the end of her being the butt of other people's bright ideas. Then he had emailed her again with a new time and place and here she was, feeling a fool.

An easterly wind whipped across the grass, throwing scraps of dead rose petals against her legs. She'd waited long enough. It was time to admit that he wasn't coming and go home. As she turned to retrace her steps the young woman looked around her, hoping to find others still in the park, but she was alone. She pulled her thick woolen coat tighter and wrapped her arms across her chest against the encroaching night. Her shadow walked before her along the flags, a comforting companion that promised lights and safety in the darkening night. It disappeared as she turned onto a path where tall bushes flanked a tunnel through shrubbery.

Some vandal had smashed the bulbs in the ornamental lamps that were supposed to light her way. Her boots crunched on newly broken glass as she walked, more quickly now. The wind was tormenting the shrubs that enclosed her, mimicking the rustle of predators in the night. Her shoulder blades twitched and she started a funny half-trot, eager to reach the safety of her car.

He was on her without warning. A dark shape leaping out and covering her mouth before she could scream. They went down together, his weight on top of her driving the air from her lungs and with it any ability to cry for help. The back of her head struck the ground and she blacked out for a second. When she forced her eyes open his masked face was inches from hers, a black leather horror that showed only his eyes and mouth. He was biting at her shoulders that were somehow bare. Her coat had been ripped open and the neck of her jumper torn.

"No!" She yelled as loud as she could, disappointed that the sound was so pathetic. "Get off me, you bastard!"

She aimed a punch at his head but he slapped her hand away and brought up a knife from nowhere. *He wasn't meant to have a knife, no one had warned her about that.*

"Shut up, bitch. Stay quiet and you might live."

She tried to concentrate on his voice, to memorize the accent and cadence so that she would make a good witness, but fear dominated her mind, making it hard to concentrate.

"Get off!" she cried out again, appalled at the tears on her face. When his hands went for her bra she fought like a wild thing, terrified of what he would do when he found what was hidden beneath. She managed to scratch his face near the eye and felt skin beneath her nails. DNA, but that would be a hollow victory if they scraped it from her corpse.

He gave up on her breasts and ripped open her jeans, using the knife to slice through the fabric in his hurry. Somehow his trousers were already undone and he rubbed himself against her. At the touch of his flesh she screamed loudly, a sound of terror, despite the threat of the knife at her throat. Surely someone must come soon. Her thighs were locked tight against his groping fingers and the beating of his fist. He jabbed the blade against her neck.

"Stop fighting me or you die. Open your legs!"

She ignored him, clamping her knees together as he punched her thighs. The pounding grew harder and seemed to radiate up from the stones beneath her. Then there were other noises, shouts, bright lights and his weight was lifted away. She kept on shouting, unable to comprehend that the threat was over.

Her shaking body was wrapped in a plastic sheet and bags were placed over her fingers routinely, as if she were already dead. Hands reached for her out of the lights.

"No." She shook them away. People stood back.

"Was there any penetration, Nightingale?"

"What?" She stared at the familiar face in disbelief.

"Was there any penetration? It's just that if there was we'll need a urine sample. It's routine procedure, Sergeant."

She heard a voice mutter *"for God's sake,"* as she brought up her fist in a swing that connected with a satisfying crack on the side of Detective Inspector Blite's jaw.

"You bastard!"

Somewhere, somebody laughed.

"Wayne Griffiths you are under arrest . . ."

The words reached him from across the grass as he watched them take his friend away. He'd been in hiding for hours, long before Wayne and the woman arrived. His plan had been simple: to observe and critique Wayne's latest efforts to graduate into his world. But now the boy was gone and there was nothing he could do to save him. He was angry and confused. The capture had reversed his sense of world order. How had this happened? How had the police traced Wayne? That woman, who was she? They'd called her "Sergeant"—was she police? How could the boy have been so stupid?

He'd succumbed to the oldest trick in the book, to grow so fixated on a woman that he'd fallen into her trap. Admittedly she was almost perfect but part of the testing was to build up immunity to their enchantments and his pupil had disappointed him. If it hadn't been for her . . . he stopped the thought. There wasn't time for regrets.

He needed to reach the flat and clean up before the police found out the address. If he removed all traces there was still a chance that the evidence would be too weak to gain a conviction. There were ways to destabilize even a strong case, particularly if it depended on a sting by the police. Provided there was no other evidence a good defense should be able to plant sufficient seeds of doubt in a jury's mind.

He had the money and contacts to arrange the best legal advice available. It would be a show of support, not that he had any concerns about his partner's loyalty; it was absolute. But he wouldn't seek bail. Some punishment was appropriate for such stupidity and a long wait in prison might teach the boy a much-needed lesson.

Meanwhile he would disappear. He'd have to go away until the trial. If and when the prosecution collapsed, they could be reunited and resume elsewhere.

Satisfied that he was once more in control, the watcher sprinted away across the grass and disappeared into the night.

ONE YEAR LATER

"Do you want to go alone? I think I should go with you, but . . ." He looked away, ashamed of his fear of what lay inside.

"No, I'll do it myself. Wait here though, for when I come out."

She pushed open a heavy iron door painted an industrial red and walked past signs in a foreign language that meant nothing to her. An unpleasant chemical smell penetrated her clenched mouth and filled her throat with an acid-sweetness that made her want to retch. The air was cold, the corridor empty. A bare window at the far end let in harsh light that sent her shadow fleeing back toward the door.

A sign bearing the stylized outline of a chapel hung from steel chains in the middle of the ceiling with a black arrow pointing to a turning on her right. She followed its mute instruction and turned, losing the sunlight from the end window. Wall lights with bare bulbs now lit the way.

Another solid door stood closed ahead of her, the little chapel sign stuck to it on laminated plastic, peeling at one corner. She tried the handle, the door was locked. There were no signs of life but then she heard the sound of fingers dancing lightly on keys and she followed them to an office door. Tapping lightly to announce her arrival, she pushed it open.

"Si?" A heavy-lidded, dark-eyed girl looked up at her, clearly annoyed at the interruption.

"Excuse me, I'm English. Louise Nightingale. I'm here to see my parents."

At the mention of her name the girl's eyes softened and she stood up.

"Scusi."

She left her standing alone in the office, staring out over a metal desk to the clear sky beyond. That's why her parents had come here after all, in search of late winter sunshine. She turned away, feeling sick again.

A man came into the room wearing an immaculately tailored black suit, red tie and sunglasses.

"Miss Nightingale, we expected you yesterday. If you would come this way."

The man walked back to the chapel door, swinging a key on a slender silver chain like a rosary.

"They are in here. I am so sorry. Perhaps you would like to be alone?"

"Yes please."

She pushed the door open; it was heavy and seemingly resentful at the intrusion. A thick leather curtain hung as a second barrier behind it. Inside the air was even colder, the light dim. There was a smell of flowers and incense and she remembered belatedly that she was in a Catholic country. A crucifix, complete with the agony of Christ in painted plaster on wood, hung on the crimson far wall. Two coffins lay open before it. As she walked toward them she was overpowered by the smell from a vase of lilies. In the cool dark they seemed eternal, perfect ivory petals clutching at the sterile, recycled air.

The faint hum of air-conditioning was the only sound to break the silence. Behind her the door clicked shut and for a moment she fought an irrational impulse to rush back and beat against it and her imagined entombment. Instead, ever the controlled and collected Englishwoman, she walked forward and placed her hand on the oak of her mother's coffin.

Someone had clothed her in her best summer dress. A pure white sheet covered her body to her breast. Her hands were folded beneath it and she felt cheated of one last look at those long fingers and the narrow pink nails that had always been so clean.

A memory came back to her of the warning delivered by the British police on behalf of their Italian colleagues: *"They were both severely injured. Your father died at the scene, your mother two hours later."*

She wondered what carnage lay beneath the cotton shroud and swallowed hard to prepare herself for the sight of her mother's face.

It was beautiful. She always had been. Miraculously the wreck had left her face intact. Even more incredible, the undertaker had resisted the temptation to paint her in colors she would never have worn in life.

Her light brown hair, no sign of gray nor need for unnatural colorings, fell soft and straight around her face. The small worry lines and the mark of a frown she'd always had when she concentrated had disappeared from her brow, leaving her looking younger than she could remember. The cruel irony of seeing her so youthful in death made her choke.

Only her mother's lips showed death. Held closed tight despite redundant muscles, they were pale, almost blue. The mortician should have colored those, she thought, but perhaps he'd wanted the naturalness of her beauty untouched in the grave.

She bent and kissed her mother's forehead, both her eyes and lastly, delicately, her mouth in an unconscious sign of the cross. Then she stood and walked to her father.

The winding sheet was wrapped to his chin, impossible to tell what clothes he was wearing. His eyes were closed but she knew their color, the harebell blue of a clear summer sky. There would be no danger of her ever forgetting what they looked like as she had only to look in the mirror to see them again. Pure white bandages bound his head from chin to crown and across his forehead, bordering his eyes, nose and mouth in a tight frame. Even so, they could not hide all his scars. One ran from the very center of his bottom lip in a vivid diagonal into the lower bandages. Another, delicately stitched and almost camouflaged, stretched from beneath the outer corner of his left eyebrow, across and up into the only wisp of hair that showed against his right temple.

It was a Frankenstein scar and the sight of it made her giggle in shock and suppressed hysteria until she had to press her mouth shut with both hands. Then the sounds dropped to whimpers as she stood looking at the corpse that had been her father. There was so little to see she wondered why they had left the coffin open but she was glad they had.

She reached out a hand and stroked the top of his bandaged head.

"Oh Dad," she whispered, "what bloody rotten luck."

Then she kissed him lightly, as she had her mother, and turned to leave, struggling to retain her self-control. There was no point in delaying her departure. What more could she do?

As she reached the leather curtain she felt the skin between her shoulder blades crawl. For one crazy second, she was sure that they were both sitting up, looking at her, willing her to turn around, bidding her good-bye. The sensation was so strong that she looked back. The only eyes on her were those of Christ, agonized, pitying and alone. She turned around, opened the door and walked away.

Outside in the sunshine of the car park her brother was waiting for her on a bench by the car, gray-faced, pink-eyed.

"You were a long time." He sounded apologetic, ashamed that he had been unable to bring himself to view his parents' bodies.

"There were a lot of forms to sign but it's done now."

"I just couldn't come with you. I'm sorry."

"It's all right, really."

"Were they, I mean, the coffins . . . ?"

He had heard the police warning as well.

"They were open. They both looked very peaceful, at rest. There was no horror."

He hugged her tightly and she felt her throat harden. She pulled away, unable to look at him, afraid of the weight of tears she felt inside her. If she once let them out, she was sure they would flow forever, like a dam breaking.

"Come on, let's go. I could do with a drink."

Her brother kept his arm loosely around her shoulders and guided her toward the car. The sun burned into her dark suit as they walked slowly away from the mortuary, their shadows sharp on the gravel.

Until today, their deaths had not been a reality. She had coped with the formalities, buying the air tickets, arranging for her parents' belongings to be packed and sent to her hotel. Even the insurance forms required for repatriation of the bodies had been a welcome distraction. There was the funeral still to organize, and the headstones. Then . . .

Her brother shut the car door firmly and she fastened her seatbelt. The sound of it slamming to had a finality that echoed her thoughts. Her parents were dead. She was an orphan. Whatever unfinished business had lain between them would forever be unresolved. Future possibilities had closed in the split second that an offside wheel punctured, sending their car spinning through the air and into the picturesque ravine she was sure they would have been admiring moments before. Regrets had replaced reconciliations in her future, guilt would have to fill a void where explanations and forgiveness might, eventually, have rebuilt their relationship. All the potential of what they might have been to one another expired with their last breaths.

The sense of lost opportunity was overwhelming. For so assured and self-possessed a person, the reality of powerlessness was suffocating. She felt damaged, detached, out of control. Her world would never be the same again. For the first time in her life she stared into an empty future and felt fear.

PART ONE

NIGHTINGALE AND CLAIRE

A man is seldom ashamed of feeling that he cannot love a woman so well when he sees a certain greatness in her: nature having intended greatness for man.

—GEORGE ELIOT

In this new experience you may find temptations both in wine and women. You must entirely resist both temptations, and while treating all women with perfect courtesy, you should avoid any intimacy.

—KITCHENER OF KHARTOUM AND BROOME

CHAPTER ONE

"And?"

The barrister for the defense leaned forward, his nose as sharp as his tone, his wig knocked askew in the passion of his assault. Nightingale tried to form a sensible reply but her mind froze. All she could remember were her mother's remarks uttered in response to some school-age failure: *"Fancy forgetting your lines. Your brother would never have let us down like that."*

The memory robbed her of confidence and she felt sweat dampen her blouse beneath her suit. She breathed deeply and pressed her fingers hard against the wood of the witness stand. For thirty long minutes she had been cross-examined. Her evidence was crucial as the rest of the prosecution's case was circumstantial. She reminded herself that it was simply a matter of telling the truth, without letting this bully of a man confuse her.

"We're waiting, Sergeant."

"Yes." She coughed as if to clear her throat and focused her eyes on a point just above his right shoulder.

"Yes what."

Nightingale squared her shoulders, not aggressively she hoped, but politely, as if respectful of his role. She knew how successful witnesses behaved: firm, confident but without assertiveness. As a police officer, every member of the jury would see her profession first and then the person. Whatever prejudices they'd brought into the courtroom would affect their interpretation of everything she said. If they had been brought up to trust the police, then they would want to believe her. Should they consider the Force corrupt or prejudiced, anything she said would be viewed with skepticism. For all of them, she had to be Louise Nightingale, victim of a serious sexual assault by a man capable of rape.

"Could you repeat your question please?" Her voice was level again.

"I asked how you came to encounter the defendant and so far, despite repeated requests for elaboration, you have said only that you replied to an email that eventually led you to exchange electronic messages in a chat room."

"That is correct. We conversed electronically over the Internet about THE GAME."

"And how did you come to meet in this way?"

"I've already gone through this several times, sir."

"Then tell us again." He was angry with her. His defense was to prove entrapment by the police and if he could force Nightingale to give her testimony in the wrong way he might yet succeed.

Details of how THE GAME was played had already been covered in previous testimony by experts from the company that had created it. They'd made THE GAME sound harmless fun, a challenge of skill and quick-wittedness, but every rape victim had played it. Eventually, when other leads failed, the police investigated it as a potential link with the rapist.

"The senior investigating officer had recovered evidence that the victims of a series of rapes had all participated in an online contest called THE GAME. There are several sites and chat rooms dedicated to it."

"And you entered one of these chat rooms with the express purpose of luring the defendant into an exchange of messages which *you*, Sergeant, made increasingly incriminating and licentious!" Spittle flew from his tongue and he dabbed at his mouth.

"Objection!" The prosecution barrister was on his feet. Reginald Stringer QC was deadly in defense, with a reputation for having a particular dislike of police witnesses. The judge upheld the objection and Nightingale answered a rephrased question.

"To join certain chat rooms you have to be given the full web address and a password. I was invited into this particular chat room by the defendant."

Nightingale felt stronger now. The police had three computer experts who'd all confirmed the email trails between herself, the defendant and the chat room. As she described her electronic conversations the judge leaned forward to interrupt.

"I still find this use of terminology confusing and I imagine some of the jury might as well. We had an explanation of what a chat room was earlier but I wonder if you could refresh our memories."

"Certainly, My Lord. The chat room is an address on the web, sometimes public but in this case private, where one can engage in a digital conversation by typing and sending messages to other participants. Many people can join in; the message is identified by sender. It is like having a public conversation. One person talks, i.e. writes a message, and someone else responds while others watch, i.e. listen. Participants can decide to leave public chat rooms and engage in private conversations using personal addresses, rather like going into another room."

The judge was satisfied with the explanation and Stringer resumed his cross-examination.

"Tell us about the characters in THE GAME."

Nightingale pointed to the board version of THE GAME on the evidence table. It was one of a dozen spin-offs from the original computer game that had made the teenage inventors multi-millionaires. The film was due out in a year.

"There are six major player-characters and hundreds of minor ones. Sometimes combatants . . ."

"Combatants?"

"Players—they call themselves combatants."

"And which 'combatant' did you elect to become, Sergeant?"

"Artemesia 30,055."

"Artemesia is based on the Greek Goddess Artemis—the huntress—is she not? Very appropriate, given what you then set out to do."

"Objection."

"Sustained."

"And the number, what does that signify?"

"I was the thirty-thousand and fifty-fifth person to join THE GAME as Artemesia. That became my ID. She's one of the less popular characters as she has fewer obvious powers."

"So, *Artemesia 30,055*, how did you encounter the defendant?" Stringer smiled at his own attempt at a joke but it didn't fool Nightingale.

She would have preferred to be called by her name. If he focused on her game character he would inevitably highlight the huntress's dark side. She was one of the players who gained strength and new powers from tracking and killing demons and trolls. The two other female characters—a healer and a sorceress—succeeded by using less aggressive tactics. Nightingale had been an exceptional Artemesia, rising quickly through the league tables. It was the reason that the defendant had noticed her. He played the Demon King, the most challenging and dangerous role, but the one with highest points potential. She looked across at him now, a mousy-haired man in his twenties. Hardly someone who would stand out in a crowd.

"Sergeant, we're still waiting."

"I first encountered the defendant in the chat room. He called himself Demon King 666. He'd worked out how to bypass the automatic character numbering and chose the one he wanted—the devil's number. He was considered an expert on THE GAME, not just on his own role but others as well. The Demon King is the target for everybody else. If you capture or kill him, you automatically win THE GAME and maximum points. Demon King 666 had never lost. He was considered invincible."

From the corner of her eye she could see the defendant shift. He was staring at her and smiling. Nightingale shuddered. Despite his situation, he was enjoying the dialogue about THE GAME and his own superiority. It was one of the reasons she'd found it so simple to engage him in electronic conversation. The more successful she became in THE GAME, the more attention he'd paid her.

"Demon King 666 was very clever. Most of the time he gave out misinformation. After all, many of the people he was advising aspired to kill him in a future game. But he also wanted other Demon Kings to be killed so that his lead in the rankings would continue, so he gave out enough genuine clues to keep people asking for more."

"Including you?"

"No, I never asked him directly for advice. It can reveal too much about your own game. I scanned the public dialogue, adding the occasional comment. He sent me the first personal message, not the other way round."

"I find it hard to believe that you would rely on the possibility of him finding you."

"That's what happened. All the records prove it." She avoided a smirk. Of course he had come to her, she'd made herself irresistible by winning and remaining silent. It had just been a question of patience.

Nightingale looked at the clock on the opposite wall. She'd been on the stand nearly an hour now and regretted her sleepless night and lack of breakfast. The timing of the cross-examination was perfect for the defense. Outside, it was an unseasonably sunny day. The windows were set along the east wall, framed by columns of carved oak that matched the heavy courtroom furniture. English air-conditioning, unused to coping with real heat, was already starting to fail. London in April was not meant to be warm. The first fingers of eager yellow light were advancing across the blue carpet toward the witness stand. Defense and prosecution tables were set further back, in the relative comfort of the shadows but she would soon be in full sun.

"Might I have some water, please?"

The judge took pity on her and a plastic glass of tepid tap water was brought to her. She sipped it and continued with her never-ending testimony. Most of it she knew by heart, but she referred to her notebook anyway to remind the jury that she was a policewoman engaged in a serious investigation, not a computer-game hobbyist.

The sun reached her. There was a hiatus when the judge ordered the blinds to be tried again, but they remained broken, sitting stubbornly at half-mast.

"You may remove your jacket should you wish, Sergeant." He was solicitous, apologetic.

Even without a jacket, the hair at the back of her neck grew damp, then wet. From time to time, the air-conditioning groaned and seemed to redouble its effort to chill the room but its only effect was to make defense counsel and witness shout over the noise. Nightingale began to lose her voice.

In contrast Stringer blossomed in the heat. His face was pink and shiny but his rhetoric sparkled. It was as if he could sense her growing weakness. Bands of shadow inched across the floor, distracting Nightingale as the colonnade of mock-Grecian columns outside barred the sunlight. Her throat was sore and her head ached. Stringer was trying once again to imply that she was a ruthless huntress of innocent prey. She fought him with every calm, considered sentence or gentle shake of her head, her temper held under tight rein. Throughout her testimony she hoped that the judge and jury could see the truth, that she'd been the hunted. A drop of sweat dripped from her fringe, making her left eye smart.

"Come on, Sergeant. We haven't got all day to wait for your answer!"

"I'm . . . I'm sorry. Could you repeat the question?"

"What?" His voice echoed in her head, louder than the air-conditioning.

"I said," she swallowed, trying to find saliva, "please could you repeat the question?"

She put fingers to her cheek, surprised at the heat she found there. It disconcerted her and she rested her free hand on the hot varnish of the dock. Black spots formed in front of her eyes.

". . . said that you . . . stretching credibility if you think . . ." His voice oscillated in and out. She blinked again and tried to focus but the black dots grew larger. Somewhere, the judge was speaking.

". . . think the Sergeant may be a little faint."

"No, I'm fine," she said, and promptly pitched forward, to be caught by an anonymous pair of hands.

As the blood rushed to her head her vision cleared and she could hear again. She drank the water that was handed to her and stood up slowly, resting heavily against the witness stand.

"Are you all right, Sergeant?"

"Yes, it's just the heat. I'm so sorry. Could I have a few minutes to sit down somewhere cool?"

In the corridor outside, the prosecution hugged her briefly.

"I'm so embarrassed, I . . ."

"That was brilliant. The show of vulnerability, reminding the jury that you're a woman. Fantastic! It was an inspired move."

Nightingale sat down, stunned into silence. What sort of person did he think she was, to be able to behave like a machine in the course of duty at no matter what personal cost? The advice of her counselor had been that she should not be compelled to take the stand as a witness. The woman rightly suspected that the trauma of the attack was deep-seated and had little to do with the physical injuries themselves. It was the memory of her helplessness, his strength and the weight of his body on hers, his fingers groping, touching her. That was her horror. She felt defiled and unworthy, but she'd been prevailed upon to testify, to relive it all, and the confidence placed in her had so far been proved right.

"Ready to go back in?"

"I don't think so. I feel very shaky. Could it wait until tomorrow?"

She felt trapped. The corridor was as stuffy as the court room. Sunshine burned through the grimy windows, intense between the black bars of shadow. She shifted sideways into the dark and leaned her head back against the wall, eyes closed.

Around and above her voices gathered to persuade her that she should continue. If the defense was left to regroup and reconsider tactics their advantage might be lost. She capitulated and pushed herself to her feet. As she entered the courtroom her knees started shaking and she felt dizzy. It was only nerves she told herself, not a premonition.

She risked a glance toward the gallery. Her brother was sitting there beside a suntanned stranger with curiously bright eyes. They both smiled back and she took a deep breath.

"Sergeant?"

Stringer had noted her glance away and raised an impatient eyebrow, anything to undermine her confidence. If only he knew how little she had left! But her smart suit and careful makeup presented a perfect, professional picture. Impervious camouflage.

"Let us turn to the night of 12th February last year. The night that the prosecution alleges the defendant attacked you."

"The night he tried to rape me." Stringer bristled. "Yes sir, I remember it well."

"Then use that recall to describe your version of events to us."

Nightingale took a deep breath. Her mouth was dry. All the remaining moisture in her body seemed to have collected in chill pools around the waistband of her skirt and under her arms.

"It was the second time that the defendant invited me to join him for a date. On the first occasion he didn't turn up, although it was from that night I had the sense that I was being followed."

"A 'sense,' Sergeant, is not evidence, as you well know, and the *facts* are that despite a significant police presence, there were no sightings of the defendant following you. Is that correct?"

"Yes, sir." She resisted the desire to tell the jury that her car had been vandalized and her rubbish searched. It had all happened in the five days between the first and second invitations but as there'd been no trace of the defendant it was purely circumstantial.

"On February 12th I followed the directions I'd received from the defendant. I arrived at the meeting point, which was by the bandstand in Harlden Park, three minutes late at five thirty-three p.m. I waited until six fifteen and then left. To reach my car, I had to walk back through the rose garden and along a path through rhododendron bushes."

"Why didn't you choose a better-lit route? It was dark, after all."

"That would have taken me fifteen minutes instead of five and normally the path is well lit."

"Continue."

"As I entered the shrubbery, there was a noise from the bushes so I looked around to find another way. There wasn't one so I walked on."

"You make yourself sound alone but you were, in fact, surrounded by police and were carrying a wire, is that not so?"

"I was wired. However, the problem with the bandstand rendezvous was that it meant the officers watching had to remain on the edge of the park. There were two posing as a courting couple, and another three playing football on the grass, but as the light went they had to leave. Four other officers were in the car park, two on benches in the rose garden—they were the closest—and the rest held a loose perimeter."

She felt the slightest tremor start in her throat. Despite the counseling, this was the most difficult part of her testimony. Memories of the attack infested her sleep, creating vivid nightmares overlaid with images of his other victims. She lost the momentum of her narrative and waited for him to ask a question.

"You have a remarkable physical resemblance to the victims of the attacks you were investigating. Did that cause you any particular distress?"

"No."

Nightingale sensed that he was changing tactics. Perhaps Stringer wasn't confident that he'd be able to convince the jury the police had used THE GAME to entrap his client so now he was going to attack her account of the attempted rape. It was a moment that she had been dreading. Apart from the police account of the attack on her and the traces recovered from her fingernails there was no other physical evidence. The rapist had never left semen, saliva or even a hair follicle on his victims. When they'd searched his flat SOCO had found it pristine, without even fingerprints and with nothing to connect him to the crimes. Faced with such lack of evidence, the CPS had decided to concentrate prosecution on three rapes that were identical in method to the attack on Nightingale. Four others, including one that had resulted in the victim's death, had been left on file. In these the victims had been attacked in their own homes, not outside, and none of them had been able to pick the defendant out of a lineup.

"Let us turn to the 'attack' in which the defendant, by the way, sustained material injuries. I put it to you that it was you who approached the defendant and encouraged him into a physical embrace, which *you* subsequently rejected, violently?"

"No, that is not true."

"Do you exercise regularly?"

"Pardon?" She was thrown by the question. He repeated it tersely.

"I run."

"Have you engaged in self-defense classes?"

"Only as part of routine police training."

"But you are fit and strong, are you not? Quite capable of taking the fight to a man."

He was deliberately baiting her and would use any show of emotion to his advantage. The thought made her angry but in a way that sharpened her wits and drove all signs of emotion beneath the surface.

"I didn't attack the defendant. He leaped out at me and knocked me to the ground. There's evidence to prove that he lay in wait within the bushes for some time."

"How tall are you?"

"Five ten."

"How much do you weigh?"

"I really don't know."

"Come, come, Sergeant, I thought all ladies knew to the ounce what they weighed."

"I don't."

"I see." His tone implied that she was avoiding the question. "Would you take a look at the defendant, please."

Nightingale licked her dry lips. She had avoided meeting his eyes since she had taken the stand. With a slight twist of her head she directed her gaze to the defendant's chest. His chin and mouth were just at the top of her vision and she flicked her eyes down a fraction.

"How tall would you say he was?"

"A giant," she thought. "I don't know."

Another exasperated sigh.

"He's five foot nine, Sergeant, shorter than you are." He left a significant pause. "Hardly an over-powering assailant for a fit, tall woman like you."

"From the ground, with a knife at one's throat, all men look tall . . . sir." Some of the women on the jury nodded in sympathy and Nightingale pressed her advantage. "And as for my attacking him, I was in no fit state to do so. I received a concussion—the X-rays show deep bruising to the back of my skull," she felt again the crack of her head as it made contact with the paving, "a sprained wrist and dislocated shoulder, bruising to my face and thighs," his strength had been terrifying, "and I had to have dental work on two of my teeth."

"So you say, Sergeant, but how does the jury know that those injuries were not inflicted by yourself or your colleagues in an attempt to build up evidence against my client?"

His callousness made her gasp and to her horror tears filled her eyes, yet when she risked a glance at the prosecution table they were hiding smiles. Confused, she turned to the jury. Five women, seven men; all looked shocked, one openly angry. Stringer had miscalculated.

"Excuse me," she whispered as she took a shaky sip of water.

"Are you all right?" The judge leaned forward solicitously. "I'm sure," he said with a meaningful glance toward Stringer, "that this cross-examination is nearing its end."

It was. The defense asked a few more questions but the heat had vanished from his attack. After ten minutes Nightingale left the stand and the judge called a recess for lunch.

As she drove home she replayed the prosecution's words of praise but they meant nothing to her. She worried over every hesitation and weak answer, convinced that she could have handled the cross-examination better.

On the top floor, high enough to have a view over the trees, Nightingale slipped her key into a sturdy Yale lock and was home at last. This was her place. The only tiny blessing from her parents' death was that she was now financially independent. They had not left her so much that anybody would consider her wealthy but sufficient to be able to put down a deposit and start buying her own home. She raised a hand to ward off a fly and brushed aside the unwelcome reality that there had been a benefit from their deaths. The thought filled her with guilt and her stomach ached in physical response.

A light was blinking on her phone; three messages. Her brother had called, sounding exactly like their late father.

"Look, come and spend the weekend. I'm off on Sunday and

Monday for a change." At twenty-seven, he'd qualified and was dutifully serving his time before moving on to try and become an orthopedic surgeon.

She shook her head. He was her only family now, but she found Simon and his wife, Naomi, depressing company. They inhabited a world where domestic bliss was commonplace and Nightingale felt like an alien whenever she visited. They also insisted on calling her Diane, her mother's chosen name for her, despite the fact that she had determinedly called herself by her middle name since senior school.

The new message light was still flashing. She felt too exhausted to care who else had called but dragged her mind away from memories of childhood arguments and pressed the play button for the second time to be greeted by silence and heavy breathing. The third message was the same. She deleted them both, cursing the crank caller who must have selected her number at random, and abandoned herself to sleep.

CHAPTER TWO

The prisoner smoothed out the three-day-old newspaper and folded a crease precisely around the article he wanted, before jerking the page sharply. The cheap paper parted obediently and he repeated the motion to isolate the exact columns with a small grunt of satisfaction. He wasn't allowed scissors. They had him on suicide watch, given the length of his sentence and the results of a psychiatric profile.

His psychiatrist had leaped at his vague hints of interest in the reporting of his crimes and had suggested the scrapbook. Griffiths found maintaining it surprisingly satisfying. He laughed at some of the ridiculous theories they'd printed about the motives for his crimes. They made him sound dangerous, erratic, a man to keep well away from. It had helped to build his reputation in here, though being inside for rape was a dangerous ride. Although he was hated, as sex offenders always were, he was no longer attacked. There was a man still recovering in the infirmary who served as a lesson to the others. But the guards made sure that he suffered and the other inmates turned a blind eye.

He'd accumulated every printed inch of coverage since the trial but press comment had reduced to almost nothing now and the realization that he was already old news depressed him almost as much as his confinement. How could he keep his demand for an appeal public? He placed the small clipping on a page beside a scrap of his own writing. His observations on life helped to keep the dark side away. As he dabbed the non-toxic glue carefully along the edges of his latest cutting he tried to decide what to do next. A few short weeks into his sentence and he was already planning. Not like the rest of them in here. Perhaps a conversion to some religion would help his appeal; a born-again Christian was always popular.

He rehearsed whole conversations in his mind. At one point he was almost moved to tears. He was a masterful role player, it was why he'd been invincible playing THE GAME, but they wouldn't allow him near a computer. One of the guards had told him it was the last privilege he would ever be granted. He knew that there were websites on him because the press reported on them. A few were vile, defamatory, set up by family and friends of the victims as acts of revenge. News of them left him cold. The one of more interest was the site that critiqued his "crimes" and proclaimed his innocence. He recognized the prose.

His door was opened without warning and he glanced at his watch, confused. This wasn't right. When he saw Saunders' grinning face he felt fear and hoped that it didn't show.

"Visitor. Come on, move your arse." The guard kicked him hard on the buttocks, reawakening old bruises. He was one of the worst abusers and the others just turned their backs whenever prisoner 35602K was the subject of Saunders' close attention.

He walked into the visitors' room and glanced around, studying the occupants openly until Saunders nudged him in the back. Desks were arranged so that the guards could walk among them, the tatty orange plastic chairs bolted to the floor.

The presence of other inmates and the curious eyes of their guests disconcerted him.

Saunders directed him to the empty chair at the end of the

line opposite a tall figure in a smart jacket who was bending down as if tying a shoelace. He tried to control his rapid blinking and squared his shoulders despite the acute sense of exposure at his back. His mysterious visitor started to straighten. The shape of the head and line of the chin were as familiar as his own. His heart lurched and his throat tightened with nerves. They hadn't spoken since before his arrest. Tripping over his left foot in his anxiousness he hurried over to the empty chair.

"You shouldn't have come! Not here, among all . . . this." The person sitting opposite regarded him silently with eyes the color of arctic ice. "It's not appropriate for you to be here. It's beneath you."

"As it is you, yet here you are." The implied criticism was clear, despite the carefully controlled tone.

"I let you down. I had no idea she was filth."

"You broke the rules."

"I . . . I wanted to meet her properly."

"Rubbish." His visitor looked away in disgust. "You were lazy, admit it."

"I was lazy."

"Say it again, 'I was lazy.' "

"I was lazy."

"I was stupid, say it."

"I was stupid. Look D—"

"No names. Are you a complete idiot?"

"Sorry." Griffiths hung his head, not daring to say more until bidden to do so.

"I watched it all in court, every day."

"I saw you. You cared enough to be there for me."

The man didn't acknowledge the remark but he smiled in a way that made Griffiths wince.

"Until the end, I thought you were going to win. The policewoman's evidence was a travesty. It should have been disallowed."

"If it wasn't for her I wouldn't be here now. I never made a mistake." There was a plea in his tone. "All I did was invite her for a second time."

"But that was against the rules. You know what happens when you get too involved. You did it once before but I was able to get you out of the mess you made in time. Remember?"

"It wasn't fair. She trapped me."

"I know, most inconvenient. After all the efforts I've made on your behalf it would be a shame to see it . . . wasted."

"What are you going to do about her?"

"Don't worry. I'm dealing with it in my own way."

"Once I'm back with you I'll do anything, everything you want and I won't ever break the rules again."

"We'll see."

Griffiths felt his ego shrivel. One look from those eyes could crush him. If the man opposite wanted him free then there was hope, but he had to make him believe that he was worth the effort. One of the guards walked over, stared at them pointedly and walked away slowly.

"Who was that?"

"Saunders, a sadistic bastard. One of the worst. He's abusive and pays me particular attention."

The visitor's eyes followed the guard's back across the room, their expression unreadable.

"He's abused you?"

"Regularly."

"You're not his property to spoil as he wishes. I dislike people who have so little personal power that they have to find positions of authority to exploit. You say his name is Saunders. I imagine he lives locally." The visitor stared at the guard, lost in thought.

Griffiths pawed at the table.

"I can't stay in here. I have to get out." There was a rising note of hysteria in his voice.

"Careful. You can't show any weakness. I'm working on it, don't worry."

"An es—?" The visitor raised a hand and Griffiths shut his mouth.

"Impossible, but an appeal . . . that's far more promising."

"But it'll take years and my lawyer says it may fail—50:50 at best."

"Have faith. If there are fresh . . . developments, shall we say, in the meantime your chances will be much greater. Leave it with me, I'll soon convince the public that the police arrested the wrong man."

"How will I know what's going on?"

"Do you remember when we were at school, how we used to send notes to each other in code? I'll send you some books but you'll need to be patient. Some things take a while to sort out, though," he looked at Saunders and smiled, "I'll see what I can do to make your time in here a little more bearable."

His visitor rose and left without another word.

Griffiths was returned to his cell, his emotions a scrambled mess. One moment he felt the most intense excitement and pleasure, the next numbing inadequacy. When he was positive, he was sure that something would happen because the visit proved he was too important to be left to rot. Then he would remember that look, the eyes tearing into his soul, revealing the depths of his failings. He paced his cell, muttering out loud against the betrayals and wounds inflicted on him since childhood. Self-pity slid into anger, familiar and warming, then rage as he thought of all the people who deserved punishment and of the scores he would settle once he was free.

CHAPTER THREE

DCI Fenwick's secretary looked up from her keyboard and gave him a broad grin of welcome.

"So you really are back. The case at the Met's finished?"

Fenwick shook his head and the light caught new hints of gray at his temples. That was what a secondment to the Metropolitan Police could do to a man.

"My part is, Anne, but Commander Cator is the expert on money laundering and he'll complete the evidence. It'll take a long time for all the strands to come together and we may never know the whole of it. But the Assistant Chief Constable has finally agreed to my return."

"The Superintendent wants to see you."

Superintendent Quinlan was on the phone but beckoned him into his office. He finished the call abruptly and stuck his hand out.

"Andrew, good to see you. Place hasn't been quite the same without you."

"I'm glad to hear it. Frankly I'm looking forward to some proper police work."

Quinlan frowned.

"Shut the door, would you. Look, I've been meaning to talk

to you for some time. Are you sure that you want to turn this transfer down? It could be the making of your career . . ."

"I think you mean the *re-making*, don't you?"

Quinlan hurried on as if Fenwick hadn't spoken.

"Commander Cator is going right to the top in my opinion, and he's asked for you specifically. It's a compliment and a great opportunity that won't come again." Fenwick opened his mouth to speak but Quinlan hadn't finished. "There's no such thing as a guaranteed promotion, of course there isn't, but with a move to his team and your track record, you'd have a shot at making superintendent."

"More than I would have here, you mean?" It was said with one of Fenwick's attempts at a wry grin but Quinlan grimaced anyway.

"I won't be drawn into that," he snapped, and Fenwick was sorry for his sarcasm. It hadn't been aimed at the Superintendent. He knew that his boss was his strongest supporter, but *his* boss, the ACC of West Sussex, Harper-Brown, disliked him intensely and Fenwick knew that he'd never win his endorsement. He simply wasn't servile enough.

"Sorry, that was a stupid remark, and it wasn't meant for you. Look, the Met really isn't for me."

"Is it the, er, commuting that's a problem because . . ."

"No, it's not the children." Fenwick substituted the word that was the real point of the question, preferring there to be no prevarication. Everyone assumed that being a single father of a nine- and a seven-year-old was a major handicap to his career but he had a live-in housekeeper who managed his household brilliantly. The children appeared to have settled at long last, and some health insurance on his wife had meant that he'd been able to pay off the mortgage more quickly. Even visiting Monique in hospital had settled into a routine, sad, to be sure, but no longer traumatic.

"So it was the politics, then. I thought as much. You never will make the extra effort to be a diplomat."

Fenwick laughed out loud and his boss looked at him in surprise. In the months before his secondment he'd rarely seen him smile. He had changed during the time away and something of the old Fenwick, the one that had disappeared with the onset of his wife's illness, was beginning to reemerge.

"I *hated* the politics and the soft-peddling way things had to be done, but I coped because I had to. In fact Commander Cator made a point of congratulating me on my performance. He'd expected far worse."

"So what is it then? Why are you turning your back on almost certain advancement?"

Quinlan looked at him in exasperation. He was an old friend and ally and Fenwick realized that he deserved an honest answer.

"It's all too remote. The investigations take years and the layers of subterfuge these criminals construct make unravelling the evidence like solving a Rubik's cube blindfolded. The syndicates are better funded than we are! And anyway I'm not very good at pursuing crime in the abstract."

He stopped short of adding the strongest negative. The complexity of the crimes frequently baffled juries and the rate of conviction was depressingly low as a result. He was a man who needed to win.

"Yet Cator says in his note to me that you have a natural talent. He called you 'remorseless and determined,' I seem to recall."

"Don't misunderstand me, I want to see Wainwright-Smith destitute and in jail. It's what the bastard deserves." The venom in Fenwick's tone caught both of them by surprise. There was a silence, then Quinlan nodded slowly. He understood.

"Of course. It wasn't a faceless crime for you, I was forgetting. Very well," he took a deep breath, "I've said my piece and I won't mention it again. There's more than enough for you to get stuck into here."

"The Griffiths case must have stretched the team to the limit." Fenwick had already noted the new lines of tension on Quinlan's face. "You took charge yourself I understand, toward the end."

"The ACC insisted. Derek Blite handled the investigation into the first attack but then that poor girl was killed, in her own home and within days of the previous rape. I had to take over. But despite all our work we were only able to persuade the CPS to prosecute three of the seven crimes we think Griffiths is responsible for. It's galling to leave the other files open."

"But you got a result. He's been found guilty and he was given life."

"Thanks to Nightingale. She did a fantastic piece of work. Without her evidence I think he might have walked. You should have heard the defense's close. He reminded the jury that they could only convict if they were sure of guilt beyond reasonable doubt and said that in his opinion, her testimony raised very grave doubts indeed."

"Doesn't matter. He lost, we won. She deserves to feel pleased with herself."

"Maybe." Quinlan looked unconvinced. "You know she lost both her parents in a car crash two months ago? Sad business."

"I had no idea. How is she coping?"

"Seems to have taken it in her stride. I offered her compassionate leave but she decided to come straight back to work after the funeral. Sometimes I think she's too plucky for her own good."

• • •

The following day the object of their shared interest was facing another, entirely unanticipated, test. As she parked her car at the police station, Nightingale was surrounded by a pack of sweaty men carrying notepads, tape recorders and cameras. The press had found her and the idea startled her more than any life-threatening encounter. She froze.

"Sergeant Nightingale, could we have a quote on Griffiths' conviction, how do you feel?"

"Look this way, darling. Lovely! And again, good, good."

"What was it like looking into the eyes of a serial rapist?"

"Word is you kneed 'im in the balls. Did you? Our readers would approve. Shame the damage wasn't permanent."

"Come on, love, just one quote, that's all we need."

Nightingale blinked rapidly as if coming out of a trance. Head down, she made straight for the station entrance without saying a word. Two of the men tried to cut her off by running backward in front of her but she kept going. Their shouted questions echoed off the brickwork in the yard while photographers kept clicking away. As she reached the first step one jostled into another who lurched sharply against Nightingale, sending her flying just as a voice shouted from above her head.

"What the devil's going on down there?"

She looked up to see Inspector Blite peering from a second floor window, his face puce.

"Get up here right now."

Nightingale stumbled into Blite's office more breathless than the two flights of stairs warranted. Her encounter with the journalists had shaken her. Her privacy had been breached and she felt grubby.

"Look at this!" Blite tossed her the day's edition of the *Daily Mail*. "Pages four, five and six. Read it."

The paper gave detailed coverage of the trial and the police investigation that had finally brought "a dangerous criminal to justice." It was positively slanted toward the police, and Nightingale wondered why Blite was so incensed. She found the answer as she turned to page six. Under an "exclusive" banner a profile featured the brave policewoman who had put her own safety at risk when she acted as bait to catch the rapist. Nightingale stared at her photograph and closed her eyes in dismay.

They had made her into a heroine. The correspondent described her role in capturing Griffiths. He hadn't exaggerated but the details were dramatic enough in themselves for that to have been unnecessary. Then he had linked her *"extraordinary bravery"* to her behavior in two previous cases, pointing out that *"such courage is characteristic of Sergeant Nightingale. Behind her cool beauty beats a steadfast heart . . ."*

She shuddered. Why would a journalist have bothered to research her brief career? She glanced at the name at the head of the article: Jason MacDonald. Well, that explained everything. She'd arrested him once as he had tried to score another exclusive from a woman she'd been assigned to protect. That had been three years ago but he had looked like a person who would bear a grudge even then. No matter how seemingly positive the coverage, he must know that it would infuriate her superiors and alienate her colleagues. There was bare mention of Inspector Blite or Superintendent Quinlan. Very cleverly, he made it read as if her bravery had rescued the case from previous bungling. Nightingale looked up into Blite's furious face.

"I have no idea how he found out all that, sir. I gave no interview."

"You expect me to believe that? Your publicity agent seems to have been working overtime!"

Nightingale bit her tongue. There was no point in arguing. If there was a leak in the station it wasn't her.

"This is disgraceful conduct, a real black mark. You can't expect your career to be unaffected by this. There'll be lasting consequences."

His voice had a cutting edge that would have left scars on a more impressionable officer. It bounced off Nightingale as she had so little regard for his opinion.

"I will personally make sure that this goes on your record, you can be sure of that . . ."

"Would you excuse us please, Sergeant." She looked around to see Superintendent Quinlan standing in the open doorway. Blite's shouting must have carried far beyond his office. "Close the door on your way out."

By the time she was finally summoned to see the superintendent, Nightingale had already suffered a range of responses to her sudden fame. Most colleagues were satisfied with a teasing comment or request for an autograph but there were enough who were jealous to make the morning uncomfortable. Her shoulders were tense as she tapped on the door to Quinlan's office.

"Come in, Louise." He looked up and gave her a half smile. "Sit down."

He studied her openly, watching her in silence. A vein throbbed in her right temple. While she met his gaze with ease, she looked young and miserable. The officer in front of him was only twenty-seven. She hadn't distinguished herself academically before joining the Force, barely scraping through college, but he didn't doubt that she was special. Yet there was something hidden about her, deliberately so, and the thought of that concealment worried him. Fenwick was like that. He had depths that Quinlan doubted anybody had discovered. Pity that he hadn't found himself a good woman after all this time. He stopped his mind from wandering and refocused on Nightingale.

"There will be nothing added to your file as you have done nothing wrong."

"Thank you, sir."

"However," he noticed her jaw tighten, as if anticipating a blow, "this case has brought you, and therefore the Division, unhelpful attention. The press love personalities and you should expect their interest in you to continue for a while."

"Surely it's just my fifteen minutes of fame. It'll blow over tomorrow."

Quinlan looked at the fine-boned face that they now knew the camera loved, her slender five-foot ten inches, the cool yet mysterious manner, and shook his head, dismissing her hopes. A beautiful young face sold papers on the back of the slightest story. Let that story include sex and violence and sales would double.

"Who is this Jason MacDonald? The name seems familiar and he knows a lot about you."

"He was a local reporter who latched on to the Rowland case just over three years ago. He did an exposé that ruined an opera singer's career."

"Of course. And now he's made the nationals." Quinlan's faint hope that MacDonald would forget all about them evaporated. "You'll be assigned internal duties for the next few weeks."

"Yes, sir." She looked relieved and her face softened into a small smile but it disappeared at his next words.

"And I'll need to consider your next posting. If you hadn't put in a special request to come back after Bramshill and your sergeant's exams, you would have moved on already. You can't just stay around here, not someone with your potential. Think about it and come back to me. That will be all."

• • •

Nightingale tried to put Quinlan's proposals, the trial and news coverage behind her but journalists haunted her for days. When they ran out of questions they took to leaving long silent messages on her answer-phone.

Instead of stopping, the calls became more frequent. At night she had to disconnect her phone to prevent its ringing disturbing her sleep. And then the emails from Pandora started: "SONGBIRD, WANT TO PLAY A GAME?"

That was all they ever said but the oblique reference to THE GAME increased her sense of paranoia. Her counselor had warned her that it was normal to feel vulnerable but Nightingale had dismissed her concerns. She had told herself that she was more robust than that, and her attempt at toughness had become an integral part of her way of coping with the stresses she now lived with every day. A few random phone calls and emails weren't going to scare her. She put up with them for a week and then decided to take a break. A weekend with her brother had become the lesser of two evils.

It was strange to walk up to the front door of the old family house and know that her father wouldn't be on the other side of it, waiting to fling the solid oak wide before aiming a kiss at her cheek. She'd never once been late for Sunday lunch but he'd had the unfailing knack of making her feel guilty from the moment she arrived.

An ancient iron chain hung from an even older lever and she pulled it, listening for the jangle from deep in the heart of the house. Seconds later her sister-in-law opened the door and greeted her with a warm smile.

"Di! Sorry, Louise—I will get used to it someday. We were

worried that you might be called away at the last minute. Come on in, Simon's in the conservatory."

They hadn't changed the furniture in the hall, but a gloomy picture of a stag at bay had at last been put down. In its place Simon had hung a gilt mirror. She averted her eyes from her reflection and glanced into the front sitting room but could see only the grandfather clock. To her surprise it showed the time incorrectly, another sign that life had changed.

"Hi, Sis." Simon was standing in the doorway to the large glass extension that her mother had insisted on calling the orangery. They were the same height but he was around fifty pounds heavier. His pale gray eyes were exactly like their mother's, and completely different from her own. In fact, they so little resembled each other that Nightingale had once challenged her mother to prove that they were twins.

Her mother had thrust a birth certificate under her nose that showed she'd given birth to a boy and a girl, Simon David and Diana. Nightingale had noticed that she had not been given a second name. Her chosen name of Louise, the one her father had always said was her second name, was missing and she'd protested the fact. Her mother had flushed bright red and shouted at her not to be so rude. Two days later Nightingale had run away from home for the first time. Two months later she was sent to the boarding school from which she was eventually expelled.

"If you don't mind my saying so," Simon's voice brought her back to the present, "you look tired."

"Thanks."

"Forget I said that. Come on, have a drink—we're both off duty for once."

Simon had changed since he'd married Naomi. The bully of a boy she had grown up with, a mummy's darling who was spoiled into meanness even before he'd started school, was a vague memory now. They had barely known each other by the time she'd finished boarding school—or rather by the time the school had finished with her. When he returned from university, already engaged to Naomi to their mother's horror, he had changed into a friendly, rugby-playing extrovert whom she had found it surprisingly fun to be with. Naomi was working steadily to rekindle an appropriate affection between them, much to Simon and Nightingale's mutual amusement.

At six o'clock they were still sitting at the dining table. Naomi went to make some tea, leaving brother and sister alone. Simon had had more to drink than usual and spoke without curbing his bluntness.

"You're too thin, you know, Di . . ."

"Louise."

"Sorry, it's the booze. You could do with putting on a good ten pounds at least."

"You sound just like Father." Simon grimaced. "Look it's been a tough year, and I'm not sure that it's going to become any easier. The superintendent wants to transfer me."

"Is that such a bad thing? Are you really happy over there in Harlden? I would've thought that you'd welcome a change while you're still young and unattached."

She didn't answer. How could she explain to him that she was quite the opposite, firmly attached to a man who barely knew she existed and feeling old before her time.

"Penny for them? You look really down."

"Don't push it, Simon, can't you tell when a girl's in love?" Naomi put a mug of tea in front of Nightingale, noticed her white face and changed the subject quickly. "Have you mentioned Mill Farm yet?"

"Has something happened? Is the house all right?" Nightingale looked at the couple with concern.

"Oh it's OK. Almost derelict because Dad let it go but still standing, just." Simon helped himself to more sugar than would be good for him in a few years' time. "We'd like you to have it."

Nightingale was stunned into silence.

"We don't need two houses," Naomi explained, "and we both feel that your parents should have left it to you, not us."

"They left me an income. There's capital in trust and I'm entitled to the interest on it. I rarely spend what I receive each month."

"That may be, but we still feel that the will was unfair, don't we, Simon?"

Her husband nodded emphatically.

"Downright Victorian. It still annoys me to think . . ."

"But it doesn't annoy me. It's very sweet of you both but you shouldn't feel obliged to change what they decided."

"It's not an obligation. You'd be doing us a favor. An old run-down farmhouse in the depths of Devon is not our sort of thing, whereas you always loved it there."

The idea was tempting. She didn't care that the house was almost falling down. It was the one place as a child that she'd been completely happy.

"We've had all the documents drawn up. It's a deed of gift so there won't be any tax to pay as long as we live long enough. I'll go and fetch the paperwork."

Naomi watched her husband leave the room.

"Please, he wants you to have it. He feels guilty about everything we've been left. Whatever you say, it wasn't fair."

"But not entirely unexpected. They virtually disowned me. When Aunt Ruth died and left Mill Farm to my father I think she had hoped it might pass to me, but I had no expectations. It's where Simon and I were born you see, and that meant I had no chance. Mother would be very unhappy with this."

"There's nothing in the will to stop us."

"I doubt the idea that you would give decent property away ever occurred to her!" Nightingale laughed then became serious. "I need to think about it. Owning an old house is a big responsibility and it's miles away. I don't want to sound ungrateful but could you and Simon hold on to the paperwork while I think this through?"

"Of course, but take the keys anyway, just in case. Simon says that it's far too run-down to live in without work but you might want to look at it to help you make up your mind."

"I doubt it but thanks for the thought."

She took the keys to keep them happy then turned the subject away from family memories and onto safer topics of conversation with practiced ease.

CHAPTER FOUR

The screams reached Fenwick in a dream in which he'd been swimming far down under water. As he surfaced, the cries became louder. For a sleep-numbed moment he lay motionless. Then he sat bolt upright and grabbed his dressing gown from the foot of the bed. He stumbled as he caught his bare toe against the chest of drawers and banged his bad knee on the edge of the door.

He was limping as he ran toward Bess's bedroom. By the time he reached her side, the noise had subsided. He lifted her head onto his shoulder and rocked the nightmare away. Gradually her breathing slowed and she settled into a deeper sleep. He laid her back down and lifted the sheet to tuck it in under her chin. What would Monique think of their little girl now? Nine already, scaring him with her occasional flashes of sophistication and feminine insight.

In his large, empty bed he lay awake, unable to return to sleep. This was the third time in a fortnight that she had been disturbed by dreams frightening enough to make her cry out. Yet in the morning she was as sunny and cheerful as ever, with no recollection of the night's distress. His children were a constant source of concern but fretting in the dark hours of the night was not his way. Fenwick got up and pulled papers from his briefcase, which he worked on until he couldn't keep his eyes open any longer. He fell asleep sitting up with the light on and the contents of an investigation file strewn over the pillow beside him.

When his alarm clock rang he groaned. Just one more day and then he could look forward to an uninterrupted weekend with the children. On his way to the station he realized that he hadn't visited Monique in nearly a fortnight. Although the doctors assured him that she would never again be aware of his or any other presence he still felt guilty. He must try and fit in a trip to the nursing home.

At six o'clock he'd finished clearing his desk and was heading for the door. When the phone rang he cursed under his breath.

"Yes?" He hoped his voice reflected the impatience he felt.

"Andrew? It's Claire, Claire Keating."

"Claire, what can I do for you?"

"I was wondering, if you weren't doing anything this evening, we're having some drinks at the College—nothing fancy, just a pre-exam pick-me-up. Life becomes frenetic for the next six weeks. This do helps to fortify us."

He had forgotten that she lectured for a living and that her work for the police was a sideline. The invitation surprised him. He liked Claire and had it just been a drink with her he might have accepted, but the idea of spending an evening drinking bad wine with a bunch of academics with whom he had nothing in common was not to his taste. And anyway, the children would miss him.

"It's a nice thought but I'm busy." A vague sense of politeness made him add, "Perhaps another time."

"Of course. It was just an idea. Have a nice weekend."

• • •

He opened the front door to sounds of television from the sitting room and a clatter of pans from the kitchen.

"Hello!" he called out. "I'm home."

Chris grunted without turning his head from the television screen. Bess leaped up and ran to greet him, a shocking vision in lime green and pink.

"Daddy, you're early!" She gave him a hug as he hung up his coat. He blinked at the fluorescent T-shirt and violently striped leggings, neither of which he had seen before.

"Do you like them, Daddy? I went shopping with Lucy and her mum after school. They were in the sale, ever so cheap."

Fenwick wasn't in the least surprised, but at whatever price they would never be a bargain.

"You went shopping?" He avoided a direct answer to her question, feeling out of his depth. He'd never thought that he would have to be a source of fashion guidance, trusting as he had in Bess's inevitable good taste. No daughter of his would ever be tempted to buy trash, or so he'd thought. How wrong could a man be?

"Yes, but do you like it?" She stamped her foot just slightly for emphasis in an uncharacteristic gesture. Fenwick began to suspect Lucy Wells of being a bad influence on more than Bess's dress sense.

"It's an interesting fabric. Oh, sorry, is that glitter meant to rub off?" He stared in appalled fascination at the spangles that had transferred themselves from cartoon apples on the T-shirt to his fingers.

"Oh don't worry, it comes off all the time. Mrs. Wells says the first wash will fix it." She looked up at him, her dark brown eyes huge under heavy lashes. "You don't like it, do you?" Her mouth turned down. There was a curious blend of defiance and pleading in her voice. Fenwick recognized the warning but plowed straight ahead anyway, honest as ever.

"Truthfully, the pink is a little babyish for my taste but the important thing is that you like them. They'll be great for parties."

She looked back at him with Monique's eyes and Monique's expression on her face. Her chin jutted out.

"They aren't party clothes. I'm going to wear them every day, except for school."

"Fine. Whatever. Just don't wear them out. I'm going to change."

He'd had the last word, or so he thought. As he walked up the stairs, she called after him.

"When I've saved up some more, I'm going to buy some leopard shoes—you can get them in every color from yellow to bright orange! Unless you'd like to buy some for me tomorrow, of course."

He turned round and came back down to the hall. This was too like the never-ending sparring with Monique to be comfortable. He sat on the second-to-bottom stair, eye to eye with her.

"Do you deserve a treat?" He wrapped his arms around her and her hard little face melted as her hands went around his neck. He tried to ignore the heavy deposit of glitter on his jacket.

"I came top in spelling."

"That was last week's test."

"What if I promise to come top next week as well?"

He had to smile at her confidence, as she never broke a promise. She was bright but not the smartest in her class. What distinguished her was her determination. Once she'd set her mind to achieve something she never failed.

"We'll see. Go back to your brother, I must change," *and take this suit to the cleaners tomorrow with the hope that it's not ruined,* he thought but didn't say.

When he came back down Chris was still lying in front of the television where he'd last seen him. The cartoon channel was on.

"Fancy a game of Monopoly, anyone?"

"This is a good bit. Maybe later." Chris didn't even glance up at his father.

Bess nodded her agreement. "Later."

Fenwick looked at the cat and mouse on the screen, both much older than he was yet somehow more appealing despite constant repetition. He bent down and ruffled Chris's hair.

"I'll collect a hug later then."

Chris nodded briefly and smoothed his hair flat. Fenwick heard a slippered footstep behind him.

"Ah, there you are, Andrew. I thought I heard you come in."

"Hello, Alice. Have you had a good day?"

"Passable. I had to do the laundry by hand because the machine broke down and they need clean uniforms but apart from that . . ." Her voice trailed away as she walked back toward the kitchen.

Fenwick followed her. His housekeeper frequently left her sentences unfinished and Fenwick had given up trying to conclude them for her. Alice Knight was a small, round woman, widowed in her early fifties and now just approaching sixty. She'd happily moved out of her rented flat and into the apartment Fenwick had adapted for the previous nanny and was clearly enjoying running a larger house.

He'd tried to disabuse her of the idea that he was a man of means, despite the size of his house, which he'd explained several times was affordable solely because of a legacy and some insurance money. In the end, the only way in which he could force her to live as modestly as he would like was to limit the weekly housekeeping. Now, he suspected, she thought him wealthy but mean and probably put it down to his maternal Scots blood. Alice was a woman who found nothing wrong in applying stereotypes as a way of saving time that would otherwise be wasted on original thought. Despite that, and her occasional extravagances on his behalf, she had proved a good addition to his household. She was warm-hearted but firm, a seasoned cook and the children liked her.

"Something smells good."

"Shepherd's pie. But don't worry. I minced the beef myself, and it was a good cut. I thought . . ."

"Delicious. When will it be ready?"

"Half an hour. You're earlier than I expected. Plenty of time for you and the children . . . They've had their tea already."

He went back and watched the cartoon, then another until his meal was ready. The pie and gravy were delicious, the cabbage good for him, or so he told himself. Two glasses of his best red wine were an indulgence but helped ease him into a routine weekend with a feeling of contentment.

The children played up a little at bedtime, probably regretting having declined the offer of a game earlier, but they settled eventually. At nine o'clock he found a film on satellite TV, poured another glass of wine and settled down with a small sigh of satisfaction. Alice was upstairs watching taped soap operas; the house was quiet, his time finally his own. He should have been content but he couldn't settle and became increasingly restless as the evening passed.

In the comfort of his armchair, he tried to work out what might be ailing him and ended up with the uncomfortable realization that he was either lonely or bored, perhaps both. Monique had been in hospital for over three years. His one affair in the year following her illness had been a disaster that could have wrecked his career and jeopardized his family. Since then he had kept his feelings, and his passions, under tight control.

That night he dreamed of Claire Keating, except that when he looked at her face, it wasn't Claire. There was another woman hiding behind her eyes. Bess had another nightmare at three in the morning and this time she woke up. He shushed her until her breathing slowed and her fingers relaxed their hold on the duvet.

In the morning they bought leopard print shoes on the strict understanding that they would be worn for parties only. They were patterned in neon purple and white, a shade that astonished him and delighted Bess in equal measure. Christopher was allowed an Action Man tank and for a few brief hours his father was a hero again. His son bestowed esteem cautiously, in irregular doses interspersed with almost savage tests of Fenwick's omniscience and affection. He could already feel the future shadow of challenge and rivalry in his son, as if having been failed by one parent he knew that it was only a matter of time before the other disappointed as well. Fenwick had barely known his own father and was determined that his son shouldn't suffer the same absence of affection that he'd had to live with.

Despite the recurring showers they all enjoyed themselves and Fenwick decided to round off the visit to town with milkshakes and a coffee in their favorite café. They scrambled into a corner table away from the crowds and the children sucked their flavored milks contentedly before Chris suddenly pushed his drink away.

"Daddy?"

"Yes, Chris."

"Is Mummy ever coming back?"

So simple, so quietly said. It was as if he was making conversation but his words stopped Fenwick's breath. Bess looked at her father, eyes intent on his face, noticing every hint of expression. He forced himself to answer normally.

"No, Chris, she's not."

"Is she dead then?" There was no trace of the nervy hysteria that used to accompany any conversation about his mother.

The absolute stillness in both children frightened Fenwick. They seemed preternaturally calm, as if waiting for a storm they knew was about to break. He was aware that his words would drop heavily into that silence, increasing or easing the tension depending on his skill in crafting an answer. He was still struggling to find exactly the right phrase when Bess took Chris's small hand in her own and said, in a matter-of-fact voice.

"No, Chris, not yet. She's very, very ill and the illness has scrambled her brains all up. They're like mashed potato now, isn't that right, Daddy? I heard you tell Alice when she came that they'd been turned into a vegetable or something."

Fenwick didn't have a chance to answer before Chris jumped in, excited.

"So she could come home then. I mean if it's only her brain that's poorly we could keep her like a pet. My teacher said that the difference between animals and us is that we can think and they can't. I like the idea of Mummy as a pet. We could all help to look after her."

Fenwick reached across and rested his large hands on top of his children's. This hope had to stop before it turned into expectation.

"No, my loves. She's too poorly to come home. She needs doctors and nurses to look after her and she's asleep all the time. There's a special word for it, could you remember it for me?"

They both nodded solemnly, their eyes huge and too bright.

"Mummy's in a coma . . ."

"A coma." They both repeated.

"That means she's fast asleep, she doesn't feel ill but she has to stay in the hospital."

"Does she have nightmares?" Bess's voice was full of horror.

"No, she can't dream. She just has a very peaceful sleep."

"Could we see her, Daddy? You visit, I know you do." Chris looked at him hopefully.

Fenwick thought of Monique's wasted white body, with machines, tubes and drips doing everything for her that her own organs could no longer.

"She's a long way away, Chris. I don't think that's possible. She wouldn't know that you were there."

He regretted his honesty now. He should have told them that she'd died. They'd be over their grieving by now instead of living this half-life of mourning. But he couldn't lie to his own children. They were too like him to forgive such a gross dishonesty. Chris opened his mouth to argue but it was Bess who shook her head and said, "No Chris, don't. There's no point. She'll be dead very soon now anyway." Her words brought both men's heads up sharply. "It's in my dream. I'm at the seaside and Mummy's walking down a long beach away from me. I try to run but I can never catch her. She's just walking and I'm running but I can't reach her. She's almost at the sea now and I know that when she gets there she'll die."

Fenwick was appalled but Chris simply nodded, understanding.

"She's walking to heaven. It's a long way, that's why it's taking such a long time," Chris said.

He looked up, his blue eyes radiating satisfaction that he had at last worked it out. "Isn't that right, Daddy?"

"Yes, that's right." His voice was thick and he took a mouthful of coffee. He hoped that they couldn't read his eyes but, ever perceptive, Bess pulled her hand free and patted his arm.

"It's all right, Daddy. I know it's sad but I think she wants to go now. It can't be much fun being in hospital all this time."

"You're probably right." He looked at them both and saw an extraordinary acceptance. To them it was simple. It was he who risked complicating matters by saying more.

"I tell you what, why don't we go home now."

"I'd like that." Chris put his coat on without protest. "I want to paint Mummy a special picture."

He painted a picture—a boat on a sea with a beach in the foreground. There were three figures on the sand, one big and two small. Their faces were sad. There was a single figure on the boat with a carefully drawn, outsized hand raised in farewell. It had long dark hair and was smiling. Across the top, Chris wrote in his best handwriting: FOR MUMMY, LOVE CHRISTOPHER. Bess decided that she wanted to do something as well and pulled out her needlework box. Inside was a piece of unfinished cross-stitch of a daisy on a blue background. The daisy was complete except for its yellow center and one leaf. She stitched them diligently before picking out in angular letters: MUMMY + BESS XXXXX.

Fenwick praised their work, gave them their tea and waited for the emotional storm to break but the evening passed peacefully. They played a game together and the television remained switched off. There were long cuddles before and after their baths. Before bed they said a special prayer for their mummy but there were no tears. They asked if they could sleep in one bed for that night and Fenwick agreed. Chris fell asleep with his arms around his new tank, Bess with her arms around her brother.

At eleven o'clock, the phone rang. Normally it would be work but with Bess's words still echoing in his ears he lifted the receiver with dread.

"Fenwick."

"It's Doctor Mortimer, Mr. Fenwick. I'm the registrar on duty at St. Theresa's. There has been a change in your wife's condition. I think you should come."

"Tonight?"

"I think it would be best, yes."

He woke Alice, who exuded a sympathy he found hard to bear.

"If you could stay close to the children, Bess sometimes has nightmares and I don't want them to be on their own." He said nothing about the source of her bad dreams.

Alice gave his arm a squeeze.

"Of course, I'll be here for them."

He drove the familiar route through heavy rain, along empty roads already filling with water in the dips. The children's goodbye gifts were securely wrapped in plastic bags on the backseat.

The hospital was sparsely lit and a kindly porter led him through dim corridors on rubber-soled shoes that squeaked on the linoleum. His wife had been wheeled into a side ward on her own. He saw at once that most of the tubes had gone. The ventilator clicked and sighed, and his own breathing adjusted to match its slow rhythm. Someone had combed out her glorious hair and it fell across the pillow in a dark halo. Her hands lay on the top of the covers across her concave stomach, pretty cotton sleeves covering the worst of the pin marks and bruises caused by long years of intravenous attention.

He became aware that a young man, probably the registrar, was at his side.

"How long?" he asked.

"Hard to say, but not very long now." They spoke in whispers in case, against all probability, the woman lying before them could still hear. Fenwick stood up and they walked out into the corridor to continue their conversation.

"Her liver's failed but she's in no pain, we've made sure of that. It's just a matter of time."

"You want to turn off the ventilator?"

"It's your decision. It always has been, but there can be absolutely no hope now."

He waited as Fenwick paused and looked at the relentless machine.

"I need a little time."

"Of course. Can I get you anything? Some tea?"

Fenwick smiled faintly at the universal English antidote.

"Yes, that's kind." He had learned that it was better to let people help.

He opened the carrier bags—one from a shoe shop, the other from a toy store, and pulled out the painting and the needlework. He propped them up on the wheeled unit to one side and realized, belatedly, that he had brought nothing himself. The tea arrived and he was left in peace. He lifted one of his wife's pale hands into his own. It was warm and soft, the nails trimmed and clean, and he was grateful to the unknown person who had attended to this detail for her.

He watched Monique's breast rise and fall but knew that it signified nothing. He sipped his tea. When it was finished he would go and find the registrar. He realized that he was swallowing a drop at a time as he held her hand, counting the pulse as if it were magic.

It was nearly dawn when he returned home. The house was dark and silent in the gray light. A blackbird, too lustful for sleep, was singing from the holly tree. Alice was asleep on the sofa, mouth sagging open. He went and made himself another cup of tea.

The anger surprised him. He had expected to be calm, not filled with this fury that wanted to destroy the order around him. All his previous denial, the rage against Monique and her melancholy disease, had been lying in wait down the years for this moment. He wanted to howl out loud. Instead he squeezed the teabag bone dry, his knuckles white, and wiped his face with his free hand. He was adding a dash of milk when he heard the soft pad of slippered feet behind him.

"Has she gone, poor dear?"

"Yes Alice, she's gone. Would you like some tea?"

His housekeeper came to his side and put her plump arm around his waist.

"Don't mind the anger, or the guilt when it comes. It's natural, trust me. We all feel it when they go." She gave a faint squeeze. "A cup of tea would be nice, thank you."

They drank in silence for a while as the dawn chorus grew from a single chirp to a raucous battle for supremacy. Light filtered into the kitchen.

"Are the children OK?"

"Slept the whole night through, not a murmur out of either of them. The funeral . . . ?"

"I've got all that to arrange. Would you mind helping me? It won't be large but I'll need to let her family know."

"Of course." She hesitated. "Will you take the children?"

It was a question that had been plaguing him during his long ride home.

"I think so. They need something tangible, to say good-bye. But only if they want to.

"I suspect that they will."

"So do I."

CHAPTER FIVE

When the phone rang she pretended that she hadn't jumped.

"Hello?"

"Sergeant Nightingale? This is Dr. Batchelor. We haven't met but I was hoping you could spare me some time. I'm a prison psychiatrist. Mr. Griffiths is one of my patients."

At the mention of Griffiths' name, Nightingale leaned back against the wall and slid down until she was seated on the cool bleached wood floor.

"Could I ask you a few questions . . . are you still there?"

"Yes." Her voice was husky and she coughed. "I'm not sure that I'm in any position to help you."

"I know that this is a little unusual . . ."

"A little!"

"But you corresponded with Wayne electronically for months."

"That doesn't mean I knew him or that I have any insight to share with you." She crossed her fingers at the lie. "A meeting would be highly irregular and a waste of your time and mine."

"Over the phone then."

"No, Doctor. I really don't want to start something like this. I'm sorry but I can't help you."

"It may do you some good."

"I have to go now. Good-bye."

She replaced the receiver and rested her head in her hands. The whole afternoon lay in wait ahead of her. She felt trapped inside her flat but when she stepped outside she had the sense that she was being followed. It was stupid, another sign of the paranoia that her counselor had warned her about, but it was debilitating just the same.

Every night her sleep was tormented by horrific nightmares. In the most recent one she was kneeling in front of Griffiths, like a supplicant, her face level with his navel as he forced her to strip naked. She'd woken shivering from the dream just after midnight. After two cups of herbal tea, she had drifted off to sleep, only to find herself on her knees again in a gutter, with Griffiths standing naked in front of her, his arms outstretched as if for crucifixion. She didn't see the knife until he brought it down in a swift arc to be level with her eyes. Slowly, he'd forced her mouth open and inserted the blade, resting it deliberately on her tongue like a communion wafer. He had forced her lips closed around it, then pulled out quickly. The razor-fine edge cut flesh and she tasted blood in her mouth.

The iron taste was still there when she woke up. When she put her hand to her face it came away bloody. In her waking confusion she'd looked around the room, searching for an intruder. It wasn't until she was washing her face in the bathroom that she realized she had a nosebleed. She shouted out in frustration at the betraying weakness of her body, swearing as she changed the stained pillowcase and musty sheets. At dawn she fell into a black slumber from which she woke unrefreshed three hours later.

She had called in sick, a lie that appalled her, but the thought of the station was worse than the idea of staying home. The phone was left plugged in as a penance and she received three silent calls before ten o'clock. Each one unnerved her. From assuming that they were nothing but childish pranks she'd become convinced that they were driven by some malign purpose. Desperate to leave the house, she had booked a hair appointment and filled the time beforehand in shopping for things she didn't need.

She'd told the stylist to be ruthless, emphasizing low maintenance while remaining indifferent to style. He called the finished effect *gamine*. She thought that she looked like a shorn Joan of Arc, ready to lead an army or face the fire. In an attempt at sensible eating she went to a vegetarian restaurant for lunch but when the quiche and salad arrived she found that her appetite had disappeared and hid most of the pastry under her untouched lettuce. Back home she drank an energy booster, ignored the flashing light on her phone and decided to go for a run.

Jogging had first become an escape for her at fourteen when she had literally run away from home with her few possessions strapped to her back. When the authorities brought her back she ran away again and again, until one policewoman by chance had impressed her so much that she had formed an ambition to become just like her. But the running had continued through college and police training. She had even run on the morning that she had been told her parents were dead.

This run was different. She ignored the park as too routine and chose instead a long track through the remnants of ancient forest that survived from the swathe of trees that had once covered the whole of the South of England. She normally saved this run for special occasions. Today it was her last attempt to break away from the paranoia that threatened to consume her, and the compulsive behaviors she was intelligent enough to recognize but not strong enough to manage. Every physical element of her life was rigidly contained. It was her mind that ran out of control.

Three hours later Nightingale's trainers were covered in dust.

Her T-shirt stuck to her back, outlining the uncompromising sports bra she wore when jogging and her hair was plastered flat to her skull framing a face drawn tight with exertion. A deceitful day off had deteriorated into an endurance test.

In the lengthening shade of an enormous oak she sucked the last drops of water from the bottle at her belt. The rustling of the leaves around her mimicked following footsteps but she shook the thought from her mind, telling herself that she was safer out here than anywhere else. She looked at her watch reluctantly. It was time to begin the long jog back to the car and then home. The thought twisted inside her, sharper than any knife and she pushed herself on.

When she reached her favorite tree she finally paused and drew in lungfuls of air. She was a long way from her car. It would be madness to exhaust herself this far into the forest but she had not yet escaped her thoughts, not even in the tedium of counting steps. She leaned forward, hands on thighs, her head hanging down toward last year's leaves lying on the packed earth under the tree. She watched drops of sweat speckle their dusty surfaces and define the faint veins in skeleton shapes. When these leaves had fallen her parents had been alive.

A sob escaped from her mouth. She covered her lips with her hands, as if trying to swallow the noise but it was impossible. Another great cry fell from her and tears joined the spattering of sweat evicted from her body. The sounds ran together until she was howling continuously. Her legs folded beneath her and she crumpled to the ground holding her head tight, as if she could squeeze the raw emotion that was pouring from her back inside. Instead she felt a counteracting pressure swell against the bone of her skull and press her lungs inside their ribcage so that she had to pant for breath.

The crying had no point of origin or purpose, it just was.

Wave after wave passed through and out of her, rocking her body backward and forward in an awkward rhythm. At some point the crying quietened and then the tears stopped. She took her hands away from her head and looked at her fingers. They were bleached white of blood from the pressure she'd exerted on them. She stared at the ring on her right hand, recalled the Christmas it had been given and felt another sob form at the memory. The tears returned and she bit down hard on her tongue in a vain attempt to stop them. The next wave of grief hit her, softer but somehow deeper and sadder, with no thread of hope.

There was a juddering in the ground beneath her that turned into heavy running footsteps and she looked up to see two curious children staring at her. Her eyes were so swollen from weeping and unshed tears that she couldn't make out their faces, but she could see that they were dressed incongruously in shorts and Wellington boots. Another picture from her mental childhood scrapbook clicked into focus. She and Simon had worn the same. There were adders in the woods and Wellingtons were safer than sandals.

"I'm OK," she said, her voice husky. "I'm fine," but they ran off. She hoped that she hadn't scared them.

It was cold in the darkening shade of the tree and Nightingale shivered as she tried to stand, protecting her body from unexpected frailty like an old woman.

"Daddy! Daddy! Come quickly. There's a sad lady crying under our tree."

Fenwick's heart sank. Since the funeral the children had assumed a disconcerting façade of babyishness, behaving badly during meals, insisting on long bedtime stories and a nightlight. When they weren't squabbling they would collapse in strange bouts of giggling over the most stupid things. They refused to discuss their mother's death and glared at him angrily whenever he tried to raise the subject. He'd hoped that this walk to one of their special places would break the mood and bring them all closer together.

He'd begun to hope that the plan was succeeding. The shell he had seen grow over both Chris and Bess had started to crack as they retraced familiar paths and splashed through memories of streams now drying to a trickle. He was inclined to ignore this woman whoever she was. Life was complicated and it was tough. Sometimes the knocks made you cry. It was usually best to deal with them in private and she wouldn't thank him for intruding, he was sure of that.

"Come on, Daddy." Bess's concern shot through him. He felt awful. She expected him to behave with common decency in response to another person's need. What had he been thinking even to consider passing by on the other side?

"Which way?"

"Over here." Chris ran on ahead, forcing Fenwick and Bess to sprint in order to catch him.

The woman was no more than a girl; thin, grubby, sweaty, in running clothes that were covered in dust and fragments of leaves. Fenwick wondered whether she had fallen and went over as she tried to stand. When she flinched at his shadow and looked up with desperate blue eyes he saw that it was Nightingale.

He stared in shock, appalled at the terrible sadness he saw so openly in her pale face. She averted her head but there was no flash of recognition in her face and she obviously hadn't realized the identity of her discoverer. His heart went out to her. It wasn't right. She would hate this intrusion.

"Nightingale." His voice was soft but she jumped as if she had been bitten by one of the poisonous snakes he warned the children about.

"Oh no!" It was a desolate wail and he had no idea what to say. He stood there, hands hanging uselessly by his sides.

"Why are you so sad?" Bess wasn't burdened by his layers of sophistry.

"I'm OK," was the whispered reply.

"Then why are you crying?" Bess peered at her then gave a little start.

"I know you. You're the police lady that came to our house last year. Daddy," Bess turned on him, accusingly, "she's not crying because you've been nasty to her, is she?"

For some reason his daughter's words triggered another surge of sobbing from Nightingale, strong enough to shake her shoulders.

"Hey." Fenwick instinctively bent down and wrapped an awkward arm about her shoulders. "Good grief, you're freezing. You'll catch your death of cold. Here," he took the jumper he had slung around his shoulders and eased it over her head. He guided her arms into the sleeves and she hugged the wool to her. "Why don't I give you a lift home?"

"No." He could hardly hear her. "I have my car. Please," she wouldn't look him in the eye but he could feel the intensity of her appeal, "it would be best if you left me alone."

"At least let me walk you to your car. Where is it?"

"Near the end of the Devil's Run."

"That's miles away. Is that how far you've come?" He tried not to let it sound like an accusation. "You must be exhausted. My car's over in the National Trust car park. We'll drive you round."

"No, I . . ."

"Does that mean our walk's over already?" Chris made no attempt to hide his disappointment.

"Chris."

"See, it will only be a problem. I can find my own way back."

"No you won't. Christopher, if we go now we'll be in time for an ice cream from the shop on the way home."

Chris's face brightened at once. Nightingale gave a huge sigh and shrugged her shoulders. Fenwick was too adept at recognizing and capitalizing on defeat to let the moment pass and helped her to her feet. As the children ran on ahead, Fenwick slowed his pace until he could match his stride to hers.

"Would it help to talk?"

She shook her head.

"Sometimes it does, you know, however hard starting might seem."

"I'd rather not."

They walked on in silence, their strides synchronized, the rustle from their feet through the leaves matched in rhythm. Fenwick glanced at her face while she stared at the ground just ahead of her feet. She appeared bruised and exhausted. Her vulnerability moved him and he felt his throat harden into an ache. He'd never witnessed this aspect of her before. At work she was tough and dependable, so logical and cool. The depth of her emotion surprised him.

He started to talk about the forest through which they walked, just as he would have done to Chris and Bess. His words were careful and measured, sentences peppered with curiosities and legends as he wove mystery into the fabric of his narrative.

They reached a stream in which the children had stopped to play.

". . . And this is where an eminent Victorian gentleman swore on the Bible that he had photographed fairies."

"Do you believe in fairies?" No respecter of silences, Bess

asked Nightingale the same question that she asked every adult she accompanied to this spot.

Nightingale stared at her, confused. A ghost of a smile tugged at her lips.

"Do you?"

"I asked first."

"Perhaps I do. They might exist. Who can say?"

Bess appeared to like this answer.

"That's what I think too. Do you believe in ghosts then?"

Nightingale slipped on the mossy stones at the edge of the stream and Fenwick caught her arm to prevent her from falling. When they reached the other side he waited for her to take it away but she didn't and he let it lie there.

"I don't think we want to talk about ghosts right now, Bess. It's not a good subject when someone's a little upset."

"Why are you upset?"

Fenwick glared at Bess but she ignored him and to his surprise Nightingale answered.

"I'm sad because some people I knew have gone away and I miss them."

"Gone away forever?" Bess's voice had dropped to a hush. Chris was listening attentively.

"Yes, forever."

"Did you love them?"

Nightingale took a huge breath and Fenwick stared at her with renewed concern but she seemed to be in control.

"Yes, I did."

"That *is* sad then." Bess trotted over to the other side of Nightingale and took hold of her free hand. Chris grabbed his father's and the four of them walked along in silence, linked together, until they reached Fenwick's car.

"In the back, you two. Wellies off. *Now* Chris . . . no, don't go in that puddle . . . Oh, I don't know." He lifted his son up away from further temptation and pulled his boots off.

"Can she come home with us?" It was a strange remark from his distant and reserved son.

"*She's* the cat's mother, Chris. This lady's name is Sergeant Nightingale and she has her own home to go to."

"Nightingale." They all stared at her. "Just call me Nightingale."

"Can Nightingale come home? Just for tea, Daddy?" Bess was as insistent as her brother.

Fenwick retreated into an elaborate show of wrapping their boots and putting them away. It would be completely wrong. There was a clear boundary in his mind between work and his personal life, particularly where the children were concerned. Yet the idea of sending Nightingale home on her own when she was so vulnerable made him uncomfortable. She saved him the problem of a reply.

"It's very kind of you both but I need to get home. Perhaps another day when I'll be better company."

"You promise, another day?" Chris was looking serious and Fenwick wanted to warn her that a promise to his children was never a light undertaking.

"Yes, whenever your daddy says it's all right to come."

He drove her around the forest to her car and watched as she unlocked the door.

"Are you all right to drive?"

"Yes thanks. Oh, here . . ." She started to take off his jumper.

"No, keep it on. You can return it any time."

"Thank you. Good-bye then."

"Good-bye, Nightingale. Look after yourself."

He watched her reverse her car carefully and drive away into the dusk.

"Come on then, you two. Do you still want those ice creams?"

"Shit!"

The man walked out from behind a tree and kicked a stone across the parking lot so hard that it chipped paintwork off the only other car in sight.

It had been easy to follow her and when he saw her take off into the forest he'd thought that his luck was in, but in the time it had taken him to park and remove his helmet he lost her. The bitch could run, he'd give her that. So he'd decided to wait for her return. Except that some do-gooding Sir Galahad had cocked it up and he was back to square one. Abducting a policewoman wasn't easy, particularly one who had zero social life.

Normally he could rely on his charm to captivate them but this one was different and he could understand why Griffiths had found it hard to leave her alone. She represented the ultimate challenge. The woman hardly ever went out except to work and when he'd tried to talk to her as she shopped for an anorexic's food she had looked straight through him.

Patience wasn't his strongest suit. In other circumstances he would have given up and moved on to someone else, but she was not a random victim. Sergeant Louise Nightingale needed to pay for her temerity. She had outsmarted Griffiths, persuaded a jury of his guilt and in so doing destroyed a perfect partnership. For that she would die but he'd decided that he wanted her terrified first. It was an unusual twist and would be a test of his creativity as well as his self-discipline, but the thought of destroying her confidence and of filling her life with fear was sufficient compensation, so far.

It was very important to him that she became dead scared

before she was dead. His game had been subtle to match her style but he thought now that he was being too delicate. She showed no signs of being concerned and hadn't even bothered to report his stalking of her—at least no police had arrived at her flat or impounded her PC. Matters would have to escalate but first he needed to make poor Wayne's life a little easier. Another trip north to prison-town was called for, then he could concentrate all his attention on her without further distraction.

CHAPTER SIX

Wednesday evenings at the Bird in Hand were normally enlivened by the appearance of an exotic dancer. Sasha was Saunders' favorite. He excused the wobble on her thighs because of her pendulous tits and the fact that she had once let him grope them when they had both of them been worse for wear. The idea that such a delight might happen again and lead on to more kept him returning to the pub-cum-club when he wasn't on nights at the prison.

Unfortunately for Saunders, on his first visit in June he found the tiny stage unlit with no sign of a dancer.

"What's up?"

"We were raided." The landlord disliked Saunders but his money was good and he could be relied upon to spend until he was so pissed that he needed help to find the door; even better he had no sense that his drinks were costing him more as the night wore on.

"Where you been anyway?"

"Shift work. Needed the money and they're shorthanded. But I was hoping to see some action tonight."

He looked around as if contemplating leaving. A beer and whiskey chaser appeared on the bar in a flash.

"A round on me. Don't worry, next week we'll be back to normal."

The landlord looked over his shoulder and spotted the new "hostess" he had hired to pull pints and keep the customers happy until the stripper could return. He didn't advertise for barmaids anymore. It was better that the girls knew what was expected of them.

"Milly! Get your pert little arse over here and meet Mr. Saunders, one of our most valued customers." He turned to the guard suggestively. "She's new—you never know your luck."

After four pints and as many whiskies, Saunders knew that his luck was out, although there was a hint of promise in Milly's eyes that meant he would be back the following day. He had chain-smoked fifteen cigarettes while he had verbally abused her in the mistaken idea that he was chatting her up, and that his lewd innuendo was a certain turn on. He wet his shoes by mistake in the Gents and was "helped to the door" when he decided that Milly should provide the striptease the evening was lacking. As he left the bar with some velocity, the landlord murmured, "fucking pig" under his breath and patted Milly's bum in thanks for keeping Saunders amused. She had expected something more rewarding and flounced off to the end of the bar and a more likely-looking customer.

There was an Indian takeaway en route from The Bird to Saunders' house. He threw up in the gutter outside, felt better and went in and bought a beef vindaloo, rice, onion bhajees, spicy poppadums and two lamb Samosas.

He peeled the lids off in the kitchen at home and took the containers into the sitting room. Saunders subscribed to The Adult Channel for evenings such as this, and watched the screen fantasizing about what he would do with the snooty barmaid next time, as he troughed through each of his cartons. By midnight the combined effects of the alcohol and heavy food had their traditional effect and he was fast asleep on the couch, head back and snoring while the TV played on.

Outside, a tall, slim figure climbed over the wall in the yard, landed silently and moved to the back door unseen. It was unlocked, a laughable lack of security for a prison officer, and led into a small kitchen that stank of curry, a week's rubbish and unwashed dishes.

The intruder was wearing a dark polo neck and black jeans. Both were expensive and in stark contrast to the cheap chain-store trainers on his feet. He carried a long hold-all like an old-fashioned doctor's bag that he opened silently. The sounds of soft porn and snoring came from the living room at the front of the house and painted a graphic picture of what he would find when he entered. He smiled. It was not a nice smile. It was the smile he reserved for night and darkened rooms. The people who saw it rarely lived to describe it.

He opened the bag and pulled out a black plastic dustbin liner that he unfolded with barely a rustle. The polo neck came off, as did the jeans, eased over the trainers. They went into the plastic bag for later. Underneath he wore a tight fitting rubber suit that stroked his skin when he moved. It too was black, unlike his skin-tone latex gloves, but the anomaly was short-lived as he pulled a pair in fine black leather over the top of them. Then he put on the mask, enjoying the smell of the leather as it covered his face. He looked around for a mirror. In bedrooms there were always mirrors in which to appreciate the final effect, not so in a kitchen but it was a minor inconvenience. He knew how he would look and the thought filled him with warm energy. He was death personified. He would be the last thing this pathetic specimen ever saw. He was God.

In the living room the curtains were already drawn, creating a cozy little hellhole. Saunders was sprawled like a beached whale on the sofa, his hairy white belly protruding from his open shirt, one foot collapsed sideways into the remains of a dark stinking curry. His belt was undone, his trousers splattered with some sort of brown gravy. A piece of burned onion had wrapped itself around an upper incisor. The intruder stared at it in fascination as the pig of a man in front of him grunted and spluttered his way through who knew what dreams.

One sharp blow to the temple with a weighted cosh drove Saunders from sleep into unconsciousness and he set about his preparations with an economy of motion that suggested planning and practice. A strip of heavy tape went over Saunders' mouth and he handcuffed his hands behind his back. He stripped Saunders below the waist, wrinkling his nose in disgust at the waft of body odor that emerged as he removed the man's pants. Leaving the socks on was an amusing touch. They made the pig look even more ridiculous. One bare shin was tied to the front leg of the couch with nylon cord that would bite into the skin when he struggled. The other he tied with a long length of flex to a radiator beside the television.

Saunders lay on his back, legs splayed wide apart with his ample buttocks on the edge of the cushion. The man ran some more rope beneath his armpits and over the back of the settee so that he was pulled back tight and immobile. He didn't want him to squirm too much, as it would make his work difficult. When he was certain that he was secure, he went into the squalid kitchen, removed the equipment he needed from the bag and set it down carefully next to his clothes, tutting at the layer of dust on the table. He threw a pile of washing up from the bowl to the floor and filled it with cold water.

Watching Saunders splutter and cough as he regained

consciousness was a sweet experience. He loved this moment, when terror replaced confusion to be followed by denial, then fear again.

"Ngh?"

Saunders struggled against his bonds, panic on his sweaty face. He pulled and twisted until the ropes bit into his flesh. When he collapsed back against the cushions, his skin was pale and greasy. For a moment the intruder feared that he was going to choke and he didn't want him to die that way, but the moment passed and he relaxed a little.

"Hello, Mr. Saunders." His voice was conversational, mild even, but he knew that his eyes would betray his true feelings and he enjoyed this moment of play. "Now, you may not know me, but I know you through a mutual acquaintance who is very displeased with you. That probably leaves you with a long list but let me reduce it for you. This person is still inside."

A look of confusion crossed Saunders' face.

"Still too many? Oh well, this is dull anyway. Do you know a nice boy called Wayne Griffiths? Yes, that's right, funny little Wayne has friends in high places. I bet you didn't count on that when you began to bully and abuse him."

Saunders was squirming again now, his eyes bulging above the gag. The man laughed, enjoying the show.

"I've been planning this little scenario ever since he told me about you and I've had plenty of opportunity to refine what I'm going to do. My only problem is that I have so *many* ideas and we have so little time. Ideally, we should spend a whole day together. I'd like that."

Saunders tried to scream against the gag. With a superhuman effort the guard lurched upward, rubbing his shins raw, and the settee jumped an inch in the air.

"Hmm, tricky. You might be more agile than I've given you credit for. I'm going to need a little more help. Don't go away."

He sprinted out to the kitchen and rummaged in his leather bag, talking to himself.

"My little bag of tricks. Ooh, Saunders, I bet you'd love to know what I've got in here for you. Here we are." He sounded like a little boy who had found a long lost toy.

He knotted a length of yellow climber's rope into a noose and forced it over Saunders' head. It tightened immediately and by the time he had secured the loose end around the bannister in the hall, Saunders was blue in the face and gasping for air.

He eased some slack through the knot and watched patiently as the cyanosis faded and his victim resumed the more normal pallor associated with terror.

"That's better. I don't want you dying prematurely. We may not have a lot of time but what we have I want to enjoy." He glanced at his new Italian watch.

"It's almost two forty-five now and I very much doubt that you'll be missed before the eight o'clock shift. What time do you normally arrive I wonder? Not early, so that gives us six hours. Plenty of time!"

Saunders had subsided into a confused stupor, exhausted by his previous asphyxia and already terrified into some sort of dumb acceptance. The man sensed that further words, delicate, almost sensual threats that he had rehearsed silently so many times, would have little effect. He brought his accessories into the living room and started to arrange them on the carpet between the television and the couch. He paused to stare at the pornography on the screen and the sight of it made him grin broadly.

"A fitting backdrop, don't you think? If the pain gets too much you can always try and focus on the three of them. But first, I want to show you what I've brought for our mutual amusement.

"I've chosen a simple theme—'do it yourself'—I rather liked that though I've never been much of a handyman so I'm afraid I haven't had much practice but I don't think that will spoil things."

As he spoke he set out his props: three sharpened screwdrivers, two pairs of pliers, electric wire, a hammer, a hacksaw and small electric drill.

"There. All set. We just need to decide where to start." He glanced over his shoulder, momentarily distracted by the sights on the screen.

"Well, will you look at that!" He said with glee. "Inspiration. Off we go then."

He picked up the hacksaw and turned all his attention to the corpulent man on the couch.

Dawn was long past when he finally packed his equipment away. He'd made more of a mess than he had intended and it took a while to tidy up before he found the shower. His nose wrinkled in disgust at its filthy state as he chose an anti-dandruff shampoo from a surprising selection in the bathroom cupboard. The shower was invigorating and he enjoyed the sensation of slipping into his clean clothes afterward. The dustbin liner was reused for his bloody rubber suit and tools. His gloves were still wet with drying blood and he was tempted to leave them behind but last-minute caution stopped him. He felt incredibly confident, almost protected, but there was no point inviting problems.

He left the house at seven-thirty, slipping out through a strip of back garden that had been left to go to seed, rather like its late owner. His escape route was already planned and he caught the number 25 bus with ease. As it passed the prison he raised his newspaper in front of his face, not so much to hide as to conceal a smile of contempt. They would be starting to wonder about Saunders soon. What would they make of his murder? The idea of their confusion and horror was a powerful aphrodisiac and he scanned the bus expectantly. There was a nurse sitting in the front seat. He sighed deeply with contentment and an old lady opposite rewarded him with a quiet smile.

"Dreadful place that," she volunteered and he nodded his head earnestly.

"Full of terrible people," he agreed.

Something in his tone must have been wrong because the old woman peered at him curiously. Perhaps the bus had been a bad idea after all. He pretended to study a poster and the woman looked away but he could sense her snatching glances at him and he decided to leave the bus at the next stop. The nurse was out of the question anyway now.

He walked the remaining mile to a small car park that he had selected for its lack of CCTV and picked out his vehicle. Intelligence was his main weapon, or so he thought, and it amused him to consider how the police would try to think when they came to investigate his handiwork.

He had never killed a man before and it had been surprisingly satisfying. There had been no urgency, no desire that needed to be held in check, so that inflicting pain had been almost scientific. As he drove away he acknowledged that he had learned a lot and it amused him to think about how he might apply it to the police bitch. Had he not been so sure that her evidence was going to be rejected he would have killed her before the trial. That had been a mistake; he had underestimated her, which meant that a simple death would not suffice. She deserved more.

The teasing was still fun and he thought that it was starting to work. She was losing weight and had grown even more isolated from her friends. He wanted her to suffer in the same way that Wayne was having to, to feel imprisoned in her own life before he ended it for her. But her time was coming. He was not known for his patience and normally thought self-control a waste of energy. As soon as she was truly scared he would kill her, right under the noses of her colleagues.

He stopped at a zebra crossing and waved a mother and child across, giving them a friendly smile as she mouthed a thank you at him before he drove on.

CHAPTER SEVEN

By the end of the week Nightingale had received a further twenty-three hang up calls, four emails from Pandora inviting her to play a game, and two requests from Doctor Batchelor for a meeting. In the end she checked out his credentials and agreed to an interview over the phone just to shut him up.

Batchelor was in no obvious rush to discuss Griffiths and Nightingale had no intention of raising the subject.

"You're not going to ask me, are you?"

"Ask you what, Doctor?"

"About Griffiths."

"Why should I?"

"All right. I'm not going to play games. It's just that sometimes a victim will show a continuing interest in the perpetrator of the crime against them. It's quite common."

"I'm not common," she said, "and I'm not a victim." She immediately regretted her protest. There was no need to explain herself to him.

"But you were attacked. And injured."

"So? It happened while he was resisting arrest."

"I see." He was meant to be asking her about Griffiths, not psychoanalyzing her and she didn't appreciate his word games.

"Get on with it, Doctor, I have work to do."

"Very well. I see Wayne once or twice a week. He has changed in that time from near suicidal to merely depressed."

"Sounds like progress."

Batchelor took her comment at face value.

"Yes, but I've brought him so far and no further."

"You've barely spent six weeks with him. Give it time."

"But I can find no way to penetrate his façade. I'm looking for an insight that will help me take his therapy on to the next stage."

"Surely it's highly irregular to contact someone like me. Speak to his family, or be patient. I can't see how I can help."

"He has no family, at least he hasn't admitted to any and there are no records of friends on his file."

"Well I'm sorry, Doctor Batchelor, but I can't help you . . . unless you're not telling me something." It was a statement, not a question, but as soon as she had said the words Nightingale wanted to take them back. She did *not* want to become involved with Griffiths in any way. She had nightmares enough and didn't need more information to fuel them. Batchelor snatched at her remark with obvious relief.

"You're right. I didn't want to worry you but it seems I have no alternative. Griffiths has kept scrapbooks of the investigation and trial. I judged that it would help him to confront and manage the guilt I believe rests at the heart of his problem."

"Oh please! The man's a sociopath. He has no concept of guilt. He's wholly driven by the desire for power and control over anyone on whom he becomes fixated."

"That's one idea," his sarcasm was unexpected, "but mine is different."

Batchelor's studied calm was starting to irritate Nightingale.

"Then why don't you share it with me?"

"My diagnosis is bound by patient privilege."

"I thought that you hadn't yet made a diagnosis."

She could hear irritation in the sigh and decided to say good-bye. Enough was enough.

"Wait." Batchelor sounded desperate. "The truth is that I do have some emerging ideas. If I could count on your discretion . . ."

"Whom would I tell?" She scoffed at his hesitation.

"Very well. I mentioned his scrapbooks. He has two, one is full of cuttings and print-outs from the Internet."

"Internet! Are you mad? That's how he found and stalked his victims." An unwelcome memory of Pandora's messages surfaced and Nightingale went cold.

"It's only under my direct supervision. I allow him five minutes use as a reward at the end of my session though the Governor is threatening to stop even that. I watch him the whole time. He can only surf and print. Under no circumstances could he send or receive a message."

"I still think it's an unnecessarily risky thing to do, but you said there were two scrapbooks. What's in the second?"

"You. It's full of pictures and photographs, and every single word that was written about you during and after the trial."

"Why?"

"That's what I was hoping you might be able to tell me."

"I have no idea. Is it just me? None of his other victims?" She bit her lip and hoped that he hadn't noticed her slip of the tongue.

"Only you. What happened that should make you so important to him?"

"I arrested him and gave evidence that led to his conviction. He's bound to resent me, perhaps even hate me."

"I don't think it's that simple. This is not about resentment or hate." The way he said the words made her think that he knew more than he was sharing.

"What aren't you telling me?"

Batchelor sighed, suddenly uncomfortable.

"When the press cuttings stopped he started to draw. He's using your photographs as a model. He makes you look like a cross between a queen and a warrior."

"He's drawing Artemesia, the huntress."

"Interesting. If that's who it is, then he sees you as a manifestation. The portraits are perfect."

"And he hasn't drawn any other characters from THE GAME?"

"Only you."

"Well, my amateur analysis is that he's fantasizing about controlling me. Now, I really have to go."

"Can you tell me more about Artemesia?"

"Buy a copy of THE GAME, it's all in there. Oh, Doctor, just one more thing," she hoped that she sounded casual, "does he have access to a phone?"

"No, not yet. The Governor's too worried about him. Why?"

"Nothing."

After she replaced the phone she replayed the conversation over again. Was Griffiths her unwelcome caller? If so then he was finding a way to access the phone unofficially and at all times of the day and night, and that was impossible. It could not be him.

"Wake up, Nightingale, they're looking for you." A ball of paper bounced harmlessly off her head. DS Randall shook his head in exasperation. "You were expected in a briefing five minutes ago."

Nightingale looked at her watch, five past three. She had put the phone down just after two and she couldn't recall doing anything since. A whole hour gone! She grabbed her notebook and ran from the room.

Sergeant Cooper was in a bad mood, something that was no

longer as rare as it had been. For nearly a year the senior officer on his more serious cases had been DI Blite, a man he found it increasingly hard to be civil to, let alone respect. As soon as DCI Fenwick had been seconded to the Metropolitan Police, Blite's ego had expanded to take his place. He had enough arrogance, in Cooper's opinion, for two men but barely enough talent for half. In fact, Cooper thought that his unique skill was the ability to lick the boots of his superior officer while having his nose stuck somewhere up their arse. Marks out of ten for being a contortionist eleven, for being a good detective nil.

Blite prided himself on being the most effective SIO in the Division. The ACC heaped praise on him for his efficiency, while the officers in his team resented the pressure he applied and the hours he expected them to work. They were dealing with a series of violent robberies on a run-down estate. Blite was convinced that the crimes were drug-related but Cooper wasn't so sure. All his instincts told him that they were dealing with something less complicated but more brutal, a gang that simply enjoyed robbing and beating up victims weaker than themselves.

"Now listen up. There are two known drug gangs operating on the Parklea estate. I want you to focus your inquiries on them. So far we've no witnesses and none of the snouts has come up with anything. The latest victim, Emily Thornton, saw them but her glasses were knocked off during the assault and she's as blind as a bat without them, so it's little help."

Nightingale arrived as copies of the briefing were circulating. One look at her convinced Cooper that something was not quite right and he worried that she might shine too bright and burn herself out. The Griffiths investigation had been a step too far. Using her as bait had been Blite's idea but to be fair she had been willing enough to go along with it. Cooper had had his doubts about her role and had gone so far as to consult Fenwick, even though he had been seconded to the Met at the time. The DCI had intervened but been told to mind his own business.

Looking at Nightingale now, Cooper regretted their joint inability to change the course of that investigation. It was widely regarded as a great success, not least by Blite who referred to it on a regular basis, but he was sure they could have achieved the same result through more traditional methods. It would have taken longer, perhaps cost more, but the human toll would have been less.

He caught Nightingale's eye and nodded, no trace of reprimand for her tardiness in his expression. She smiled back but the gesture didn't reach her eyes, which he noticed were blue-ringed.

At the end of the briefing she hung back waiting for him.

"Hello, Sarge." Despite her recent promotion, Nightingale couldn't yet bring herself to call Cooper by his first name. It amused her that he had a similar problem with her, but she took no offense as none was intended.

"Afternoon, Nightingale. So you've drawn the short straw to work with me again have you?"

"I'm looking forward to it. I haven't had a decent case to get my teeth into for a while. Can I be on surveillance? I've been inside for weeks."

It wasn't often that Cooper had a volunteer for surveillance duty and he agreed quickly.

"You'll be on from oh-seven hundred tomorrow. Your partner will be DC Rike. He's experienced. Keep your mouth shut and your eyes open and you might learn something."

He watched her walk away and went to see if Fenwick was back from compassionate leave. He was, and the Chief Inspector motioned him into his office.

"Any chance of two coffees, Anne? Plenty of milk and sugar for Bob." Fenwick motioned Cooper to sit down in one of his visitor's chairs. The Sergeant regarded the skimpy, metal-framed thing with a feeling close to hatred then eased back into it. The Chief Inspector looked at him expectantly. He wasn't a man for small talk or gossip.

"Just came to say that it's good to have you back. We sort of miss you, me and the others, and it would be good to have you more involved in the day-to-day again . . ." His voice trailed away. What was he saying? He'd just implied that Fenwick was being sidelined despite their growing caseload.

"I'll bear that in mind."

Cooper winced. He had never grown used to Fenwick's sarcasm. It was as sharp as raw vinegar and about as palatable. He cleared his throat.

"And I also wanted to say that I am sorry for your loss. Me and the missus were both very sorry to hear about Mrs. Fenwick."

It was as if a fine veil descended across Fenwick's face. As far as Cooper could tell, the expression hadn't changed but he had withdrawn behind a mask that obliterated any emotion from his expression.

"Thank you. Now, if that's all . . ."

Cooper left still holding his untouched coffee and rubbing the back of his right thigh to encourage feeling to return. He should have known better than to stop by.

Behind him Fenwick closed the door. In the privacy of his office he sat down heavily and rubbed his forehead, trying to shift the dull ache that had tormented him since the funeral. Sleep was almost impossible and he refused to take sleeping pills. He had started to miss Monique again as desperately as he had when she had first gone into hospital.

The headache had grown with the fierce sunlight of morning and painkillers had failed to shift it. He rummaged in his desk drawer for some more aspirin and found half a strip. Knowing that he should wait another hour, and only take two, he swallowed three with the dregs of his coffee. There was a tentative knock on the door.

"Phone for you. It's Claire Keating." Anne took one look at his face and took his empty cup away for a refill.

"Claire."

"Andrew, at last. I wanted to say that I'm so sorry for your loss. How are the children?"

"Coping. I'm in a bit of a hurry. What can I do for you?"

"I know that this isn't a good time but I was hoping to see you. I'm writing up the McMillan investigation as a case study and there's a deadline. I wouldn't have troubled you this week otherwise."

"It's years old."

"Yes, but it represents a breakthrough in forensic psychiatry and it would be very helpful to have your input. You were the SIO."

"I see." He tried to keep the sigh from sounding over the phone. "Can it wait until next week?"

"Of course. My deadline is Friday but I'll call and beg some extra time."

They agreed to a time and place to meet and Fenwick put the phone down with relief.

The prisoner had put on weight. He performed press-ups, squats and sit-ups for hours every day, but the weight had still crept up on him. He imagined yellow globules of fat coagulating under his skin and the thought repulsed him. On the rare occasions that he was allowed out into the yard, he jogged for the whole hour, sprinting in short bursts. During that too-short time he could feel the burn in his muscles and the pain was exquisite. They were brief flashes of orange-red in an otherwise gray life.

For some reason he had been denied further computer access. No amount of argument had persuaded the Governor to relent. Instead, the doctor had brought him the board version of THE GAME. Griffiths had ignored it, too insulted even to acknowledge its existence in his tiny cell. For over a week it had lain undisturbed, wrapped in plastic, accumulating a layer of gritty dust from the walls.

He had been a Grand Master. His score on capture had been a magical, and purely coincidental, 666,106. It was an unchallenged record for the Demon King, or it had been. One of the many reasons he was desperate for release was to ensure that he still reigned supreme. What was moulded plastic compared with the reality of a live game?

Today had marked the low point since his capture and he was filled with self-loathing. He had long nails and wasn't allowed a manicure set to neaten them. His hair curled over his collar, inches longer than he had ever worn it in his life. Prison trousers pinched at his thickening waist. And last night he had opened the board game.

The sight of the Demon King in crude black plastic had brought tears to his eyes. It was so grotesque, as if his own weight-gain had blurred the shape of his alter ego. He had stared at the figure, detesting it, before collapsing onto his bunk in a black mood. For the first time the idea occurred to him that he might indeed spend his life in this cell as the judge had intended. When he woke before dawn, the depression was still there and he contemplated suicide for the first time.

It was ironic that he had mimicked a self-destructive motivation before without any intention to do himself harm. Now the authorities were more relaxed, convinced by his play-acting that he was beginning to accept his fate, yet for the first time the idea of death appealed. There was comfort in the idea that he could kill himself, and the intellectual challenge of working out how would keep him occupied. He still had no belt or braces, and his uniform could not be torn. No sharp instruments were allowed anywhere near him. Perhaps if he could feign illness they would take him to the hospital and an opportunity would present itself.

He was practicing expressions of intense agony when a warning rattle of keys announced an intruder. He expected to see Saunders, it was his shift, but instead another guard jerked his thumb at the open door.

"Your shrink's here. Get a move on."

Batchelor was waiting for him wearing that sports jacket again, the one that looked mouldy, and there was a spot of dried food on his woolen tie. He hid his contempt behind a half smile.

"Dr. Batchelor. How good of you to come and see me again."

"Are you keeping well?"

Thoughts of suicide, the infirmary, perhaps even escape whirled in the prisoner's head. Did he want to die? He wasn't sure. Best to keep his options open.

"So, so. I keep getting this twisting pain in my stomach. It doesn't last long but it's uncomfortable."

A look of immediate concern showed on Batchelor's face.

"Have you seen a doctor?"

"Only you."

"I meant a physician."

"No, haven't asked to. I'll see how it goes. I'm sure it's nothing."

The conversation drifted into the usual psychobabble that passed for analysis. Now that he knew he wouldn't be granted further access to a personal computer, the prisoner saw little purpose in these conversations. He was placid and formless yet never out of control. In order to prevent the doctor from becoming too frustrated he would throw in a fit of gloom or introspection that kept him coming back.

An unwelcome thought ambushed him. Today he had no need to fake his depression.

". . . you'd be interested," the doctor said.

"Pardon?"

"I said I spoke to DS Nightingale."

He felt as if he had been struck a blow to the chest. For a fraction of a second he didn't know how to react, then he realized that the shock must have shown in his expression. There was a brief look of satisfaction on the bastard's smug face. Griffiths felt tricked, outsmarted by a quack, and his self-esteem shrank even further.

"Why did you do that?" Griffiths was proud that his voicc was level.

"Oh, a chance conversation. I thought you'd be interested."

He said nothing. When it was obvious that he was going to remain silent Batchelor tried his next move.

"I can see why she took the role of Artemesia. She's almost the perfect huntress, don't you think?"

Griffiths said nothing. Anger smoldered inside, banked up against the future.

"What was her best score against you?"

"27,500."

"That's good, isn't it?"

"Almost the best." He would not meet the doctor's eyes.

"Are you enjoying the board game?"

How he would love to have said that he hadn't even opened it, to thrust the shiny plastic bundle back into Batchelor's arms, unborn. But that wasn't true now.

"I haven't played it. There's no excitement without competition."

"Why?"

Here we are again, he thought, back with the same inane questions. These he could parry for as long as he liked. With a smile Griffiths went into his routine.

Back in his cell, after hours of agonizing over the decision, the prisoner finally re-opened the box and unpacked its contents. The six main characters stood three inches high, their acolytes a mere one-and-a-half. As well as the Demon King, which was black with highlights of red and silver paint, there was the Sorceress—blue and silver—and the Knight, a laughable character, all blond hair, white armor and golden weaponry. Every male newcomer to THE GAME wanted to be the knight. Most of them "died." He was brave, courageous, honest and thus easy to defeat. Whatever he said had to be true as laws of chivalry bound him. On average the Demon King triumphed over him three times out of five but one hundred percent of the time whenever Griffiths had played.

The Mercenary was a more interesting challenger. He frequently teamed up with the Sorceress, although his loyalty could never be relied upon. And the Maiden—ah, Griffiths loved her, as did the Mercenary. One could never be sure whether he would follow the rules of money or love, but capturing the Maiden was usually a successful way to neutralize his skill.

He fingered the white plastic dress and long blond hair. She carried a spray of red and white roses, symbols of her maidenhood and vulnerability. She never attacked, but if rescued in the wrong way she absorbed the strength of her would-be savior. Griffiths thought her the most corrupt of the characters. Whenever he caught a Maiden he used them as bait before killing them; not against the rules exactly but always a shock to the other players.

He picked out Artemesia. For some reason her features were

finer, better articulated then all the others. The modeling of her weapons—bow, arrows, knife, and spear—was detailed and precise. He stared at her for a long time.

She was wearing a long, green Grecian-style tunic, slashed at both thighs. It flowed around her as if blown by a phantom wind, moulding her breasts and pelvis like Botticelli's Flora. He imagined warm flesh hiding beneath the thin material and grew excited. He placed her down gently and sorted out his drawing materials.

Despite the growing pressure inside him he followed his ritual. Paper set exactly in the middle of the tabletop; chalks and eraser to the right; water-color pencils and a small plastic bowl of water to the left. With a fine piece of chalk he started to sketch the figure. His lines were long and fluid, gliding easily over the smooth paper. He drew in the bitch's face exactly, but the body beneath was more voluptuous. In his drawing, he stripped her of her robe. The breeze had raised her nipples to hard pink points; her sex pouted, pretty as a kiss beneath luxuriant pubic hair the color of aubergines. Looking at her made his breath come in short gasps and he forgot about his drawing.

When he climaxed he cried out—a growl, a name, he didn't know, but the release was exquisite. For once he was oblivious to the peephole in the door as he sprawled back in the chair, exposed. He hadn't felt like this since . . . well, in a long time, before that bitch had ruined his life.

He washed fastidiously. When he was quite clean he bent to pick up his latest drawing, to slip it into his scrapbook. The paper was torn. In his ecstasy he had stabbed her. A great gaping red wound had ripped apart her paper breasts and throat. He stroked the drawing with his fingertips, lingering over the face and crimson tear.

It would have to go. The guards searched his cell regularly

and Batchelor insisted on looking through his scrapbook, yet he couldn't face the thought of simply screwing up the picture and throwing it away. It had become a totem, a promise of something beyond the prison cell. The idea that he could always draw another didn't appease his desire to preserve this one. He wanted to sleep knowing that he had it, to wake and be able to unfold it secretly and remember the taste of her tears. He would be revenged for this imprisonment. A promise had been made and he knew it wouldn't be broken, it was only a matter of time. Meanwhile the picture would be a talisman.

He looked for a hiding place. His gaze was drawn to the game, lying scattered on the floor. The laminate on the glossy moulded board had split, peeling away from the cardboard backing. He picked it up and with a long fingernail began to prise it apart. The drawing, folded once, slid neatly between the plastic surface and card backing. He squeezed the board together again. No one would notice the damage.

Instead of packing THE GAME away he started to read the rulebook. After his evening food he began to play, throwing the elaborate set of five varicolored dice with increasing dexterity. He memorized the possible combinations and the implications of each score. There were tens of thousands of variations, even in this non-computerized version. With a small grunt of pleasure, he pulled his paper and charcoal toward him and began to note down his first ideas for mastery of this new Game.

CHAPTER EIGHT

Parklea Estate had been built late enough in the 1970s for there to have been no excuse for the mistakes of design. The towers rose sixteen stories, with half-covered walkways joining them in an ugly concrete spider's web. They criss-crossed above long-dead patches of lawn, casting shadows and providing a perfect launch-pad for the missiles that were cast down by the younger generation on the old.

On Monday morning the estate was dry, hot and airless. The stench of urine and dog or human excrement from numerous hidden corners made the officers concealed in flat 6B Compton gag. Past tenants had run ahead of eviction and trashed the place. The Council had not bothered to repair the damage and it had become a squat, then a doss-house for down and outs. After a fire had threatened to spread to the occupied part of the block, the Council finally took steps to secure the premises. They had been empty ever since.

Unfortunately, 6B was the perfect location for police surveillance of the open ground that lay between the towers, half in shadow, the other half burned white. DS Nightingale was on first watch, her partner wore his undercover five-day growth of beard and long greasy hair with pride. He was currently in a café on the other side of the estate buying breakfast.

DC Rike had taken one look at her designer jeans and freshly laundered T-shirt and suggested that she should stay concealed until the end of their shift. So she was condemned to this stinking cell for another six hours and twelve minutes exactly.

Tomorrow she'd remember to bring some bin liners to sit on but right now she had the choice between enduring the discomfort of remaining standing or the horror of being contaminated by whatever had been smeared on the walls or deposited on the floor. She chose pain.

The door banged open and she jumped. It was Richard Rike, returning with hot drinks for them both.

"Jesus, it stinks in here!"

"I hardly notice it now. They say that after about twenty minutes the olfactory system adjusts, neutralizing the odor."

"You what?"

He handed her one of the cups and she lifted the lid from the Styrofoam to reveal a weak, milky drink. She had asked for her coffee black, no sugar. She took a sip. It was lukewarm, and sweet.

"Your nose doesn't smell anymore—the brain sort of blocks out the stench."

Rike looked at his watch.

"Only nineteen minutes and thirty seconds to go then. I couldn't remember whether you said you wanted tea or coffee so I got you tea, just how I like my women: white with two lumps." He grinned in anticipation of her disapproval.

Nightingale kept a straight face.

"Pity, I'd asked for coffee, just how I like my men: black and strong."

He barked with laughter and threw one of the bags at her.

"What's this?"

"An iced doughnut. They're yesterday's. The van with the fresh stuff hadn't arrived, but they're OK. I've had one."

Nightingale looked at the sugar-coated wedge of greasy dough and tried to feel hungry. She'd only had an apple for breakfast and that had been two hours ago.

"You going to eat that?"

"Not if you're still hungry. You have it."

He demolished the cake in three large bites, cramming them in with barely a pause. It was gone in thirty seconds. She tried not to stare and looked away from the goo-covered teeth of his triumphant smile.

"Fastest in the canteen," he spluttered proudly.

"I can believe that."

The conversation proved to be the high point of their day.

They were relieved from duty at four o'clock and Rike went off to deliver their brief report to Blite.

It was gone half past four by the time she reached home. She padded up the stairs to her flat in socks. As soon as she was inside, every stitch of clothing went into the washing machine with an extra load of powder. For once she didn't care if her T-shirt and underwear turned blue, she just wanted them clean. She showered twice.

There was a pub opposite the park and she decided to go out for her wine instead of staying home. That way she could pretend that she wasn't a solitary drinker, honest. It was turning into a glorious evening, cool after the heat of the day. She'd almost walked to her destination when she cannoned into a good-looking man who stepped out in front of her.

"I'm sorry, I didn't mean to startle you."

"That's OK." She moved to walk around him but he spoke, preventing her.

"You wouldn't know of a place where I can get a decent drink would you?"

He had amazing eyes, a charming smile and looked vaguely familiar so she took the time to answer, although part of her thought it odd that he should ask so close to a public house.

"This place is pretty good."

He looked around as if surprised to see the swinging sign above his head.

"I hadn't even seen it! You must think I'm stupid. Is this your local? If so, can I buy you a drink in apology for being dumb?"

Nightingale was almost tempted but she was saved the problem of giving an answer by a shout from across the road. She recognized the familiar voice.

"Hello, Sarge." Cooper dodged the slow-moving traffic and joined her. When she turned to speak to the mystery man he had already melted away into the evening. She shrugged and forgot him.

"I was on my way home. Dot has me walking it at least once a week, says it's healthy. Fancy a quick drink now that we're here?"

"Well I . . ."

"Come on, the Dog and Duck does a good pint and the wife tells me the wine's quite decent."

Despite the temperature he was wearing his customary tweed jacket. It had to be quite new as the elbows didn't yet display leather patches. His face was glowing as they entered the beer garden, a cobbled yard into which trestle tables and benches had been squeezed between tubs overflowing with geraniums. They chose a table in the shade by the wall.

"What'll it be?"

"A glass of white wine please, and a still water if that's OK."

He was back quickly, carrying their drinks on a round tin

tray promoting the last surviving local brewery. There were two packets of crisps wedged between the glasses.

"There you go. Plain or cheese 'n' onion?"

"I'm not . . ."

"Plain it is then. Go on, eat them. I bet you didn't have a proper lunch."

She couldn't argue because he was right. As she opened the packet, the smell of salt, potato and fat made her mouth water.

Cooper told her about his last case, then about his daughter and her baby that was due any day. He followed up with news about his son's job, his wife's garden and the diet that she had put him on. At the end of a quarter of an hour he stood up suddenly and went to buy fresh drinks. Nightingale waited, feeling surprisingly relaxed by his easy chatter.

All the tables had been taken and there was a pleasant buzz of conversation. She tuned out of it and stared over the post-and-rail fence to the cars parked beyond. A silver Saab pulled into the car park and her stomach lurched at its familiar shape. Fenwick stepped from the driver's side and went round to open the passenger door. She recognized the woman's reddish brown hair and the profile was familiar but a name escaped her. She said something that made Fenwick laugh and Nightingale had to look away.

"There you are, another glass of Chablis, some more water and these." Cooper passed her a plate of sandwiches. "Smoked salmon on brown bread with lemon, no mayonnaise for you, and roast beef and mustard for me," he paused, frowned suddenly at his presumption, and said, "unless you want to swap. This is only a snack before dinner."

"You shouldn't have, Sarge."

"Don't be daft. You need to eat. You're skin and bones these days, although I'm probably not allowed to say that. I bet you've nothing but rabbit food in your fridge."

She opened her mouth to protest but closed it quickly with a wry smile. He was right. Cooper grinned and arranged the plate and paper napkin in front of her. He was about to demolish a quarter of his own sandwich in one bite when the sound of a familiar voice made him twist and look over his shoulder.

"Evening, Bob."

"Evening, sir." Old habits died hard where Cooper was concerned.

"Relax, don't get up. Hello, Nightingale, how are you?" He sounded happy.

"Fine, thank you." She forced herself to smile.

"Have a pleasant evening, both of you." He turned away to join his companion who had been waiting at the door.

Cooper put his sandwich down untouched.

"Well, that's a bit of a surprise!" He took a sip of beer and shook his head at the closing door. "I hadn't expected to see him out like that so soon. Not that there's anything wrong with it, mind."

"So soon after what?"

The Sergeant stared at her in surprise.

"You haven't heard? His wife died. She'd been in a coma for years, of course, but she's passed away at last. It was a blessing really."

He took another sip of beer and looked at her with concern. "Are you all right?"

"I . . . I hadn't heard." She blinked a few times and looked down at her wine as she sipped. It was impossible to meet his eyes.

Cooper held his silence but she could feel him watching her as he munched steadily through his sandwich and washed it down with beer.

"Would you like another?"

She stared at her empty glass in surprise.

"No thanks. I really ought to be going."

"You should eat something."

"I'm not hungry right now. Can I take them home with me?" She was already wrapping the sandwiches in a paper parcel, folding the edges precisely.

"Just promise me that they're not going to end up in the dustbin."

Her fingers hesitated for a moment.

"I promise. I must go. Thanks for the drink, it was very kind of you."

Inside her flat she was greeted by a soft whirring from the fridge as it pumped out hot air in an effort to chill its contents. She opened the door and changed the temperature setting, confused as to why it should have been on fast freeze in the first place. Had she done that this morning? A shrill bell sounded as she locked the front door. Instinctively she checked the smoke detector but it was silent. As she pushed open the bedroom door it grew louder. Baffled, she silenced the alarm clock and studied the time it had been set for, seven-twenty, yet that morning she'd had to be on duty by seven.

The skin between her shoulder blades prickled. She was sure that she hadn't re-set the clock. There had to be a logical, non-threatening reason for the change in time but she couldn't think of one. Her hands were shaking as she replaced the clock on the bedside table. If she hadn't reset the fridge and alarm clock then someone else had and that person could still be in her flat.

She slammed the door of the bathroom back hard. The handle hit the wall with a thud and bounced back. The shower was on full but no one was lurking behind the curtain. The spare bedroom was empty, the built-in wardrobe crammed so full of clothes that there was no space for someone to conceal themselves. That left her sitting room.

Nightingale took a large knife from the wooden bloc in the kitchen and checked that no others were missing. Forcing her breathing steady and silent she crept toward the partially open door. She bent down and looked through the gap along the hinges. When she was sure that no one was hiding behind the door she moved into the room, aware that sweat on her palms was making the knife handle slippery. The sofa was in its normal place, flush to the wall. That left the curtains on the two picture windows. One faced south, the other west. The curtains had been pulled closed. Had she done that this morning to keep the room cool? She didn't think so and her hands started to shake. It was almost impossible to keep her breathing under control, her throat was tight and her heart was beating so hard that the blood in her ears deafened her.

Nightingale switched the knife to her other hand and dried her palm on her shirt before gripping it again even tighter. In self-defense class she had been taught to move surely and only to carry a weapon if she was confident that she would be able to keep control and use it. She took a long, silent breath and frowned. Which window? Choose the wrong one and she would present her back to the intruder.

She was about to choose south window when the right hand curtain in the west window twitched. It was the faintest movement. When she blinked the material was hanging still again but it was enough to decide her. In one fluid run, she reached the drapes and yanked them back, her right hand raised to strike.

There was an awful shriek and a massive black cat twisted toward her, arching its back and spitting in fury, as ready to attack as Nightingale had been. She jumped away in shock and checked the other curtain quickly to confirm that nobody was there. The cat regarded her with pure hatred, its claws gouging great tufts of wool from her cream carpet.

At first she didn't know whether to laugh or cry, then she found that she was doing both. Whoever had set this practical joke, for that is what it had to be, couldn't have known of her childhood fear of cats, particularly black ones. Her mother had had a cat very like this, a malignant animal that had hated her for no reason. One day it had lain in wait on the stairs for her to pass below and had laced its jealous claws beneath the skin of her scalp.

It had to go. With this creature in the flat she couldn't think straight. Yet it stared up at her, confidant and quite at home. Nightingale edged back toward the hall where she had left her bag without taking her eyes from the cat. She opened the clasp and pulled out her wrapped sandwich, wrinkling her nose in displeasure at the smell of the warm smoked salmon. There was a click of claws on wood as the cat walked into the hall, nose and tail twitching in time. She threw a piece of salmon and it took a few steps forward watching her with deep suspicion. She backed off toward the front door, giving the animal more space. It settled into a preparatory crouch. Nightingale waited, hoping that greed would overcome distrust. Minutes passed then its hindquarters shivered and the tail flicked, just as her mother's monster had done as it stalked baby birds. Another quiver and it finally pounced.

The slice of salmon disappeared and the cat licked the floor where it had lain before looking up expectantly for more. Nightingale opened the front door and set another piece of fish just outside, then a third on the top of the stairs before throwing the last piece onto the half-landing below her.

The cat made a run for the second piece, grabbed it and swerved away as she went to push it outside. She missed but it ran along the landing anyway and she slammed the door behind it. Through the peephole she watched it turn and stare at her flat before eating the third sliver and heading down the stairs.

Her hands were shaking as she locked the door again and wedged a chair beneath the handle. She scrubbed the floor clean, vacuumed the carpet and dusted everywhere that the cat might have touched, then she ran a bath. The intrusion into her flat, the sight of Fenwick with Claire, and the news of his wife's death had stretched her feelings to breaking point. It occurred to her that she had at last arrived at a clear choice. She could give in to the self-pitying malaise and fear that had threatened to overwhelm her since the trial or pull herself together.

Whoever put the cat in her flat must have hoped to scare her witless and make her paranoid but they were going to be disappointed. She felt something of her old courage return, a grain of tough self-sufficiency that she feared had been lost forever.

As her bath filled, she checked the answering machine: six calls, five silent heavy-breathers and one message. "Welcome home," a man's voice said, then laughed. The fine hair on her arms rose and she rubbed them vigorously. On her PC she had three emails from Pandora. She deleted them all.

In the warm, lavender-scented water she laid back, closed her eyes and tried to think. She should report the break-in and the phone calls. They were linked—the last message made that clear—and somebody had invaded her home; she had to take that seriously. But would her colleagues at Harlden treat it the same way? One or two of them would; George Wicklow and, of course, Bob Cooper, but there were plenty of others who still resented her promotion and would spread the story about with a negative twist. Neurotic, that's what they'd call her; attention-seeking. And Quinlan would insist on her moving away for her own good. The thought of the consequences of making a formal report made her shudder but she could no longer ignore the fact that somebody had decided to try and terrorize her. It was time to do something about it and she would after her shift finished tomorrow.

Mentally she was beginning to feel better. Physically she was a wreck. She could count her ribs even if she didn't breathe in; her wrists and anklebones were sharp; her head ached and her eyes were hot and dry. It was possible that she had a temperature. She told herself that all she needed was a decent night's sleep and a good meal to put her right, and she almost believed it.

After her bath she cooked herself scrambled eggs on toast and made herself eat it all. She felt sick but more alert than she'd been for some time. Before going to bed early she re-checked every possible entry into her flat. They were all secure, with no marks to suggest how her intruder had gained access but she looked up the name of a locksmith to call in the morning anyway. At nine o'clock, she took a half a sleeping tablet, hoping that its effects would have worn off by six when the alarm would wake her. The next thing she was aware of was the bell from the clock, faithful to time, summoning her to the morning. With gritty eyes and a dry mouth she rose to confront the new day.

Blite met the team at the rendezvous point. It was already twenty degrees even though it wasn't yet seven o'clock. Despite the heat, the Inspector was wearing a jumper beneath his jacket and he looked terrible. The whole team was to be positioned out of sight around the estate. One of the more experienced officers objected.

"There are only ten of us, including you. Shouldn't there be more?"

"Waste of resources. We know where the post office is and all the attacks have been within three hundred yards of it."

He jabbed a grubby handkerchief at a plan of the estate opened on the bonnet of his car. In two dimensions it all seemed logical, and Blite had only visited the location once. Perhaps he'd forgotten the walkways and stairwells, the ants' hill of passages that made up the site. They would never be able to cover it.

Nightingale stifled a sneeze and took a sip of water from one of the bottles she had remembered to bring with her. Two others were frozen solid within a rucksack in the hope that they would hold their chill during the heat of the day. Blite coughed again and spat phlegm onto the cracked tarmac before putting a hand to his ribs. Mentally she shook her head. Blite didn't have the instincts of a wombat and was a useless operational officer.

She studied the plan, superimposing onto it her limited knowledge of the estate. If the attackers doubled back, away from the post office, they had a choice of at least four escape routes, one of which passed close to the derelict flat in which she was sentenced to spend the day with Richard Rike the doughnut monster. Even with her limited experience she estimated that they needed another four officers. She opened her mouth to add her concern to that already raised.

"With respect, when one takes into account the walkways above, and the alleys, it will be very difficult to cover all possible escape routes. The teams on the periphery will be too far away if there's an attack."

Blite looked at her in astonishment, his disdain undermined by his bulbous red nose and watering eyes.

"When I want your opinion, Sergeant, I'll ask for it. Now shut it and get into position before the whole estate is awake."

Rike pulled at her sleeve and she followed him.

"That took balls," he glanced at her, "so to speak, but it was hopeless, I could've told you that. I've worked with him too often to even bother any more. We'll be OK though, he usually has the luck of Old Nick. I reckon he's sold his soul."

"As long as he doesn't sell ours as well while he's at it."

Rike opened a greasy bag and shoved it toward her. "Bacon sarni? Home made by Linda, my better half. She got up early to see me off."

It was said with pride and she took one to avoid hurting his feelings.

"Why is Superintendent Quinlan giving Blite so much of the tough stuff?"

"Instead of DCI Fenwick you mean?" He eyed her shrewdly but she was a good poker player. "Rumor has is that the ACC wants to see more on Blite's CV asap. Thinks Quinlan's kept him in the backroom too much."

That made sense. Word on the evergreen and usually healthy grapevine was that the promotion boards were looking for more "real" police experience these days. Front line skills were in demand again.

In their stinking hide, Nightingale shivered and stifled another sneeze. She cursed Blite's germ-ridden briefings. The first bottle of water went quickly but she was sweating so much that she didn't need to go and find another room to squat in to relieve herself. The shivers started before eight and she took two Nurofen. Rike seemed fine.

"Never catch cold, me. Constitution of an ox. Me grandad lived to ninety-three, and two of his sisters are still alive. A long-lived family we are. Doughnut? Feed a cold, they say."

Nightingale shook her head and rubbed one of the icy bottles against her forehead. Sweat trickled between her breasts and down her back. Richard slipped out for coffees and this time he remembered her order. She sipped the bitter, black liquid and turned from hot to freezing cold. This felt more like flu and she cursed her stupid body for its weakness. It's all in the mind, she tried telling herself, then sneezed three times. Her radio transmitter squawked loudly and Richard rushed to turn down the volume. The operations center had DI Blite back with them and he ordered Rike to another vantage point about thirty meters away. He slipped the radio into his pocket and turned to go.

"Don't forget this." Nightingale handed him his Kevlar vest and he touched his forehead in thanks.

An hour later, she could see him pacing back and forth in his tatty shirtsleeves, trying to walk the cramp from his legs. Her own muscles spasmed sympathetically and her back ached. Part of her brain said that it would be sensible to call in sick but then she remembered how much worse Blite had been and guessed that he would only tell her to stay put. But when she found herself about to the leave the flat for some fresh air her stupidity made her shudder. There was no question in her mind now that she had to go home. One call to Operations and a replacement would be on its way.

She looked around for her radio but it was nowhere to be found. Rike must have taken hers with him by mistake after he had silenced it. All she had was her mobile phone. One button dialed Harlden station and she waited impatiently for the switchboard to answer.

There was quite a stir in the Operations Room when DI Blite collapsed. Sergeant John Adams, the nearest first-aider enjoyed being at the center of attention but his pleasure faded as he stared down at Blite's corpulent form and the contagious air around him.

"It's this viral flu," said Sergeant Wicklow knowingly as he watched John check vital signs and call an ambulance. "My next door neighbor's got it. He's been terrible. In bed for a week, doctor out every other day." He jerked his hand toward the man lying unconscious on the floor. "Should have stayed at home. All he's done is bring his germs in here."

John wasn't a fan of DI Blite but he recognized a very ill man when he saw one.

"This might be pneumonia. Be a bit more sympathetic, poor bugger's not well."

Wicklow sniffed without compassion and turned his attention to his duties. The first priority was to alert the Superintendent that his SIO on a live operation was out cold. Quinlan's response was predictably direct.

"Find Fenwick, quickly."

The Chief Inspector was tracked down to another endless meeting on new procedures that the Superintendent had delegated to him. He listened, suddenly attentive, and went to find Cooper for a briefing. Despite the Sergeant's studied neutrality it took Fenwick less than five minutes to share his concern that the surveillance was under-resourced. He swallowed a sharp remark that would have betrayed how little respect he had for Blite and called Quinlan's office. On his way up the stairs, with Cooper increasingly lagging behind, he asked about the gang's MO.

"Are they armed?"

"A baseball bat. No guns or knives so far." Cooper paused at a turn in the stairs and gulped in air.

"That's bad enough. What back-up's been arranged?"

"The minimum and an alert in Ops to be on standby."

"Bloody stupid, penny-pinching prick."

"Pardon, sir?"

"Nothing. I'll see you in Quinlan's office."

Then he was gone though the door.

"We need more resources, sir."

"So soon!" Quinlan laughed. "I had expected ooh, at least," he pretended to consult his watch, "another hour before this request."

"I'm serious. I think this operation could be heading for disaster. At best it might fail, at worst someone could be hurt."

"How many more."

"Eight, six at a pinch, just for the rest of the day. I'll reconsider tonight if nothing happens."

There was a hesitant tap on the door and Cooper walked in.

"Bob, help Andrew find another six. It's got my backing. You'll be going straight out there yourself, I imagine."

"Of course I will."

Perspiration was dripping from Nightingale's chin onto the bare wood of the windowsill where it evaporated in magnified sunlight within thirty seconds. She watched in fascination as the dark blot shrank and faded from sight, almost hypnotized by the process. The operations center had told her to stay put until a relief officer could reach her. She'd given up counting seconds, now she marked time by keeping note of the number of sneezes per minute. The record so far was six.

Every joint in her body ached, even the knuckles in her fingers and toes throbbed. Occasionally her vision blurred, nothing dramatic, just a faint fogging around the edges. Whatever virus Blite had given her, something in her body had supercharged the germs and she was failing fast. At one o'clock she drank the last of her water and tried to eat an apple she'd brought with her. After some unsuccessful scrapes at the skin she threw it away. Rike hadn't returned to the flat and he still had her radio.

There was a noise from outside, not alarming just unusual. She peered out of the window and Richard's head popped up over a wall, but there was nothing for either of them to see.

She heard another sound, an obvious shout this time, and straightened up, flexing her toes within her trainers. Across the square, about two hundred meters away, she saw two figures creep around the corner. One looked no older than sixteen, his companion was even younger. They were hiding, so tense that even at this distance she could feel it, like cats waiting to pounce. An old man ran through a passageway into the square, glancing back fearfully over his shoulder. The gang must have split into two—drivers and catchers.

Nightingale watched the boys waiting to spring their trap, unable to alert the others because Richard had taken her radio. The old man had almost reached his hidden attackers yet the square remained empty. She had to decide—watch and wait in the hope that help would arrive or break cover to save the old man from hurt but risk his attackers escaping. There was really no choice.

Her legs felt like jelly but she moved as fast as she could, buckling her vest as she went. Outside it was like running through water. The square was massive, the old man too far away. One of the boys already had an arm around his throat.

"Police." Her cry was a feeble croak. She cleared her throat and tried again. "Police!"

That was better. There was another shout, Richard's echoed "Police," as he reached the square far behind her. He too was wearing his Kevlar vest.

The teenagers dropped their victim in an untidy heap on the ground and started running toward Nightingale. She had thought that they would turn away but she'd underestimated their aggression. As they closed on her she studied their eyes and realized that they were high on something. When they saw Richard, they hesitated and the younger of the two started backing away toward the passage. Two against a single woman might have been good odds but Richard looked as if he meant business.

Nightingale slowed, waiting for Richard to catch up.

"Come on! Get the fuck out of it." The younger one decided to run but his partner ignored him, confrontation flaming in his eyes as he squared up to Richard.

"Stay away, fucker."

Richard stopped when he reached Nightingale. The youth waved a knife in wild arcs as Richard held up his hands, palms out in a gesture of peace.

"It's OK, son. Drop the knife." He was out of the crazy boy's reach but not beyond a sudden lunge.

The kid wasn't listening. He was swinging the knife again, agitated and dancing from foot to foot. The old man lay still on the ground.

"Stay the fuck away, you fucker. Any closer and I'll fucking kill you, I mean it."

"No need for that. Look, I'm just going to stay here." Richard glanced at Nightingale. He whispered softly, from the side of his mouth.

"Where's back-up? I called this in. They should be here by now. Chase them."

"You've got my radio," she murmured, trying to keep her voice from the boy, who was panicking now. His eyes slid from side to side, as if figuring out how and when to attack.

"Stop talking, you pigs." The boy chanced a step closer. Adrenaline rushed through Nightingale. Child or not, he was capable of killing them both.

There was a shout from behind them. Six officers came pounding around the corner of the furthest block. The boy saw them and freaked out. Instead of running he leaped forward and slashed out at Richard. The blade slid off his protective vest but caught the flesh of his forearm. Blood welled up instantly through his shirt. The sight of it threw the boy into frenzy. He struck out in all directions, cutting Richard's palms as he tried to ward off the attack.

Blood was everywhere, pumping out with arterial force. She tried to attract the boy's attention, shouting at him, urging him to attack her but the boy only had eyes for the man. As she watched, Richard stumbled, his face bone white, and she reached out to support him. She clamped her hand over his gushing arm, pressing hard, and they backed away, giving the boy more room, but he paced forward. A wild animal crazed by the chemicals in his brain and the smell and sight of blood, he was circling in for the kill.

She saw people running across the square but they were too far away. The boy lunged again, aiming for Richard's neck, the hatred in his eyes shading them red and black. The blade scratched the skin and pinpricks of blood bloomed on the surface. Nightingale tried to angle Richard behind her, out of the boy's line of sight, hoping to break the spell of aggression that bound them together. He let out a scream of rage and jumped, knocking them both to the ground.

"Die, you fuckers!" He screamed as he stabbed at them.

Nightingale felt the blade jar her protected back and nick her arm before it slid toward Richard, narrowly missing his eye and slicing a thin piece of skin from the top of his ear. He raised his bloodstained hands in defense as the blade swung again.

"Help me. For God's sake!"

Nightingale heard the fear in his cry. With a superhuman effort she pulled at him and rolled them both away. Their attacker was on his hands and knees, his teeth bared in a snarl. She raised herself up and dragged Richard further out of reach as the front runners of their rescue party slammed into the boy, knocking him flat and jarring the knife from his grasp. One hundred and sixty pounds of pissed-off policeman collapsed on top of him and dragged his arms behind his back, cuffing him so tight that the flesh went white.

As two officers held the spitting, cussing boy, the rest attended to the old man, Richard and Nightingale, muttering meaningless words of reassurance. In the distance she could here an ambulance siren and pressed harder on her partner's gushing wound.

CHAPTER NINE

"Come in, Louise." Superintendent Quinlan looked up at her and smiled. "Sit down. How are you feeling?"

"Fine, thank you." She sat obediently, her face expressionless.

"Ah, Andrew. Good."

Nightingale started but kept her face forward. She'd been away sick for two weeks, during which time a discreet internal investigation had exonerated her completely. Blame had been placed firmly where it belonged for once, on the flu-ridden shoulders of Inspector Blite. He had explained away his error of judgment as a consequence of his illness and the Assistant Chief Constable was inclined to concur. Quinlan had held a diplomatic silence but in the locker rooms and at canteen tables, views were expressed freely and the verdict was that Blite's penny-pinching habits had been found out at last.

DC Richard Rike would be off work for at least a month, perhaps longer if he needed further surgery on the severed tendon in his wrist. Nightingale had refused the offer of further counseling. After one obligatory visit for assessment she'd locked herself up in her flat with flu remedies, aspirin and Mrs. Cooper's soup. The counselor who visited her came away concerned and her report was one of many that Superintendent Quinlan had been studying before his officers arrived.

For such a youngster Louise Nightingale's personnel file was surprisingly thick. It included a commendation for bravery, references to two hospital visits for injuries received in the line of duty and a letter from the barrister for the prosecution complimenting her performance at the Griffiths trial.

He glanced down at the papers, deep in thought, comfortable with the silence that had fallen in his office and unsurprised by it. Neither Fenwick nor Nightingale indulged in small talk. He used to think that there were a lot of similarities between them but now he was less convinced.

Andrew Fenwick seemed to have grown younger. He looked tanned, fit and full of energy. The awful tightness that had locked his mouth and lower jaw rigid during the years of his wife's illness had softened at last. In contrast Nightingale was paper white and gaunt. Her wrists looked like thin bundles of twigs that could be snapped in a firm grip. The purple half-moons beneath her eyes were the only color in her face. Although neat and tidy as always, her hair was lifeless and her clothes hung on her body.

Sergeant Cooper had visited her while she had been away, taking with him the best of his wife's home cooking. He hadn't formally reported back his deep concerns but had talked privately and his views eventually reached the Superintendent's office. Cooper's story was that she had been on her own with only some stray cat for company, which he suspected of eating most of his wife's meat pies.

The woman needed a complete change. The transfer he was going to recommend would be perfect for her.

"Are you sure that you're completely recovered, Louise?"

"*Completely*, sir. I would've returned on Monday if the doctor hadn't been such a wimp." There was a new harshness in her tone.

"I see," Quinlan was frowning, "in that case, I can see no

point in delaying further a discussion about your future. As I said when we last spoke, there is absolutely no suggestion of any problem with your progress but a move would be highly beneficial. There are two openings you should consider."

Nightingale opened her mouth to speak but Quinlan raised a hand for silence.

"Now I happen to know the chief constable in Leeds and I could put in a word. She's a first-rate leader, runs an excellent operation. You'd fit in very well."

She couldn't contain herself any longer.

"But, sir, I don't want a transfer. I'm very happy here."

"You can't stay in Harlden forever."

But Nightingale would not see reason. She argued with a passion that Fenwick hadn't believed she possessed. He could see Quinlan become agitated and realized that Nightingale had no idea that his "suggestion" was nonnegotiable. Her obstinacy would alienate an influential senior officer and he decided that he had to intervene.

"Nightingale," he could not bring himself to call her Louise, it sounded unnatural, "you don't understand. This isn't a debate. It's time for you to leave Harlden."

She looked at him as if he had struck her. Bright spots of color flushed her cheeks and for an awful moment he thought that she was going to cry. She stood up, her eyes fixed on his, her face a blank.

"I see. In that case, if you will excuse me." She walked out of the room without waiting for permission. Fenwick leaped up after her.

"Nightingale!" She didn't even hesitate.

"Leave it, Andrew. God knows what's got into her. The sooner she's back in a normal environment and not moping around on her own the better. Women!"

Fenwick raised his eyebrows and Quinlan laughed.

"I know. I'm not allowed to say that anymore but I tell you they're a race apart."

"Well I certainly don't claim to understand her, but I think there's something not right here."

"It's pretty straightforward to me: she's lost her parents, survived an attack by a serial rapist and now this, just as life should have been getting back to normal. Oh, and she hasn't got a boyfriend. A decent man would put her right."

"Bloody hell, sir. Don't let anyone else hear you say that. Anyway," Fenwick frowned, confused, "it can't be true. Someone as attractive as Nightingale must have plenty of offers. Why would she be alone?"

"Search me. I told you, it's women, they're a perverse lot."

Nightingale stared at the scarred wood of her battered corner desk and tried to force her mind to think straight. After a lot of thought she hadn't reported her break-in and the anonymous calls because they'd seemed less substantial after the attack on Richard and also because she knew they'd give Quinlan another excuse to ask her to move. Her silence hadn't done any good. They—he—wanted her out of Harlden. When the Superintendent first raised the idea she'd thought it a temporary overreaction to the publicity surrounding the Griffiths case but she had been wrong. They wanted her to go and she found that she couldn't bear it.

Who's life did they think they were messing with? To them Harlden was simply a convenient posting, one to be written down on a CV, then as promptly written off. They were so wrong, this wasn't just a job, it was her life. Harlden was where Fenwick worked. He may be in this relationship with Claire Keating but word was that she had pursued him very hard. It might not last.

Her face felt hot. Perhaps she should return to her flat. Blackie would need feeding. The stray was a greedy, graceless cat that had refused to leave her alone. He made it clear that she only represented a convenient meal but she'd become attached to him in the last two weeks despite her original fear. The sight of him sitting outside her door or digging up one of the flowerbeds made her grin. She realized that this need to be needed, even by a mercenary animal, was pathetic but told herself that at least she was honest enough to acknowledge it.

Someone wished her well as she walked the length of the room. Another voice told her to take care of herself. Her face formed itself into the shape of a smile.

At home she made some tea then forced herself to check the answering machine. She dreaded the constant flow of non-messages. Perhaps it was only in her mind but Nightingale felt that the nature of the silence had changed.

Blackie batted her calves with his head so she found him milk and corned beef. The smell of cat food disgusted her but Blackie would eat anything as long as it was meat. Mrs. Cooper's steak and kidney was his favorite. The sight of him munching his way through the mush, favoring the side of his mouth that still had all its teeth, was comforting.

As she put his bowl down on an old newspaper the phone rang, startling her.

"Hello."

She could hear the familiar soft breathing from the other end of the line but this time there was the noise of traffic in the background and the unmistakable echo of a mobile.

"Look, this is becoming a bore. You're very tedious, whoever you are." She replaced the receiver and wondered again whether she should have her number changed.

Blackie climbed onto her lap smelling of food as she cleared the rest of the messages. Four hang-ups. The cat yowled in protest as she stood up and scratched at the door to be let out. He stalked off in a sulk and Nightingale switched on her PC.

There were eight emails waiting; all of them from Pandora. The first was almost lyrical except for its menace:

WHY DON'T YOU FINISH IT, ARTEMESIA? BRING ON THE NIGHT AND IT'S DEADLY SONG. BEAUTY AND DEATH. HOW OFTEN ARE THEY LINKED IN ART? WHY NOT IN LIFE? DON'T HIDE UP THERE ON YOUR OWN IN THE DARK. COME OUT AND PLAY WITH ME.

This had to stop. Perhaps if she replied dismissively Pandora would go away. She typed in a reply:

TO WHOM IT MAY CONCERN. THE FIELD IS YOURS. I DON'T NEED THE GAME ANYMORE.

When she read the rest of the emails she was glad that she'd been abrupt. The language grew progressively more insulting with each one. Nightingale deleted them all then did what she always did when she didn't know what else to do, she went for a run. The concentration on physical effort followed by exhaustion usually stopped her thinking but on this occasion her remedy failed.

When she returned two hours later she was still confused and angry, and the sight of the new message light flashing on her phone made her kick the door closed in frustration. She yanked the phone cord out of the wall and pulled an energy-boosting drink from the fridge. The message on her PC screen told her that she had new mail and she jabbed at the keyboard savagely to call it up.

YOU FUCKING WHORING BITCH! WHO DO YOU THINK YOU ARE, USING YOUR BODY IN PEVERTED PROSTITUTION IN THE NAME OF A LAW TOO COR-

RUPT TO BE WORTHY OF THE PEOPLE YOU CONDEMN. YOU'RE NO BETTER THAN AN ANIMAL. A STINKING PUTRID CAT RUTTING WITH ANY TOM, PRICK OR HARRY. YOU WAIT. YOUR TIME WILL COME SOON. DON'T THINK YOU ARE SAFE. IN YOUR PRISTINE AERIE UP THERE ON THE FIFTH FLOOR. YOU'RE NOT. LOCK AND BOLT YOUR DOORS AND WINDOWS AS MUCH AS YOU LIKE. I'M COMING TO GET YOU. ONE DAY, ONE NIGHT, WHEN YOU LEAST EXPECT IT YOUR TIME WILL COME.

Nightingale stared at the rambling text in horror, rereading the stream of hate directed toward her. The sender knew where she lived and that she had changed the locks since Blackie's arrival. She sipped her drink and tried to direct her analytical detective's mind to the message despite her shaking hands. She had to accept that her stalker wasn't going to go away.

It was the first time that she had used that word to describe what was happening and it frightened her. A stalker typically became more violent as their obsession grew. She had no choice now but to alert the station to what had been happening. It would be embarrassing because the threats had been going on for so long but they had become too serious to ignore.

Midnight. It was stiflingly warm. Fenwick raised himself on one elbow and looked down at Claire. A cotton sheet covered her long body. He tried to ease his weight out of bed without disturbing her.

"Are you going?"

He stifled a sigh and made his tone light.

"Yes, I must. The children will expect me for breakfast."

She sat up and switched on the bedside light, letting the sheet fall to her waist. The glow caught her body and he automatically compared her with Monique. He shook the thought away with a guilty jerk of his head.

"One of these days, darling, you must stay. I'd love to see you here when I wake up in the morning. I could make you breakfast . . ."

He bent over and kissed her mouth quickly, stopping the words and the picture they conjured up of shared domesticity.

"At least let me make you some coffee so that you're awake for the drive home."

"All right. I mean, thank you." He dressed quickly as she pulled a dressing gown around her nakedness and went downstairs.

The coffee was far too hot but he didn't want to hurt her feelings by rejecting it. She had made herself some tea.

"Well, if we can't talk tomorrow morning why don't you tell me about your day now? We barely spoke last night." She giggled and Fenwick groaned silently. Conversation was the last thing he wanted but he felt that he owed her some companionship.

"Not a good day. Too much paperwork, a visit to see Richard Rike, which was depressing, and then a meeting that Quinlan wanted me to join that went badly."

"Oh, what was that about? I thought you two got on well."

"We do but it wasn't just us."

"The ACC? What was he doing slumming it in Harlden?"

Fenwick laughed.

"No, the other end of the scale. A young sergeant who doesn't want to take advice and has no idea of what's good for her."

"Who?" Claire loved human drama. She had an insatiable curiosity for accounts of life at the station that he was beginning to find tiring.

"You won't know her, Louise Nightingale."

Claire's eyes narrowed and she stared at him as he tried another sip of coffee.

"Of course I do. Tall, a bit thin and intense. Good, but accident prone. Well, well. What's she done now?"

Fenwick experienced a spurt of indignation on Nightingale's behalf.

"Oh nothing much. Saved a man's life, was hurt in the process, had viral flu and refuses to take her medicine. By that I mean that she refuses to accept our advice."

"Tell me all about it." Claire sat down on one of her smart kitchen chairs, her eyes intent on his face. He found her scrutiny disconcerting but in the interest of a quiet life he told her about the meeting. In response to her astute questioning—she was a psychologist after all—he found himself explaining Nightingale's terrible year and his fears for her future. When he came to describe his encounter with her in the woods he paused, feeling it too personal to disclose.

"Well go on. Don't stop just as it's becoming interesting."

He continued, paring the story down to its bare essentials.

"Now tell me," Claire smiled and he recognized the expression; she was enjoying the exercise of analysis, "was the jumper washed when she returned it or not?"

"What would that signify?"

"Just tell me."

"Neither. It hasn't been returned. In fact I had forgotten about it until now."

Claire raised an eyebrow disapprovingly. She seemed annoyed and rinsed her cup under the tap in silence. Her kitchen was immaculate in its stark modernity. The cup was dried and put away.

"What?"

"What do you mean, what?"

"What have I said to offend you?" Fenwick washed his cup, surreptitiously tipping away half its contents under the running tap. He turned around for the tea towel only to have the crockery pulled from his hand.

"Nothing. I'm not offended. If you have to go, make it soon. I need my sleep. I have a busy day tomorrow."

"Claire . . ." Fenwick paused, baffled. "I don't understand."

"There's nothing to understand, though you should be asking for that jumper back. Not a good habit to get into, giving your clothes away to waifs and strays."

Confused, he kissed her cheek and bade her good night. Claire went back to bed but didn't fall asleep for a long time.

CHAPTER TEN

For a second time he was summoned to the visitors' room but this time he went with a sense of impatience.

"You've taken your time coming back."

The belligerence in Griffiths' tone was new and not to the liking of his visitor. He made as if to leave, a small gesture but it provoked the desired reaction.

"No, I'm sorry. Don't go. You have no idea what it's like in here. Stay, please."

There was enough supplication in Griffiths' tone for his visitor to sit down again.

"But life's better without Saunders, isn't it?"

"Yes, he was the worst." The prisoner hesitated, knowing what was expected of him but unusually reluctant to oblige. At last he said. "Thank you . . . thank you very much."

"Anything for an old friend."

"And can you do anything more for this old friend?"

"Oh I haven't finished yet, I still have your nemesis to deal with."

"My what?"

"Artemesia, do keep up. You could at least read and improve your mind while you're in here. I think you'd approve of the little scenario I have going with her. Obviously I can't go into detail but let's just say that I have engaged her in a game of my own devising, one that she's losing even as we speak. I have one last trick to play on her and then I shall finish it. I'm starting to grow bored."

"It's not like you to hesitate. You usually go straight for the k—" Griffiths stopped himself in time.

"This way is better, trust me. My usual approach wouldn't have worked as she's far too suspicious but you won't have to wait for long now. You must be patient."

"That's fine for you to say, you're not stuck in here." He lowered his head and hissed. "I need to get out; please, you have to help me."

"You're going to have to resign yourself to some more time in here but I have a plan. It may not be as rapid as you might like but it will work."

"What do you mean?"

His visitor shifted in his seat. In someone else Griffiths would have taken it for a sign of discomfort. He knew that the man opposite didn't like enclosed spaces though it was not a subject that was talked about.

"I am going to work on giving you grounds for an appeal."

"I told you, my solicitor says I have no chance."

"Well, we need to create that chance. Think about it. What is the simplest way to convince the authorities that they have the wrong man?"

Griffiths scratched his head with the effort of original thought. "I don't know."

His visitor sighed with impatience and leaned forward so that he could whisper.

"The way to convince them is for the, ah, incidents that put you in here to continue while you're inside. Of course, it will mean that I won't be able to visit as you'll come under renewed scrutiny. Just remember to keep quiet about me."

"I always have." Griffiths reached out for the man's hand but it was pulled back and he changed the subject to cover up the rejection.

"The books have arrived. I've already deciphered the message."

"Excellent, then we're done. I must go. Remember, be patient and be smart."

The person who had been Griffiths' only friend walked away. If the plan didn't work he would never see him again and the thought made him even more depressed. Back in his cell he looked again at the letter he had received and at his carefully concealed deciphering, of which he was inordinately proud. The original ran:

Dear Friend,

I have been thinking about your request for suitable reading materials. The enclosed book is one of my favorites. It tells the story of a remarkable seaman who pioneered sailing around our coasts in the twenties. Pages 2, 12, 46, 33, 18 and 15 are particularly interesting. The author shares a birthday with me; month and day, and by coincidence lived in a house with the same street number, 125. Of course we shouldn't forget your birthday, nor how important Christmas is to us all. Now in the other books the pages to note are . . .

The letter continued with the same strange sequence of pages and references to apparently random numbers until it ended abruptly with: *I'll write again soon, yours, Agnes.*

First he'd marked pages 2, 12, 46, 33, 18 and 15 of the book. Then he counted to the words indicated. The birthday was 17th July, which meant that he needed the 17th word on page 2 and the 7th on page 12; the 125th word on page 46 came next, then the 1st on page 33, the 8th on page 18 (his own birthday), and the

25th and 12th on page 15. At the end of fifteen minutes he had his first sentence and proof that he could decipher the code:

He cannot escape From confinement Better Plan.

Half an hour later he had the whole message: *He cannot escape From confinement Better Plan. to strike again, same tack As before while prisoner Inside. First finish bird then move on. London perhaps. Keep constant.*

He flushed his work away, tucked the original letter into the back of one of the books and lay down on his bed. "Agnes" was going to continue a spree of rape using his method. That would make the police look stupid and give him grounds for an appeal. But Agnes did not stop at rape these days. The thought warmed him like a good brandy. He drifted into a sweet sleep, the smile on his face cherubic.

"Well, don't hang around, the Superintendent wants to see you." Cooper shook his head in exasperation.

He watched her drag her feet through the door, his sympathy running out. As his dear mother had been known to say, "*You can't help those who won't help themselves.*"

"Never a truer word," he muttered to himself, "never a truer, bloody word."

She reappeared ten minutes later, face pale as marble but composed.

"A month. I transfer at the end of July."

It was pronounced with the same enthusiasm as a death sentence. Cooper spoke some platitudes in an effort to sound encouraging but it was impossible to tell whether she heard him. With a shrug he returned his attention to the paperwork before him. One of his cases was due in court later. When he returned at three o'clock he looked automatically at Nightingale's desk and was surprised to see it empty. He asked around and was told that she'd left early again. Cursing, he called her flat but couldn't get through. When he checked, the operator told him that the phone was off the hook. The mobile was no better so he left a brief message with her answering service.

From time to time during the rest of the afternoon he tried both numbers without success. Eventually he decided to call at her flat on the way home. He told himself that it was because she had no business slipping off early like that without an explanation; it made him feel less of a fool.

The flat was too hot and the air stuffy. The windows would normally have been left open but Nightingale's concern for security had meant that they remained shut. Now that she was home she risked pushing them wide. The breeze from outside started to stir the heavy air as she changed into baggy cut-off jeans and a white vest. Like her doors, the windows boasted new dead locks and individual bolts. The improved security had worked so far and her flat remained inviolate.

She had no appetite and no inclination to force herself to eat. There was a self-destructiveness within her that she held on to like a disturbed adolescent. She poured herself a large glass of chilled Sauvignon and nibbled on breadsticks as she listened to her messages.

Only four, but they were all hang-ups. She shrugged her shoulders and deleted them before disconnecting the phone and turning off her mobile. She had been determined to tell someone at the station about the calls and emails but then the summons from Quinlan had come and she'd allowed herself to descend into a pit of self-pity.

On the computer she had a new email from the server ID she'd come to dread. She pressed enter and waited for the screen to fill. A black box with white lettering appeared in the middle of the screen *"warning explicit picture."* She swallowed more wine and unconsciously clenched her hands into fists.

The picture took a long time to form. Blocks of abstract color flashed onto her computer screen, gradually building a coherent image. She gasped as she recognized an authentic-looking scene-of-crime photograph. The naked body of a woman lay at an angle, her feet to the top of the screen with the left arm lying across her naked abdomen. There was something disturbingly familiar about the hand. White blanks filled the rest of the picture.

The upper torso arrived in a sudden rush of color, complete with bruises and lacerations, then the dead head, with a terrible throat wound. It took Nightingale fully thirty seconds to work out what was wrong. It wasn't an anonymous mask of horror that stared back at her from the screen. It was her own face.

It was *her* hair that was matted with congealed blood, *her* eyes that stared sightlessly into the photographer's lens, *her* neck that had been strangled and then slashed.

The taste of bitter wine filled her throat and she nearly retched. Whoever had done this had taken a lot of care to create his victim. The work was painstaking and precise. She looked again at the hand flung across the naked belly. No wonder it was familiar—it was her hand. Her signet ring graced the little finger.

Nightingale closed her eyes and felt perspiration form along her brow and at the nape of her neck. It dribbled down her back. Who could hate her this much?

In the kitchen she drank a glass of tap water and it helped to settle her stomach. Shock had been replaced with anger more than fear. True, it disturbed her profoundly to think of the stalker spending hours creating that picture but she refused to be victimized by it. There was no option now but to report the terror she had been living with and accept the consequences. She would take her PC into the station first thing in the morning.

At four o'clock she took tablets for a pounding headache. There was no sign of Blackie but that didn't surprise her. He was an independent animal and rarely turned up unless he was hungry. She opened a packet of smoked salmon and divided the contents between a sandwich and his bowl, putting slightly more aside for the cat than for herself.

As she finished eating there was a ring from the doorbell, making her stiffen instinctively. When she looked through the peephole the landing and stairs were empty so she opened the door. There was a large parcel on her doormat wrapped in brown paper, with her name written in block capitals. It had been hand delivered and the hairs on her neck prickled as she immediately considered the worst. Would her stalker really send her a parcel bomb?

She took it inside and placed it on the floor in the hall, closing and bolting the door behind her. It would be very stupid to open the parcel, yet her mood of reckless fatalism was strong. The wounded adolescent in her that had never left, had only been concealed under layers of fragile self-assertion, whispered in her mind *"it would serve them all right."* After staring at the package for a long time she took a knife from the kitchen and sliced through the tape that bound it before lifting the paper away.

Inside there was a cardboard box wrapped in layers of sellotape. A bad sign, but she ignored it and applied the knife delicately until she could work out how to open the lid. At that point she paused and went to find her duvet cover and pillows, which she arranged as sandbags around the box. Behind them she piled the sofa cushions and long foam seat.

She noticed a strange smell as she came back into the hall. If the increasingly unpleasant odor was anything to go by the package was more likely to be unpleasant than dangerous. Even so, she tensed as she extended her left arm and the longest knife she could find through a gap in the improvised sandbags.

At first, the top held fast but she was patient and by levering it up in stages around each side she raised it sufficiently to flip the lid. The smell was overpowering. It made her gag as she pulled the cushions out of the way so that she could look inside.

"Oh no."

Nightingale went to find newspapers and placed them in a thick layer on the floor. Tears blurred her vision as she lifted out the contents carefully, as if she was afraid to inflict further pain on the creature inside, but Blackie was clearly dead. His killer had slit his belly so that some of the slippery gray intestines spilled out as Nightingale laid the matted fur bundle gently on the floor.

The overpowering stench helped to take her mind off her grief. He hadn't deserved this. Whoever had indulged in such torture was a sadist of the worst sort. She forced her thoughts from sadness to practicalities as her anger toward the perpetrator grew.

When the doorbell rang for a second time she gripped the long kitchen knife in her hand and jerked it open, prepared to confront the bastard who had done this.

Cooper recoiled in horror from Nightingale and the smell that engulfed him.

In the circumstances they both reacted with remarkable calm.

"You'd better come in." When he hesitated she reached out and pulled him over the threshold in a disconcertingly strong grip.

"Don't look, it's Blackie. Someone has just sent me his body in a parcel."

"What?" He looked at her baffled.

"It's my cat. Someone tortured and killed him, then left his carcass in a parcel on my doorstep. I thought when you rang the bell that you were them, coming back."

He reached for the knife and she let it go passively. Once it was safely back in the kitchen he bent down and peered closely at the body.

"It's not a cat, look; it's a furry Davey Crocket hat with a tail. Someone's tipped offal and blood on top of it. Who would do such a thing?"

Nightingale had to struggle to control her sob of relief before replying.

"The same person that's been stalking me since the trial, leaving heavy-breathing messages on my phone and sending me obscene emails."

She saw doubt in his eyes and took him into the tiny second bedroom that she'd made her study. The computer had timed-out but when she pressed the space bar, the screen kicked into life, revealing the photograph from her most recent email.

Cooper looked at it and sat down heavily in the chair.

"This is . . ."

"The most recent abusive email I've been sent. I opened it shortly before the parcel was delivered."

"But how is it your face?"

"With patience it's possible to adapt any photograph." She stretched over him and clicked on the zoom button until a section of the picture was magnified beyond recognition. "You see those little squares? An expert can adjust the color and tone of every one. Someone spent hours creating and perfecting this."

"Why didn't you report it?"

"I was going to, tomorrow." Something in her icy tone cracked. "Honestly. When I opened this today, I knew it had gone too far—and that was before . . ."

Cooper's suspicion changed to concern as he went to find her phone and call the crimes in.

"It's disconnected, hang on." She bent and plugged the line into the wall.

"You do that a lot?"

"All the time. Otherwise I'd never get any sleep. The calls can go on all night."

He spoke to Sergeant Wicklow, whom he could rely on to be discreet, then found bin liners and bundled the box and its contents inside, securing the necks tightly. While he waited for officers to arrive he began to take Nightingale's statement, using a discretion and sensitivity few would have believed he possessed. Now that the immediate crisis was over and someone else had taken charge, Nightingale's composure started to crumble. When she tried to drink some tea her hands shook so much that she spilled most of it, which gave her the excuse to ask for wine.

Cooper coaxed the facts from her without judgment.

"Do you have any idea who might be doing this?"

"None. The silent calls and hang-ups started about the end of the trial I think, then the emails. I thought they were pranks. When someone put Blackie in my flat it seemed like a stupid practical joke but I changed all the locks and fitted security bolts to the windows even though I'm on the top floor. I was going to report it tomorrow," she looked up, willing him to believe her. They were still talking when SOCO arrived with additional officers.

"It might be a good idea to stay with your brother until all this settles down."

"No."

The statement was nonnegotiable. The pouted bottom lip and shake of the head reminded Cooper of his two-year-old grandchild just before she had a tantrum.

"You can't stay here, Louise."

The words were gentle but tears filled her eyes.

"I could book into a hotel."

"No way. Not after what you've been through. You must

have a friend nearby who'd be happy to put you up for a couple of nights."

Another shake of the head and tears splattered onto her shirt.

"You don't understand. I don't want people to pity me."

"That's silly. There's nothing wrong with sympathy."

In the end, Cooper persuaded her to stay with him and his wife for the night while SOCO worked on the flat. He arranged for a WPC to take her there and stayed behind long enough to hear feedback from the officers going door-to-door. No one had seen or heard anything. They found the cat though, munching happily from a bowl of food in another flat while the neighbor protested that they'd had no idea that "Sooty" had another home.

Had the victim not been an officer previously involved in a murder trial Cooper would have written the incident up and left it with the minor crimes unit. As it was he decided to retain personal control. He felt stupid for having missed the signs of Nightingale's distress, so obvious in retrospect.

Belatedly he recognized that there'd been something almost willfully self-destructive about her recently, as if she didn't care about the consequences of her actions or her own safety. He wondered what might have happened to allow her to consider herself as of such little value.

Sergeant Wicklow told Fenwick about Nightingale's stalker when he arrived at the station the next morning and he bore the brunt of the Chief Inspector's anger that he had not been called the night before. Anne recognized the symptoms of one of Fenwick's black moods and brought him in an extra strong coffee.

"Superintendent Quinlan's assistant has just called asking for you. He wants to see you immediately."

The atmosphere in the Superintendent's office was even darker than Fenwick's mood.

"Bloody woman's resigned! After I'd called Leeds to smooth the way as well. Absolutely typical . . . women, they just . . ."

He caught himself in time, perhaps cautioned by Fenwick's frown.

"You know what happened yesterday?"

"Yes but that's not the point. It's damned stupid. And she doesn't even have another job to go to."

"She handed her letter to you?"

"Obviously." Quinlan waved a piece of paper under his nose.

"*Just* to you?" There was something in Fenwick's tone that made Quinlan answer slowly.

"Yes."

"Who else knows apart from us?"

"Nobody. What are you suggesting?" He regarded Fenwick with suspicion, confused that an officer typically so black and white should sound complicit.

"Why not keep it to ourselves, give her some time to think. If anyone deserves it she does."

"But she's *resigned*, Andrew. And in the most direct terms, I can assure you." Quinlan was angry as well as disappointed.

"May I?" Fenwick pulled the letter gently from the Superintendent's hand. The words were grouped into three close-typed paragraphs. He read them and winced.

"See what I mean?" Quinlan regarded him with baleful eyes.

"She was angry and frightened. I expect that she's already regretting this."

"The resignation or its tone?"

"Certainly the latter, possibly the former as well. I think we should offer her an extended leave of absence, with or without pay, whichever you prefer."

"And the letter?"

"Ignore it."

"I can't do that. She'll expect an acknowledgment and knowing Nightingale she'll have kept a copy. In her current mood she's not beyond sending it to the ACC."

"I'll go and see her, try to talk her into postponing her decision for a few weeks."

The irritation that had puffed up Quinlan like a pink baboon dispersed. He was not a vindictive man. He strutted up and down his office, tapping the folded letter against his cheek.

"She's one of our best officers but to write to me like this . . ."

"The best, in my book."

"She has had a bloody awful year."

"Lesser officers would already be on long-term sick."

"Hmm. Very well. Give it a try. It would be such a bloody waste—of tax payer's money if nothing else."

Fenwick exhaled slowly.

"I'll call her to make sure she's back in her flat and go round straight away."

"What am I going to say to Leeds?"

"You'll think of something, sir. You always do."

As Fenwick was driving to Nightingale's, Claire Keating called on his mobile. He hadn't seen or spoken to her for over a week and had been ignoring growing feelings of guilt.

"Hi, Claire. Good to hear from you." He forced himself to sound warm and relaxed.

"Are you free for lunch, Andrew? I know it's short notice but I'd really like us to talk." Her tone made him grimace.

He checked the dashboard clock—eleven forty-five. Lunch was the last thing he wanted. The conversation with Nightingale was going to be difficult enough without having a deadline to work to.

"I could do a late lunch, one-thirty, say?"

"No. I have an appointment at two. You couldn't do an early one instead?"

It was unlike her to be so persistent and his guilt made him concede.

"OK. I'll change my plans and see you at twelve, at the Dog and Duck."

When he called Nightingale again to explain that he would be late she sounded indifferent, already disconnected. He experienced a momentary flash of panic that his delay would undermine his ability to persuade her to stay, then dismissed the thought as fanciful. Nevertheless, he was impatient and inclined to be irritable by the time he saw Claire sitting at their usual table in the near empty pub. Two drinks were on the table: a spicy tomato juice and a glass of white wine.

He kissed her cheek as he sat down and forced a smile.

"Good to see you. Is there a problem? You sounded anxious on the phone."

Claire raised her eyebrows in a way that was starting to irritate him.

"I don't think I did, Andrew, at least I didn't feel anxious." She paused, a classic psychologist's trick, but detectives knew even more about the power of silence, particularly on the guilty, and Fenwick said nothing. The absence of casual conversation grew into an uncomfortable void.

Eventually they both looked up from their drinks and laughed.

"OK," Claire shrugged, "this won't do and we're both too busy to waste time."

"Agreed, but I have no idea what you want to talk about so you're going to have to start."

"I want to talk about us, well you, really, Andrew."

Fenwick felt his face harden.

"I see."

"Do you?" There was an answering firmness in her expression that reminded him of his mother, not a comforting thought. "The trouble is that I've grown increasingly fond of you over the past few weeks. I've always liked you but now it's something more and that scares me, because I still have no idea what you think of me.

"Before things go any further I need to know what I mean to you." A trace of hurt had crept into her voice, making Fenwick cringe inwardly.

She looked at him intently but he was even less able to think of the right words now than he had been before. He was sorry for her obvious discomfort but wasn't sure that he could take it away.

"Would you like another?" He pointed to her empty glass. She winced and looked out of the window. When he returned from the bar she was still staring determinedly at the garden.

"Claire, I'm sorry. What do you want me to say?"

"I'm not asking for pat answers, Andrew. But some sort of show of emotion, other than acute embarrassment—which you do very well by the way—would be nice. It's as if you daren't reveal the real you inside." Her voice turned sharp. "Or perhaps there isn't anything there and you don't care much about other people."

Fenwick sipped a single malt and water and tried to suppress his irritation. He hated this sort of encounter. However unexpectedly, the friendship that he'd seen as casual and easy for them both, meant a lot more to Claire.

"I thought we were having fun. I didn't realize that you saw us as a serious item. The last thing I wanted to do was hurt you."

"But you encouraged me!" She turned away from the window to fix him with a stare that refused to believe his innocent shake of the head. "Yes you did. In bed you . . . What was I meant to think?" Her voice broke and he put his hand on her arm.

"I had no idea . . ."

"Absolutely correct." She interrupted him, her voice suddenly loud enough to make a couple at the bar look round. "You have absolutely no idea. You're completely closed up. God knows how you manage your job, reading other people's emotions. You don't even know your own."

She finished her second glass of wine in one last swallow and he decided not to offer a third.

"Come on," he stood up and stretched his hand toward her, which she ignored, "let's go outside. I need some fresh air."

In the garden the sun filtered through lifting cloud, raising the humidity to an uncomfortable level in the windless day. As they reached the fence around the car park Claire swung to face him. He was relieved to see that she'd calmed down, though her cheeks were still pink.

"You're doing it again, Andrew, and this time I simply won't let you."

"Doing what?" He was genuinely confused.

"Avoiding the issue. As soon as you have to deal with your personal life you're hopeless."

He bit back a retort that he was managing single-parenting very well, thank you.

"I can normally work people out," she rubbed her forehead, perplexed, "it's my job after all. And I really thought that I was getting to know you but I was wrong. You're so manipulative."

Fenwick's resolution to remain calm evaporated.

"That's unfair. I hate trickery."

"I'm not saying it's deliberate but you're a past master. I don't know who you learned from but they were an expert. You portray this tough-but-broken image, the strong man bearing grief with stoic resolution for the sake of his children. You hint at a warm heart just waiting to respond to the right woman's love, then when that person tries to reach inside what does she find?"

Fenwick couldn't speak. Her taunts had provoked an anger in him he could barely manage. Claire took his silence as an invitation to continue.

"Nothing. Behind the outer wall is an inner one, smooth and impervious."

"I thought we could be friends," his lips said with control, "good companions enjoying each other's company. I hadn't meant to imply more."

"That's because you haven't any more to give. You're like a brilliant robot with a poor-little-me attitude."

He heard tears in her voice and reached out his hand instinctively. She jerked away as if burned.

"Don't, please. You're not worth the heartache. If you'd only once let me see the real you and not the charming stranger then I might have persevered."

With a bitter shake of her head she stalked to her car and drove away without giving him a chance to reply.

Fenwick watched her go, his face expressionless. Inside he felt as if someone had taken his vital organs and pulverized them. She had summed him up as a heartless cipher, a hollow, false man wrapped about with meaningless charm. Because she hadn't been able to find his heart she had assumed that it didn't exist. He knew that wasn't true. Monique had found a way through his armor. For years he'd been helpless, writhing on the barb of her love. Every day, Bess and Chris pierced his protective layers, provoking extraordinary emotions within him—joy, fear, anger, love, protectiveness—sometimes all at once.

He had to admit that Claire was perceptive though. She had discovered his armor-plated shell. The destructiveness of

Monique's madness and her long, slow death had hurt them all. The idea of facing such loss again paralyzed him and he was honest enough to admit that he was relieved that Claire had broken off their relationship.

He bought a sandwich and a bottle of water at a petrol station and ate deliberately. The energy of the food worked its way through his system, expelling any effects of the whiskey he had half consumed. When he was in control again, calm, professional and correct, his shield once more in place, he felt ready to see Nightingale.

For perhaps the tenth time, Nightingale rubbed at a non-specific gray smudge on her wallpaper left by the SOCO team. Apart from that her flat was spotless again and the prolonged wait was driving her mad. He'd never been here and the initial phone call announcing his intended visit had thrown her sense of perspective.

At eleven forty-five she ground Arabica beans, filtered fresh water and was about to switch on the machine when the phone rang. He was running late. She abandoned the coffee and went for a run.

The park was full of mothers and children. She sprinted around them on each circuit, feeling the hidden sun draw moisture from her body. There were puddles still from the weekend's rain, and every now and then she would slap into one rather than shorten her stride and break her rhythm. Her pace settled. The drumming of her own blood in her ears was as comforting as a mother's heartbeat, and she matched her arms and legs to its pace, feeling energy course out of her with each step, to be sucked back in on every breath.

Sometimes it happened, this almost magical pulsing run that could eat up the miles without a stitch or cramp, as if she could complete a marathon with ease. On her fifteenth lap, her ninth mile, a duck rose flapping and quacking from the pond and the momentum vanished. Suddenly she was hot, tired and thirsty. The enchantment had gone. She remembered to check the time and was horrified to see that she was going to be late. Not just late, she was steamy, muddy, disheveled and late. With an audible curse she changed direction and headed for home.

He was waiting in the visitors' car park as she jogged into the drive.

"Chief Inspector." She nodded at him, conscious of her shorts and sweat-stained vest.

"Nightingale. Is this a good time? Do you want me to come back later?"

His question confused her, as did his expression. There were new lines of strain on his face. She imagined a difficult case interrupted and felt unworthy.

"Now's fine. I'm sorry. I went out for a run and forgot the time. Come in."

She led the way into the vestibule and they waited in silence for the tiny lift. Blood was pumping like a brass band in her ears. She took shallow breaths so that she wouldn't need to smell her own sweat and could pretend that he didn't either.

The flat felt empty to her, too clean to be real.

"Is that fresh coffee?" The smell of the abandoned beans hung in the air. "I'd love a cup. Would you mind?"

For the first time she noticed a trace of whiskey on his breath.

"I need to take a quick shower, if you don't mind waiting."

"No problem, I can make it . . ."

"No! I mean, there's no need."

"Please, I make great coffee. Trust me."

He smiled and she gave in. She pointed him in the direction of the kitchen and left him to it.

Ten minutes later she was back, in jeans and a short sleeved sweatshirt, hair towel-damp. He had a pot of coffee ready.

"I wasn't sure whether you wanted regular or iced—you looked hot when I arrived but now . . ." He stopped and busied himself with putting the airtight lid back on the unused beans.

There was silence as she poured their drinks. It was his usual tactic, forcing the other person to talk, and she was usually curious to see how long it would last. Today though she just wanted the conversation over and done with. She had no expectation of anything meaningful emerging and none at all that there was personal motivation behind his visit.

"You came here to talk to me about my resignation, sir. What did you want to say?"

He seemed taken aback by her bluntness but rallied quickly.

"Don't do it, as simple as that. I think you're making a mistake."

"Do you? Well, I don't. It's not an easy decision and I can assure you that I thought about it long and hard."

"You've been stressed for months and that's not a good time to make big decisions."

"What stress?" Her voice was level but Nightingale could feel indignation building at his presumption.

"You know what I'm referring to—the trial, other cases, health, this stalking thing, ghastly . . . and your parents. It's a huge burden to carry on your own."

"And who else can carry it? You've just described *my* life. No one else can live it for me."

"No, of course not, but sometimes it helps to share problems, talk them through."

"And you're assuming I have nobody to do that with—I think that's bordering on the patronizing." She turned away and bit her lip to stop her anger.

"I wasn't making any assumptions. Look, let me start again. I don't think you should resign. You are an exceptional officer with a great career ahead of you. You should stay. You'll be a huge loss to us."

"You were losing me anyway. I was to leave Harlden, had you forgotten?"

"Is that's what's behind this? Your first major move? Well, I sympathize. I felt the same. No sooner are you settled than you're urged to move on. It's understandable to feel a little unwanted but really, it's the best thing for your career."

"A little unwanted!" She heard the tremor in her reply and took a gulp of coffee as she walked to the window, keeping her back to him.

"Look, I'm not good with words. If you left the Force you'd be hugely missed."

"Would you miss me?"

"Me? Of course, we all would. I enjoy working with you. You have a very good reputation for thoroughness and delivery."

"Thoroughness and delivery. Wow!" Her view of the trees blurred.

"Come on, Nightingale, don't take every word I say and see the negative."

Fenwick walked over to her and placed a hand briefly on her shoulder.

"What other words do you want me to use? Professional, brilliant, insightful, tough, a great role model . . . they all apply, take your pick."

"Thanks." She had meant to keep the sarcasm at bay but it leaped up unbidden. Even she could feel the sting of its sharpness but she was scared to say any more in case her voice betrayed her.

If he'd only said "fun to be with," "a good mate," even

"pleasant" would have done, anything that suggested she was a person with substance behind the role. Had he spoken like that she would have had something to take away with her. Instead, he had simply confirmed that she meant nothing to him beyond their convenient and productive working relationship.

She blinked away the dampness that had somehow accumulated in her eyes and disguised a small sniff in another swallow of coffee. She turned round to face him, momentarily put off by their proximity. He was well over six foot, but she was five ten in socks and their eyes were almost level, his full of barely concealed frustration, hers, she didn't doubt, over bright. For a moment she said nothing, then she smiled, a wry one-sided affair.

"I really appreciate your concern for me and I know how busy you are . . ."

"Nonsense, this is important."

"Even so, it's taken time out of your day, which is very kind . . ."

"You're going to say no, aren't you. Why? I just don't understand it."

"There's nothing to understand. People make career choices every day. This just happens to be mine." The stone in her throat threatened to choke her.

His mobile phone rang and he checked the incoming details.

"The station, excuse me."

"I think we're done."

"No we are not! Just hang on." He stepped away and spoke into his phone. "Yes? He's early . . . very well. No. I can't say when I'll be back . . . Yes, I'll call when I'm on my way."

"No one important I hope."

"The ACC."

Nightingale's mouth opened in shock.

"He's here to see the Superintendent. I'm only on standby in case he needs to see me."

"Even so, you should go." She took his empty coffee cup from his hand. "Oh, before I forget, I have a jumper of yours. Wait a moment, I'll go and get it."

She returned with it washed and pressed.

"Here," she said too briskly, "in case I don't see you again."

"I'd forgotten about it. Thank you." The frown was back on his face. "Nightingale, this just doesn't feel right. I know that's not a logical thing to say and you'll hate it . . ."

"No, go on."

"Well, I've tried all the sensible arguments and you seem as pig-headed as you always are when you're sure that you are right and the rest of us are too stupid to see it."

She raised her eyebrows in a question.

"Am I that bad?"

"Terrible. Stubborn as the proverbial mule."

"You make me sound like a menagerie. I'm surprised you haven't tried to drum it out of me, or have Sergeant Cooper do it for you."

"I've thought about it but," he paused then shrugged as if he might as well be honest, "I like it. It's part of what makes you so good."

"I see. Any other character weaknesses you would like to mention by way of farewell?" She was smiling now, enjoying the spectacle of him walking on thin ice.

"How about lack of respect for senior officers, a smart alec with more brains than are good for her?" He'd caught her mood and was smiling in return. "Over zealous, aggressive . . ."

"I think you mean assertive."

"Whatever. Shall I go on?"

"I've got the idea. And you *still* want me to stay? Why?"

He shook his head as if baffled.

"I don't know. Perhaps I like the idea of you in the Force somewhere. Who knows, we may even work together again."

"That's unlikely isn't it? If I transferred that would be the end, you know that."

"Probably. Personally, I hate the idea of your transfer but it's for your own good."

"You've never said that before, that you didn't want me to go."

"No, well and I shouldn't have now. It's none of my business. But I do care about what happens to you."

"I see." The conversation was confusing yet she felt elated. She had enjoyed his insults. They had been personal and somehow showed that he cared. "I don't know what to say. I still think I should resign, I really do."

"Give it time, take some leave; compassionate, sick, holiday, whatever. Go away and think about it. We'll hold the letter until you return. Just give yourself the chance to reconsider."

"Let me sleep on it. I'll call you in the morning and let you know."

Fenwick picked up his laundered jumper and turned to go.

"Sir . . . Andrew, thank you. Whatever my decision, this conversation means a lot to me."

He flushed at her compliment and left without another word.

CHAPTER ELEVEN

"Louise Nightingale wishes to see you."

"Tell her to come in, Anne." Fenwick put the file he was reading to one side and looked up, his smile fading at the expression on Nightingale's face. Instinctively, he stood up. There were some blows he preferred not to take sitting down.

"Morning. Cup of coffee?"

"No thank you, sir. I won't be taking up much of your time." She took a deep breath and continued. "I don't think I can go on working, not right now, but I accept what you said about this being a very big decision and I'd like to take up the offer of unpaid leave. Just for a month or so to give me time to think."

"And your resignation is on hold?"

"For now. Would you tell the Superintendent?"

"Of course."

Some of the strain went from her face, leaving her looking exhausted. Fenwick felt an inexplicable urge to put his arms around her shoulders and give her a hug. She needed looking after and as far as he knew there was no one else to do it. Something of his feelings must have shown in his face because she blushed. He stuck his hand out.

"Good luck then. I hope it all works out."

She shook his hand and looked up at him while still holding it, her eyes full of questions.

"Yes?"

She shook her head.

"Never mind. It's nothing."

Fenwick watched her leave, straight-backed, precise, and felt that he had missed something significant but he had no idea what it was.

"Keep in touch," he called out, but she appeared not to have heard him. He started toward the door but his phone rang and he automatically reached to pick it up. It was the Superintendent's assistant, reminding him that he was late for an appointment. He shrugged his shoulders and made his way to the meeting.

Cooper had had no luck tracing Nightingale's stalker. The computer technicians hadn't traced the source of the emails and interviews at the flats had produced nothing. He was used to failure, what policeman wasn't, and was usually phlegmatic in defeat, but this time his lack of progress was giving him acid indigestion, a sure sign that he was really upset.

He repeated his problems to Fenwick.

"I just can't stand the idea of her being terrorized. It's not fair."

"Maybe she'll be away for a month or so—she's taken leave of absence. That will give us time to find the bastard."

The next day Cooper was interrupted with a message. One of Nightingale's neighbors had heard sounds of a disturbance from her flat.

"Is it still going on?"

"It's quieter now but I think someone's still there."

Telling the woman to stay inside he rang Fenwick and the two of them were soon driving through Harlden in a squad car with Fenwick urging the driver to go faster every time he braked. They tried Nightingale's phone but it was off the hook. There was no answer from her mobile.

Fenwick led Cooper and a uniformed officer at a run up the stairs while another stayed on the door. The neighbor, alerted by the siren, was on the landing with a spare set of keys.

"I haven't seen her since yesterday when she gave me her keys and said that she was off on holiday. That's why I was worried when I heard the noise."

"Any sounds from in there recently?"

"Nothing for the last ten minutes."

Fenwick asked her to wait in her flat and pushed open the door, noting the smashed locks. Inside was a scene of devastation. Nightingale's neat, precise hall had been sprayed from floor to ceiling with foul-language graffiti. Pictures had been ripped from their frames; pieces of mirror crunched under his feet as he walked in.

He told the officer to stay on the door and beckoned Cooper inside. The kitchen was a mess; crockery and glasses had been broken and thrown around the room. In the living room the curtains and sofas had been slashed with a knife, furniture smashed and the expensive CD player wrecked. There was more graffiti. Only the bathroom had been ignored. His eyes watered from the smell of the bleach that had been poured over a heap of her clothes on her bed.

"Good grief, I want SOCO here right now. We need to find her. Put out an alert for her car and check with the airports. If she's gone abroad it might explain why her mobile isn't picking up calls."

Cooper listened to his boss trying to talk himself calm. He had never seen him so agitated.

"She has a brother somewhere. He may know something."

Cooper called Simon Nightingale's home, using the number he found in a battered address book. A woman answered.

"What's happened?"

"Her flat has been broken in to and we are trying to reach her."

"Well, she'll be at work. Why are you calling here?"

He explained about Nightingale's extended leave.

"She didn't tell us. I'm sorry, I have no idea where she might have gone."

"What was her typical holiday choice?"

"I'm not sure there was anything typical."

"Are there any friends or family she might have traveled with or be visiting?"

"We're all the family she has. Apart from this house there's an old farm but it's derelict so she couldn't stay there."

Cooper was about to finish the call when an idea occurred to him.

"Mrs. Nightingale, have you given Louise's address to anyone recently?"

"Of course not! I wouldn't do something like that."

"Please, think hard." Cooper didn't doubt the woman's integrity but she was the trusting kind. She had taken him at his word when he said he was a policeman and hadn't bothered to check him out in any way.

"Well . . . but that can't have been significant, it was nothing, an old friend that's all."

"Go on."

"It was a few weeks ago. A man about Louise's age was collecting for the Lifeboats. He came to the door and we got talking. He said, "You're not Louise Nightingale's sister-in-law by any chance are you? It's such an uncommon name." I said I was and it turned out that they were at school together. He said that he'd like to get in touch with her again. Apparently they'd been good friends but had drifted apart."

"So you gave him her address."

"Yes, and phone number and email. Was that wrong?"

"I don't know, but somebody has been making Louise's life hell for the past few weeks and we want to find out who it was."

"Oh no." Mrs. Nightingale sounded close to tears. "But he seemed so nice, a really pleasant man."

"Can you remember what he looked like?"

"Vaguely. Attractive, tall, nice eyes. He was wearing smart clothes."

"I'll need a full description from you later. In the meantime if Louise calls, please contact me at the station."

Cooper went in search of Fenwick and found him staring at the wrecked coffee machine.

"Another neighbor has been asked to water her plants. Looks like she'd already left."

"So she's safe." Cooper sagged with relief.

"Maybe, for the moment. This all started after the Griffiths trial. Look at the hatred and anger in this destruction; it goes beyond vandalism. What if the person behind it is seeking revenge for Griffiths? They're not likely to give up easily. But I don't see who it could be. He wasn't married and didn't have family or friends." Fenwick started to pace. "Supposing there *was* someone that we didn't know about, could they have done this?"

"It's a possibility. I remember thinking when Griffiths was interviewed by DI Blite that it was odd there was nobody in his life."

"Go through the file again, identify anyone who might have known him personally and reinterview them. I'm going to go and visit the man himself."

* * *

Prisons made Fenwick's skin itch. The smell of hundreds of male bodies, averagely washed and sweaty in confinement was so strong that he imagined it settling on his face and clothes like fine dust. During the long journey north to the prison he had listened to tapes of police interviews. Griffiths sounded an arrogant man, confident of his superior intelligence. It was as if he had been so certain that the physical case against him was minimal, that all he needed to do was admit nothing and wait for his release.

If Griffiths had a friend or relative he had managed to keep their existence a secret, yet when he arrived he was told that the prisoner had had a visitor. The prison log recorded the name of a man who'd visited twice and had signed his name as Tony Troy. There were hundreds of A. Troys in England alone, including one poor man with the middle names of Steven Henry Ivan, but none of them with an address that matched the one given by the visitor.

Fenwick was surprised when Griffiths entered. He was not the man he had been expecting. Instead of intelligence he saw furtiveness and cunning. His eyes were set too close together, the jaw was weak and the top teeth a little too large. He gave the impression of being a scavenger not a hunter and Fenwick felt a deep disquiet.

Griffiths affected boredom to mask his curiosity as Fenwick introduced himself and started questioning without preamble.

"Do you have any living relatives?"

"What's this all about?"

"Just answer my question. Do you?"

"No."

"Who is Tony Troy?"

A look of genuine confusion appeared on Griffiths' face.

"The man who has visited you twice."

"Look, I don't need to do this."

"It might be in your best interests to cooperate. I understand that you intend to seek an appeal. Declining to answer police questions won't help."

Griffiths thought for a while then shrugged.

"Troy was some weirdo gay ponce. A stranger who read about the case and wanted to be my 'friend.' I told him to fuck off." Griffiths kept his face angled away but he found something in what he had just said funny.

"Who is Agnes? You have had letters from her."

A flicker of concern then calm again.

"An old school teacher. She befriended me."

It was a lie but a good one. Griffiths thought quickly.

"And we can reach her via the address you write to? Odd for a school teacher to use a P.O. box."

Real furtiveness now about the eyes but the rest of his face remained impassive.

"She travels a lot, in a caravan. I don't think she likes post to pile up at home."

"Could I have her phone number?"

"She's not on the phone."

"A mobile?"

He shook his head.

"I see. Well, her full name, permanent address and approximate age should be enough."

"About sixty now I think. I can't remember her surname and I only know her post office box number."

He wrote down the answers, intrigued to see the sweat break out on Griffiths' forehead. This was not the line he had intended taking but he had caught him out in a lie, which was always a promising start.

"What family do you have?"

"I don't."

"You must have had once."

"I never knew my father. My mother left when I was a kid. I was fostered after that."

"No aunts or uncles?"

"None that cared to know me." It was said with real feeling and Fenwick suspected it was the truth.

"I'd like their names anyway, please."

"Can't remember."

"You must know them if they were your only living relatives."

"No. We didn't exactly keep in touch."

Fenwick tried other questions but nothing else shook Griffiths and he eventually left to meet with the prison psychiatrist.

Batchelor had a practice in the neighboring town and was waiting for Fenwick with a look of anticipation on his face. He talked nonstop about the prisoner, how fascinating he was, the intricacies of his mind, his increasing remorse. Fenwick found it sickening and struggled to suppress a growing dislike for the doctor.

"Do you think him capable of inciting violence while still in prison?"

Batchelor flushed with indignation.

"Certainly not, it would be quite out of character. Why?"

Fenwick described what had been happening to Nightingale. The psychiatrist started shaking his head in denial within half a sentence. By the time Fenwick had finished he was sitting with arms and legs crossed.

"Impossible. He would never encourage something like that."

"Are you sure?"

"Of course. In fact, the more I think about it, the more likely it is that this is some hysterical response on her part."

"My sergeant saw the blood and offal. It was not imagined, I can assure you."

A more sensitive man would have recognized the warning in Fenwick's tone.

"Even so. She's a nervy young woman. You never can tell with that type."

"And what type is that, precisely?"

"So straight and correct, always in control."

"You've met her?" It was an accusation.

"Spoken on the phone, just once. She agreed to help me."

"Willingly?" Fenwick's mouth and the edges of his nostrils were white with self-control as he waited for this vainglorious man to justify himself.

"Well, er, yes."

The pause betrayed his lie and Fenwick shook his head in disgust.

"You deserve to be reported."

"Now, see here! It's none of your business. You come in here, throwing your weight around. He's behind bars, can't you leave him alone?"

"He *deserves* his sentence, for the sick bastard he is." Fenwick stood up, reminding Batchelor of how tall he was. "*She doesn't* and her punishment is just as real, believe me. If you try and have that psycho out on appeal or medical grounds, you will fail. There's me and a dozen other officers standing between you and success."

"He's mentally disturbed, not a psycho."

"Really? What makes you so sure? He might just be very good at manipulating you." He muttered under his breath, "It wouldn't be difficult."

He saw himself out, angry with himself for losing his temper and depressed that a prisoner as obviously guilty as Griffiths could stimulate sympathy. On his way back to the station he called the prison governor and thanked her for her help. He asked that the next letter Griffiths sent be held for his personal examination. While he couldn't prove a link to the attacks on Nightingale, his instinct told him that there was a connection, however unlikely, and he felt uneasy, as if he was driving away from something important.

At ten o'clock that evening, Superintendent Quinlan returned to Harlden police station after a dull dinner. He was surprised to see a light coming from an office on the second floor and went to investigate

"Anything I should be concerned about, Andrew?"

"No, just catching up on some reading."

All ranks from inspector upward were having to do increasing amounts of unpaid overtime but working past ten o'clock when there were no serious crimes to investigate was excessive.

"Looks like a closed file." Quinlan took a step forward and Fenwick suppressed a sigh. He had been hoping to avoid this conversation.

"It's the Griffiths case. I went to see him in prison today, trying to establish whether he's connected with the attacks against Nightingale."

"And is he?"

"I don't know." Fenwick leaned back in his chair and rubbed his forehead wearily.

"He's locked up and has no known acquaintances or family to act on his behalf."

Quinlan raised his eyebrows, as articulate as a spoken word. They had known each other for too long for him to be fobbed off with half a story.

"OK. For some reason he lied to me, and on the most trivial matter—the name and address of someone who is writing to him in prison. Why would he do that?"

"To be awkward?" Quinlan sat down in one of the chairs facing Fenwick's desk and winced as the metal frame bit into his legs. "Why don't you have these replaced, man? They're so old there's no padding left in them."

"Really? I never sit there." Fenwick dismissed the chairs from his mind and went over to a large corkboard attached to the wall opposite his desk. It was full of photos of Nightingale's flat and printouts of hate mail from her computer. To one side was a photograph of Griffiths. "Are we sure that he doesn't have a friend or relative?"

"Never saw any sign of them."

"No family at all?"

"None. You've read the file."

"Yet he was socially well adjusted enough to hold down a decent job at a software company for two years and be regarded by his colleagues as, I quote, 'a normal bloke, a bit quiet but all right.' There should be someone."

"Maybe they cleared off when he was arrested. Happens all the time."

"True but why no mention at all on file? There's another odd thing about him. He never stayed put in one place." Fenwick pointed to another piece of paper. "His first job was in Telford, then Birmingham. Both software development companies and well paid. Seems he was highly skilled, so why move on?"

"You should ask Blite but be sensitive, it was a bloody awful investigation. The attacks against women went on for nearly a year and putting the case together was incredibly difficult, even after we caught him."

Fenwick looked at him, intrigued.

"Of course, you weren't here, but you can imagine the flak when woman after woman was assaulted and we appeared powerless to catch the man doing it. Using Nightingale to draw Griffiths out was a last ditch idea. If it hadn't worked we would have had to wait and hope that a friend turned him in. There was no trace evidence you see. And his method kept changing. One minute he was stalking them outside, the next he had charmed himself into their homes."

"But you were certain that it was the work of one man?"

"Positive. We received anonymous letters from the perpetrator boasting of the crimes and giving us details that only he could know. And then there was the souvenir taking. In each incident the poor girl lost part of a finger. We missed it at first, thought the injuries were defensive, but when the bastard mentioned them in his bloody letters we realized they were a link."

"But despite that CPS wouldn't let you take all the cases to trial."

"No, our evidence was so thin. When we searched his flat it was spotless. No clothes to link him to the attacks; no PC, printer or paper to connect to the letters; and definitely no fingers!"

"What about DNA on the envelopes or stamps."

"Letters were sent unstamped and the envelopes were sellotaped. Now you can see why Nightingale's testimony was so crucial. Without it he could have walked. Only the cases that were identical with the attack against her were tried. The others remain open on file and there they'll stay, including the murder—a poor woman who died of her injuries. It's bloody for the relatives but at least when we caught him the attacks stopped."

"Why wasn't there more about the souvenirs in the papers at the time."

"It was in our interests to play it down because they were a link to the crimes we weren't able to bring to trial, and for some reason the defense didn't use it. We never released the information to the press. Check that confidential folder there and you'll find more information." He turned to go. "Goodnight. Don't work until the small hours, not when you don't need to."

Fenwick opened the red-edged envelope and pulled out a bundle of photographs and medical examiners' notes. Victim one had the top of her little finger sliced off. She had been semiconscious when it happened.

The second victim had the top of her ring finger taken. Another, the poor girl who later died, lost several fingers. The missing fingers intrigued Fenwick. He logged on to PACE and input his search criteria then waited impatiently while it checked hundreds of thousands of cases. There were ten matches, but eight were domestic incident injuries so he dismissed them and concentrated on reports of two women who had lost parts of their fingers during sexual attacks. One woman had been raped and later died of her injuries, making the case murder. She had lived in a village five miles from Birmingham and had invited her attacker into her own home. The other lived in Telford and had been raped at a nature reserve.

Given the problems that Blite had faced bringing his own investigation to trial Fenwick could see why he'd been unwilling to follow up unsolved crimes outside his own patch, but the detail of the missing finger joint was compellingly similar and Griffiths had lived close to where both attacks took place. He checked the file again and found notes of conversations that Blite had had with the forces involved. At the bottom he had typed in capitals:

NO OBVIOUS CONNECTIONS OTHER THAN FINGER AMPUTATION. LIKELIHOOD OF A LINK REMOTE. HAVE FAXED MATERIALS TO TELFORD AND BIRMINGHAM FOR THEM TO FOLLOW UP AT THEIR DISCRETION.

It was typical of Blite not to pursue tangential leads that he would have seen as a distraction. True, he hadn't had enough to suggest a firm connection but at the very least he had been faced with interesting coincidences that Fenwick would have found impossible to leave alone. He printed off the information and tacked it to his corkboard.

"There is no record of an Agnes teaching at any of the schools Griffiths says he attended."

"So he was lying. Why?"

Cooper trotted out the same theories that Superintendent Quinlan had a few days earlier but Fenwick remained unconvinced. Something about the stalking of Nightingale and the whole Griffiths case disturbed him. He even spoke to Blite and asked for his ideas but the inspector didn't respond well to what he saw as Fenwick's dabbling in one of his cases.

"Your problem," Blite had said, "is that you're bored, Andrew. Your secondment to the Met has spoiled you for our more provincial way of life."

At the time he had treated the remark as a joke and laughed it off but there was an element of truth on its barb. He was bored. His detection rate was impressive, the highest in the Division and good enough to warrant a call of congratulation from the ACC, but his brain remained unchallenged. The Nightingale case, with its potential link to Griffiths, intrigued as much as it concerned him. If the connection was real then there were elements of Griffiths' past that remained hidden.

He sent Cooper off to dig deeper and studied the printouts from PACE. On impulse, he called Birmingham City Center Police and was eventually put through to an inspector involved in the original inquiry.

"We never found a trace of him. The girl's body had been thoroughly washed, there was no physical evidence and no one saw her leave the pub she was in. One minute she was there, the next gone."

"Where was her body found?"

"That was the strange thing, on her own bed. The bastard hacked her about so the missing finger didn't seem significant at the time, though I wondered later whether it was linked to a couple of other cases we had up here, but it was so tenuous . . ."

"What other cases?" Fenwick sat up straight in his chair and reached for a pen to take notes.

"We had three other sex attacks within eighteen months of each other. One was a sexual assault where the bloke tried to cut the girl's finger off but failed. It received a lot of publicity at the time. The next was a rape out in the suburbs but the hand injuries looked incidental. It was my case and we never caught the bastard. I didn't make a connection as the description of her attacker was different but I thought I should mention it all the same. The third one was a murder. The medical report described the injuries to her hands as defensive cuts. She lost two fingers and the tendons of the rest were damaged."

"Could you send me the details? I know you're short-handed but it would be helpful. I think we may have your man in prison but proving the connection will be difficult."

As he replaced the receiver, Fenwick wondered again how Blite could have ignored such a tantalizing coincidence but he knew why. He would have concentrated on securing a prosecution

VICTIM

Location	Sex	Age	Height	Build	Other	Crime
B'ham 1	F	22	5'9"	slender	well educated	Rape
B2	F	18	5'6"	petite	student	Assault
B3	F	23	5'7"	slender	graduate trainee	Murder
B4	F	19	5'6"	thin	p/t sudent	Rape
Harldn 1	F	24	5'8"	slender	junior mgt	Rape
H2	F	26	5'7"	slim	nurse	Murder
H3	F	20	5'10"	slender	student	Attm'd murder
Telford	F	25	5'9"	slim	teacher	Murder

MO

Location	Evidence of planning/ stalking	Am’t of violence	Weapon	Prior dia-logue/social invitation	Location	THE GAME
B’ham 1	N	Med	Knife	Y	Flat	N
B2	Y	Low		N	Outside park	N
B3	?	High	Knife Ligature	Y	Home	N
B4	Y	Low		N	Outside	Yes
Harldn 1	Y	Med	Ligature	?	Outside	Yes
H2	N	High	Knife Ligature	Y	Home	N
H3	N	Med?	Knife	?/Y	Flat	Yes
Telford	?	High	Knife	Y	Friend’s bedsit	N

on the local crimes. It would be the expedient thing to do and Blite was nothing if not expedient.

The fax from Birmingham arrived at six o'clock and Fenwick called his housekeeper to say he would be late. By seven o'clock he had summarized the facts and added to them details of the unsolved crimes from Harlden. He studied his notes, the frown line between his eyebrows deepening as he recognized significant consistencies yet baffling contradictions:

DESCRIPTION OF ATTACKER

Location	**Height**	**Build**	**Hair**
B'ham 1	6'2"	Light	Dark Brown
B2	5'10"	?	?
B3	?	?	?
B4	?	?	?
Harldn 1	5'11"	Stocky	Fair
H2	over 6"	Big	Black
H3	5'10"	Average	Lt Brown
Telford	?	?	?

He circled the attack in Telford, the first and third in Birmingham, and the second and third in Harlden, where there had been extensive violence. The women involved had spent time with their attacker beforehand in a pub or club and were then taken home. That suggested a highly confident, socially well-adjusted individual. In the other Harlden and Birmingham crimes, the interaction had been limited.

He went home, ate a decent meal and looked in on his sleeping children, feeling guilty. By six the next morning he was awake, sweaty from a forgotten dream, and forced himself to wait until the children were up so that he could serve them a hurried breakfast before leaving. On his way to the station just before eight o'clock, he called Telford.

A bemused constable in CID heard him out, repeated back a faithful transcript of his message and said that he would pass it on. Telford rang him back at noon. A detective explained that they'd had a spate of sexual assaults that coincided with the dates Fenwick had given him but nothing that matched the crimes Harlden were interested in. Fenwick rang off feeling disappointed and tried to return his concentration to the rest of his caseload but his mind kept wandering to Nightingale's ransacked flat. Perhaps it had been an act of random violence and the stalker was a freak who had become obsessed with the trial. He could identify with obsession. By the end of the day he had almost persuaded himself that Quinlan was right and that he was just being fanciful. The thought brought him no comfort.

CHAPTER TWELVE

Driving was exhausting, or rather it would be fairer to say that driving down to the West Country through a three-day rainstorm had been one of Nightingale's less sensible ideas. She took her time, breaking her journey in remote yellow-stoned villages and avoiding the motorways. When she reached Dorset she sent emails to her brother and Sergeant Cooper explaining that she had left on a long holiday far away.

She had pledged never to replay her final conversation with Fenwick again and concentrated on her driving. This flight from her previous life was about more than him, but the absence of his presence was the most significant aspect of her journey so far. Instead of experiencing renewed freedom, she was oppressed by a sense of emptiness. Some lines by Keats kept circling in her mind:

Then on the shore / Of the wide world / I stand alone, and think / Till love and fame to nothingness do sink.

They made her think that the only thing standing between existence and oblivion was her own force of will. If she once stopped moving she might cease to be, but she was exhausted with the effort. She was in need of R&R and where better to relax than in the depths of ancient Britain. Her father had insisted that his family came from Celtic stock, a romantic notion that

Nightingale thought unlikely given their name. What she couldn't deny was that he came from an old Devonshire family. His sister had lived and died here, in the family farm built around their original mill.

Aunt Ruth had been Nightingale's favorite relative and she had cried for a whole day when she died suddenly in her forties. She left the farm to Nightingale's father. Inevitably, he had willed it to his son along with every other scrap of property, save a small annual income for Nightingale. She would never starve, but she was hardly rich. The lack of a fortune did not matter to her, but the careful measuring out in monetary terms of her value to her mother and father hurt deeply. On their deaths they had confirmed what she had always suspected, that she counted for very little.

As she peered through the windscreen and rain, she started to look out for signposts. Mill Farm was in the woods, set back from the wild north Devon coast. No one would think to look for her here. Only Simon and Naomi knew of the farm and they thought it uninhabitable. She drove past Okehampton and expected to see familiar landmarks but the road layout had changed and she passed through an unfamiliar landscape. On a side road deserted of traffic, she saw a small gray church, dripping disconsolately beside a cluster of giant yews. It looked familiar. An elderly man was walking along the road toward her, head down against the Devon rain. She drew alongside him and spotted a white flash of dog collar beneath his coat.

"Excuse me, could you give me directions to Mill Farm please?"

He turned round, head still bent and took a step closer to the car, a hand cupped around his ear. She repeated her question, feeling guilty for sitting in the dry while he waited in the rain.

There was no doubt that he had heard her this time, but instead of answering, he stared at her intently. The rain matted the cashmere of her sleeve as she waited for a reply.

"It's a while since I was asked directions for Mill Farm. Are you family?"

She nodded.

"A Nightingale then, well, well. You don't look like your . . . aunt?" He was fishing for information in exchange for his help.

"I don't have the typical family looks."

"True, but it's odd, you remind me of somebody."

"Mill Farm?" she repeated hopefully.

"Yes, yes. I can take you there if you want. It's hard to explain now that the sign's fallen down. You'll need to spare me a few minutes to check the church though. The Cubs are marvelous of course, but not always reliable and our insurance is void if the doors aren't properly locked. You can pull in here."

Rather than wait in the car, Nightingale found her umbrella and followed him down a gravel path, slippery with moss. The churchyard was crowded with ancient graves, headstones pressing upon each other and leaning out eagerly toward the path. Some plots had ornate crosses mimicking the old Celtic style, others were more traditional with rounded headstones from which the inscriptions had been erased by time and lichen.

Inside the church was dark and cold. Pale unlit candles on the altar glimmered like ghosts in the faint light from the narrow side windows, a silver crucifix glinted between them.

"Good, everything's off. We can go."

"You don't want to check the vestry door?"

He muttered and shuffled off, leaving her alone in the dark. Goosebumps sprang up along her arms and she shivered. To distract herself she went to investigate one of the stained glass windows. Beneath it stood an extraordinary font. Carved from green-gray marble, the creatures in its relief seemed to spring to life from the stone. The quality of carving was almost freakish in its naturalism. She ran her fingertips over the nose of a fawn. The chill of the church made the nostrils feel wet and she twitched in shock. Despite the font's sacred use it was one of the most pagan things she had seen.

The priest returned.

"We can go, come on."

He ushered her outside and pulled the door closed before walking away briskly.

"Ah, excuse me." Nightingale hovered in the wooden porch. He turned round looking impatient. "The door? Does it need locking again?"

He almost flounced back and she had to turn her head to hide a smile. How many times had the Cubs been blamed for his forgetfulness?

"This way, young lady. Come on. I haven't all day."

For an old man he walked fast and she broke into a jog to catch up. In the car their damp clothes steamed up the glass and she had to drive with the heater full on and windows cracked open.

"Left!" The priest thrust out his right hand, almost hitting her nose.

"Left, left, come on!" He gesticulated fiercely with his hand, suddenly caught sight of it and said without pausing, "indicate then, right just here, yes, up the hill."

Nightingale changed down and eased her car onto the narrow track that ran between two stone posts. An iron gate lay in a ditch to the side of the road, smothered by ivy and brambles.

"I think I know my way from here; can I take you back?"

"It's no trouble, come on." There was a sense of excitement about him. "I haven't been up here for years, not since Ruth died."

"She was my father's sister."

"Went mad and threw herself into the sea. Coroner called it accidental so I couldn't avoid burying her by the church in the family plot. Pity. Strange woman. Ran in the family."

At that moment Nightingale had to negotiate a string of potholes and a sharp bend so she had an excuse for her silence. She wasn't so much shocked by his callousness as by the priest's wholly unchristian attitude.

"Maybe you should get out here if you really don't need a lift home."

"Yes, I think I will and no, no lift, thank you. I take my constitutional whatever the weather. Come on, unlock the door then. Oh, it is unlocked. The house is at the end of this track, two miles or so. Holy Communion is at eight on Fridays and Sundays. The main service is at eleven and there's a prayer group at six. I'll see you then."

He was gone before Nightingale could reply, strutting off down the hill like an old crow. The car protested as she slipped it into first gear and the back wheels span in the mud until they caught and she lurched forward. After a mile the thick woodland started to clear and she could see another gateway ahead, this time bordered by a wall that disappeared off into the margin of the wood. One of the keys her brother had given her opened a rusty padlock on the gate. Beyond, the path dipped down to follow a fold in the hill and crossed a stream before rising again through a stand of rowan trees.

This part of the journey was familiar. The sudden descent, even on the sunniest of days, brought with it a chill of mystery. As a child she had felt that she was crossing into another world as they cleared the stream and had said as much once to her father. He had accused her of being fanciful and dismissed such feeblemindedness with a customary wave of his hand but he had then grown expansive with his own memories.

"It was a mill as well as a farm," he'd said. "Water powered the wheel. When I was a boy we had a bridge here, don't need it now unless there's a flood.

"There's a spring by the house, runs all year, the purest, cleanest water in the world. Until the Seventies it was just enough to keep the wheel turning but it doesn't now. The mill was the original source of our money. There were so few in this part of the world. Family changed to retailing in the nineteenth century when we bought those shops and never looked back. Wouldn't have had any money without the mill though. That's why it's so important."

Nightingale smiled as she recalled her father's words. It had been a long speech for him but then it had been about money and family, his favorite subjects. To Nightingale, Mill Farm hadn't represented wealth but something far more important, security. Crossing the ford took her into a private place, cut off from the outside world, in which as a child she had felt happy.

Her Aunt Ruth had loved her as no one else ever had before or since. During the summers here her dreams had been filled with adventures in which floods or snows cut off the hill from the rest of the world, and she and her aunt had survived on food grown in the garden, fish from the sea and game in the forest. Week after week she walked in the hills, swam from the rocky beach or read her favorite books snuggled by the big green Aga on rainy days.

That same sense of adventure returned as the car crept forward, dipped into another fold in the hills and then climbed steeply up the final slope. Only a few miles behind, people huddled under umbrellas in busy towns but here it was as if they had ceased to exist.

The rain eased and she switched off the wipers. Ahead, the last of the saplings gave way to tall grass and thistles. Beyond them, as faint as smoke, was a hint of gray slate and her heart leaped. The roof came into view, then a badly pointed chimney, and at last, the farm. She drove over weeds and nettles, hearing brambles scratch at the paintwork of her car until she reached the front door. She turned off the engine; she was home.

A gust of wind splattered heavy drops of rain on the roof of the car, then there was silence. She stared at her house. One window on the ground floor was broken, another above the front door swung on its hinges. Birds had built their nests in the guttering and old swifts' nests studded the walls under the eaves. There had been hollyhocks once and sunflowers in a perfect cottage garden. Now, a crop of dangerously green nettles fought with docks and a dog rose, showing pink-white petals among the remaining hips from last autumn.

A large iron key fitted neatly into the front door lock. It turned easily but the door held fast. In the end she slipped through the broken window into the musty flagstone hall, treading carefully over glass on the floor. The front door had been wedged shut with a chair, which she moved to one side. A flight of stairs rose up before her; the fireplace opposite held the skeleton of a large bird. Beyond, a passage led to the back of the house and the kitchen. At some point someone had camped out here. Most of the kitchen chairs had been broken up for fuel and an old mattress lay mouldering against the chimney wall. Despite the desolation she felt elated and went to explore the rest of the house.

Whoever had squatted had been selective in their invasion. The dining room with its enormous dark oak sideboard was untouched. With a smile that her aunt would have recognized, she skipped forward and pressed her fingers beneath the top. With a deft twist she released the lock of the secret draw and it sprang free. As a child she had been trusted with this most important confidence on condition that she promised never to look inside. She never had until now.

As she pulled the drawer open a small sigh escaped into the room. Inside, she found a bundle of correspondence tied in faded blue ribbon, a diary, a photograph and her aunt's rosary. On top was a letter, written in her aunt's sloping hand. With a chill that raised the hairs on her neck, she saw that it was addressed to her. It was as if the ghost of her aunt had been waiting for her to return all these years and she felt guilty that it had taken her so long. It was unthinkable to read the letter in the cold of the house so she took it back to the car, her new-found energy already drained by the discovery. But she had to read it; after all this time how could she ignore her Aunt's words? She broke the seal on the envelope. Inside there were two handwritten pages.

My dear Louise, [her aunt had always called her by her preferred name] *I doubt that I shall see you again and there is still so much I have to tell you. Firstly, you are a wonderful girl, never forget that.*

You have special gifts, not least your intelligence, your warmth of spirit and your insight into human nature. Never let anyone persuade you that you are not creative because you are. I don't know what form your creativity will take but it is there, it must be, because you are like your mother in so many other ways.

Nightingale stopped reading in surprise. She had thought that her aunt and her mother had barely tolerated each other.

After I'm gone, people will say a lot of unpleasant things about me but my love for you is strong and I shall be looking over you from where I go next.

I have been trying to decide, these last few weeks, how much to tell you of matters I doubt you even suspect. You are too young to know the full truth and it would be unfair to your father to reveal what he should tell you himself. He made a promise to me once that he would speak to you when you come of age and I must trust to that.

But then I worry. What if he breaks his promise or forgets? So I have done the next best thing. In our drawer with this letter, you will find some of my diaries and letters. If you are clever enough, and I think you are, and when you are experienced enough, which you will be in a few more years, you will be able to work things out for yourself.

Nightingale shook her head in confusion. Her father had never revealed a secret to her. At seventeen she had been sent away to what her mother liked to call a finishing academy but in effect had been a school of last resort for difficult girls, so her "coming of age" had been a muted dormitory party.

Instead of feeling closer to her aunt, the letter with its odd language and strange ideas had alienated her. It was as if the aunt she remembered so fondly had betrayed her by growing strange with age—just as the priest had suggested. As for reading her other letters and diaries and delving into some mystery invented by a disturbed Aunt Ruth, that was the last thing she felt capable of doing. She had come here to live simply, to escape her old life, not to become entrapped by her Aunt's fantasies.

The sudden joy of her arrival faded and she felt cheated. The only antidote to her discomfort was action. Nightingale unloaded the cleaning materials she had thought to bring with her from the backseat and took them inside. She started in the kitchen, checked that the flue was clear and lit the Aga. Three hours later hot, filthy but happy, Nightingale stood in the middle of the damp stone floor and turned full circle to admire her handiwork. A few coats of paint and it would be an attractive room again. Her spirits had bounced back.

After demolishing half a loaf of bread and a bottle of orange juice, she explored. The sitting room was dominated by an ingle-nook fireplace that she had been able to stand up inside the last time she was here, but she was too tall now. Upstairs, one of the bedrooms was so damp that plaster had fallen from the walls but the other three were sound and the old-fashioned bathroom was in better shape than she had feared. The stairs groaned under her weight as she returned to the hall and she held on tight to the bannister. It was just as well, as the tread at the corner gave alarmingly under her weight.

She was tempted outside by the sunshine glinting off the remains of cold frames in the kitchen garden where summer had vanquished winter in an unwitnessed battle. Moisture steamed off the overgrown vegetation within its walls. Unpruned fruit trees dominated the neighboring field and a grapevine sagged, pregnant with flowers, from the south wall.

A tough, low-lying shrub sprang up as she stepped out of the door and a wonderful aroma reminiscent of Sunday lunch filled the air. In the rest of the herb garden purple heads of chives fought their way through marjoram and blue sage. A massive rosemary muscled its way over half the bed, and the mint had escaped from its terracotta prison and was making a run for freedom. *This* would be her first project once she had finished inside. She would plant salad crops, renovate the herb garden, and after that the vine and anything else that looked as if it might respond to some tender loving care.

At nine o'clock she stopped for the day and washed in streamwater, warmed on the Aga and infused with rosemary, a natural antiseptic for her cuts and stings. She ate sandwiches then set out her sleeping bag on the floor as the sun set. Her breathing grew heavy and slow, and she imagined that she could hear the clip clop of ponies' hooves as smugglers hid their cargos of spirits and silks away from the Excise men in the caves in the cliffs below.

PART TWO

LUCINDA AND WENDY

The rarest gift to Beauty, Common Sense.

—GEORGE MEREDITH

Gentleness, docility, and a spaniel-like affection are, on this ground, consistently recommended as the cardinal virtues of the sex . . . She was created to be the toy of man.

—MARY WOLLSTONECRAFT

CHAPTER THIRTEEN

Lucinda Hamilton had had a frustrating day trying to persuade a very snooty magazine to cover her client's launch party. With her connections from school and her family background, Lucinda had assumed that a career in public relations would be a cinch. She had persuaded one of the newer agencies of her credentials but unfortunately working life was proving somewhat tougher than she had expected. Her first client had insisted on another representative within a week; her second had been fulsome with praise . . . until an impromptu dinner with one of Lucinda's friends from school, now a society columnist, had resulted in a ghastly piece in one of the Sunday papers.

Her current client was her last chance. He was opening a themed restaurant to be launched with an innovative and lavish party—Lucinda's idea—and surrounded by appropriate publicity. The expenditure on the party was enormous, well over budget, but so far the acceptances were pitiful, even from the C-list she was using as backup.

People who didn't know Lucinda assumed that she was frivolous and disconnected from the life the majority of the population was forced to lead. The reality was quite different. She was ambitious and determined to prove herself without having to rely on a family inheritance. She made up for what she lacked in intellect (and it had to be said, sometimes, common sense) with abundant charm and a ruthless streak that took friends and colleagues alike by surprise. There was a sense about her that, if she once had a lucky break, she might surprise the world with her determination to succeed. Most acquaintances wished her well and worked to stay on the right side of her, just in case.

It was in a typically audacious frame of mind, masked by a buttercream smile, that she had joined her boss and a senior representative from the client for a review of the party arrangements that afternoon. After a grueling thirty minutes she had just managed to save the account, and her own role representing the client, but she had only five days in which to deliver a decent guest list that would guarantee quality press coverage. Lucinda left the meeting feeling that she would rather die than accept defeat.

The Frog and Nightgown pub in Knightsbridge had become a popular meeting place for the smart set who enjoyed pretending that they liked beer, not wine or cocktails, these days. After decades during which there had been no limit to experiences and experimentation provided one had money, it was considered cool to return to basics. But the "Frog" was hardly slumming it. The range of beer matched Belgium's best and the chef had already been approached by a White restaurant. It had become one of Lucinda's favorite haunts.

She arrived earlier than usual and the bar was almost deserted. Brian, the reserve barman, offered to mix her a cocktail but she shook her head and ordered champagne. As she sipped from the long chilled flute, she confronted the idea of defeat for the first time. If she failed there was no way she could accept demotion and she would have to move on. The spicy bubbles didn't cheer her but she finished the drink anyway and decided that it was time to leave.

A fresh glass of champagne appeared on the polished wooden bar in front of her.

"From the gentleman at the far end," Brian explained. "He thought you might need cheering up. No obligation, he was quite specific."

Lucinda looked toward the man at the end of the bar. He was smoking despite the law, with a shot glass in front of him almost full of colorless liquid. She took in the designer watch, Ralph Lauren shirt, with a soft sweater looped over his shoulders. The blond hair was longer than fashionable but well styled, and she liked the tan that spoke of sun, not a bottle. After a moment's pause she raised the glass in a salutation she hoped was casual and took a small sip. He saw her watching, raised his own glass in the briefest of acknowledgments, then returned to his perusal of the *Evening Standard*. She waited for his next move but he didn't make one. In fact he barely looked in her direction as she sipped her champagne.

The bar started to fill and a couple of friends invited her to join their table. She acknowledged their offer but stayed at the bar, becoming piqued by the man's apparent indifference. Two glasses of champagne on an empty stomach didn't help her equilibrium and as she drained the last drop she had almost decided to go and talk to him despite his cool demeanor. Almost.

It was difficult to decide whether the man at the other end of the bar was worthy of her attention. The gallant gesture of the champagne without strings had been appreciated, but the goodwill created was being undone by his studied indifference. Lucinda was used to being the pursued, not the pursuer, and the fact that he was attractive only added to her irritation.

His blond hair was thick and wavy. It tickled his collar and gave him a raffish look. The eyebrows were the same color, almost sculptured like a girl's, and beneath them his eyes were beautiful, dark brown and impossible to read. She watched him take a drink from his glass. Either he was a slow drinker or he'd had a refill. His hands had the long elegant fingers of an artist.

She ran through a familiar routine of summarizing her strong points. The act of repetition was like a litany against the powers of doubt and darkness. She was attractive—very, quite a catch in fact. She was more accustomed to fending off advances than standing in line. Her dark hair was long and silky, her eyes gray and her skin creamy-white. Breeding showed in her bone structure, poise and demeanor. Above all, she was naturally slim, bordering on skinny. No wonder some of her friends found it difficult to love her, but she pitied and forgave them.

Two women arrived. Well made up, dripping jewelry, they might as well have worn a sign around their necks that said "available." They spotted the lone attractive man at the end of the bar and went into a classic courtship routine. He remained unmoved, but raised his mysterious eyes to Lucinda's and smiled at her, inviting her to join in his ridicule of the women he had already dismissed as unworthy of his attention. She smiled back and brushed aside a momentary sense of guilt as she betrayed her own sex to his censure.

On impulse she raised her hand to buy another drink but before Brian had turned around to see it, the man was at her side.

"Allow me."

"No, it's my turn."

"Those words don't exist in my vocabulary. Please."

He wasn't condescending so she accepted the chivalry, surprised at herself. Brian served them immediately and delivered a little plate of olives to accompany their drinks.

"Your very good health." He raised his glass in a formal toast that made the corners of her mouth twitch.

"Cheers."

"I'm Edmund, Edmund Althorpe."

"Lucinda Hamilton." For an awful moment she thought he was going to offer to shake hands but he didn't. Instead he pulled up a stool and arranged his long-legged body on top. He had wonderful shoulders and while his mouth was too thin to allow him to be truly handsome, he was stunning. She wondered whether the tan extended below the V of his open-necked shirt and blushed at the thought.

"Are you too warm? Would you like to move to the terrace?"

"No, I'm fine . . . Edmund," she smiled, in her element, "and thank you for the champagne."

"It was my pleasure. You deserve it. I saw you sitting there, your face framed by your beautiful hair and I hated to see a frown mar that perfect complexion."

She smiled in a one-sided way that suggested she was used to more skilled compliments.

"I'm sorry, but you are beautiful. It puts a man on the defensive to see someone so lovely. I wanted to come straight over and say hello but I didn't know how to."

His childlike candor was disarming. Gradually she began to talk to him about herself. It was easy; he listened patiently, like an old friend. He had a lovely voice, with a trace of an accent she could not place, and an old-fashioned turn of phrase that Lucinda found appealing. The dried crustiness of her miserable day flaked away as their conversation flowed. When he was kind or complimentary she didn't push his remarks back in his face but accepted them as her due. Her defensiveness melted as she finished her third glass and they asked for another round.

"It sounds as if you've had an awful few weeks." He looked

at her with genuine sympathy and she found that she had tears in her eyes.

"Oh that's not the half of it." She found her tongue a little difficult to manage but he didn't seem to notice. "This restaurant is a blend of sci-fi and mystic. *Star Wars* meets King Arthur, if you know what I mean."

"Very retro," he said and something in his tone made her frown. Was that sarcasm?

"Pardon?"

"I said, you don't say so." There was a sudden tension in him. "This is extraordinary. I can't believe that I just met you by chance. I was attracted to you as soon as I saw you, I admit, but I had no idea that the meeting would be so . . . relevant."

The excitement in him was obvious and she felt slightly disconcerted. He made a visible effort to relax and smiled at her, his eyes sparkling, his teeth brilliant white.

"What do you mean?"

"Are you familiar with THE GAME?"

"Of course I am. Thousands of people play it. The inventors are multimillionaires."

"I wish," he murmured, but ignored the question in her look. "You've never played?"

"No, I'm not good at computer games."

"That would explain why you haven't made the connection with your party. It's perfect. You should invite all the celebrity players of THE GAME—and its creators—they would attract headlines too. It's a perfect fit."

Lucinda listened, entranced. His enthusiasm and ideas were exactly what she needed. As she finished her fourth glass of champagne her stomach rumbled loudly and she giggled in embarrassment, hoping he hadn't heard. She wanted to keep him talking. If only she could persuade the producing company of THE GAME to back her party—it would be a great advertisement for them, she told herself—her problems would be over.

"How come you know so much about THE GAME? Are you a star player?"

He stared at her and a light flickered deep in his eyes, like the sun catching the flanks of a tiger between thick trees.

"I am, yes, but I'm more than that." He looked at her solemnly and raised his hand to cup her chin so gently that it was barely there. "I'm one of the inventors of THE GAME. I still own the copyright."

The smile on Lucinda's face was beatific.

"Your party sounds a perfect opportunity to promote THE GAME among a more upmarket audience. I know we've only just met but you don't have much time and I've always believed in capturing the moment. Could I take you to dinner? I know the perfect place. Quiet, not ostentatious."

Lucinda didn't give the negative option a thought.

"I'd love to. Is it far?"

"No. Shall we?" He grinned at her boyishly and she wasn't sure whether the jelly in her knees was due to alcohol or her reaction to him. Outside he offered her his arm, just as her father did, and she took it, leaning in to him.

"Lucinda means light. Were you born at dawn?"

"I have no idea." She hiccoughed and almost tripped but he didn't seem to notice. She looked up at him, the perfect coquette. He stroked her cheek lightly, making her senses shiver in anticipation of his next touch. They were walking easily through thinning crowds.

"So tell me, as you know so much about names, what does Edmund mean?"

He turned and gave her a flash of his eyes, then pulled her gently closer to the warmth of his body.

"Well," he said, "here is another coincidence. It is an old name and it means 'happy protection.' Which is exactly what I am going to be for you."

Lucinda relaxed her weight into his supporting arm, feeling the cares of the week evaporate. She didn't believe in any particular god but as they turned away from the traffic into the quiet evening, she did offer thanks to whom- or whatever was responsible for her meeting Edmund. She was positive that her troubles of the day were about to disappear and, in a way, she was right.

CHAPTER FOURTEEN

On Tuesday Fenwick received a call from the prison. Griffiths had sent a letter to Agnes and a copy had been made for him. Anne brought the fax into him and he asked her to read it out as he had forgotten his reading glasses. Halfway through she stopped and look at him, puzzled.

"This doesn't really make sense, does it? He keeps referring to some book, then he goes on about his hellish life in prison and how he is working on his appeal. It hasn't faxed well. I'll call the prison for another copy."

He was in a meeting with Superintendent Quinlan when they were interrupted with a message that the Metropolitan Police were anxious to speak to the Chief Inspector.

Quinlan raised his eyebrows at Fenwick, who shook his head, baffled.

"I've no idea what they want. Do you mind if I take it?"

"Put them through, I'm as curious as you are."

Quinlan switched the call to the speakerphone so that he could listen in.

"DCI Fenwick."

"This is Superintendent MacIntyre. You placed a marker on the National Criminal Computer last Friday about assaults involving amputated fingers." Quinlan looked at him with exasperation and Fenwick shrugged in half apology. "May I inquire why?"

Fenwick explained quickly, not just about Griffiths' attacks in Harlden but also about the information he had secured from Telford and Birmingham.

"Why are you interested, sir?"

"There's been a murder on my patch. A young woman. Her index finger was removed. Her body was discovered today by a colleague worried that she hadn't turned up for work. I haven't received a confirmed time of death but it was at least forty-eight hours ago."

"Tell me, is she in her twenties, dark-haired, slender, perhaps a student or professional woman?"

"Yes—does that match your victims?"

"Exactly. And was she very badly beaten or mutilated before and after death?"

"Yes . . ." Fenwick heard the hesitation in the man's voice and had a flash of insight.

"Before we go further, I appreciate that you'll need to eliminate me from your inquiries. I can give you a statement and I have alibis for the weekend and for Friday."

"Thank you. Ridiculous, I know, but it's just the timing."

"I'd be the same in your position. I'll make the statement here and have it sent to you?"

"Perfect. Then we can talk fully."

Fenwick broke the connection.

"Why on earth did you suggest a statement, Andrew? It's completely unnecessary."

"If my interest had been noted at the time of the original inquiry I'd agree with you but I only entered it on Friday, perhaps hours before this woman was killed. Any coincidence like that has to be checked out. I'd do it, no matter if it caused offense."

"Well hurry up and come back here before you call him. This could have major implications."

He returned within fifteen minutes. Quinlan had canceled his next meeting and was waiting impatiently. Fenwick laid out the bare facts of his work since Nightingale's flat had been broken into. Quinlan studied his tables, comparing victims and MO for a long time. The expression on his face changed from irritation through anger to concern.

"So you are suggesting that Griffiths was involved in these earlier crimes?"

"Griffiths and/or someone else. There are two distinct methods here, despite the amputation of the fingers, and Griffiths is nowhere near six foot."

"Rape victims always overestimate their attacker's height. And anyway, there's the matter of the letters we received linking all the crimes."

"It might still be two men but working together. I know it's rare but it has happened."

"Do you realize what you're implying? How could you charge off on this hair-brained line of inquiry without consulting me first?"

Fenwick knew that he was very exposed. He'd intended to share his work with Quinlan at an appropriate time but had wanted to digest the information first, to avoid jumping to conclusions on too little evidence. As he tried to explain this to Quinlan he was cut off abruptly.

"Never mind that now. Have you sent this to MacIntyre yet?"

"No, sir. I thought it required careful explanation."

"Damn right it does. Have you had the courtesy to consult the original SIO?

"I've spoken to Inspector Blite," Fenwick paused and sighed deeply, "it was almost the first thing I did but he was pretty dismissive."

"As he has every right to be. He identified the other cases but the connection was so shaky that we jointly agreed not to pursue it."

Something in Quinlan's blustering tone, so different from his normally straightforward manner, put Fenwick on alert.

"Whose call did you say it was not to pursue the connections?"

"A *joint* one, Chief Inspector."

Fenwick noted the warning, suddenly sympathetic.

"I would imagine that a step of that importance would have to be ratified from the very top, so we'll need to be sensitive to the ACC's position on this as well?"

Quinlan turned away in his large swivel chair and stared out of the window. As he waited for him to calm down, Fenwick worked through their dilemma. The ACC and Blite had always been tight, two of a kind, often an unhelpful alliance. Fenwick could imagine what had happened once Griffiths was in custody. Blite had made the same phone calls that he'd done but instead of digging deeper he'd had a quiet word with his mate, ACC Harper-Brown. There was a choice to be made: a quick, aggressive prosecution of a multiple rapist who had been spreading fear in the county for months versus a drawn-out inquiry based on superficial similarities in evidence. Blite would have had no guarantee of success, as the CPS was even refusing to support a prosecution for the murder and two of the rapes because of lack of evidence.

Quinlan had probably been involved but with his boss and

SIO against the idea of a complicated extension of the inquiry he would have found it difficult to change their view. After a suitably contrite pause Fenwick spoke again.

"I have a suggestion if you'll hear me out."

"Go on." Quinlan kept his back to him.

"My idea's this. After Griffiths was safely locked up you decided that the vague similarities with other crimes outside the Division could be investigated during a quiet spell in Harlden. An intensive workload preparing the case for trial and the very tentative nature of the connection meant that this couldn't be initiated straightaway but last week you asked me to reopen the file."

"Why you and not Blite?"

"I had come to you asking for more work . . ."

Quinlan laughed dismissively. That would not be credible.

"All right, I came to you because I wanted more of a challenge. My detection rate for the last few months had been exceptional, you recognized that I was bored, in need of a more stimulating case and you gave me this . . . having checked first that Blite did not mind, which he didn't being newly back from sick leave and fully stretched."

"Blite would need to corroborate the story."

"What choice does he have? He's not exactly in a strong position, is he?"

"And the ACC?"

"Call him. Tell him that my work was only partially complete and you had been going to brief him at your next progress meeting when this murder happened."

The Superintendent swung his chair back and raised weary eyes to meet Fenwick's.

"Very well. But I won't take credit for your own initiative. You pursued the connection and followed through without guidance from me and that's what I shall say. I'll call the ACC now. Talk to the Met along the same lines then revert to me. I want to know what they're going to do next."

Fenwick was almost through the door when Quinlan called out to him.

"Were you really that bored?"

Directness and diplomacy struggled within Fenwick. Unusually, diplomacy won.

"I was on a winning streak, that's all."

MacIntyre was relieved to hear from an alibied Fenwick and launched into a full description of the murder. Lucinda Hamilton was twenty-four and lived in Knightsbridge. She was the middle daughter of the chief executive of one of Britain's largest companies, a man who happened to be a personal friend of the Home Secretary. The case was being handled with utmost urgency.

Lucinda had been found dead in her flat at ten-twenty that morning by a female colleague. She'd been beaten, raped, strangled and stabbed, and her index finger taken. So far there were no physical traces of the killer. He had washed the body and spring-cleaned the flat. MacIntyre was hopeful that they might recover trace evidence from the waste pipes but Fenwick was unconvinced. In the Harlden attacks nothing was left to identify the perpetrator.

Fenwick sent through his analysis of the previous crimes and went to find Quinlan, who had made his call to the ACC and was looking more relaxed.

"We are to volunteer to help the Met provided it doesn't take much resource. The ACC has agreed that you can act as Liaison Officer rather than DI Blite because of your experience of working with London."

When MacIntyre called, Fenwick outlined the suggested West Sussex contribution to his investigation, treading carefully and making it clear that they would be subordinate to his control in all matters relating to the Knightsbridge crime. He'd acquired tact during his secondment that tempered his typical bluntness but it was wasted. Harper-Brown had already contacted the Met and an edge in MacIntyre's tone warned him to proceed with care.

"I was proposing to spend the rest of today and tomorrow reexamining the cases here and reinterviewing the victims, if they're willing. I'll also make up a dossier of photographs for you to compare with the injuries to Lucinda Hamilton."

MacIntyre accepted the olive branch.

"OK. We also need e-fits of the perpetrator as well. There are witnesses who saw Lucinda leaving a pub on Friday night with a man they hadn't seen before."

Anne interrupted him half an hour later with an envelope from the prison.

"The photocopy of Griffiths' letter has arrived."

She was showing an unusual interest in this correspondence and blushed when he stared at her.

"Do you have an idea you'd like to share with me, Anne?"

She wouldn't meet his eye, but kept her attention on the letter.

"Do you believe in graphology?"

"I'm not even sure that I know what it is."

"The study of handwriting." She rushed on before he could say anything. "I'm studying it at evening class. I'm a novice but my teacher is fantastic. I'd really like to give her this to study."

"I don't think so. It wouldn't be something I'd like to have public, even if she could help us, which I very much doubt."

"It would provide an insight into the writer's character. I realize it's a strange idea, and of course to do it properly she'd need the original, but I do think it might help."

It was rare for her to become involved in the operational side of his work so he was understated in his rejection.

"I'll think about it. Have you asked the prison to hold any incoming letters for me?"

"They want an authorized request in writing, something about prisoners' rights."

"And the envelope. I want it handled carefully, to preserve any prints. I'll draft the paperwork today."

The request depended on his being able to give substance to an assertion that Griffiths had an acquaintance *and* that the person had stalked Nightingale and posed a danger to her. Yet this remained only a theory. Perhaps an analysis of Griffiths' handwriting would tell him something new. The idea was absurd and any evidence wouldn't be credible but the thought prompted another idea. If he could persuade MacIntyre to have his profiler look *beyond* Lucinda's murder, their analysis might provide substance to support his hypothesis.

He would have to work his way closer to MacIntyre first and he sensed that the ACC had already compromised his chances with his high-handed style. A visit to London would be the perfect excuse to build rapport. He would take all the information he had and practice his charm on the way.

The journey to London was usually quicker by train than car but Fenwick sat in a near empty carriage just outside Clapham Junction for forty-five minutes because of signal failure. He apologized for his lateness but MacIntyre waved the words away. It was Wednesday. Lucinda's body had been discovered twenty-four hours before.

"She'd been dead for between 60 and 72 hours according to the post-mortem. So far we can't account for her movements from around nine o'clock on Friday when she left the Frog and Nightgown pub until the Saturday night/Sunday morning when she died, but there's one possibility." MacIntyre paused and opened the post-mortem report in front of him. "There are signs that she was tortured before death, and she'd been raped and sodomized repeatedly."

"You're saying that he kept her alive?"

"It looks likely. I haven't told her father yet, for obvious reasons. I want to be as sure as I can be before I do."

Fenwick's eyes naturally went to the boards on the walls of the incident room with their smattering of photographs.

"Dear God."

"Is this consistent with the other crimes?"

"There was a murder in Harlden that the CPS wouldn't allow us to link to the rapes. The MO is similar, though the violence here is even worse. Any joy with trace evidence?"

"Nothing. She'd been thoroughly washed and the flat scoured clean. Bleach has been poured down the drains. In the kitchen, he put any utensils he'd used into the dishwasher and we have nothing."

"He ate in her flat?"

"Must've done if you think about it. He was there for a day at least. We're searching the rubbish bags now in case we can find anything. Our only real leads are eyewitness accounts of the man seen leaving the bar with her." He passed an e-fit over to Fenwick. "Ring any bells? He's tall, about six foot, lean build, wavy blond hair, brown eyes."

"It's so general. Any distinguishing characteristics?"

"None, that's my problem. The eye-witness descriptions vary. The one you've got there is a composite of the most reliable."

"What about his behavior at the bar?"

"He stopped smoking when asked and was 'charming and discreet'; I quote from a girl standing next to him. The barman said that he didn't drink much."

"Fingerprints?"

"The bar was wiped down when business closed and chairs put up to allow the floor to be cleaned so we don't even know which was his. At last count we'd identified over seventy individual prints. None of them match records on file.

"This is going to be a long haul, Fenwick. I'm grateful for your cooperation, and if anything comes from your inquiries I'll be delighted, but at the moment I'm managing expectations away from an early result."

Fenwick recognized the dismissal but he had unfinished business.

"I have one other suggestion—and I apologize if it's already in hand. Do you have a good profiler? One possibility is that the person who killed Lucinda is behind our unsolved cases in Harlden and connected to our prisoner Griffiths. Superficially the crimes on my list look like the work of two men. If we could establish that with more confidence then it's worth pursuing the possibility and Griffiths would be a real lead for you. With the resources at your disposal, you'd be able to set up a hunt that we could link into."

MacIntyre frowned, sending worry lines into his receding blond hair.

"My priority is to find Lucinda Hamilton's killer, simple as that. I'll be straight with you, I'm not convinced that the killer's connected to your prisoner but I'll keep an open mind."

"I appreciate that . . ."

MacIntyre raised a hand. He hadn't finished.

"But, if all my current lines of investigation fail, I'll be forced to consider other strategies. I've already engaged a Home

Office profiler and the Home Secretary has asked for support from the FBI—God knows why. Meanwhile, I suggest we keep things simple."

A week passed without a word from MacIntyre. Fenwick returned to his other work and scythed through it relentlessly. His secretary, Cooper and the rest of his staff kept out of the way and wished that his previously sunny mood would return. Ten days after he'd seen MacIntyre, the prison called to say that Griffiths had received another letter from Agnes. It was placed in a plastic bag and sent to Harlden, where Fenwick passed it immediately to forensics.

On Friday, he had all the results except DNA analysis from the envelope and he called Cooper to his office.

"We have a set of prints from the letter, too many from the envelope to be helpful but," he paused, his excitement obvious, "those from the letter match a partial taken from Nightingale's wrecked apartment."

He had been working on the theory of a connection between the stalking of Nightingale and Griffiths for weeks, without any supporting evidence. This physical proof changed everything.

"The letter was posted in Birmingham two days ago and we know that the P.O. box address Griffiths writes to is in Birmingham as well. Now we should have enough of a case to have it watched. I was denied a surveillance order before but they can't stop me now."

He didn't mention that he had given copies of the letters to Anne the day before, then deliberately turned a blind eye as she slipped them into her bag. Somehow, he didn't think Cooper would understand.

"What about the message?"

"Nonsense again. Quotations from those books, the odd half sentence. It doesn't make sense. I'm going to ask the prison governor to keep a watch on Griffiths when he receives the next letter to see what he does. I won't be rebuffed with a civil liberties argument a second time."

Fenwick had learned more than he ever wanted to know about prisoners' rights.

As soon as Cooper left, Anne came in. She was flushed, but not with embarrassment.

"The letter from Griffiths first. Here's my friend's assessment."

As Fenwick read the single page, his skepticism gave way to suspicion.

"What did you say to her, Anne?"

"Absolutely nothing, I pretended that he was a potential recruit, that's all."

He believed her but the graphologist's words were uncanny.

The subject is an interesting and complex individual. He exists on many levels at the same time. Outwardly quiet, he may give the impression of diligence and application and indeed he has the capacity for this, although he is easily bored. However, beneath this show of adaptation he is an insecure individual prone to wildly changing moods. He is distrustful of people yet may have the tendency to be easily led. He enjoys games and any pursuit that brings speedy gratification. Think carefully before hiring.

"She determined this from one letter?"

"Uh-huh. Had it been the original you would have had even more." She handed him another page. "This is about the letter sent to Griffiths. Her findings are rushed, but still . . ."

Fenwick read, his features impassive.

An assessment is difficult as there is much about this character that is elusive. However, with a heavy caveat and not for any file, this subject has plenty of charm, is articulate and quick-witted. There is considerable intelligence here, combined with daring. He has courage and an urge to do things that take him to the edge. He is entirely self-directed, dislikes authority and can be arrogant. He probably considers himself more intelligent than others.

There are strong indications that he is manipulative, perhaps even a bully. I have the sense again of many levels in this person but they are more carefully concealed. There is passion here, strong sexual energy, and there may be a violent tendency, though this needs to be probed fully . . .

"Thank you, Anne." Fenwick gave no hint of his deep concern. If she was right then this unknown man was far more sophisticated than Griffiths and he was roaming free. He was left with few choices but one was obvious. He needed to visit the prison again. While Griffiths was reinterviewed by Cooper, Fenwick planned to search his cell. The timing of the visit would be arranged to coincide with an activity period. Provided the guards remained discreet his search would go unnoticed.

Griffiths still had a cell to himself. Doctor Batchelor was convinced that he was a suicide risk and it suited the Governor, at Fenwick's request, to maintain the additional privacy. The cell was tiny and sparsely furnished: a bunk, toilet, sink, table and chair, with one shelf for his few personal possessions. Fenwick asked the guard to check the bed and under the mattress while he scrutinized materials on the shelf and desk. There were three books. He noted their titles, checked the pages for any markings, and then opened them upside down by their covers to see what fell out. He sent the single folded sheet from the back of *Around the British Isles* for photocopying and continued his search. When he opened the scrapbooks he gasped in shock.

"Good grief!"

The sketch was drawn in flowing lines: a young woman in torn robes. Her hands were tied around a post tightly enough to draw her shoulders back and curve her spine. The front of her gown had been ripped open, revealing nakedness beneath. The woman's head was thrown to one side, her eyes averted from a dark formless shape in front of her.

It was Nightingale, drawn with almost photographic clarity, no doubt copied from one of the many press cuttings in the other scrapbook. Fenwick sat down and looked at the next study. Nightingale again. She looked like a doll. Griffiths had drawn her naked, stretched out on a stone altar, arms and legs tied wide. The detailed anatomy drew a blush from Fenwick. He hated the idea of Griffiths creating then lusting over these images.

"Is it usual for prisoners to be allowed to draw stuff like this?"

"It's part of his therapy. Dr. Batchelor supervises him. It's all legit."

Fenwick shook his head in disgust and returned the scrapbook to its place.

"When he received his last letter do you know what he did with it?"

"I was on duty and watched him. He read it, made lots of notes, left it while he read some of his books, made some more notes, then finished at lights out."

"What else does he do when he's in here?"

"Plays that game over there for hours on end. I've seen them do more stupid things."

Fenwick opened the box, making an effort to remember how the pieces, board and cards had been stacked. He removed them then shook his head.

"Means nothing to me." But as he was replacing everything, he noticed that the board was warped. Thinking he had folded it incorrectly he opened it and tried again, without success. He ran his fingers over the surface and around the edges.

"There's something in here."

At last the guard looked interested.

"Probably his stash."

"I don't think so." He prised the edges of the board apart wide enough for him to reach the paper folded inside. Two more pictures, both of Nightingale.

In the first the paper had been gouged where her heart should have been, with enough savagery to leave a hole. The second image was even more violent. It showed a naked woman with Nightingale's face. She was tied to an altar and there was a wound in her chest. All her fingers had been severed. Above her the gray shape had been drawn in detail. The Demon King: black wings, scales, a long articulated tail and a gaping red mouth. He was holding aloft a steaming bloody heart.

Fenwick shuddered at the graphic detail, so reminiscent of Lucinda's murder.

"He's seriously sick."

The guard laughed, a cynical sound that annoyed the detective.

"Not according to the good doctor. He thinks Griffiths is getting better."

"Bollocks!"

"So you say, and I might agree with you, but it's Batchelor who's the expert. What do our opinions count?" He looked at the picture in Fenwick's hands. "He's good though, isn't he? Wonder who the models are?"

Fenwick stared at the guard, then at the picture a second time. He had failed to notice that the face on the Demon King was not that of Griffiths.

"Do you have a color photocopier here?"

"The Admin officer might have one but I doubt it."

"I need to borrow this to make a copy but he mustn't know it's gone. What can you do?"

"Confiscate his game for a few days. He'll go ape, and we'll have Batchelor all over us but what the heck," he smiled, "it'll serve the pervy shit right."

In the car park, Fenwick debriefed Cooper and showed him the picture. His sergeant blushed.

"Recognize the face—the man's I mean?"

"No." He folded the image away fastidiously and handed it back to Fenwick.

"Well, I think I do. We need a copy made and the original returned—would you see to it while I visit the good doctor."

Doctor Batchelor was in his consulting room with a patient when Fenwick arrived and he had to wait ten minutes. The patient left through a side door and Fenwick heard sobbing from the stairwell.

Doctor Batchelor opened the door and frowned when he saw Fenwick waiting.

"You again. I thought I was finished for the day, Cynthia."

"I need to talk to you again about Wayne Griffiths?"

Batchelor's mouth settled into a thin line.

"The man's in prison. Can you not leave him alone even now?"

"Please, Doctor, I'm one of the good guys. We have so few resources, why waste them on a man who has already been sentenced. I'm hoping by speaking with you to put a stop to all this."

"Hmm." Batchelor eyed him suspiciously. "I'll give you five minutes. Cynthia, note the time and interrupt accordingly."

Fenwick took a moment to judge his surroundings, as he

hadn't seen the consulting room before. The carpet was of warm burgundy wool, the couch and doctor's chair a matching leather shade. All the walls had been painted a dark pinky-cream and were hung with abstract paintings of spirals and valves that looked as if they had been bought at a car boot sale. It was his desk though that convinced Fenwick he was dealing with an egocentric with pretensions of world salvation. The top was solid smoked glass, arranged on steel legs and cross-pieces that braced to give it strength. And it was completely empty. Even the dark red phone was on a side cabinet.

He kept his face blank but nodded appreciatively.

"Does the sense of reentering the womb help your patients?"

"Perceptive, Chief Inspector, but it doesn't mean I'll talk to you."

"I'm just curious to gain your assessment of Griffiths as a man, not as a criminal. His strengths, concerns, his character if you like."

Batchelor said nothing for a long time. He had not invited Fenwick to sit but had positioned himself in his leather chair behind his desk, hands raised, fingers steepled against his lips.

"I will not give you my clinical assessment of him."

"Of course."

"However, I will answer specific questions if I feel they are of a sufficiently general nature."

Fenwick hid his irritation at the man's powerplay in an acquiescing nod of his head.

"Very well. Is he intelligent?"

"Yes."

"Is he artistic?"

"Oh yes."

"That must help in terms of therapy."

"No comment."

"Does he have a good imagination?"

"Not particularly."

"So when he draws he copies what he knows?"

"One could say that. I really don't see where this is leading?"

"But it is helpful, I assure you. So he would be good at copying or drawing from memory?"

"Yes." There was exasperation in his tone now.

"Let me change the subject. Does he follow rules well?"

"Yes. He believes in rules. It is why he plays THE GAME so well and why he hasn't gone mad, despite his false imprisonment."

"So you don't agree with the jury?"

"In my opinion it was a clear case of entrapment."

"Despite the attack?"

"I accept that Griffiths has a few problems, not least his response to disappointment."

"Is he making progress in therapy?"

"Excellent progress. If ever there were an appeal against the sentence I would have no qualms now about testifying in his favor."

There was a tap at the door. Fenwick didn't wait to be dismissed.

"I'll see myself out. Thank you, Doctor," he paused, "you've been most helpful." He could see Batchelor's disconcerted expression from the corner of his eye and allowed himself a silent chuckle.

CHAPTER FIFTEEN

One of the few passengers on the delayed late night service to Birmingham New Street was dozing when the ticket inspector shook him softly by the shoulder. The passenger woke with a start and his hand seized the inspector's wrist.

"Easy now! I just need to see your ticket." The gentle Welsh voice was reassuring and the dangerous light died in the passenger's eyes.

The inspector clipped the ticket and walked away without looking back but the space between his shoulder blades itched. As soon as he left the compartment he hurried through the remaining empty carriages and tucked himself up securely inside the guard's van. He radioed the driver, just to hear a friendly voice, then moved slightly so that the heavy fire extinguisher was in easy reach. The guard, Eddie to his friends, had been a useful middleweight in his younger days. He hadn't felt this threatened since his final bout, when his opponent had beaten him to a pulp. Until tonight it had been the only time that he had seen murder in someone's eyes and known them capable of carrying it out. He shivered as he waited in the van, his eyes on the door handle, but the rest of the journey was uneventful.

He watched the passenger leave the train at the end of the line. Instead of going straight home for a pre-prepared meal, bottle of beer and bed, Eddie sat on a cold metal seat in the station and wrote down a description of the man. He was tall, around six feet, blond hair, slightly wavy, strong features, wearing an expensive sports jacket and smart trousers. The rucksack had a logo on it that he didn't recognize so he drew it instead. He folded the piece of paper carefully and placed it in his pocket. If there was a violent crime that night he wouldn't have to rely on his dodgy memory. Past punches had made it unreliable and he was constantly writing notes to himself. His main problem was then remembering that he had done so.

The next morning the man with the rucksack stepped off a bus within miles of the Welsh border and breathed in the clean air. He was carrying supermarket bags, their weight a minor inconvenience as he walked three miles to the small development of holiday cottages. They were well spread out, providing privacy and a view of a lake in the distance. One cottage was set well back from the path. It was his bolt-hole when he needed to retire and take stock, usually after an "event" like last weekend. He used it roughly twice a year but at no set season.

The cottage was really a bungalow with an extra bedroom in the roof. Over the years he had stripped out the old furniture. In its place he had installed a camp bed, simple prefabricated wardrobe, desk, chest of drawers, TV, and single armchair. Only the kitchen was unchanged. He wasn't in to plumbing and electrics so he put up with the old-fashioned fittings and ignored the memories that lingered in corners.

He made himself tea and then found the stash he had left in the bread crock. The mouse-proof wrapping was intact and he rolled himself a joint. He took the mug and roll-up into the sitting room and switched on the TV. There was a supply of violent porn videos in a drawer. He chose one of his favorites and eased into an hour of fantasy, the fiction on the screen in front of him blending with the facts of recent memory.

He drifted into a contented sleep, waking at five in the morning. Breakfast was a mound of bacon and eggs from his new supplies. He felt invigorated but restless, eager to resume the previous pattern of his life but aware that it was impossible. It had been stupid of Griffiths to be caught and he was disappointed in him.

For years they had been able to operate in a loose partnership, becoming more confident as their skills grew and their imaginations developed. The ability to share their experiences and to talk openly, yet operate with complete independence had been addictive. He was the cleverer of the two, bolder and more original. Griffiths was too in awe to be a worthy partner but good enough to be accommodated. Subconsciously his hero worship was one of the things the man missed.

And now he had to find a way to extract Griffiths from prison. It was too tedious. The game of codes and books had amused him briefly but it was already beginning to pale and the police had failed to connect the death of the woman in London to the crimes of which Griffths had been convicted. He had taken a finger, throwing it into the Thames from a bridge later. Surely even the most stupid copper could work out a connection.

He was reluctant to send another letter. Only the previous week he'd watched an episode of *Forensic Detectives* on TV in which a man had been caught because of letters he'd sent, despite his care, and he didn't want to take unnecessary risks. A phone call then? Maybe, but it struck him as clumsy and he preferred his methods to be elegant. Like his tormenting of the policewoman, except that when he had finally decided to finish her the flat had been empty. The bird had flown. Now he needed to search again from scratch, but he thought that she would be worth it. Normally he would have resented this need to plan, preferring to let inspiration guide him, as it had the previous weekend. The memory made him smile. He had enjoyed her for over twenty-four hours, until her friends had started to ring when she was late for a party, and then he had finished it.

Some of the restlessness within him arose from an unusual lack of direction and it needed to stop. He looked at his watch and was relieved to see that it was time for him to leave; he rarely spent very long in any one place. His motorbike was at the back of the cottage, covered by a tarpaulin. It was a discreet but powerful machine. He let out the clutch and drove carefully to the National Trust Car Park and his appointment.

She was waiting for him alone, her face drawn and anxious. His anger bubbled up as it always did when he saw her after a period of separation. She was useless. Look at her, dressed in smart but unfashionable clothes that did nothing for what remained of her figure. Her face was a dead giveaway, eyes nervous and darting, her lips chapped. He scorned the fear in her, yet it also made her his perfect companion.

He drew up at a distance from her car and climbed off his machine, his leathers creaking. His face was impassive but hers betrayed every thought as she scanned his expression, hopeful yet scared. She was trying to work out whether he was in a good mood or not. Well, he'd keep her guessing.

It took him three long strides to reach her. With his left hand he grabbed a handful of her long blond hair and twisted it so that she was forced to raise her face to his. He leaned down and kissed her hard, pressing with his mouth until he could feel her teeth grate and taste the sweet saltiness of blood in her saliva. With his free hand he reached inside her jacket and squeezed her breast until she whimpered with pain mixed with pleasure.

The sound excited him and he pulled down her jeans, then

opened his fly. He took her, quick and hard over the bonnet of the car. Later that night, the sight of her fresh bruises would excite him and he would have her again.

When he'd finished, he zipped up and stepped back to have a smoke, leaving her to pull up her jeans from the muddy gravel. Only when he'd stubbed out his cigarette did he speak to her.

"I'll stay at the flat tonight."

"Have you seen Wayne?"

"What do you care?" He let the anger he felt at her interest harden his voice. "He's nothing. I'm your only family, I always have been. You'd better remember that, Wendy." He rarely used her name and it brought a smile to her face despite the harshness of his tone.

"Sorry, Dave." She bowed her head submissively.

"Time to make a move."

He followed her, keeping a few vehicles between them all the way back to Birmingham, confident that she would remain as biddable as he needed her to be.

Wendy was asleep and it was still dark outside when he woke up. He had been dreaming about Lucinda tied to her bed and was excited all over again. Without bothering to wake her, and with no foreplay of any kind, he rolled Wendy onto her side and took her. She cried out but the noises changed from pain to pleasure as he continued. As soon as he had finished he got out of bed. She reached out a hand to him but he ignored her.

The second bedroom in the flat was his domain. She wasn't allowed to dust or vacuum and he kept the door locked when he was away. He had the only key despite the fact that the computer was password protected. Even so, he paused at the threshold and checked that everything was as he had left it. He thought that the chair was slightly out of place but as everything else was exactly as it should be he dismissed the minor irregularity. Before he sat down he opened the window wide and wedged the door so that he couldn't be shut in.

His computer was a top-of-the-range model, linked to the Internet through an ISDN line. He connected quickly and checked his mailbox. There were no messages from her and he cursed out loud. Since the trial he had been unable to entice her into playing THE GAME. He and Wayne had made a lot of money helping to develop it, and could still have been raking it in if they hadn't been asked to leave the company. That had been Griffiths' fault. He had this habit of becoming over-attached and the object of his attentions would eventually complain. Janie, the bitch, had made a formal complaint against them both. "Harassment" was what they put in Wayne's letter of dismissal. Fucking overreaction he'd thought.

After they had been forced to leave, Wayne wanted to teach Janie a lesson but he had been able to persuade him against it. Instead they had gone after her sister at Sixth Form College. Wayne had raped her at a nature reserve and came back with virginal blood still on him, against the rules. Three weeks later they had followed Janie and a group of friends at a discreet distance as they enjoyed a Saturday night out. One of the girls was particularly attractive and he'd followed her home himself to a bedsit on the outskirts of Birmingham. After watching the house for an hour he concluded that no one else was in. He had made himself a dog collar from folded white paper and knocked on the door holding a bundle of *Big Issues* that he bought from a seller at the end of the road, and that was that.

The following week the police had called without warning. Fortunately Wendy had been at home and had lied for him, as she should. He had remained calm, not least because he knew that he had left no trace evidence at the woman's flat. The Detective Sergeant interviewing him wouldn't say how they had come by his name but he guessed when they started asking questions about Wayne. Janie must have fingered them, it stood to reason.

As soon as the police had gone, he'd called Wayne on his mobile and told him to leg it and say nothing if they traced him. He had packed and left the same day, pausing only long enough to reward Wendy for her loyalty in the way she liked best. Since that experience he only returned to Birmingham to keep her sweet.

He clicked his way into the specialist sites that formed the core of his recreation. They catered to particular tastes. Some contained scenes of torture, others wartime atrocities, yet more showed injuries to children. He wasn't that interested in the latter, not that he had anything against them in principle, they simply didn't turn him on.

There was a tentative tap on the partially open door as the dark behind the curtains gave way to gray.

"I've put your tea out here." Wendy wouldn't dare push the door wider.

Her knock had broken his reverie. He turned his mind to the problem of finding the policewoman. There was a way to track her through the web if he was lucky and if she went online. He could mail her a virus that would attach itself to everything in her computer and send it back to his own. It would be difficult to construct but he knew someone who still worked at the games company who was a genius developer. Iain would help him as he had a penchant for kiddy porn, which he had once helped to supply.

Iain would not be in the office before eight so he had time to kill. He might as well go and be sociable with Wendy, just to remind her of what a good boy he could be when he wanted. She was drying her hair at the dressing table when he came up behind her and took the hair dryer from her hands. He brushed the thin blond hair until it shone. When he had finished he lay back and watched her dress, donning thick tights, cheap cotton striped dress, elastic belt and sensible shoes in ritualistic order. Her freshly laundered cap would already be in her bag. He had once thought her almost pretty, now she was merely convenient. That she loved him, he knew. That Griffiths loved her made him smile. That they both feared him made him laugh.

He had made Wayne lend her the apartment in the heady days of the technology boom. It tied her to them and it was convenient. When he was feeling generous he rebated some of the low rent she paid him. Neither he nor Griffiths had given her any of their money, so she had to exist on her nurse's pay. He had invested most of his wealth with a private bank on the Isle of Man. The rest was in a bank account he shared with Wendy. In theory, she could have plundered the money and run away but he knew that she would never dare.

She bent over to kiss him and he turned his face away so that her lips brushed his ear. Then he reached out, snakelike, and grabbed her by the back of the neck, forcing her down into the bed so that he could kiss her mouth hard, smearing the red lipstick like a gash across her cheek.

"Don't be late back," he instructed.

"You'll be here?" He saw hope in her eyes and enjoyed the flash of power.

"Maybe."

He kissed her again and felt the passion of her response. She liked it rough, to a point. He always made sure he went beyond that point, so that he could see the lust turn to fear in her eyes. One day he would go all the way. That would be so good. Something of his desire must have shown in his face. Wendy pressed her hand against him, inviting, but he didn't want her again so soon or so easily.

"Get going. And see if I have any mail at the drop."

When he called Iain's office they said that he would be in late so he left the flat for some breakfast.

Wendy waited around the corner until she saw Dave's back disappear toward town. She wasn't expected at the hospital for another two hours but he didn't know that. As soon as she was sure that he had really gone she ran back to the flat. Her heart was thudding painfully against her ribs and her hands shook as she took a copy of the bedroom key from the hiding place in her Tampax box. If he found out that she had made it she was certain that he would kill her.

She was making small whimpering sounds as she switched on the PC, appalled at the risk she was prepared to take, but she had to know. Ever since Wayne had been arrested she had been tortured by doubts. Could Dave have been involved? It was impossible to think of Wayne acting on his own initiative but it was equally difficult to accept that Dave might be implicated. When Wayne was sent down and Dave went traveling, she had found the key in its hiding place and had a copy made. It had lain unused in her bathroom cupboard ever since, until that poor girl was killed at the weekend.

Lucinda Hamilton. Dave had been in London the weekend she died. The way he'd made love to her in the car park the day before had been so reminiscent of the times he'd returned from his jaunts with Wayne that she'd resolved then to act on her fears. She wasn't sure why she was doing this while he was in the city but she couldn't face another night without sleep or day with no appetite. Breaking through Dave's security would be a desperate attempt to remove her suspicions once and for all. While she waited for the PC to warm up she remembered that she had bought rubber gloves and went to find them.

After a bacon sandwich he bought a paper to read over a decent coffee in a café he thought did the best in Birmingham. A pretty student, no more than nineteen, came into the crowded shop and asked if she could share his table. She had long legs, good skin and eyes as brown as coffee beans. From time to time she would flick them up to him, then look away quickly. It was fairly typical behavior. Women found him attractive.

He toyed with the idea of picking her up and taking her away to a place where he could enjoy her properly but she was bound to live in Halls—she looked like a Fresher to his trained eye. Besides, he no longer indulged his interests so close to home since the police attention that had almost hooked him. As his coffee cooled, the idea of taking her became more attractive and he indulged his fantasy while he read the paper. When she saw him smiling at her she smiled back and he began to have second thoughts. She almost seemed to be inviting him to take her, and she would be a good one, he could sense it. She would struggle. And he needed to act again quickly, otherwise there was a danger the police would think Lucinda an isolated attack, which would delay Griffiths' appeal. Perhaps he could risk it just this once. He leaned toward her.

"Beverly! There you are. I've been looking all over." A plump girl with wire-rimmed glasses and frizzy hair flounced up to their table.

"I said I'd be here." The young beauty opposite him suddenly looked sulky and the idea of biting down hard on that plump lower lip was delicious.

"You said *Starbucks*, not here. Just as well I remembered this was your favorite. Come on we'll be late."

Beverly looked at him with a disappointed smile, and he raised his eyebrows in an invitation to stay. She hesitated a moment but her dumpy friend dragged her away. He watched them go, vaguely disappointed. It was time to call Iain again anyway and that was best done from the flat. He cleared his drinking debris away like a regular citizen and started the short walk home.

Wendy searched the desk in the hope of finding Dave's password. She unearthed some dope, pornographic magazines and details of an account in the Isle of Man that she didn't know he had, but no trace of what she really needed. Now that she was actually sitting at his desk she felt as if she had already taken the most difficult decision. The problem was that she had already tried twice to log on and the system had rejected her. If she tried again and was still wrong, the PC might lock her out. That was what happened at the hospital and then the password would need resetting. She could not risk that—Dave would know next time he went online and then her life would not be worth living.

A small voice told her to stop. If she took much longer she might be late for work and then the hospital would call and her deception would be discovered. Her palms were as wet as her cheeks.

"I have to do this!" She told herself, knowing that she would never be able to find the courage again.

She stared at the letters she had written down from watching through the crack of the door. His right hand had been visible and she had seen: _ O U_ I _ I quite clearly. In the weeks since she had spied on him she had done her research. There were only two words in her dictionary that fitted those letters and she had tried both without success. Now she was faced with the choice of using her last idea and risking a lock out and discovery, or abandoning her search. Wendy looked at the sweat-dampened paper in her hand and offered up a silent prayer before typing in the missing letters: H, D, N. Her finger hovered over the enter key, then with an audible sob she hit it.

HOUDINI, the great escape artist. His face appeared in the screen and smiled at her. She was in. She opened Internet Explorer and found his favorite sites. Dave had no idea that she knew how to do this, that she had paid for the class at night school with cash saved from her housekeeping. She maneuvered the mouse until she found the address he had used most recently. It too was password protected and when HOUDINI would not work she selected the next one. On the fifth attempt she was given access. The site featured pictures of sadomasochistic sex and she browsed through it unmoved. What she saw was tame compared with the realities of her life.

Time was running out. She opened the next destination on the web and watched in horror as close-up photographs of train wrecks and natural disasters filled the screen, each with explicit images of human carnage. A severed foot lay next to a red mess that looked like pulped tomatoes with white beans floating in it. When she recognized the white lumps as remnants of a shattered jawbone she had to rush to the bathroom. She cleared her vomit away scrupulously and sprayed perfume in the air to disguise the smell.

It was hard to return to the screen. There was little reason to look further, and she had no desire to see what pictures lay behind password protection. They would be worse and the thought sickened her. The necessity to log off and disguise her intrusion occupied her mind, forcing all other thoughts to the far reaches but they kept intruding nevertheless. Dave liked this stuff, he had searched the net and found it. What more did he like? Could she openly admit that he was a sadist, turned on by pain and violence? She already knew the answer but while horrified, she was also relieved. Nothing she had discovered suggested that he was capable of murder.

Wendy turned off the PC, aware that she was running late because she had been sick. She was slipping into her shoes when she heard the front door below slam shut. Their two neighbors had already left for work, which meant that it had to be Dave. She let out a squeal and looked around for somewhere to hide. There was nowhere. Her only option was to climb out of the bathroom window and onto the flat roof of the ground floor flat's kitchen. From there she would be able to jump to the ground.

Wendy wasn't a brave person, nor was she fit or agile but the thought of being trapped by Dave, with the PC still warm from her use, was more terrifying than any physical trial. She would have to take the risk about the PC and just hope that he thought that it was from his earlier use. There were footsteps on the landing outside and she could see a silhouette through the frosted glass of the front door. She grabbed her bag and ran to the bathroom, closing the door behind her as his key slid into the lock. "Please, God, don't let him come in here," she thought as she opened the window and pushed her bag through. It was narrow but by standing on the lid of the toilet she was able to squeeze through and onto the asphalt of the roof three feet below.

As she pulled the window closed the bathroom door opened. Wendy shrank back flat against the wall and started to pray. She heard the noise of the seat being raised and a long stream of his pee spraying the bowl as he relieved himself. When the toilet flushed she counted to one hundred and then risked the jump to the concrete yard. She didn't look back as she opened the gate and ran to her car, hidden three streets away.

During her drive through the city traffic she began to sort through the images in her mind. This was something at which she was practiced. Self-deception was relatively easy when the alternatives were unthinkable. By the time she arrived on the ward her thoughts were under control, excuses prepared and explanations in place. After a day of dealing with other people's traumas she managed to regain a semblance of routine in which her main concern was whether Dave would still be there when she returned and, if he was, what she should buy him for supper.

CHAPTER SIXTEEN

Thunder directly overhead woke Nightingale and she lay in the dark, disorientated, as she tried to shake away the cobweb of a dream. She didn't know why she should start having nightmares again but after a wonderfully blank sleep on her first night she had dreamed of Griffiths repeatedly. He was stalking her through a wood. It was night and a heavy bird was flying through the trees above her head, scattering twigs and leaves onto her. She was wearing a diaphanous, pale green dress with nothing on underneath. Griffiths was masked and much taller than she remembered.

Every night she woke up as his fingers grabbed her hair and pulled her backward. Tonight, as she had struggled up out of the depths of sleep, she had felt the heat of his breath on her neck seconds before her eyes flew open in alarm. She pulled on a jumper over her T-shirt and went to find wood for the Aga so that she could make a cup of tea. While she waited for the fire to heat the water she lit a tilley lamp and laid out the contents of her aunt's secret drawer. She had lost count of the number of times she had done this, but she had not yet discovered their secret.

There was a diary for the year of her birth, in which there was reference to a January house party that had ended in a fearful argument between her mother and father, and another at

Easter when her parents were again among guests at Mill Farm. Nightingale compared the names of the people at the party at Easter with those from New Year. Five matched apart from her aunt: her parents, a married couple called George and Amelia Mayflower, and a guest called Lulu Bullock. The way her aunt described Lulu and the depth of their relationship had convinced Nightingale that the women had probably been lovers. In August her father had arrived with his heavily pregnant wife on condition that Lulu should reside somewhere else during their stay. Her aunt had prevailed on Amelia to take in her friend.

Nightingale studied a packet of photographs as she sipped her tea, trying to put names to faces. The girl she imagined might be Lulu reminded her of someone and she was still trying to remember whom as she drifted into a dreamless sleep.

A light tapping outside the window woke her at dawn. The air was full of birdsong, triumphant after the night of rain. A thrush had a snail in its beak and was beating it determinedly against the stone windowsill. Sunlight angled low through a gap in the trees. During the morning she finished cleaning the bedroom she had selected upstairs and cut some dog roses to place in a creamware jug on the dressing table. She decided against curtains. The idea of waking and sleeping in rhythm with the sun appealed to her. She was on her way downstairs when she heard someone knock at the front door.

"Miss Nightingale, good morning." The old priest touched the brim of his hat lightly in salutation. "Glad to see you up and about. I've come to invite you to church. You've missed early morning mass but we have another service at eleven should you choose to celebrate the Lord's day of rest."

He eyed the mop and bucket in her hand meaningfully and there was a distinct emphasis to his final words. The priest managed to irritate her all over again but despite this the idea of church and some company appealed. She had been on her own for too long.

"I'll do my best to make it, Father, once I have finished here." She was not going to give in that easily.

He nodded and peered over her shoulder.

"My word, you've transformed the place already. All your own work?"

"I'm here on my own, if that's what you mean."

"Indeed, yes, well. As I say, transformed. The garden is back under control, and you've put in seedlings, I see. Until later, then."

Nightingale watched him walk away across the rutted track, his cassock caught up neatly in his belt to avoid the puddles. If the service was at eleven she barely had time to finish her chores and wash. She lit a fire under the copper in the scullery and filled it with water from the stream. In the twenty minutes it took to heat to luke warm she finished weeding the herb bed. The rosemary bushes had been hacked into submission, clumps of lemon, variegated and garden thyme had been shaped, and the sages sculpted into almost oriental proportions. Their mixed aromas filled the warm air as she worked.

She cut some lavender to throw in her bath and stripped off to wash there in the scullery. Her skin was tingling and pink by the time she finished, her hair glossy wet but drying quickly in the increasing heat of the morning. The blouse she took from her case was a little creased but the long floral skirt flowed wrinkle free. She put pearl studs in her ears, applied lipstick and a spray of perfume; she was representing the Nightingales, after all.

Bells were already ringing as she parked. An old lady leaning heavily on a stick was hobbling hastily to the door and she followed her down the path. Yew trees crowded the gate and shadowed the lichen-covered graves. Mixed oaks and rowans surrounded the church, proud in their summer green.

The church door creaked loudly as the old lady pushed it open and a dozen heads turned. Two dozen eyes widened in surprise to see a stranger step inside. Nightingale walked a short way down the aisle, crossed herself and bobbed in an action that sprang unchecked from her childhood. In front of her, she was conscious of the dry rustle of old people's whispers. The priest arrived and with him a choir that included the only people in the church below the age of fifty. They raised the number in the congregation to twenty-five.

The organist played the opening bars of the first hymn and Nightingale joined in unselfconsciously, comfortable that her contralto voice would pass muster. As she sang she studied the organist, a woman about her mother's age, who worked the stops and keys vigorously, inspiring the few voices to sing out. The service was traditional, the hymns the same as she had sung as a child. There was no clapping, no shouts of joy and not the faintest echo of a tambourine. It would have been entirely possible for this same service to have been conducted twenty-five years previously. Perhaps it had been and was only now being recycled.

As she left the priest was waiting to shake her hand. Beyond him, clusters of congregation and choir were hovering on the pretext of engaging in casual conversation but Nightingale was not fooled.

"A lovely service. Thank you."

"Thank *you* for coming, Miss Nightingale. Shall we see you next week?"

"I hope so." She shook his hand and he turned to go. "Oh, one thing, Father could you show me my Aunt's grave?"

The priest colored and looked around for rescue.

"I'll do that, Father Patrick." A voice came from behind her and Nightingale turned to see the organist bearing down on them.

"Ah, thank you, Amelia. Into your capable hands then . . ." He went to join safer members of his small flock.

"I'm Amelia Mayflower. You must be Henry's daughter. You have exactly his eyes. Well, well. It's amazing," she narrowed her eyes and examined Nightingale openly, "the similarity is astonishing."

"Hardly. It's my brother Simon people say resembles my parents. Apart from my eyes I have nothing in common with either of them."

The woman blushed an unbecoming red and gestured with a beefy arm.

"Your aunt's grave is over here." She strode off to the west of the church. Nightingale followed her square rump into the shadow cast by the church wall and shivered.

"There." The brisk tone softened. "I'll leave you alone for a moment."

Nightingale could not believe what she was seeing. The headstone was carved out of gray marble without any sign of age. It was a sculpture of a young woman kneeling on a mossy stone covered by heartsease and forget-me-nots. Above her another woman rested her hand on her shoulder. It was just possible to think of her as a guardian angel but to Nightingale's enlightened eye the imagery was clear. This was her aunt's lover and protectress, Lulu. It must have been carved when the two women were living together.

There was no inscription, nothing to suggest any sense of grief at her passing, only her aunt's name and the dates that marked her life. She felt tears gather in her eyes.

"You were fond of her then?"

Nightingale blinked hard before turning to face Amelia. "Yes. We were very close."

"She doted on you. If you had been her own daughter she could not have loved you more."

"Did you know her well?" It was a test question. The diaries and photographs had already given her the answer but she was curious to see whether this woman was honest.

"Very well at one time. Less so as we grew older. I had three children to bring up and a husband who was dogged with ill health. It was because of me that this stone was erected. The priest was fearfully against it but he can't run the parish without me and I threatened to change churches so that was an end to it."

"Thank you." Nightingale stretched out her hand in a proper greeting. "I'm Louise, and I'm very pleased to meet you."

"So you stuck with that name did you? A real chip off the old block." She laughed and released Nightingale's hand. "Shall we go, or would you like more time?"

"Let's go. I'll come back with some flowers later."

They walked away together, Amelia chatting by her side, explaining that she had been at school with her aunt.

"We were inseparable, the three of us."

"Three?"

"Your father, Ruth and I. They were wonderful days. How is Henry? He's always kept in touch."

The expression on Nightingale's face must have told her that something was wrong.

"Put my foot in it, have I? I'm always doing that. My late husband used to say it was my only distinguishing characteristic! Have they separated at last? I knew it would happen . . ."

Nightingale cleared her throat.

"He's dead. He died earlier this year, in January."

It was as if she had punched Amelia. The breath went out of her and she sagged against the gatepost.

"I didn't know. News hasn't reached here yet. Henry's

dead . . ." She said the words as if testing them and Nightingale saw tears in her eyes. Instinctively, she put her arm around the woman's broad shoulders in comfort. "I thought I would have known, that he had gone I mean. I should have known. What date was it?"

"January 27th."

She shook her head.

"No, that means nothing to me. All this time, I've been thinking . . ." She shook herself and stepped away from Nightingale's protecting arm.

"You must have been very fond of him."

"Oh yes, I was. At one point I thought we would marry. But then, I was a silly empty-headed girl of eighteen. He went away to university and came back with a good degree and your mother."

"And you married and had children," she prompted, hoping to move the subject on.

"Of course. George had always wanted me. His family was the wealthiest in the area and his prospects were promising, then. You should've seen the wedding present his parents gave us!"

"What was it?"

"The house I still live in. Imagine that. Your fate sealed at twenty-one. Hard to believe, isn't it."

Nightingale, who still had no real sense of who she was, let alone her destiny, could only nod. Something in her expression returned Amelia to her normal capable self.

"Listen to me wittering! Tell me how's your poor mother coping? I would have thought that his death would be hard on her."

"She's dead too. It was a car accident. They died together." Nightingale tried to sound composed but there must have been something in her tone that betrayed the rawness of her feelings.

"Oh my dear. You poor thing. And you're down here on

your own with all those memories. Let me give you lunch, no I insist. Follow me in your car, it's not far." She was not to be denied.

Mrs. Mayflower lived in the heart of the village in a small Georgian house next to the old post office. "Some wedding present," Nightingale thought as she pulled up outside.

The smell of roast lamb greeted them as her hostess opened the door.

"It's all done bar the gravy and greens. Help yourself to a sherry, it's on the sideboard. Be a dear and pour me one too. I think we both need it."

Sherry was not exactly to Nightingale's taste but when she poured a glass for Amelia she noticed it was pale and smelled deliciously of smoked almonds. She served a second glass and took them through to the kitchen. Her hostess sipped but did not speak as she boiled peas then used the juice to make the gravy.

"Knives and forks are in the top drawer. Place mat is by your elbow and napkins are in the dining room. Take your sherry through and lay your place. I'll be right behind you."

The plates were served ready filled, which meant that the meal was hot. There was fresh mint sauce and the potatoes were roasted a crispy golden brown.

"I have a roast every Sunday and I always make plenty in case one of the children turns up unannounced. Some wine? I know you've your car outside but there's a back way up the hill to Mill Farm."

She poured herself a very large glass and did the same for Nightingale. As they ate Amelia refilled her own glass while Nightingale sipped from hers. She talked almost nonstop, pausing only to chew and swallow. Nightingale forgave her hostess her loquaciousness as she was easy company. If she occasionally said a stupid or thoughtless thing it was soon forgotten in the following flow as there was little apparent malice behind the words.

Amelia opened a second bottle of wine although Nightingale had only just finished her first glass and frowned at the measure that replaced it. Over cheese and home-baked biscuits, Amelia spoke of the early death of her husband after years of illness. Family money had kept her children housed, fed and educated and a small pension from the family business meant that she would never starve. Nightingale could understand why a woman with Amelia's passion and industry had thrown her energy into village and church life.

Over coffee, during which Amelia worked diligently at her wine, they talked of Aunt Ruth.

"She was a good friend. She helped me hold the family together when George was ill and after his death."

"I don't think my father knew that side of her."

"Your father!" Amelia shook her head dismissively and rose to clear the last of the plates.

"Please, what about my father? He was so secretive that I never truly knew him."

Amelia kept her back to Nightingale as she stacked the dishwasher.

"I think it would be better he was allowed to rest in peace."

Amelia, previously talkative beyond the point of indiscretion, suddenly became close-mouthed. Despite all the wine she had drunk, she would say no more. They were drinking tea and admiring the herbaceous border when Nightingale made her next attempt to learn more about her family.

"This is a wonderful place. I feel so at home here."

"Well of course. You were born here."

"In this house?"

Her hostess looked as if she had been snared in a trap, then laughed in a silly schoolgirl way.

"No, you were born at Mill Farm with your brother, Simon."

She fanned herself while Nightingale studied her surreptitiously. Somewhere in that effusion, she sensed a lie.

"So where does Lulu Bullock fit into the story?"

Amelia was ahead of her so she couldn't see her face, but she didn't need to in order to judge the impact of her question. The woman went rigid and her teacup fell from her hand. It smashed on the path but she barely noticed. After a significant pause she said, "Fancy you knowing Lulu's name. Who was that from?"

"Just letters at my aunt's house but I saw her initials on the statue by the grave and I was curious."

"She was an old friend of your aunt's."

"I believe she was staying here the year I was born. She was a sculptress?"

"Yes indeed. And a very fine one." Amelia's relief at the change of subject was palpable. "She was commissioned to sculpt our new font. Vandals had destroyed the fifteenth century one. A collection was organized to raise money for a replacement and Lulu's uncle, who used to be a chorister here, pledged to donate pound for pound whatever the villagers raised. There was only one condition, that he could select the artist. Everyone agreed but then Lulu was chosen and all hell broke loose."

"Why?"

"Well, she was so . . . bohemian and a practicing Buddhist at the time. She'd lived in a commune near Glastonbury. Imagine!"

"And she and my aunt were *very* close."

Amelia's face darkened to purple. Her assumption had been correct then, Lulu and her aunt had been lovers and the conventional lady in front of her was embarrassed by the fact. Nightingale said her thank-yous and promised to keep in touch. An invitation for lunch the following Sunday was offered and accepted, and she drove back carefully to the church to place flowers from Amelia's garden on her aunt's grave.

After the service the following Sunday, she waited inside the church door for Amelia to join her. To fill in time she studied the font, conscious that her aunt's lover had been the artist. The paganism in the work was redeemed by the portrayal of the Lamb of God, which had been carved with exquisite delicacy. It was standing in a field of thorns. Behind the Lamb a panoply of birds, animals and fishes twisted in confusion. Facing It was a wolf, vast and menacing, a figure of terror: massive shoulders, a lolling, slobbering tongue, legs strong enough to cover infinite distances in search of prey, the nose sensitive enough to find them, wherever they might seek to hide.

Its eyes were fixed on the multitude behind the Lamb. In them Nightingale could read an eternal hunger large enough to devour the world. This was Satan, the Devil stalking the earth. Looking into the wolf's eyes, Nightingale shivered, seeing reflected there the expressions of lust, depravity and greed of all the people she had ever arrested. For a shocking moment she felt vulnerable, as if the wolf was somehow seeking her out, even as she stood in this quiet place of God. But if the wolf was endless terror, the eyes of the Lamb spoke of eternal peace. In His face was the essence of compassion, redemption and love. Yet it was also sad, as if He knew of the sacrifice He would have to make to save those sheltering behind Him.

"Come on, let's go."

Nightingale left reluctantly, as if she had been dragged away from the edge of an important discovery. Stepping into Amelia's immaculate house the smell of roast pork made her mouth water. In what was now an established routine, Nightingale poured their drinks while Amelia prepared the vegetables.

"Another ten minutes," she called out and Nightingale went to explore the drawing room, across the hall. Sunlight filled the far end in a golden pool. In the shadows by the door was a baby grand piano. Music for a Chopin Nocturne was open, waiting. She recognized the tune and her throat tightened. She had played this for grade eight, when she was fourteen, in the winter before she had first run away from home. She took another sip of her sherry and sat down.

Her fingers were stiff and she fumbled the first arpeggios, then she found her rhythm, slower than her previous fluid style but safe. The music settled over her like a gentle net, trapping her in its silken chords. As the harmonies developed, she ceased to think about the individual notes. The sound, the sensation of being part of it, the glorious heat at her back and the memory of the sculpture in the church melted together until she could feel their connection. Everything was as it was meant to be, and for once her place within it was clear.

She looked up to find Amelia staring at her.

"You're very good." She opened her mouth as if to say more then said simply, "Lunch is ready."

During the meal she quizzed Amelia again about her family. Amelia parried the questions with skill, sometimes open and expansive, at others cautious, pleading ignorance or loss of memory. When apple pie and ice cream was served, she changed the subject to her aunt and Lulu Bullock.

"I know they were lovers, you know. It's clear from my aunt's diary. That must have been a scandal."

Amelia sighed in resignation as she refilled their glasses from a fresh bottle.

"It was. A big one." She twirled her wineglass and smiled. It was not a pleasant smile. "However, one of the advantages of being middle class in a rural district is that one has to be tolerated. Your aunt, all the Nightingales, were almost gentry. Lulu's uncle was a local JP and benefactor."

"So they were politely ignored?"

"Ignored at first. After a while most people spoke to them in the local shops."

"Why did they split up?"

It was an innocent question but Amelia flushed and drained her glass.

"Why does any relationship fail?"

"And my father?"

"He was a wanderer, never staying anywhere for long, quite the free spirit, until he met your mother."

She looked around for more wine and raised the bottle in invitation to Nightingale, who shook her head. After the sherry she had paced herself but it hadn't slowed Amelia. Something about the woman worried Nightingale. She was friendly and warm yet she was also evasive, as if she couldn't trust her guest or had a secret to hide.

What could there be that was even more scandalous than female homosexuality all those years ago? Whatever it was, she would need to find out another time. Amelia had returned to the defensive and she would learn nothing more today. She gave the older woman the expected peck on the cheek and invited her to lunch at the farm the following week. Being there might stimulate more memories.

CHAPTER SEVENTEEN

It was Monday July 15th. Schools were beginning to break up and along the coast of North Wales tourist money was starting to flow once more. The unoriginal but accurately named Sea View Caravan site was half full. Within a week all the vans would be let and the site heaving. One of the reasons the Mackie family came early was to enjoy the relative peace for a few days, though their teenage children did not appreciate that fact.

The eldest, Tasmin, or Taz to her friends, was sixteen going on twenty, and already miserable because she'd had to leave her boyfriend behind. Her younger sister, Dawn, was just thirteen and the baby of the family, but she wasn't beyond taking Taz's makeup. Nathan was fourteen, lanky and greasy haired, with shoulders that had just started to burst the seams of his school shirts. As the only boy and middle child he'd led a curious existence, both spoiled and overlooked.

This was the second year that they had used the site. Mrs. Mackie, Irene, liked it because there were two restaurants, a café and a takeaway Chinese all within walking distance, which meant that as the week went on and her husband, Hugh, became more relaxed about money, they would eat out more and her real holiday would begin. But this was day two, one of the tricky days. The children would be fractious until they had made new friends at the site and Hugh stressed out because memories of work would be fresh and he'd be tired from the previous day's drive. Irene was snappy because she *did* have a job as well, had packed, unpacked, acted as peacemaker, dog-walker, nurse, cook and home help in the previous twenty-four hours, and this was her holiday too! At least the weather was kind.

Taz put on a miniscule bikini, halter top and micro shorts and flounced out of the caravan with a beach towel as soon as she had done her share of the drying up. Dawn whined to go with her but she was gone before anyone could stop her.

"Be back for lunch by twelve-thirty, young lady!" Irene called before telling Dawn to grow up and asking Nathan to take her with him to the campsite activity park. The dog bounded off after them happily, on a long lead. Nathan thought himself too old for slides, swings and climbing frames but had little option other than to obey.

At the beach, Taz's long-limbed, slender body soon attracted attention, some of it welcome. By eleven o'clock she had made two new friends: Chloe, who talked posh and came from somewhere near London, and a girl whose nickname was Boo and who refused to tell them her real name because it was gross. Chloe and Boo were the same age and attractive in different ways, not least because of the freshness of their youthful skin and bodies. Some young men on the beach started a game of football nearby and redoubled their efforts when the girls began to watch.

"I'm hot. Fancy a swim?" Boo stood up and brushed sand from the back of her calves.

"Yup." Chloe sprang up and started off down the beach. Taz stayed where she was.

"You coming?"

"No thanks. I'll wait here."

Boo shrugged and sprinted to the sea, jiggling nicely. Taz

breathed a sigh of relief. She had a fear of the sea so strong that she still held her father's hand if she went for a paddle. She had never learned to swim and the idea of having her face under the water terrified her. Even being splashed made her shudder.

The newly formed group parted for lunch and went back to their respective families, watched by most of the men on the beach, attached or otherwise. One in particular studied them well.

They regrouped at two and concentrated seriously on their tans. Taz avoided the water all afternoon, finally having to admit to Boo that she had a phobia of the sea.

When she returned home to the caravan, early for a change, she helped her mother prepare supper without being asked and tidied her siblings' mess away. Irene knew at once that she wanted something and waited with a mixture of irritation and amusement for the question to be asked. The family was finishing ice creams for dessert when the request finally came.

"There's a disco on in The Barn tonight . . ."

"No." Hugh didn't even look up.

"I'd be going with Chloe and Boo. Chloe's eighteen."

"I said no."

"I promise I'll drink water and fruit juice all evening."

Hugh eventually looked up.

"Can't you hear me? No."

"You let me last year and I was younger then."

Now he looked confused.

"Did I?" He turned a questioning face to Irene.

"Yes, you did. On the strict understanding that she would be back by eleven. And she was."

"Oh."

Taz waited in silence.

"Where did you say it was?"

"In The Barn. Only ten minutes away. And it has to stop at eleven-thirty anyway because that's all the license allows."

"Well, all right then." Hugh received a hug and a kiss. "But I will be there to pick you up at eleven, not a minute later."

Taz opened her mouth to argue but caught her mother's eye and shut up.

"Are your friends coming here?" Irene was curious to see them.

"No. We're meeting at the gates at seven thirty."

"Pretty confident, weren't you." Her father raised his eyebrows.

Taz bit off a sharp retort, not wishing to antagonize him.

"We agreed that they'd wait for ten minutes and then go without me, in case you said no."

"You'd better hurry, Taz, it's gone seven already." Irene knew how long it would take her daughter to get ready.

"Can I go?" her brother asked.

"No, you can't, Nathan. Dad and I are going to have a quick drink after we've washed up and you and Dawn can come with us."

It was twenty-five past seven by the time Taz finally found the right shoes and earrings. She shouted good-bye and left the van quickly, hoping to avoid the comments that she knew parental scrutiny would give rise to. Her skirt had little more material in it than had her shorts, and her blouse was fine enough for the color of her purple bra to show through.

She was in such a rush to reach the site entrance that she missed her way and ended up in the wrong part of the camp. Cursing, she looked around, trying to regain her sense of direction. It was already half past and she knew that Chloe and Boo wouldn't wait long. After a couple of false turns she found the main tarmac road that ran through the middle of the camp and trotted along it as fast as her heels would let her. She ignored the wolf whistles and concentrated on finding her way. Of course by the time she reached the gates Chloe and Boo had already left. The problem was that she wasn't sure of the way.

"Lost?"

The man had come up behind her silently and his voice made her jump.

"Just trying to remember my way to The Barn."

"Oh, I'm walking past it. It's not far, come on, we can go together."

Taz hesitated. He was a stranger but a very good-looking one. He was a tall, with sleek dark brown hair and bright blue eyes that were set off by his tan. When he smiled his teeth were very white. It wasn't as if he was asking her to get in a car, after all.

"OK." She followed him and he solicitously made sure she was walking on the inside.

He said that his name was Des and that he was on holiday with friends. She noticed that his fingernails were neat and impeccably clean, like his white shirt and fawn trousers. He had a small pack on his back that he carried easily and his jokes made her laugh.

Half way along the empty road he turned right down a footpath.

"A short cut. Saves several minutes. You might even catch up with your friends."

She followed him after a bare moment's hesitation. It was just wide enough to walk side by side provided she kept her left arm angled in front, away from the nettles that ran along the bordering hedgerow. She noticed that the brambles among them were bearing tight green fruits.

When she landed hard on her back in the wheat she thought

at first that she had tripped, but then she realized that he was kneeling over her, his weight on her arms, and she opened her mouth to scream. Something was stuffed into it so far that it touched the back of her tongue and made her gag. Tape went over it before she could work her jaws to spit it out, then her hands were tied behind her back.

He pulled her to her feet so hard that she felt something give in her shoulder, and pushed her ahead of him through the waist-high crop. They cut at an angle away from the footpath toward another field separated by barbed wire. At the fence he raised the top strand of wire and forced her through. She scraped her thigh on a lower barb and nettles stung her calves but she was too scared to notice.

Her mind had become a blank of white terror that overwhelmed her and made it impossible to think. At some point she noticed that she was crying and long trails of snot ran from her nose. The realization brought her to her senses. She was behaving like a pathetic victim, just following this man's tacit instructions obediently. He had abducted her and was taking her far away from the possibility of rescue. Men only abducted girls for one reason. Her mind shied away from the word *rape* yet at the same time sought to define it. Was it like sex but with violence on top?

She had lost her virginity at the end-of-year disco only days before in a fumbling adventure that had left her confused and a bit sore. It hadn't been as exciting as she had expected, but it hadn't been too bad either. If she pretended to like what this man was going to do to her would it please him enough to make him gentle? She risked a glance back at his face. One look into his eyes made her heartbeat skip as another rush of adrenaline surged through her. The pleasant young man who had been chatting her up minutes before had disappeared. In his place, in the same perfect body, walked a monster with eyes that were already lusting after her, and a snarl on his face that spoke of a taste for blood. Instinctively, she knew that this man fed on fear and any sign that she was willing to cooperate would inspire him to violence and excess. The tears that had stopped while she had started to think started again. When she sobbed loud enough to be heard through the gag he laughed.

They had crossed a second field and he paused to look around. She could hear waves in the distance and realized that they were completing the third side of a square. The caravan site would be on her right. It was set in a dip so she couldn't see any sign, but she thought she would be able to find it given the opportunity.

When the man bent down to ease through the fence his grip on her arm loosened. Taz took her chance and broke away. At first she tried to run fast but with her arms tied behind her back that was impossible so she settled into a shambolic jog. Of course it wasn't fast enough. He caught her easily and delivered a punch to her temple that knocked her to the ground.

"You'll fucking pay for that, bitch."

He yanked her to her feet again, sending a fresh jolt of pain through her shoulder. This time he held on to her in a grip tight enough to burn her skin where the friction of their uneven pacing twisted her arm with every step.

He dragged her through yet another barbed-wire fence, scratching her arms and back in the process. She realized that she was not going to escape and for the first time wondered whether he intended to kill her. Her knees gave way at the thought and he was half dragging, half carrying her by the time they found what he had been looking for. A sheep shelter, reduced to a tumbled cross of dry stone walls, appeared in a fold of the hill and he grunted in satisfaction. Stubby trees hid most of it from view.

The man threw her to the ground in the shelter of its walls

and gave her a look that dared her to move. Taz was petrified. She lay where she had fallen and watched him start a bizarre ritual. From his pack he took out more rope and tied a length to each of her legs, looping the free ends around heavy stones in the wall so that she was spreadeagled. Her arms he left tied behind her back. There was the stink of urine and to her shame she realized that she had wet herself in terror. He delivered a stinging slap to her cheek.

"Filthy bitch."

He pulled her skirt and knickers away, leaving her bare below the waist. Then he took a large thermos from his pack, opened it and poured some of its contents over her, washing her. He reached into a pocket of his trousers confidently as if expecting to find something but then started to search frantically.

"Fuck it!" He emptied his pack, then tried his pockets again but whatever he had been expecting to find had gone. His loss earned her a kick in the ribs.

"Never mind. I still have enough imagination for us to have some fun, sweetheart." He knelt over her and began to undo the tiny buttons of her blouse, the tips of his fingers cold against her skin.

"Who had too much sun today?" He traced the white outline of her bikini on her flesh. "I saw you lying there, flaunting it for every man and boy that passed. And all the time I was thinking about what we would be doing later. It was a lovely way to spend the day."

He continued talking in an almost conversational way as he stripped her remaining clothes away. The normality of his voice persuaded her more than the violence that he was completely insane. When she was naked, he stood up and stared at her as he removed his fawn trousers, then his pants. At the sight of him she closed her eyes and turned her head away, making him laugh.

"Yes, it affects most girls like that. Now, let's see. Oh, it's only eight o'clock . . . and it won't go dark until ten, so we have plenty of time. I'm not going to leave you here, you see. Normally, I'd wash you thoroughly afterward but outside I'm having to improvise, so the sea will suffice. Don't shake your head like that. I know you hate the water, I heard you tell your friend today. That's what's going to make drowning you later so much fun. But in the meantime," he bent over and stroked a breast, "shall we begin?"

He sat on the cliff top smoking a cigarette and watched the tide rise. His damp clothes were spread on the grass beside him and he was wearing the spare trousers from his pack. Two hours hadn't been long enough to do things properly but he had managed to have some fun. To make the link to Griffiths he had worked outside this time. Apparently the police hadn't made the connection between Lucinda and the crimes for which Wayne had been imprisoned, and his sometime friend was starting to complain that the attacks weren't similar enough, despite the missing fingers. That detail was possibly too small for the bungling coppers to notice.

He inhaled deeply and thought about the girl. She had been younger than he usually liked but with a body mature enough to satisfy his tastes and she had been suitably terrified. In fact she had behaved exactly as he had hoped and imagined as he lay on the hot beach all day, waiting.

The tide was rising. He found a point, a rock just in front of the cave where he had hidden her, and watched as the black peak above the water became smaller. It had been difficult not to finish her off at the sheep pen but the idea of her terror as he forced her, conscious and open-eyed, beneath the waves had stayed his hand. And it had been exciting, knowing her fear of the sea, and watching her struggle as the air bubbled up from her lungs and the seawater flowed in.

He had pushed her under three times, counting to sixty then pulling her up to retch and gulp air, before returning her to the water. The last time, he had counted up to one hundred and when he pulled her up, her eyes had stayed closed. But as he had stuffed her into her rocky tomb he thought that she had coughed. Far from displeasing him, the idea of her conscious as the tide rose around her made him excited all over again. He imagined her claustrophobia as the water inched over her knees, to her waist and finally into her nose and mouth. Unexpectedly he was reminded of his mother's death and the link between the two women brought a new variation for him to use in his fantasies.

The water was well above the top of the cave mouth and he knew that he should go. She would be missed soon, and searches would start during the night, so he needed to be well away. Since his one serious encounter with the police he had become ultra cautious. There would be no trace evidence on her, and he doubted there was any on him, but a man with wet clothes in a pack might be uncommon enough to be remembered.

It was a real shame that he had dropped his knife and he cursed Griffiths all over again. He had lost his talisman. While he carried it he remained lucky. Now that it had disappeared he was superstitious enough to fear that his good fortune might change.

The tip of the rock vanished and he rose with a sigh of satisfaction. He packed his clothes into a plastic rubbish sack and placed them in his backpack, then stubbed out his cigarette, put the butt in his pocket and left the sea behind him.

CHAPTER EIGHTEEN

Nightingale prepared a substantial Sunday meal despite her rudimentary kitchen. There was plenty of wine and Amelia had second helpings of everything. Afterward Nightingale suggested a stroll outside to keep her awake. Summer had returned and this time the forecast was for it to stay. In the walled garden the temperature was in the low eighties.

"It's amazing to think you've only been here six weeks. You've fitted in so well. Oh, what a pretty wild orchid."

Her guest wandered ahead with a wide reminiscent smile on her face. Nightingale watched her from a distance, leaving time for the memories to settle.

"It must have been wonderful here thirty years ago."

"Oh yes, it was." Amelia's voice was wistful.

"I wonder why my grandparents left the house to my aunt and not my father."

"He didn't want to live here. He thought the village too small for him." Amelia plucked a long strand of wild grass by the wall and started to chew it thoughtfully. "It was time for him to go away."

"Why?"

Amelia looked at her with narrowed eyes.

"Your father had a penchant for pretty women. He kept it

secret from his parents for years, but eventually things got out of hand and he made quite a few enemies. When your grandparents moved from the farm to live in town, they left it in your aunt's care. Your father didn't argue. His new in-laws had rented a very nice house for the newlyweds near them."

"Did you love him very much?"

Amelia took a quick, short breath then fell silent. Nightingale let the quiet deepen, in no rush to hurry the revelations along. After all these years the urge to confide must be strong. Eventually Amelia spoke.

"We were at school together. He was the boy all the girls wanted to go out with, yet he chose me over the others. It lasted one summer. In autumn he moved on to someone else and that lasted to the Christmas dance. The third relationship went on to Easter and the fourth until he hitchhiked to a festival of some sort.

"When he came back, three girls came with him and camped up on the hillside. They were older, eighteen or nineteen, but then your father was a precocious lad. He used to sneak out to spend the night in their tent.

"And so it carried on until he had an affair with one of his schoolteachers' wives. There was a scandal and he went to another college to finish his A-levels, then off to university."

"Where he met my mother?"

"Yes, but he kept her secret for years, until after he graduated. Whenever he came back it was on his own and I would be waiting for him. I realize now that I was simply a convenient way to fill in time during the holidays but back then I thought I was his true love." She laughed at herself but Nightingale could hear the echo of heartache.

"It must have hurt like hell when he became engaged to my mother."

"It was terrible but I didn't believe that it would last. She was so different from his other women." She hesitated then continued, her expression determined. "She wasn't the nicest of women, I'm afraid. Perhaps her power over him lay in her selfishness. She bullied him into dropping his old friends. After they were married there were terrible rows and they separated almost straightaway."

"What did they row about?"

Amelia looked away.

"Go on, please, I need to know."

"Your father had a final fling in the months before the wedding. Some busybody in the village sent a letter to his new wife, which was waiting for them when they came back from honeymoon. She walked out and went to live with her parents."

"That was a bitchy thing to do to a new bride. Was he so unpopular?"

"A bit but it was really because the woman your father had an affair with upset the villagers. On one occasion she was found with the son of a local publican, both stark naked on top of one of the tombs in the churchyard. On another she and half a dozen young men went skinny-dipping from the beach. The stories of the orgy that followed may or may not have been true but they sealed her reputation. For someone who arrived in the spring and stayed a mere twenty months she left a lot of memories and myths. She broke too many hearts around here, until your father broke hers."

"What was her name?"

"Why, it was Lulu, I thought you knew. She swung both ways, as we said in those days."

"I had no idea. So when my mother left did my father go back to Lulu?"

"Probably. She was living with your aunt at Mill Farm and

your father would stay each weekend. Then he was reconciled with his wife, she was pregnant after all, and both sets of parents put a lot of pressure on them."

As the shadows lengthened toward dusk Amelia decided to leave. At the front door Nightingale asked the question that had been preying on her mind for most of the afternoon.

"So do you regret it, knowing my father I mean?"

Amelia looked shocked.

"Of course not."

"But you said you've loved him all these years, wouldn't it have been better never to have known him and avoid the heart-ache?"

Amelia shook her head, as if at Nightingale's stupidity.

"For the whole of that summer when I was fifteen, he loved me."

"Surely that's even worse. To know for however brief a time what it means to be loved by the object of one's desire must be far worse than to live in ignorance."

"No. For me it was definitely better to have loved and lost than never to have loved at all. Trite but true."

Nightingale shook her head vehemently.

"Butler was an idiot. Imagine being blind from birth, learning to cope with it, never knowing what you were missing. Then for one incredible day, when you woke up you could see! The colors, sunlight, trees, the smiles on people's faces, the eyes of the people you love. Then you go to bed only to wake up the next morning blind again. Nothing could be more cruel than to learn what you are going to miss for the rest of your life."

Amelia rested a hand on Nightingale's arm.

"People are different, Louise. For me that summer was a blessing. Perhaps for you it would have been a curse, but I think that very sad. It means that you will go through life avoiding pleasure in case the absence of it causes you pain. Do you really want to live like that?"

Nightingale tried to forget Amelia's parting words. Until that afternoon, she had been happy here. Her retreat had started as an escape but had turned into a new beginning. Now her fragile contentment had been challenged and inevitably her thoughts turned to Fenwick. She wondered what he was doing. Was he still seeing that Keating woman? Did he ever think of her?

Twilight was creeping into the evening but she was too restless to sleep and started to prowl the house. She found a torch and climbed the crooked stairs that led up from the kitchen to the landing at the back near the mill. Shadows flickered on the wall ahead of her as the light found the carved newel post, a remnant from some long winter during which a distant ancestor had found occupation in carving. The faces were crudely formed, rising one above the other in a totem pole. Without thinking, she touched the noses of each one and whispered the password she had invented for protection as a child.

It was necessary to have a very good sense of direction in order to navigate through the upstairs of her aunt's house. In the past visitors had been heard to call out for directions to the bathroom even though they were standing less than ten feet from it. By coming up the kitchen stairs Nightingale had entered the old servants' quarters, two small bedrooms knocked into one.

At first glance, the room and tiny landing appeared to be completely separate from the rest of the house but Nightingale knew they were linked. In the attic room she had used as a child, there was a low door in the wall, papered over so as to be almost invisible. It led to the roof above the milking parlor.

She went into her old bedroom and found the door to the hidden passage that ran between the eaves and the wall. It was dark and unwelcoming and she was in her Sunday clothes so she closed the door flush to the wall again and pushed the bed against it. The mood to explore had vanished and she went to find a book to read until she became too tired to focus on the words and fell asleep.

The warm weather that had started on Sunday turned into a heat wave. Instead of going into town on the Monday she gardened, read and sunbathed naked in the kitchen garden until she became too hot and went to swim in the sea. She followed the same pattern for the rest of the week and was surprised at how good her laziness made her feel.

The idyll came to an end on Friday when she finally ran out of food and she felt an urge for company. She ventured into Clovelly to find a pub. There was a lovely old place on the high street full of tourists. Fortunately, most of them wanted to drink outside in the sun so the saloon bar was quiet. She pushed her way through the crowd by the door and into the dimness beyond. A long, dark oak bar curved away toward a bottle-glass window. Two drinkers, locals by their proprietorial stare, were playing dominoes at a table beneath the window.

The barman had his back to her, polishing a glass, and turned as the door banged shut.

"Can I help . . . Good God! When did you get back?"

Nightingale moved closer, smiling in surprise. As the light from the window picked out her features the barman's look of surprise changed to one of confusion.

"You can't be . . ."

"I can't be who?" she asked with a small chuckle.

"Never mind. Someone from long ago. You're the spitting image."

One of the domino players by the window looked up and nodded.

"Spitting," he said, then returned to the table and knocked twice. But Nightingale could feel their eyes on her and it made her uncomfortable.

"Half a pint of cider, please."

She sipped her drink, perched on a stool at the bar, her long bare legs golden brown in the dim sunlight. When she ordered a ham sandwich it appeared promptly, and gradually the normal conversation of the pub returned. Unusually, Nightingale felt the desire to join in. Whenever the barman had a brief pause from serving she talked to him, asking questions about the area and its history. He answered in short sentences: he had grown up here, his father had owned the pub before him, his family went a long way back.

She finished her sandwich and ordered another cider. When he served it she asked him the question that had been on her mind all along.

"Whom do I remind you of?" She smiled at him and her charm, rarely used but devastating when applied, had its customary effect.

"An old girlfriend if you must know."

"I'm flattered."

"You could be sisters, only your eyes are different. Hers were almost lilac."

"I have my father's eyes, or so everyone says."

"Well, they're lovely, don't get me wrong."

She laughed, enjoying the attention. Suddenly, she felt sexy. Whether it was the heat or the cider she couldn't tell. If only he had been twenty years younger.

"So what brings you here then?"

"I'm on holiday." It wasn't the complete truth but she didn't want the conversation to be about her. "Tell me more about your old girlfriend, I'm curious."

"She wasn't from around here. Had family, an uncle as I remember, in the neighborhood. Stayed here about a year I think."

"More like two." One of the domino players interjected.

"Don't mind George, he's my father's second cousin. He never did like her."

"Didn't do you no good, my lad. Bad day for the village when she come."

"Why did she come here?"

"She was an artist. Had a commission here."

"A painter?"

"No, a sculptor."

Something clicked in Nightingale's brain.

"Was she called Lulu?"

The barman dropped his cloth. George scattered dominoes. Nightingale smiled.

"How did you know that?"

"Amelia told me about her. I guessed." A simple answer but it didn't fool George or the publican.

"And how come you know Amelia?"

Nightingale's survival instinct was stronger than the cider.

"Oh, I go to church. A very nice lady."

"Aye, mebe." The barman turned away and went to "sort out" the kitchen.

The game of dominoes finished and George's partner rose stiffly to make his way home before " 'er in doors come to get me." As the saloon door closed, George came to the bar and leaned on it.

"He was in love wi' her. Gave up fishing and all sorts 'cos of her. Even said 'e'd marry 'er. No good. She 'ad her eyes fixed on flashier prizes. But you are the dead reckoning, except the eyes mebe. And the hair. You've got your'n under control. Hers were so long she could sit on it. Like silk it were, midnight silk."

Nightingale said nothing, not wishing to remind the old

man he had an audience. It was obvious that Lulu had managed to stir hearts beyond her own generation. Whoever she had been, she'd had an ability to make even the most unlikely of men fall in love with her.

Even her father.

The barman returned. George called him Dan. They talked about cricket, how poor the fishing was and their doubts about tourism for late summer. Nightingale disappeared to find the ladies. When she came back it was obvious that they had been discussing her. She drained the last of her cider and slipped her sunglasses down from the top of her head.

"You off then?" Dan picked up his glass cloth and started polishing furiously. Neither man would look at her.

"Yes, must be getting back."

"That would be back to . . . ?"

She could sense his keen interest. Perhaps it was because of the cider, whatever, but for some reason she answered openly in a break with her habitual discretion.

"Mill Farm, at the top of the hill. It was my aunt's house."

It was as if an electric current had been passed through both men. There was a dull crack and Dan looked down in surprise as the glass parted in pieces within the cloth.

George spilled his beer.

"You're Ruth Nightingale's niece?"

"You'd be the daughter then." They said together.

"Well, yes. Did you know my family?"

But the men were no longer listening to her. They stared at each other and a knowing look passed between them before George opened a newspaper and Dan found another glass.

"Er, I'll be off then."

"Good day, miss." Dan examined the gleaming glass for spots.

"Good-bye." George turned the page.

Frustrated by their sudden indifference, Nightingale left the pub and stepped onto hot cobblestones. The crowds parted and reformed around her as if she didn't exist. She felt lonely and confused, and all because two grumpy, inbred old men had given her the cold shoulder.

The steep street led to the harbor. She walked down, stared at the boats and then walked back up. Her phone remained useless, with a weak signal and low battery that kept frustrating her attempts to call her brother. There was a queue outside the public call box. In the end she found a tiny Internet café in a side street that also sold Devon violet sweets and cheerful pixies. It was busy but she waited patiently and was soon online.

She had mail. Mentally calling herself stupid she opened the inbox and found twenty messages, from Harlden Division, Fenwick and Pandora. The sight of the screen full of her past made her feel queasy. Pandora's sustained correspondence intrigued her, but she considered email from Harlden an intrusion. It angered her that they should presume to contact her when she had made it clear that even unpaid leave was a concession so she deleted all their emails unread with a few angry keystrokes. She couldn't bring herself to do the same to Fenwick's two messages and opened the first:

NIGHTINGALE, DON'T BE ALARMED BUT I THINK THAT YOU <u>MAY</u> HAVE ATTRACTED THE ATTENTION OF SOMEONE WHO THINKS GRIFFITHS WAS WRONGLY CONVICTED. BE EXTRA VIGILANT. DON'T TRUST STRANGERS. PLEASE CALL ME. MY HOME PHONE NUMBER IS HARLDEN 526592. YOU KNOW THE STATION'S.

REGARDS ANDREW FENWICK.

It was dated two days after she'd left Harlden. Since then she had only spoken to strangers and had never felt safer so it's warning had been unnecessary. She deleted the message and opened the second, sent only a week before:

DEAR NIGHTINGALE,

THINGS ARE VERY SERIOUS. THERE IS SOMEONE OUT THERE WHO MAY SEEK TO REVENGE GRIFFITHS. YOU COULD BE IN IMMINENT DANGER. YOU MUST CALL ME, OR AT LEAST EMAIL TO LET ME KNOW THAT YOU ARE STILL OK AND WHERE I CAN REACH YOU. ANDREW.

There was no mistaking his meaning but Griffiths hadn't had an accomplice, had he? Fenwick must be harking back to his worries about a sympathetic supporter who was convinced of Griffiths' innocence. She couldn't decide what to do in response to the warning so she opened the first of Pandora's messages instead.

WANT TO PLAY A GAME?

Nightingale typed in a succinct reply.

NO. I AM NOT PLAYING AGAIN, EVER.

She hit send and deleted the message before opening the next.

YOU CAN'T IGNORE ME. I AM IN YOUR LIFE NOW. NAME YOUR FORFEIT OR I WILL DO IT FOR YOU. IN MY GAME, I PLAY FOR REAL.

The tone was different. There was impatience here and a veiled threat. She deleted several more messages unread then opened one that had been sent that week:

I HAVE CHOSEN YOUR FORFEIT. IT IS DEATH. THERE IS NO RIGHT OF APPEAL. THE MANNER AND TIME WILL BE OF MY CHOOSING, NIGHTBIRD. WHEREVER YOU ARE, WHEREVER YOU HIDE YOUR NEST, I WILL FIND YOU. I WILL THROW YOU

TO THE GROUND AND CRUSH YOUR BONES TO POWDER. YOU CANNOT FLY FROM ME, FOR I AM EVERYWHERE.

Sweat broke out on Nightingale's forehead. The small hairs on her arms rose as a shiver passed over her. She tried to tell herself that the message had been sitting in her electronic inbox for days and nothing had happened to her. Why should she fear it now? Yet it was a death threat. Perhaps it was what Fenwick had been trying to warn her about. The detective in her argued that this might be evidence so she took a copy, standing defensively over the printer until it delivered its single page. The café owner watched her with a smile on his face. When he leered at her knowingly she ignored him and slipped the paper into the pocket of her shorts. She deleted all the other messages unread and was about to return to Fenwick's when the pleasant electronic voice of the machine spoke softly: "You have mail." Curious, she opened the message from Pandora that had arrived seconds before:

THANK YOU! START THE COUNTDOWN, SONG BIRD. IT'S ONLY A MATTER OF TIME NOW.

She could see no significance in it. What had she done that deserved thanks? She deleted it before considering Fenwick's email again. When she had first read it she'd considered it an unnecessary warning. Even if he was right and there was somebody set on avenging Griffiths, they'd never find her in deepest Devon. Nobody knew where she was; no one from Harlden had a clue of her address and even her brother wouldn't consider looking for her at the farm. But what if the threat was real and there really was someone searching for her? Maybe it was Pandora, frustrated that she wouldn't play THE GAME, unable to call her on the phone anymore . . . She stared at the screen-saver with blank eyes as her detective's brain awoke sluggishly from its sun-induced holiday. There probably was a link and Fenwick, good old determined Andrew Fenwick, had somehow made the connection. Nightingale smiled; how like him. And she'd be able to help him a little without revealing her whereabouts. Her brief reply gave no hint of the time it took to compose:

ANDREW, THANK YOU FOR YOUR MESSAGES. I AM FINE. I HAVE BEEN RECEIVING THREATENING EMAILS AND WILL FORWARD YOU THE MOST THREATENING IN CASE YOU CAN FIND THE SENDER. BUT EVEN IF SOMEONE IS LOOKING FOR ME YOUR FEARS ARE GROUNDLESS. I AM TUCKED AWAY QUITE SAFE AND NO ONE COULD EVER FIND ME HERE—NOT EVEN YOU! PLEASE DON'T WORRY ABOUT ME BUT THANK YOU FOR YOUR CONCERN. NIGHTINGALE.

As she drove to the farm, Nightingale felt confused by her brief encounter with her old world. The certainty that she would be able to face it again at a time of her own choosing had disappeared in the last hour. When she reached home she made a mug of herbal tea and took it into the garden to an old chair she had placed in the sunniest corner. It was time to think.

Before Griffiths' trial she had read a book on cyber-stalking. The majority of obsessives were content with an electronic pursuit. Relatively few of them lured their victims into a physical encounter. Griffiths had been an exception, not the rule, and she refused to be intimidated by Pandora. Man or woman, she would simply delete all future emails unread.

The messages from Fenwick were more disturbing. He wasn't someone to give in to nameless fears, and he had issued a significant warning, yet she found herself disinclined to worry. Even if Griffiths had a defender, and they had taken it into their mind to be vengeful, they would never find her. The farm was the safest place she could be; no one from her old life knew where she was and the few people she'd met here had no knowledge or interest in her previous life. If anything, the possible threat meant that she should stay put for a long time. She finished her tea and drifted into a gentle sleep.

He logged on to the Internet in the tiny second bedroom of Wendy's flat. After Wales he had waited a few days in the hills, in the holiday home he now thought of as his safest retreat. Not even Wayne Griffiths knew he still owned it.

The sultry voice of the machine told him that he had email. His pulse quickened as he opened his inbox. Yes! She had been online and opened his latest email, releasing the little surprise he had left for her. He had spent days crafting the virus with Iain's help, which he had then hidden in the white space of his last message. When she had opened it the virus had greedily gathered up her documents from within the machine. It would take him days to sift through to find her messages and, within them, a clue to her location but he didn't mind. Simply by opening his message she had exposed herself and it would only be a matter of time before he found her.

While the machine saved the rifled information he decided to amuse himself by reading some of the recent emails. The most recent was someone called Fenwick. The contents shocked him. There was no way that the police should have been smart enough to work out that Griffiths had a senior partner. Had Griffiths talked? The bitch's reply made it clear that she had disregarded the warning. More fool her.

"Shit!"

There was a creak from behind him and he swung round, instantly on guard.

"What?"

"I'm sorry. I heard you cry out. I thought you needed me."

"You know you cannot come in here. It is absolutely forbidden." He had a number of rules, drilled into her with repeated beatings. He stood up, his face impassive.

"I'm sorry, really. I didn't see anything. I was worried." She shrank back from him as he advanced but didn't dare run away.

He caught both her wrists in his left hand in a familiar gesture that brought fear to her eyes. The sight excited him and he squeezed harder until she winced. He dragged her along the tiny passage, enjoying her whimpers of pain. When they reached the bedroom she pulled back, forcing a snort of annoyance from him, despite his preference for silence. The sound made him even angrier.

"Please, Dave! No don't. I didn't do anything, honest. It will never happen again."

He ignored her bleating and kicked open the door. Her dressing gown was hanging on a hook behind it. He yanked the cord from it and bound her wrists tight behind her back. Her clothes, summer-light cotton, ripped away easily, leaving her skinny body bare for his scrutiny. It left him unmoved but the sense of power that filled him when he threw her back onto the bed and he saw the faint traces of bruising from the last time was all he needed.

He didn't bother taking off any of his clothes but his belt, which he wrapped once around the palm of his hand. She was crying now but she didn't bother to protest as she knew it would do no good. When the leather bit into her flesh on the first lash she let out a small scream.

"Ah, you want the gag."

"No! Please. I won't make a noise. I can't breathe when you do that, it suffocates me."

"We'll see." He hit her again, harder and smiled to see a thin line of blood bloom on her thigh. She bit down hard on her lip but didn't make a sound. After a while his arm started to ache so he decided to end it. As he forced himself into her she buried her head in the pillows, keeping her face away from him. He bit her shoulders, enjoying the salty taste of her blood. He stared at the thin twig of her neck, imagined snapping it, and with that it was over quickly.

She lay very still beneath him, waiting for him to finish, barely breathing. She could almost be dead. He smiled and bent down to kiss her cheek, wet with tears.

"Don't do it again," he whispered in her ear. "You know I don't like naughty girls."

He untied her hands but she didn't move so he left her there, almost certain she was still alive despite her pallor and stillness. It would be inconvenient for her to die. For the last eight years he had been able to rely on her and know that she was too scared to do anything against him. All in all she was too convenient to kill.

As he soaped himself generously in the shower he heard movement in the bathroom beyond the curtain. He twitched it open and watched unmoved as she washed her cuts and smeared Savlon over the worst. When she had finished, she turned her ghostly face toward him.

"Cup of tea?" she asked and managed to smile.

CHAPTER NINETEEN

The weather forecast had promised sun and Fenwick planned the weekend accordingly. He made the mistake of sharing his plans with the children on Saturday evening. They loved eating outside. Chris called it camping even though all Fenwick did was place some old blankets over the washing line and put a groundsheet down inside the makeshift tent.

Early Sunday morning he was woken by a loud clap of thunder overhead and the children arrived in his bed within minutes. Around ten o'clock the cloud started to break up. Bess spotted this at once and said that it was time to go outside. She slipped on her Wellington boots and splashed into the garden. Chris followed and Fenwick's heart sank. This was not the weather for blankets over the line nor did he fancy a barbecue. But then he looked at them running about, falling over, arguing as to who would have the favorite swing—although they seemed identical to him—and his mood softened. It was the first weekend that he had spent with them uninterrupted for a long time and he wanted it to be special.

He was clambering about in the loft when Chris found him.

"What are you doing, Dad?"

"Stand back, I'm going to drop something. No, right back by the door."

The canvas sack fell with a dull thud and clatter of aluminum poles. Chris stared at it wide-eyed and followed his father into the garden in silence.

It took nearly an hour to erect the tent. Bess and Chris were determined to help, which slowed him down a lot. It was old but didn't seem to have perished, and it had a built-in ground-sheet. As soon as he'd driven in the final tent peg, Chris and Bess took their toys inside, leaving their muddy boots on the grass. The novelty of a real tent lasted long enough for Fenwick to make progress with lunch, which they finished eating just as the rain started again. The children didn't mind as they ate second helpings of ice cream in the rubbery warmth of the tent.

They were about to start a three-way game of Monopoly when Fenwick's mobile phone rang.

"Yes?"

"DCI Fenwick? It's MacIntyre. We think he's struck again, in Wales this time. I'm going there. Thought you might want to join me."

As Fenwick took down the details, his mind ran through options of what he could do with the children until seven o'clock and the housekeeper's return. His regular standby babysitters were both away on holiday and there were no close friends of whom he could beg a favor. In the end, with deep-seated reluctance, he rang Sergeant Cooper and explained his predicament.

"No problem. I'd like to join you and it would stop the missus having a go if she had your kiddies to look after. She'll be in her element."

Fenwick left the tent up, doused the barbecue, then packed the children and selected toys into the car. Half an hour later, he and Cooper were heading toward the M25 en route to Wales. Traffic on the motorways was heavy and it was ten o'clock before they met up with MacIntyre in a mobile incident room. He introduced them to Superintendent Amos, the local SIO, who took them through the investigation to date.

"Tasmin Mackie, age sixteen, disappeared from Sea View campsite on Friday. She was last seen by her family at about seven twenty-five as she left to meet friends on the other side of the site. She never made it."

Fenwick and Cooper nodded. The disappearance of the schoolgirl had received national coverage.

"Despite intensive searches and inquiries we couldn't find a trace of her until Saturday morning when one of her shoes was discovered on a beach three miles up the coast. We concentrated our search along the seashore and one of the dog teams found her at six twenty-five p.m. yesterday. She was alive."

Fenwick, that most poker-faced of policemen, merely nodded. Cooper's mouth dropped open.

"We imposed a complete news blackout. This morning she regained consciousness enough to give us a description of the man who raped her. Apart from the eyes, which she insists were blue, it was so similar to the Knightsbridge murderer that we added the e-fit Superintendent MacIntyre sent through to photographs of known offenders for her to look at. She picked him out at once."

Fenwick scratched his head in puzzlement.

"I don't understand why he left her alive. Was she badly hurt?"

"The sexual assault was brutal. She'd been beaten and half-drowned but for some reason he didn't use a knife. He washed her body in the sea and hid her in a shallow cave. The mouth is covered at full tide, that's why we didn't find her on the first search."

"Why didn't she drown?"

"A pure fluke. The cave rises from sea level and he'd pushed her right to the back, her head was above the water level."

"And nobody on the beach saw them?"

"We think he attacked her away from the beach, though she has no recollection of the incident. There are definite drag marks on a path down to the sea. We think he waited for the beach to empty then carried her down in the dark."

"Risky," Fenwick shook his head, "and out of character. Last time he used charm then killed at home with his own knife. Why this dramatic change in style? It's more reminiscent of Griffiths' attacks. If it wasn't for the identification we wouldn't have made the connection."

"I think we would have done, Andrew. He tried to sever one of her fingers, we think with a rock."

Cooper went white.

"This is bizarre. Why attack without a knife? Is it a deliberate change? I can't believe he forgot it, he's too methodical and clever for that."

"Perhaps he lost it." They all looked at Cooper in surprise. "A hole in his pocket, or it falls out when he climbs over a stile. You never know. Accidents do happen."

"We've done a finger tip search of the area around the caravan site and found nothing but we could widen the search and put up posters in case somebody found a knife and decided to keep it. I'm increasing the search perimeter anyway as we're still trying to determine how he arrived. We have bugger all to go on." But Amos didn't look despondent. Finding Tasmin alive had been beyond their hopes and the significance of the discovery was still motivating the whole team.

"No trace evidence?"

"None. We're lifting the sand from inside the cave in case

he left hair or a broken nail when he put her in there but that's going to take a while."

"When are you going to interview Tasmin again?"

"In about seven or eight hours, when she wakes up, provided the doctor says it's OK. Her parents are being cooperative. As soon as they found out that her attacker might have killed before they promised to do anything to help us catch him before he strikes again."

Fenwick shivered at the reminder of this man's capacity to attack and kill. There was still no trace of Nightingale and he was convinced that she could be the ultimate victim, despite a more cautious stance from Superintendent Quinlan and the ACC. They accepted the link between the ransacking of Nightingale's flat and the anonymous sender of letters to Griffiths in prison but drew the line there. In their combined opinion, the Knightsbridge killing was unconnected.

"Do you have a photograph of Tasmin?"

Amos passed a copy over to Fenwick, who took it and shook his head in dismayed resignation. He passed it to Cooper, who couldn't resist blurting out, "Just like all the others, just like Nightingale." The picture of the pretty, smiling dark-haired girl, long legs draped over the back of a settee, made him shudder. MacIntyre took it from him and studied it closely.

"Very similar to Lucinda, striking and looks older than sixteen. This could be the same man, despite the lack of knife wounds. Do you need any extra officers?"

"You'll never find me saying no to that!"

"They're yours. I thought you'd be interested in the reports from the forensic psychologist in London and the FBI profiler." He glanced apologetically at Fenwick who still hadn't seen them.

It was gone midnight but Fenwick was as awake as if it were midday. He accepted a cup of bad coffee while a junior officer ran off copies of the profiles. In twelve tightly typed pages the psychologist had classified all the murders and rapes on Fenwick's original list and had concluded that, despite there being striking physical similarities in the victims, they were the work of two men. Subject "A," who could be Griffiths, was in behavioral terms different from Subject "B," the Knightsbridge killer who was described as an expressive killer.

Claire Keating had explained to him once that for a serial killer the murder is simply an expression of the desire to kill, an end in itself. Having life-or-death control over their victims stimulated expressive murderers. The significant degree of violence pre- and post-mortem, and the delay before killing the Knightsbridge victim suggested that the true source of pleasure was not the sexual act itself but the killer's ability to exercise sustained control.

With Subject A, Griffiths, the profiler admitted some confusion. The entrapment through THE GAME and the stalking all suggested a form of enjoyment through control but the crimes themselves, though brutal, were clearly sexually motivated. Statements from the rape victims who survived all supported the suggestion that enough violence was used to coerce the victim and to force sex upon her but no more.

The FBI analysis was consistent. They had gone into even more detail on Subject B and had summarized their key findings:

Physical Description: Male, Caucasian, late twenties or early thirties. Well dressed. Attractive. Employed, with reasonable income and life style.

Social and Cultural Background: Victims are female, post-adolescent, young adult, which means there should be no automatic assumption of abuse as a child. It is entirely possible that B led a relatively normal childhood. However, it is also possible that his relationships with his parents (mother in particular) may have held tensions, e.g. he felt he had never met expectations; emotional relationships were under-developed; there was sibling rivalry; father may have been (or B felt him to have been) distant.

A well-adjusted, social, charming personality suggests well-integrated family life, regular schooling. B's confidence and lack of respect for social norms may mean that he dabbled in minor crime during adolescence, seeking thrills. If he escaped punishment for these, he will have a reinforced a sense of superiority toward society and law enforcement.

Clear evidence of sociopathic behaviors: He is unlikely to have any guilt for his crimes and does not respect rules. B is likely to be impulsive. There is no evidence of planning in his crimes, rather they appear to be driven by desires that he has no inclination to control. He will react negatively to challenge and is likely to be deeply frustrated with a society that is not providing him with what he thinks he deserves.

It is possible that he is in a medium-term relationship with a woman: either engaged, married or partner. This may be a "normal" relationship on the surface, but is merely convenient (for sex, food, money, routine tasks or a useful "cover" to prove his normality to society).

Method: There is extreme violence pre- and postmortem, inflicted over a sustained period. Some of this is likely to accompany the acts of rape (e.g. the biting and beating) but the scale of genital injury and mutilation after death is an expression of hatred toward women and their sexual power. Subconsciously, he despises his need for sex as it implies that women have ultimate power over him, a concept that is deeply threatening to him. Consequently, he uses violence as both a disguise for his need and in revenge for his dependence.

The taking of a finger is not consistent with the extreme violence of the attacks and seems contrived. If A and B are acquainted it could be a simplistic means of linking their crimes to confuse investigation.

His confidence will be growing. This may lead him to make mistakes but it will also mean that he is more likely to attack again more quickly.

The incident room remained quiet after the officers had finished reading the report. Fenwick felt sullied by its contents, despite the detachment of the writing, as if looking inside the killer's mind had contaminated his own. He eventually broke the silence.

"This makes it all the more strange that Killer B should copy Griffith's methods in this latest attack. Why would he do so?"

MacIntyre yawned and stretched.

"The question's only relevant if they are connected and that is unproven." MacIntyre glared a warning at Fenwick not to confuse Amos with his theories. "I'm going to catch a few hours sleep before the press conference in the morning. I can't wait to see their faces when they learn that she's alive."

Caravans had been set aside for police use. Cooper and MacIntyre headed off but Fenwick stayed with Amos, studying the incident boards, already full of information.

"Any ideas?" Amos appeared to be a confident man who didn't mind the insights of others. He was about the same age as Fenwick but heavier set and shorter. He looked as if he might have boxed and the break in his nose supported the idea.

"Killer B is an intelligent man. Why did he hide her so close to the site instead of taking her body away by car?"

"We still didn't find her for thirty-six hours. We tried dogs but they lost his trail. It was raining yesterday and that helped to clear the scent as well."

"He couldn't rely on the rain. It doesn't feel right."

There was a map on one wall with pins indicating sites

linked to the crime. Fenwick pointed to a blue pin by the railway line.

"What happened here?"

"A sighting of a young man about midnight."

Fenwick stared at the map.

"There's no evidence that he has used a car in any crime. What if he came here by train and left the same way?"

"I have posters going up at all stations and officers interviewing people on and off the trains." He eyed Fenwick with interest. "Why are you so keen to find this man? You don't have any open cases to worry about?"

Fenwick paused, then decided to risk the man's cynicism by telling him of his fears for Nightingale. He emphasized the link between the ransacking of her flat and the letter to Griffiths.

"And you think the murderer is Griffiths' secret pen pal?"

"Yes."

"Isn't it more likely that the stalker is a friend of Griffiths who is simply harassing her? Why do you think that he knows the killer and that they chose to work together?"

"The similarities of the victims, the unsolved crimes, two distinctive MO's in proximate locations, the pristine state of Griffiths flat, so consistent with the lack of trace evidence. There's plenty of circumstantial reasons."

"But no hard evidence."

"None, but I just know. It sounds crazy, and I'm used to being told I have conspiracy theories on the brain, but I'm often right."

"It's odd but not daft. I hope this Nightingale of yours is worth your worry."

"Oh she is."

Eddie read the *Daily Mail* in his van on Tuesday as the express hurtled back to Birmingham. The picture on the front cover made him spill his coffee. It was the man he had seen on this train a week ago, the man he had been so concerned about. He read the story twice, raising his eyebrows at the name of the officer in charge who was an old sparring partner. As soon as the train pulled in to its final stop, he was off to a phone at a run.

"Derek Amos, please. It's urgent."

"The Superintendent is unavailable, can I help you?"

"No you bloody can't! I want to speak to Derek. Tell him it's Eddie Swaine and it's very urgent, about this case he's on."

He had to wait and the supervisor was giving him black looks for staying on the phone for so long but he ignored him. Derek sounded irritable when he eventually came to the phone.

"This had better be bloody good, Eddie."

"I saw him. The bloke you want. Two weeks ago on the train from London to Birmingham." He described his encounter and his concerns.

"Are you sure this is our man?"

"I wrote the details down and I've got them here. There's no mistaking him."

"I'm going to have someone from the local force come over to take your statement right now. Don't go away."

CHAPTER TWENTY

Fenwick left for Harlden with Cooper and a copy of Tasmin's file and arrived at the station by noon. In Quinlan's office he spread the contents on his desk and waited in silence.

"My God, this is grotesque. And they think it's the same man?"

"Can't be sure, but he tried to take her finger and the face is identical to the Knightsbridge killer. Only the hair and eye colors are different but they're both easily changed."

"How long since the killing in London?"

"Two weeks." The statement hung in the air. "I'm worried for Nightingale."

"You've got to let that drop, Andrew. I accept that there's a remote chance this killer is somehow linked to Griffiths but Nightingale is fine. There have been reassuring emails so we know that she's safe. Let it go—it's an unnecessary complication based only on your conjecture."

"Her original emails to Cooper might have been reassuring but the one she sent me acknowledges she's still receiving hate mail."

"Which says what?"

"I don't know; I can't open the attachment with it in. Every time I try to my system shuts down. IT support are trying to open it for me."

"And what else did she say, Andrew?"

Fenwick looked away, unwilling to repeat Nightingale's words of reassurance.

"Exactly," Quinlan said, vindicated, "she doesn't feel threatened does she?"

"She says she's in a place no one can find but . . ."

"She should know."

"But the physical similarity . . ."

"Nightingale was chosen for the operation *because* of that. Now look, MacIntrye has asked for you to be seconded to his team. It'll mean virtually living in London until the case is closed, and you can't carry that crusade with you there. Are you up for it?"

Fenwick thought of the children, home for the holidays, and took a deep breath.

"Yes. I'll go." If Quinlan shared MacIntyre's skepticism it was the only chance he would have to pursue his theory, and screw the consequences.

The problem of how to persuade Quinlan and MacIntyre that Nightingale was in real danger stayed in his mind for the rest of the day, even when he was with Bess and Chris. When he told them he would have to go away there were tears and sulks but by the time he put them to bed, far later than normal, they were friends again. Mrs. Knight was kind enough to say she would forego her days off if need be and he packed his overnight case with a growing sense of anticipation.

Before he could reach the offices of the Metropolitan Police the next day, MacIntyre rang and directed him to Doctor Batchelor's house. He would meet him there.

"I still think that B is unconnected to Griffiths but I need to exhaust every angle. If Griffiths is a link he'll be suspicious with too many interviews but we can ask the Doctor whatever we like. Anyway, I want to form my own opinion."

Batchelor was waiting for them and opened the door before they rang the bell. Fenwick was delighted to see that concern had replaced his sanctimonious expression.

They followed him down a narrow hall and into the womb-like room. Batchelor positioned himself safely behind his desk. MacIntyre took the lead.

"It is possible that Griffiths may be linked to a man who is raping and murdering young girls. We need to identify this person before he attacks again and information from Griffiths may be helpful. As I said on the phone this morning, if you claim patient-doctor privilege I shall do whatever is necessary to compel you to assist. This case has the Home Secretary's personal interest."

"There's no need to threaten me, Superintendent. The Govenor has given her support to your request. For my prison work the patient signs a disclaimer in case the authorities require detailed reports." Nevertheless his hands shook as he found and lit a cigarette.

MacIntyre put a tape recorder on the desk and switched it on. He identified the people in the room, the time and date, then looked expectantly at the doctor.

"How would you describe Griffiths? What sort of man is he?"

"Reasonably intelligent. I ran some IQ tests. His scores averaged 105. Reserved, shy, not always articulate. It came as no surprise to me to learn that he had made his living as a software developer."

"Was he a successful one?"

"Very. In one interview he told me that in his peak year he made £100,000. He also had some stock in one of the companies he had worked for. The idea of being a shareholder appealed to him although he was frustrated that he hadn't sold his shares as others had done, when they were worth ten times what they are now."

Fenwick raised a hand and MacIntryre nodded.

"You said when others had sold. What others do you think he meant?"

"I don't know."

"Yet it was someone he knew well enough to have a conversation with about personal financial affairs?"

"Yes. Well, let me see what else I can tell you about the man." He leaned back in his oversized black leather chair and stroked his wispy beard. Some of his confidence was returning. "I've had many patients who have committed violent crimes. Griffiths is different. In fact, I find it hard to believe him guilty of such violence toward women."

"Did he mention any normal relationships with women?" MacIntyre took up the questioning again.

"He assured me that he'd had healthy sexual relationships in the past and no problems relating to women—not sure I believed him. He was abandoned as an infant and lived in a series of children's homes until being fostered by a family as a teenager. He describes that as the turning point in this life."

"What else did he say about growing up?"

"I have a tape of an interview with him. Would you like to hear it?"

Batchelor rummaged in a filing cabinet then inserted a numbered tape into his own machine and forwarded it to the right moment. Griffiths' voice filled the room.

"*The early years were difficult. None of the homes was well run and there were always fights. I stayed out of them but it was hard to. Some of the carers beat us.*

"I never expected to be fostered, but my life changed. The house was out in the country—I'd never seen a real sheep before then. I started to enjoy school. It was weird. I found I was good at some subjects: maths, computer studies. We didn't have a computer in the house so I stayed behind to use the school one."

"What do your foster parents think of your imprisonment?"

"They're dead, a while back. I told you before I have no relatives."

"Were there other children at home?"

There was a pause, then Griffiths' voice.

"No. Just me. I told you. There was no one."

MacIntyre reached across and stopped the tape.

"Sounds like a lie, don't you think, Doctor?"

"Very probably. Prevarication, certainly. Do you think this other person was fostered with Griffiths? How fascinating!"

"Did he ever mention any names of friends or family?"

"Never. I'm sure. It was something I noticed about him. He would talk quite freely, if with no show of emotion, but it never once sounded personal. Sometimes he would go back over old ground but his descriptions and statements were always identical. He never once contradicted himself."

"Did he ever talk about what happened to his foster parents?"

Batchelor's eyes sparkled.

"Oh yes! That was a most fascinating interview. You must hear it. Let me change the tape."

More fussing in the filing cabinet and with the machine, and then the doctor could be heard speaking.

"Tell me more about your foster parents. Were you fond of them?"

"Fond? Sort of. They were nice."

"How did they die?"

"I've told you before, I don't want to talk about that."

"I think it would be good for you to do so, Wayne. Even a simple comment will really help you."

(Pause)

"What do you want to know?"

"What would you like to tell me?"

"Don't know. I've never talked about this."

"How old were you?"

"Seventeen. It was on my birthday . . ."

"Go on."

"My mother had baked a cake. We finished tea at six thirty. It was dark outside. The house was in the country, by a lake, not far from a wood. Very quiet. My mother decided to take the dog for a walk even though it was snowing. She put on her big tweed coat and took the torch with her.

"When she hadn't returned by quarter past seven Dad started to worry. At half past, he decided to go and look for her. He put his cap on and took a torch. When he opened the door to go out, the dog ran in. It had its lead on and was sort of yipping.

"My father became very agitated. He pulled on his Wellingtons, black ones with the tops rolled over, and picked up the lead. He tried to take the dog out with him but it wouldn't budge. So he went alone. Mother's footprints were clear in the snow and he followed them. I never saw either of them again."

"What happened?"

"She fell through the ice on the lake and drowned. It was a very cold winter so I imagine they thought it would be solid but it wasn't. Father went to find her and fell in too. That was it."

The tape stopped. There was silence in the room. Batchelor was first to speak.

"Poor little blighter. No love or family life for years, then a decent home, and that happens. Absolutely terrible."

"Maybe," said Fenwick. Something in the tone of his voice made them turn and stare at him, "except that Griffiths' date of birth on file is the 1st August. Not a lot of ice and snow at that time of year."

MacIntyre shared Fenwick's car on the way back into London. The flyover was jammed solid so they listened to the borrowed tapes of Griffiths' interviews as they crawled forward, trying to distinguish lies from truth. As they inched into west London Fenwick asked MacIntyre to play a section of one of the tapes again.

"I started going out with girls when I was at senior school but I didn't date seriously until work. Very often I didn't particularly like the girl, they were so stupid some of them, but it was the accepted thing to do and the sex was good."

"Did you find it easy to get dates?"

"Oh yes, particularly with the prettier ones. They were so used to the boys being all over them, which was something I never did, so I was a challenge to them."

Fenwick glanced at MacIntyre. "What's your immediate reaction to that?"

"Arrogant prick."

"I agree, but what else?"

"It sounds a little rehearsed, slightly artificial? What are you getting at?"

"Remember the profiler's report. They described Griffiths' crimes as the work of someone who was not socially confident, poorly adjusted, unlikely to have normal relationships."

"Yes but they also said he probably lived with an elderly parent and that was clearly wrong."

"Bear with me. The report also said that killer B was far better adapted, and we know he's smooth-tongued enough to be invited back to his victims' homes. I think Griffiths is using his words, not his own."

"Possible."

"They might have met at work, perhaps even in the children's home, and formed a bond."

MacIntyre stared at Fenwick in silence. The scrutiny made him self-conscious. After a considerable pause during which they actually managed to hit thirty miles an hour, MacIntyre said, "You're an interesting copper, aren't you. I bet if anyone said to you that you were intuitive you'd argue against it as a matter of principle but I think you are, exactly that."

"Some people just call it lucky." Fenwick smiled, trying to turn the conversation into a joke.

"Maybe, I'm a great believer in intuition myself. My father was a superintendent in the Highlands. He believed in his gut, said he got more convictions that way than any other."

"Well, you said yourself that Griffiths sounded artificial on that tape. How did you know that?"

"Years of practice." MacIntyre laughed. "OK, so maybe we all have an ability to interpret beyond fact but I still think yours is more than that."

Fenwick shrugged. The car accelerated across an amber light as the traffic of the metropolis closed around them.

MacIntyre handled the team briefing with authority, mentioning the possibility of a link with Griffiths with cautions that it was only one theory. He wasn't a tall man, but he had presence that suggested leadership and toughness. While he was in discussion with the NCS, he said, he reassured them that the investigation was still all theirs.

"DCI Andrew Fenwick here was responsible for identifying a potential link between Lucinda's killer and other crimes and has played an important part in the investigation to date. I am placing him in charge of a small team that's going to focus on past crimes with similar MOs. Brown and Knots, you are to be attached to the Chief Inspector."

Fenwick's habitual poker face meant that there was no show of surprise at his welcome responsibilities. The two officers who were going to work with him introduced themselves and he explained that he wanted one in London as an anchor and the other would travel with him to Telford the next morning where Griffiths had gone to school. Knots volunteered to go. Brown didn't argue. He gave them Tasmin's file to read while he went for a walk in the fume-laden London air.

PART THREE

GINNY AND AMELIA

Why was it that upon this beautiful feminine tissue, sensitive as gossamer, and practically blank as snow as yet, there should have been traced such a coarse pattern as it was doomed to receive.

—THOMAS HARDY

A man keeps another person's secret better than his own; a woman on the contrary, keeps her own secrets better than others.

—JEAN DE LA BRUYÈRE

CHAPTER TWENTY-ONE

He was on his own again. At first light he'd left Wendy asleep and returned to the cottage on his motorbike. He avoided driving a car unless it was an absolute necessity, although he never once linked this aversion to his past. To do so would have been to admit the possibility of a weakness and he had never done that.

His mood was somber. Imagine leaving her alive! Even though he'd fantasized on the cliff top about her regaining consciousness as the sea rose around her, only to drown in the claustrophobic blackness of the cave, he had thought her dead. It was all Griffiths' fault. To create stronger grounds for his appeal he had decided to work outdoors. It should have been easy but he'd found it strangely difficult. There were too many areas of uncertainty outside. What if somebody had walked by? It was different in their homes where he was completely in control and could take as long as he liked. That was the other problem. It had to be quick. No sooner had he started to enjoy himself than he'd had to stop. But everything might still have been all right if he hadn't lost his knife.

Fortunately he hadn't told Griffiths about the girl in Wales so the mistake remained his secret. His frustration mixed with a black mood that he couldn't shake off and the anger grew. With anger came a release of power and energy. He could feel it building now. A decision needed to be made. Did he try and copy Griffiths' clumsy style once more or go back to his own ways?

In the cottage he paced the sitting room, slashing the air with his hand as if it held the lost knife. When the idea came to him he smiled at its genius. His best solutions were always the most simple. He needed to look younger, so the mustache he'd started to cultivate would have to go. It didn't matter. He could grow a plausible beard in a week. The side burns had been coached longer but he razored them away. He showered vigorously, using a tough exfoliant to remove surface skin and loose body hair. There was always a risk that it wouldn't be enough but he'd been successful so far and his confidence in the technique had grown.

Now to the last details: he chose his contact lenses color and clothes, not too expensive this time. He wasn't in London now and the style that had enabled him to blend in there would make him stand out back here, but he needed to look fashionable—a pair of light chinos and a black T-shirt would do. His shoes needed to be strong, good quality for walking as he would not be taking his bike where he was going, but he had a thick-soled pair that would also pass as a fashion statement. Finally he took a wig of short dreadlocks from a cupboard and found his diamond ear stud to complete the effect.

The excitement was building. It made his eyes sparkle and brought a smile to his face. He snorted a line to keep the high then left the house. The air held an electricity that tasted like blood at the back of his throat. The hairs on his arms rose and the back of his neck tingled as he walked briskly along the footpath. He knew then that this was going to be a very special night.

Dana, Rachel and Virginia (Ginny to her friends but never to her family) were regretting their decision to visit Shrewsbury instead of staying in Telford as they usually did on a Friday night. They'd tried all the bars and discos they knew in a vain attempt to connect with whatever might be happening, only to conclude each time that it must be happening elsewhere. Low on adrenaline, makeup fading, they started to argue as they left the final bar on their list and walked out into the drizzle.

Under cover at a nearby bus stop they argued about what to do next. Dana was in favor of taking the train to Telford. Rachel thought that the bus would be quicker. Ginny kept quiet. She felt as if she had a cold coming. When the others couldn't agree she suggested that they go back to Dana's house and watch late-night *Buffy* with a glass of wine and a take-away but Dana and Rachel were having none of that.

The night was still promising as far as they were concerned and they weren't bound by Ginny's curfew. They were still enjoying their first year of legal drinking and didn't see why they should waste that at home, away from the boys. The girls finally agreed that the train back to Telford offered more pick-up opportunity and set off toward the station. Dana and Rachel strode ahead under an over-sized golf umbrella. Ginny followed, lagging further behind with each step. She huddled beneath a pink polka dot, see-through plastic umbrella. It belonged to her younger sister but had been the only one she could find before leaving home in a hurry.

Neither Dana nor Rachel was wearing a coat and Ginny figured that Dana *had* to be cold with that bare midriff, even if her new stud did catch the light. Rachel always looked good no matter what she wore but it was irritating the way her hair stayed sleek and shiny even in the rain.

At the station they discovered that they had just missed a train and would have to wait half an hour for the next one. There was a bar nearby to which they retreated to wait. Ginny ordered

Hooch but when it arrived the chilled sweet liquid made her shiver and she set it to one side. She huddled into her raincoat feeling poorly but trying to look bright, attractive and interested in their mindless chatter. Two men in their twenties came over and bought them all a drink, raising their eyebrows when she changed her order to whiskey.

Dana and Rachel started to have a great time. One of the blokes definitely fancied Rachel and the other seemed prepared to take an interest in Dana. As the half-hour wore on, then passed, Ginny felt herself increasingly pushed to the edge of the group. She sneezed a couple of times but didn't even warrant a "bless you," let alone any sympathy. When the others stood up to go back into Shrewsbury, suddenly a foursome with a convenient car, she decided that joining them just wasn't worth it. Dana and Rachel were briefly guilty enough to make a passing attempt to persuade her but accepted her third negative with a "suit yourself" and left Ginny to decide how to get home.

She had missed the previous train and there was over half an hour to wait for the final service. The barman was calling last orders as she checked how much money she had left—£47:52p—more than enough for a taxi even at this time of night. She had three numbers in her bag, carried at her dad's insistence.

There was a queue for the payphone by the loos and by the time her turn came around there was only a handful of other people still in the pub. The first taxi firm's number was constantly engaged. The second quoted her a thirty-minute wait and the third explained that all their drivers were booked or sick with flu. She was re-dialing the second number as the barman tapped her on the shoulder.

"Come on, love, time to go."

She didn't protest. At the station she dialed the second taxi firm again. It was engaged and she started to shiver, really cold now. She thought of the words of the last dispatcher. Perhaps she had the flu. If she couldn't find a taxi to take her home before midnight she decided that she'd call her dad. It was what she really wanted to do but they'd had a row that morning about her reluctance to go to university and she didn't want to behave in a way that suggested any weakness.

The phone booth was full of cards for taxi firms. She picked one at random and her call was answered straight away. They could have a cab to her within twenty-five minutes. The dispatcher sounded a friendly woman. *"If you're unlucky, it'll be my husband. Just don't complain about the suspension—his or the car's."* She chuckled at her own joke with a smoker's throaty laugh.

Ginny's spirits lifted. Twenty-five minutes was nothing and it was almost dry under the awning. She sneezed twice.

"Bless you! Are you all right? You shouldn't be out alone on a night like this."

It was a nice voice, sympathetic and cultured. Ginny softened her dismissive shrug with a superficial smile.

"I'm serious. Are you going to get home OK? Do you have enough money for a taxi? Sorry for asking but you remind me of my younger sister and I'd hate to think of her out on a night like this. I can order you a taxi if you like, my pleasure. I would never forgive myself if a pretty woman like you caught a chill because I'd abandoned her in the rain."

Ginny looked at him for the first time and smiled properly. He was tall with lovely green eyes, broad shoulders and crazy hair. But he was a stranger and he was a man. Ever since she had been a little girl she had never spoken to strange men. It was one of the reasons she tagged along with Dana and Rachel. They had no such inhibitions.

"I have a taxi booked, thank you."

He frowned but it disappeared quickly.

"Then I bet you have a bit of a wait. Can I buy you a coffee?"

The idea was tempting. A hot drink in attractive company was better than waiting outside in the damp. What harm could there be in a coffee?

The station buffet was closed but there was an Italian-looking place (that is the awning was red, white and green) over the road and they went in there. He told her his name was Graham and left her at a table near the door while he went in search of a waiter. If she twisted her head she could see the taxi rank and she started to relax.

Graham was gone for some time. He returned eventually looking triumphant with two large cups of thick cappuccino.

"Success! And I managed to persuade him to give us these as well." He pulled two packets of Amaretti biscuits from his pocket and handed her the pink-wrapped one.

"Thank you." She wasn't hungry but it felt rude to decline. He watched as she unwrapped the paper and started to nibble the sugary nodules from the top of the macaroon.

"That's no way to eat them!" He laughed and dunked one of his own into the froth of his coffee before popping it into his mouth whole. "Delicious. Go on, try it."

Ginny still didn't feel like eating but he was kind and friendly so she copied him and ate both halves of her own biscuit. He chatted to her easily as she sipped at the froth and watched for the taxi. It still hadn't arrived when she decided to leave to be on the safe side.

"I must go. Thanks for the coffee."

"You haven't touched it. At least drink some. It will warm you up."

"Oh, OK." She took a long swallow and grimaced. "What's in it?"

"Grappa, just a splash. It's a great cold remedy and it won't do you any harm."

Ginny gulped more of the cooling coffee to be polite then rose to go. She sneezed twice as she said goodnight. Feeling decidedly undignified she picked up her coat and walked toward the door. Somehow he was there, opening it before she could stop him.

"I'll walk you to the rank and wait until your taxi arrives. No, I insist. You shouldn't be on your own at this time of night. I'm amazed that your boyfriend left you to fend for yourself."

Ginny let the remark pass, it was simpler. Besides, she was having difficulty putting her arm into the sleeve of her coat.

"Here, let me help you. There you go. And button it up tight, it's still raining."

The restaurant felt hot and steamy. She put her hand to her forehead, expecting to find it hot but was surprised to touch cold clammy skin. She must have a temperature. Her hand trembled and her knees felt wobbly.

"Are you OK?"

"Hot, just hot. Fresh air. That's good."

Ginny was shocked to find that full sentences were difficult. The words were there in her head but they bunched up in her mouth when she tried to say them. She stepped out into the drizzle and waited for the dizziness to clear. Instead it became worse. She tried to open the stupid pink umbrella but her fingers felt like immovable sausages. He opened it and held the plastic over her head as he guided her over to the rank. When she stumbled he cupped his free hand under her elbow to steady her then put it round her waist as she started to sway. He was holding her too tight.

"Nah." She wanted to say, "no go away," but her lips wouldn't open. She tried to push against him but her arms were useless unresponsive lumps by her side.

He was pulling her really hard against him now and panic grew inside her.

"Don't wriggle. You'll have us both over. Ah! Is this your taxi?"

A car pulled up and the driver opened the front passenger window enough to shout.

"Virginia Matthews?"

"Virginia? Oh yes, Ginny, that's us."

Ginny tried to shake her head. This was all wrong.

"She's drunk. I won't have drunks in my car. They sick up all over."

The man who said he was Graham laughed.

"Don't worry, she's been ill already. There's nothing left. I just need to see her home safely."

Ginny heard him give an address in the wrong direction and opened her mouth in silent protest. The taxi driver looked at her and frowned.

"Nothing left? You sure? It's twenty quid extra if she throws up. In fact . . ." The driver seemed about to drive off.

Graham thrust something through the open crack in the window.

"Here's a tenner, on account. If she's ill you can stop the car and chuck us out, and I'll give you another. Have a heart. Look at her, her dad'll be worried sick."

Ginny attempted to shake her head but only managed to wedge her chin on her shoulder. The taxi driver unlocked the doors reluctantly and she was bundled inside.

"Thanks, mate. You won't regret this." They climbed in and Graham immediately opened his window wide. "Fresh air will help," he explained but even in her drugged state Ginny could feel the tension radiating from him.

No one spoke as the tires swished through puddles and the

orange streetlights became less frequent, then stopped altogether. The car left the town limits and Ginny felt drug-induced indifference build inside her, more sickly than vomit. She moaned, softly at first, then louder.

"She all right?" The driver cast a worried glance over his shoulder and edged out of potential vomit range.

"I think so. Where are we?"

"'Bout a mile from Cressage."

"Hmm," Graham appeared to consider the distance to their destination. Ginny groaned again and managed a brief struggle against his restraining arm. "Tell you what. Take us another mile, then we can manage to walk from there."

The driver didn't answer. He just looked skeptical, as if he doubted that the woman in the back of his cab could walk anywhere. The minutes passed in silence. Ginny struggled against the fog that was enveloping her. She knew that something was wrong but the thought brought confusion and dull compliance, not fear.

"Just here will do. Pull over. Here, keep the change and the ten quid." He paid, and if the driver noticed his hand shaking, the tip dulled his curiosity.

A sensation close to terror struggled to fight through to Ginny's consciousness and failed. She knew that if she left the stuffy heat of the car something horrible would happen. The thought hammered away at the inside of her skull with puny fists as her body followed his lead and unfolded obediently, onto feet a thousand miles away that stood on a wet grass verge.

The driver took another look at the couple he'd left standing on the muddy margin of the road. The girl looked high on something more than booze. Disgusting, couldn't be more than eighteen, letting herself get into a state like that. He shook his head in condemnation as he reversed into a layby and pulled away. As he did so, he glanced in his rearview mirror one last time. The bloke was trying to get the girl's arm over his shoulder but she seemed to be lolling away from him. Her face was turned toward his car, head heavy, her shadowed mouth open. From this distance it looked exactly as if she was screaming. He moved up from second gear and accelerated back toward the lights of town.

Ginny felt numb. Her eyes were wide and staring, trying to focus on the night around her but she could barely make out her surroundings. Darkness and drugs were blinding her to everything but the immediacy of her body. The man beside her was dragging her away from the road and she hadn't the strength to resist him. He was pulling hard and her skin burned. There was a stone hidden in the grass and she tripped, falling onto her knees. The ground beneath her felt as soft and insubstantial as a cloud.

"Get up!"

He yanked at her arms but her weight had settled low and he had to drag her toward the five bar gate set back in the hedge. Once he reached it he dropped her to use both hands to push back the heavy fastening. Then he was pulling her through the entrance into an empty pasture. She could smell dung from the milk cows that had passed through earlier in the day and coughed.

"Shut up." He sounded angry now and there was a dull stinging sensation against her cheek, forcing her half-closed eyes open. Had he hit her?

"Don't you laugh at me, you fucking bitch."

She saw the boot raised and swinging toward her. There was a thud that made her whole body shudder but no pain. Only her sense of smell stayed true and she recognized the taint of blood as it joined the manure.

Ginny lay flat on her back. He lifted her arms and dragged her as the drizzle fell on her face. Her body was completely passive by the time he reached the shelter of a hedge where the ground was dry and firm. Even when he ripped open her coat, tore her blouse and pulled her skirt up around her waist, she felt formless, like a paper doll left outside in the rain. As he kicked her legs apart she gave in to welcome unconsciousness.

As a taxi driver, Geoff was familiar with the local radio station but he'd had enough of their mellow midnight sounds, thank you. He needed something to keep him awake in the closing hour of his shift and selected Radio Four. He listened passively until the item about the abduction and rape of a young girl in Wales captured his attention. It was almost local news. He tut-tutted over the details and thought how lucky she'd been to escape with her life. Young women these days needed to be more careful. The thought brought back a memory of the lass he'd just dropped off. Just as well she had a boyfriend decent enough to see her home.

The radio journalist was interviewing the policeman in charge of the investigation, a Superintendent Amos. He was describing the attacker: white male aged about 25-30, six foot tall and slim but muscular, with brown hair and blue eyes. Amos emphasized that he frequently altered their coloring. The presenter described him as dangerous and a serious threat to young women, particularly those who were dark haired and attractive.

Geoff Minny slowed his cab. A bright flash of memory brought a picture of that young girl into his mind, her mouth open in a soundless scream as he drove away. All at once the sensible, well-tipped ride he was returning from became sinister and he pulled over to think.

It had been a legitimate fare he told himself. She'd been

drunk, young, out late. All he'd done was take her home . . . except of course he hadn't, had he. He'd dropped a kid no older than his niece on her own in the middle of nowhere, with some strange bloke who claimed to be her boyfriend.

"Oh bugger!" he said out loud, feeling a bit sick all of a sudden. He'd wondered about the age difference and about her state when he'd picked them up, but he'd seen worse. Guilt ambushed him, making him hot and queasy.

He turned the volume up so he could hear the end of the report.

". . . and you think he may be the same man who killed a young woman in Knightsbridge in June?"

"We are keeping an open mind but there are similarities that I can't go into now."

"Any other sightings of him?"

"We believe that he may have caught a train from London to Birmingham, and potentially from there on to Telford in the weeks before the abduction of Tasmin. Residents of these areas should be particularly vigilant."

"Just a regular fare," he muttered to himself and wiped his palms on his trousers, leaving damp traces. His wife was on the blower chasing him for another pick-up but he ignored it. Supposing . . . the thought was too awful. No, he was being over imaginative. It was late and he was tired. He put the car into gear and relaxed the clutch and handbrake. He traveled less than fifty meters before he stopped again.

What if his instincts we right? What if that young girl had been in trouble, not drunk but drugged? He'd read more than once about that date rape thing—Rippi something or other. What if . . . ? He shook his head to try and clear the confusion from his mind. He was going daft. Too many night shifts for the extra money and too much coffee to keep him going. He'd look a right burke if he gave in to his fears and called the police only to find he was fingering a courting couple. The old bill would be unamused and he'd lose the rest of the night's fares into the bargain.

He lit a cigarette but the worry wouldn't go away. What would his wife and son say if they ever found out he'd turned away from a girl who was later murdered? He shuddered at the thought.

"Bugger, bugger!" He stubbed out his cigarette and turned the car around.

"Graham" sucked deeply on the roll up and watched the tip glow red and die, glow and die, unlike the anger inside him, which just kept growing. He'd never used drugs before because of his confidence in his ability to seduce women. Tonight he'd decided to experiment and combine some of his usual skill with medicinal help to speed the process along. Bad idea. He'd used too much. It looked as though the biscuits he'd prepared beforehand would have been enough, but the thrill of doping the coffee and watching her drink it had added to the excitement. He'd really got a kick out of persuading her to drink the stuff. When she'd started to become dizzy he had enjoyed the charade of assisting her and the original helplessness had been erotic. But then she'd blacked out on him and with her unconsciousness his passion had died.

He kicked the inert body lying at his feet. What was the point screwing that? There was no fear to feed his desire. Stupid bitch. He kicked her again. Instead of the terror he was used to seeing in acknowledgment of his supreme power, there had been nothing. No matter what he did, or how much pain he inflicted there was no response. He was left feeling unfulfilled and angrier than ever. His body was temporarily satisfied but even now he could feel the knot of tension tightening deep in his stomach.

He would either have to find someone else or start over again with her. He bent and slapped her hard.

There was a faint moan and the body on the ground stirred slightly. He smiled briefly, a flash of white teeth in the moonlight. If she was coming round perhaps he could have his fun with her after all. He dragged her deeper inside a small copse. It was little more than a few trees and brambles but was better than nothing. He decided that he hated this outdoor work and regretted his commitment to his sometime partner. This one, then the police bitch, and he would go back to his old ways. If that wasn't enough to provide grounds for appeal then tough, Griffiths would have to handle it himself. His anger bubbled like an erupting boil under his skin as he tried to shake her back to consciousness.

Geoff slowed to twenty miles an hour. The rain was a faint drizzle now, making it easier to see the roadside but for the life of him, he couldn't remember where he had dropped them off. The man had asked for Sheinton and he'd stopped a good mile before their destination but each hedgerow and gateway look the same. A car came up fast behind him and he opened his window and waved them past. Someone in the back gave him a single finger salute, which he thought summed up his evening.

There was a heavy five-barred gate to his right tied with bailer twine. Something about it was familiar and he braked to a stop, then reversed so that his headlights lit up the scene. The mud was rutted with old tire tracks and there were dark depressions that might have been footprints. He lit a cigarette as he decided whether to investigate. It was warm and cozy in the car and he regretted his impulse to go in search of the girl. She was sure to be home already while he was out here wasting petrol and building up a sweat. Now that he was here though he might as well check the gateway.

He stepped outside and stretched. The ground was black and featureless in the starlight, the night silent. There was another gate further along the road close to a lay-by. It looked familiar . . . perhaps he'd used it for his three-point turn. He walked up the road toward it, muttering to himself that this was the last time. A final look then he'd head back into town for a bollocking from the wife and a nice cup of tea.

There was a clump of stinging nettles hidden within the brambles. He sucked his hand, spitting on the cluster of white bumps, then rolled her over so that she was on top of them, to be rewarded with a cough. About bloody time. He pulled the remains of her tights from her legs and used them to bind her wrists tightly behind her back.

The sense of anticipation was acute now and he slapped her face until her eyes flickered open. They closed again and her head lolled to one side. He cursed her out loud and shook her until they reopened. It was too dark to read her expression but when he raised his hand to strike her she flinched and his blood surged. He undid his belt and let his trousers drop, ready again. This is what he had been put on earth to do, to search out weakness and destroy it.

He carried on long after he was finished, unwilling to let the moment pass, but eventually he could see again as the red mist cleared from in front of his eyes. He was sweating like a dog after its kill and wrinkled his nose in disgust. Was she dead? God, he hoped not yet. As the drumming in his ears quieted he strained to catch the sound of her breath. Moonlight was fighting through the clouds but the trees cast barred shadows across her face. There was blood where he had bitten her but he checked his pocket and was relieved to find his knife unused inside—for a moment he hadn't been sure. He bent his head to her open mouth and thought he felt the faintest breath on his cheek.

After all that, she was still here with him. The thought made him smile like a child at Christmas. He needed another cigarette but his hands were trembling so much that he dropped the first paper. At his third attempt he managed to seal a roll-up well enough to light it. He sucked in the smoke and held it in his lungs until it burned, then exhaled slowly.

Life was so good that he could cry. He looked at the girl, her white limbs splotched black, her once pretty face bloodied and bruised, and howled with delight. For the first time he began to understand why Griffiths worked outside. With it came a sense of freedom, of behaving as nature intended. He had already perfected the arts of seduction and entrapment indoors, now he could add to them a new skill. He was a master.

Another deep drag on the cigarette and he started to relax . . . and think. If he left her like this the police would find his traces all over her. He needed water. One of the reasons he'd selected this place was that he recalled there was a stream nearby. He never used fire as it had serious disadvantages. A body was too wet to burn without accelerant and even then there was no guarantee that all the evidence would be destroyed. During his long days between jobs he went to the library and read every available book on forensic investigation. He considered himself an expert. Even the police knew less than he did. Only other specialists would appreciate his insight. Sometimes he fantasized about giving a lecture, illustrated with slides of his own work. They would be astonished, those forensic scientists; they would have no choice but to acknowledge his supremacy.

He caught himself daydreaming, a potentially dangerous habit. She wasn't even dead yet and here he was mentally debating slides of her autopsy. Time to move. He found the fast-running stream and dragged her into the shallows, careful to keep her face out of the water. The night was young and he could afford to wait before he finally killed her. If he held off using the knife he could keep them alive for hours. He was always in control, not like some of the sad cases he read about in the papers, driven by primitive sexual urges to perform unimaginative crimes that deserved punishment. He spat and started to wash her.

Geoff stumbled and almost fell into a puddle at the entrance to the field. Despite the growing light as the clouds shredded and cleared, he could make out very little of his surroundings. Had he not heard the hawking cough as he peered over the gate he would have abandoned his search already. It had been distinctively human. There was no mistaking it for the bark of a fox or grunt of a hedgehog. At the sound the hairs on the back of his neck had risen. He moved into the field as quietly as he could and instinctively hunched into a crouch of which he was unaware.

Something flickered in the grass and he bent to pick it up. A diamante hairslide, cheap, plastic and clean. His heart beat faster. Had the girl been wearing it? For the life of him he couldn't remember but how else would something like this be here sparkling in the mud? This was becoming serious but he'd never felt more stupid or out of place. Despite the hairslide in his hand he almost turned back. Then he heard another cough from the trees less than a hundred meters ahead of him. He crouched lower and crept forward, suddenly conscious of the noise he was making. His heart was hammering in his ears and he was sweating profusely beneath his shirt.

As he reached the hedge before the copse he saw something white glinting in the ditch. A Gap T-shirt, ripped open with something dark down one side that might have been blood. To his credit his first reaction was one of fear for the girl, then anger toward the man who might be attacking her at that very moment. His next thought was to call out, to give her hope and scare her attacker, but a rush of common sense stopped the impulse. All he would be doing was warning the man of his approach.

His mobile phone was in his pocket and he backed away a few steps to create what he hoped was a sound break then dialed: nine-nine-nine. When prompted he whispered "police and ambulance" and gave succinct directions to the field, emphasizing that he thought a girl was being attacked. They started to question him for more details but he didn't have any and rang off.

For the first time he acknowledged that he was scared. The idea of waiting in the car was very appealing and he almost turned around to retrace his steps, but the thought of what might be happening to the girl was too horrible to ignore. Instead he followed the line of the hedge back to the copse and crouched down on his haunches to peer inside.

The first thing he noticed was the silence beneath the rushing of the wind in the trees. Then there was a rustling and the faintest, lowest moan. Feeling smaller and lonelier than he had done since his first cub pack holiday, he started to creep forward.

He was smoking another roll up when he heard the girl moan. It was long past midnight. On impulse he decided to finish her off and dump her body. He pulled out his knife, a replacement for the one lost in Wales, and opened the sharpened blade. His excitement returned. This was the best part.

The water had roused her and she was trying to raise herself on one elbow. She was a disgusting creature, entirely unworthy and it was good that she was going to die. The heat in his stomach increased as his pulse quickened.

"About fucking time!" He brought his free hand up and hit her temple, driving her back into the river bank. She cried out in pain and his body exulted.

He put his hand over her mouth and felt her whimper against his palm. Her eyes were wild as he held her tight against his thigh. The sight and smell of her drove the stale adrenaline from his system with a surge of fresh excitement. She was crying now, the tears wetting the back of his hand. She screamed against his palm and he cried out with joy.

He was laughing as he raised the knife. When she saw the blade she tried to fight her way free but she wasn't strong enough and he made the first delicate cut easily, enjoying the way she arched her back in agony.

Geoff raised himself from his knees, appalled at the sounds coming from the bushes ahead of him. The girl was moaning in pain while that bastard was laughing and enjoying himself. He looked hopefully back toward the gate and the road beyond but it remained empty. If the girl was to be saved there was no option but to do something himself, but he wasn't a hero and he remembered the man as tall and muscular. He tried to stand but his knees were like jelly. Geoff was petrified. As the sounds of the man's attack filled the night he clamped his hands over his ears. Tears soaked his cheeks unnoticed. Then the girl cried out, a real scream full of horrified pain, and he could crouch there no longer. There was a wooden branch in the brambles and he picked it up, ignoring the sting of nettles. With a loud cry he leaped forward, swinging the makeshift club wildly.

The man raised himself to his feet and hitched up his trousers. He ducked easily under the swing and stepped away to open the distance between them. Geoff swung again and almost overbalanced. He struggled upright and aimed a kick at the man's groin. It connected but not with enough force to inflict real damage. The man leaped at him wielding a knife. There was ice in Geoff's belly now as he tried to keep out of range. The girl was screaming, or was it the man? He could no longer tell as he was forced to use the branch to deflect a vicious thrust.

The other man was younger, fitter and he kept coming. There was a stinging pain along his arm and he glanced down to see his jacket gashed open and blood on his wrist. He had to use both hands to hold the branch now, alternatively thrusting it forward like a sword or swinging it as a club. It made no difference. His opponent seemed to dance around him, just out of striking distance until he darted forward with a lunge that increasingly brought with it numbness or pain.

In the dark he tripped over the girl's legs and stumbled forward. When he looked up his opponent had gone. As he tried to stand, there was a blow to his back and Geoff fell forward, winded. He forced himself up but his legs wouldn't lock and he collapsed gently into a kneeling position on the mud next to the girl. She was screaming again and he wanted to tell her to stop but his mouth wouldn't work.

Another blow, on his neck this time, and he rolled sideways, the branch held above him like weights. His attacker was standing astride his legs looking down with an expression of joy far worse than any snarl. Geoff tried to hold the branch between them but it was so heavy. He felt desperately tired suddenly and kept yawning. It was freezing cold and there was a buzzing in his ears. The girl's screaming faded, then there was only silence. Above him, the man knocked the branch casually to one side. As he watched, the knife was lifted high in the air in a sacrificial gesture. It glinted blue, silver and red in the night, a sight that Geoff knew was good, though he could no longer remember why.

He waited for the final killing strike, too weak even to raise an arm to deflect it. The solid world was fading away from him. He thought of his wife and son, his sister dead these thirteen years, his own mum and dad, and still the blade didn't fall. His eyes strained to see but the man was gone.

From somewhere he heard a voice shouting his name but it was too far away. Then inside his head he thought he could hear his sister calling him downstairs. Late for church again.

"Come on!"

He could see his feet on the red hall carpet and brilliant sunlight streaming through the open front door of his parents' house.

"Come on!"

She was always such a little madam. He stepped outside.

"Come on, come on! Don't you go now! Come on, you can do it."

The paramedic stopped the cardiac massage as fresh air was blown into the man's lungs and felt for a carotid pulse beneath the thick blood on his neck. Still nothing. He repeated the sequence again and again. Nothing. After another ten minutes his colleague pulled him back gently.

"He's gone, Steve."

"There's still a chance. We should keep going until we get to emergency."

Steve continued relentlessly as the ambulance careered through deserted streets toward the hospital. On the opposite stretcher the girl had sunk into a semi-comatose state of shock but at least her vital signs were stable and the knife wound to her shoulder was superficial. Which was more than could be said for the poor bugger they'd found with her.

Steve was still massaging dead muscle as they wheeled Geoffrey Minny, fifty-two, married father of one into A&E, where he was pronounced DOA. His mate pulled him away from the stretcher.

"You need to change."

Steve looked down at the bright arterial blood that was stiffening on his uniform.

"Yeah. Right."

"You OK?"

"Sure." Steve waved a casual hand. "It's just that we were so close. You know how sometimes you can feel them still there? He was almost ours, that's all."

"You win some, you lose some. Happens every week, you know it does."

"Right."

Steve found his locker, a change of clothes and an empty shower cubicle. Under the camouflage of running water he wept for a man he had never known.

CHAPTER TWENTY-TWO

Griffiths folded the newspaper precisely and placed it square on the library table. Normally he enjoyed the Sunday editions but today was different. Wearing the poker face he was so proud of he waited, seemingly patient, until it was time to return to his cell. Once there, he had exactly forty-five minutes in which to work on his next letter. The simple but effective code system had become second nature to him. As he wrote his anger forced its way onto the page.

Hidden beneath layers of nonsense words he chastised his sometime partner for his pathetic failure.

You used to be so superior, so smart, but you can't perform like me, can you? Get it right! I've had my solicitor in, told him that I was the wrong man, that the real one was still outside. He didn't believe me!

The light went out. He threw himself onto the bed in a flounce that made the bedsprings rattle. The police still weren't making a connection between the attacks outside and his previous crimes. Taking the fingers had always been part of the grand plan but it hadn't even been mentioned in court. He had reasoned that if the pattern continued the police would have to conclude that they had the wrong man. At the very least it would create substantive grounds for appeal. He'd had high hopes of the master and now he felt badly let down, to say the fucking least.

His letter would create a powerful negative reaction. He had dared to criticize. Unthinkable. Despite his anger he felt scared. Without Dave's help he would never be released. He'd have to change it in the morning and beg for help. That night he dreamed of Wendy, a sweet satisfying fantasy that made him long for freedom.

Police in Wales found a knife two miles from the scene of Tasmin's abduction, at seven in the evening on Thursday. They'd been able to lift partial prints and had found a match against a set from the underside of a stool at the Frog and Nightgown. Fenwick almost ran to the incident room in London to see the only tangible evidence they had so far on Killer B. It was crowded but MacIntyre beckoned him round to look at the weapon. He had expected a serious blade. Instead he was staring at a large penknife.

"This is it?"

"Look at it, the tip has been honed to a fine point."

"Does it match any of Lucinda's wounds?"

"We don't know. He used Sabatier knives from the kitchen to torture her, then washed them clean in the dishwasher but the PM suggested the wound that killed her, the one to her heart, had been made by a finer blade, perhaps this one."

"Why would a killer of this viciousness resort to killing with a penknife? It's almost a child's toy, which makes me even more convinced that whatever bound Killer B and Griffiths together had its roots in childhood."

MacIntyre shook his head skeptically but held his peace. He'd given Fenwick responsibility for investigating a potential link between Griffiths and Killer B and wasn't about to undermine him in public.

Fenwick paused, aware he was about to ask a favor.

"Is your relationship with the Governor good enough to ask for Griffiths to be interviewed by another psychologist? There's someone I've worked with before. She's good and I'd trust her assessment more than I do Batchelor's."

"I'll try, if you really think it's worth it."

"I do."

An hour later MacIntyre told him they had approval. That left Fenwick with the problem of how he was going to persuade Claire to help him. He hadn't spoken to her since their break up and he knew that she had been avoiding him on her visits to Harlden.

He dialed her number, hoping for the answering machine but she was there.

"Claire, how are you?"

"Fine."

"Um, Claire, I wonder if I could ask you a favor."

She listened to his request in silence.

"What do you think?"

"I need a fuller briefing before I can decide. What is the name of the psychiatrist seeing him now?"

"Doctor Batchelor."

"*Maurice* Batchelor?"

"Yes. D'you know him?"

"We've met. Look, I may be able to help you but I think we need to meet. How urgent is this?"

"Very, I could be in Harlden this afternoon."

"Not good for me. How about tomorrow?"

"It's Saturday."

"I thought you said it was urgent."

"Well, yes it is, it's just that I'm babysitting while the housekeeper is away."

"I could come to the house."

Fenwick hated the idea but he was asking a big favor and needed her cooperation.

"Fine. Tomorrow afternoon then."

They said their good-byes, leaving Fenwick concerned about the following day. He did *not* want to renew their relationship and he hoped that she didn't think his request for help was a come on.

The children were playing in the tent in the garden when Claire arrived. He offered her a glass of a Pimms. It was a drink he took care to make well and was suitably rewarded by her appreciation.

"Delicious. Exactly what the day needed."

She smiled at him, sunglasses shading her eyes from the brilliant light on his terrace. He had chosen to sit beneath the parasol but Claire bared her arms to the sun. She was wearing a sleeveless white shirt and khaki pants that stopped mid-calf to reveal slim ankles. He noticed that she had a great tan.

"It was good of you to come round. And I appreciate your time."

"Andrew, stop sounding like a stuffed shirt. We both know that you're human really. Relax, I'm here to help, not to seduce you."

Her laugh was light and easy but he smiled uncomfortably. She might be relaxed but seeing her again had brought back a conflicting bundle of emotions that were as unexpected as they were unwelcome. She looked lovely—golden, fit and, admit it, desirable, but he told himself that he had no regrets.

"Penny for them?"

"What?"

"Your thoughts, a penny for them." She smiled into his eyes.

Fenwick looked away, feeling trapped.

"Nothing, just the case, you know."

"No, I don't. I have no objections to your being distracted, Andrew but I do resent being lied to."

The sharpness of the word lay between them, made harsher by the sound of the children's laughter from the tent under the apple trees. There was an uncomfortable pause. Eventually, he spoke.

"I'm sorry." He stood up and paced the terrace, draining his drink. "Do you want another?"

Claire raised a glass that was still well over half full, and shook her head.

"I haven't come here to put up with Fenwick the mystic for the infiniteth time, Andrew."

"Is infiniteth a word?" He tried a lopsided smile.

"Don't try to joke your way out of it."

"I'm sorry." He needed her help and was prepared to grovel to get it.

"Sorry is as sorry does."

"Did I hurt you?"

"Yes, but it's not terminal."

He stood up, wishing that he hadn't asked the question.

"I'm not escaping but I really would like another drink and yours has gone warm."

He brought back two large tumblers of Pimms, crammed with ice, mint and cucumber, together with a plate of Alice's homemade cheese straws.

"So why are you here? Apart from the fact that we're new best friends of course. Are you willing to help with the Griffiths case?"

"I was as soon as I found out whose advice you were relying on."

"You don't rate Doctor Batchelor?"

Claire snorted and took a drink.

"Not based on my one encounter with him. We attended a seminar together. I found that his ego got in the way of his analysis. He was forever reminding me that *he* was a psychiatrist while I was 'only' a psychologist, as if that mattered. What really worried me were his opinions on typology and the motivations for criminal actions. I found them deeply flawed."

"He seems thorough, though."

"Oh yes he's that but, to put it bluntly, I thought he was thick."

"Why don't you say what you mean. I've never heard you be so damning. He must really have upset you."

"Forget about him. I'm interested in the Griffiths case, I have been since I first heard about it. I was frustrated that Blite never let me in, so this is a chance to indulge my curiosity. I should be able to read the files over the weekend and visit him next week."

"What excuse will you give for seeing him?"

"I don't know yet but the files will give me ideas. I want to avoid lying if possible. Now, why don't you tell me about what is happening in Andrew Fenwick's life?"

The Pimms had relaxed him but he still squirmed.

"Dull, as usual."

"Your life is *never* dull, Andrew. Come on."

"Why are you interested?"

"Because everyone should be able to talk about what's happening to them, share the day-to-day things as well as the momentous. I believe it keeps us sane."

"And you doubt my sanity?"

"No, I think you're lonely."

He felt as if she had punched him in the stomach and tried to scoff her observation away.

"I have no time to be lonely. I work six days out of seven and spend any spare hours I have with the children. Most nights I fall into bed too exhausted even to think."

"And on the nights you don't?"

He turned away and took another drink.

"Don't retreat again. This isn't a come-on. Just because I like you doesn't mean I need you back as a lover. There is an in-between, you know. I had hopes once," she paused and smiled with a bitter twist at odds with the sunshine, "but I was wrong. I should've realized that your heart wasn't free to give."

"Not free to give?" He thought of Monique and felt guilty. He knew that the desperate, passionate infatuation he'd once had for her had finally passed away with her death and he was embarrassed that Claire should attribute to him more than chronic grief.

"Did I say that?" She looked evasive and drained her drink.

"Another?"

"No thanks, I must go."

"Can I ask you a question first?"

She looked at him cautiously.

"I'm curious; why do you think that I'm not free?"

She flushed and it was her turn to look away.

"You need to pluck up the courage to answer that yourself."

"I don't think I can."

"Rubbish!" She kissed him quickly on the cheek and left.

Griffiths stared boldly at the woman opposite. She had come to see him instead of Batchelor but he didn't yet know why. He waited. He had all the time in the world and psychiatrists' games of silence left him cold.

"My name is Claire, Mr. Griffiths. I've asked to see you because I am conducting research into the effects of wrongful arrest and conviction on the mental state of prisoners."

"So you think I'm innocent?" This was more like it.

"I think that you think you are."

Typical, bloody clever, mincing words. He was inclined to ignore her, but on the other hand, she was the first person other than his lawyer to raise the subject of wrongful arrest.

"Go on."

"Well, that's it really. I don't know all the details of your case and I have no opinion of whether you are guilty or innocent. In fact, I'm completely open-minded on the subject. But I am very interested in the impact your imprisonment has had on you. Could you tell me about that?"

Could he fuck. He wasn't prepared to have another can-opener brain picking around inside his mind, but he could tell her about his grounds for appeal. It would be an interesting test, to see how well developed his argument had become.

"To understand that, you really need to know what happened to me and why I can prove I'm innocent."

She looked interested.

He told her how the bitch policewoman had assaulted him then claimed that he'd knocked her to the ground, being careful to keep his tone sad rather than angry. He allowed tears into his eyes when he described being remanded in custody; it was disconcertingly easy to do.

"Why did imprisonment hurt you so much?"

"Are you mad?" Careful. That was a little too close to anger and he wanted her sympathy, not fear. "Sorry. I still get choked."

"I understand. The reason I ask is that you lived alone. You said during interviews that you had no close friends, so what did you lose when that door was locked?"

"My freedom, my self respect. The ability to go out for a beer when I wanted, pick up a girl, have fun."

"I see. Is that how you get your fun? Down the pub?"

He just glared at her. That didn't deserve an answer.

"What I mean is, you seem more intelligent than most prisoners I've met. I can't imagine you being satisfied with an evening out around a few beers."

She was perceptive this one, better than Batchelor. And she wasn't scared of him, though it would be easy for him to make that change.

"What is it?"

"What?"

"You were smiling. You looked nostalgic. What was the memory?"

"Nothing. Look, do you want to hear about why the charges against me are a load of sh . . . rubbish?"

"Yes. Of course."

He told her about the other attacks based on what he'd read in the papers, nothing else. She made a lot of notes. When he stopped she re-read them with a frown on her face that produced two parallel lines between her eyebrows and made her look a lot older.

"This is very interesting, Wayne. May I call you that?"

He shrugged. His name meant nothing to him.

"Wayne, can I ask you to clarify some points?"

She asked a lot of questions, good ones, and he enjoyed making the links for her and teasing her with snippets of information.

"You'd make a good detective, you know." She smiled as she complimented him.

"Thanks."

"What is it that makes this other man attack and kill women?"

The question took him by surprise. She was asking him for information about Dave and he was sworn to secrecy. But a few hints wouldn't do any harm, would they? It might even impress her.

"Killing them isn't the point, it's just a consequence."

"Go on."

"He's smart, really clever, but life hasn't been good to him. He's too good, under-appreciated."

"Why women, not men?"

He felt the flush start in his neck and burn into his face. Even his hands went hot. He broke eye contact and opened one of the bars of chocolate she had brought.

"Was that a difficult question?"

"No, just a stupid one."

"But men do kill other men and boys as result of sexual assault, don't they."

He felt too warm in the room and slightly sick from the chocolate.

"Could I have some water?"

"Of course."

They waited in silence for it to arrive. He drank it down in one gulp.

"Let's return to this other killer. What do you think motivates him?"

What a good question. He'd asked himself that once a long time ago, but it had ceased to have any significance before he had been able to answer it. He shook his head and gave his first completely open answer.

"I honestly don't know."

She started asking about prison life and his state of mind—routine stuff that he parried with ease.

"One of the guards mentioned to me that a colleague had been murdered—a Mr. Saunders. How did you feel when he was killed?"

He started in surprise, then made himself relax. She had a habit of doing that, throwing in the odd trick question but he was too smart for her.

"I didn't care."

"But you didn't like him, did you?"

"None of us did. He was a bullying prick."

"He died horribly, you know."

He'd heard rumors, of course, and Dave in one of his letters had hinted that it had taken a long time.

"Really?"

"Yes. He was tortured."

She was breaking the rules. She shouldn't be telling him this. Perhaps he'd got to her after all.

"How?"

"With an electric drill." She was half smiling, as if she found the idea intriguing.

"Fuck!" He glanced at her quickly but she didn't seem to object to his language. The warmth from his face spread down his body in a wave.

"The killer worked his way through a whole tool kit."

"Nails?"

"Oh yes. Skewered to his couch."

She was leaning forward. He could see skin between the buttons of her blouse and the heat in his groin became intense.

"And a staple gun. As well as a Stanley knife of course." She tossed the last out as if it was too banal to be worth their interest. He leaned forward, closer to her. Her perfume was light and flowery and he could smell her body beneath it. The skin on her forearms was tanned and covered in soft hair. He was only inches away from being able to stroke it.

She was still smiling as if enjoying the secrets they were sharing.

"Have you ever wondered," she said, "what it would be like to do that? To kill a bully of a man? Pay him back?"

Her lips were moist. She looked excited. He'd heard about these women who hung around prisons because deep down they were aroused by the crimes of the men they visited. Some even married prisoners. He imagined that happening. What would the others say, when they saw him with her?

His left hand strayed beneath the table but she didn't seem to notice. The guard was outside; she'd insisted on privacy and they were quite alone. He touched himself while she carried on smiling at him. Should he reach over and rip that blouse open? Would she cry out for help or lean back with pleasure?

She stood up abruptly, surprising him.

"My time's up. If I don't go now they'll come in and I'd rather that didn't happen."

"Will you come back?"

"Would you like me to?"

He told himself to be careful. No woman could be trusted, Dave had taught him that. But he had Wendy didn't he? Quiet, obedient Wendy whom he had been allowed to share so rarely as a reward. He felt angry. Fuck Dave. He was still in here because he'd screwed up the copy-catting so badly that not even the press had made a connection. He was entitled to his own woman, and if this one fancied him who was Dave to tell him no.

"Maybe, yes, OK."

"You'll need to ask for me to replace Batchelor. Can you do that?"

"No problem. When will you be back?"

"When was your next appointment with him?"

"Day after tomorrow."

"I'll see you then."

And with that, she was gone.

Claire sat down in Fenwick's office in Harlden and rubbed a hand over her face.

"You look shattered."

"It's been a tough week."

"How many times have you seen him?"

"Three. Any more and he would have grown suspicious."

"I wasn't implying you should have done more. This is fantastic." Fenwick tapped a thick report on his desk. "How did you get all this out of him?"

"Don't ask." She closed her eyes for a moment.

"What did you do, Claire?" Fenwick was suddenly concerned.

"You said you were desperate for a lead, didn't you?"

"Yes. But not at any cost." He stood up and closed the door to his office, giving them privacy.

"Oh, don't worry, it wasn't at *any* cost." She sounded bitter.

"What did you do?"

She looked away and shook her head.

"Claire. What happened? You'd better tell me."

"Well, let's just say I'd rather that you didn't have to use my report in evidence."

"Go on."

There was a long pause, then she said, "Promise me this is between us? That you'll never tell anyone else?"

"I promise."

"We indulged in a fantasy game the second time I visited, in which we devised ways of killing people."

She looked up as if daring him to comment. Fenwick kept silent although the implications of what she had done horrified him. If this ever got out her professional reputation, possibly even her career, would be ruined.

"It made him very excited, sexually I mean, and he ejaculated in front of me. I think it was spontaneous."

"Oh, Claire, you poor thing." Fenwick flushed with embarrassment for her.

"It's OK. I'm fine, really."

"Sure you are!" He shook his head in disbelief. "And that was during the second visit?"

"Yes. Afterward, he told me about his childhood, well, his teenage years, how he'd always had a problem climaxing too quickly. I told him I found that arousing and he told me about the women he'd had and what it was like."

"Was he telling the truth?"

"I don't think so. He's very confused about his own sexuality. Something happened to him in puberty. I don't think it was abuse because he has some residual self-esteem, more than if he had been molested. Maybe it was experimentation; whatever, it was mixed up with violence in some way."

"He didn't have a criminal record before his arrest."

"That's what's so bizarre. Perhaps it was S&M, consenting adults, or involving animals. I've known that."

"And I thought I saw filth in my job."

"Oh you do, Andrew, you do."

"And the third interview."

"That could have been difficult. Fortunately I'd had the presence of mind to ask the guard to interrupt us early, otherwise . . ."

"Did he touch you?"

"Yes, but it's all right, don't worry. He held my hands. That's when he told me about his family."

"Are the names in here real do you think?"

"Yes, or very close. It was after he asked me to marry him . . ."

"Claire!"

". . . so I think he was telling the truth. Anyway," she sighed deeply, "the name of the foster home is accurate. I checked."

"You shouldn't have done this."

"Don't be a hypocrite, Andrew. I can tell that you can't wait to get started on all that lovely information."

"So long as the price wasn't too high."

"Look I'm screwed up but I'm OK. He didn't get beneath the surface. A good bath, or ten, and I'll be fine." She stood up to leave. "But Andrew, promise me one thing."

"Yes?"

"Never, ever, let him get out of prison. OK?"

"I promise I will do my utmost to keep him inside forever."

She left. Before the sound of her footsteps had died Fenwick was on the phone to MacIntyre. Five minutes later his driver to London was waiting in the car park and the siren was on before they cleared the gates.

Griffiths waited for Claire to come back. For several days he lived in a warm fantasy that made prison bearable. He didn't even mind that Dave hadn't written. There was someone on the outside now who believed he was innocent, would fight for his appeal and marry him on his release. It didn't matter that she was older, in fact he loved the idea. She would teach him to be slow.

After a week he began to doubt. At first he thought maybe she was ill, or hurt in an accident, but when Batchelor turned up for their regular appointment and would say nothing about her, he began to suspect the truth. She was gone. Like all women she had opened him up and rammed a knife into his heart. Immediately his fantasies changed and he wanted her dead.

CHAPTER TWENTY-THREE

On the way to London Fenwick read the report until he felt car sick, and even then he re-read key passages in snatches. When the journey slowed in heavy traffic he made notes, summarizing the lines of inquiry that had been opened by Claire's interviews. MacIntyre was waiting for him, which told Fenwick that the investigation into Lucinda's murder was making little progress.

"You said that you'd rather not have to disclose the source of this information so Knotty's going to help you fill out Griffiths' background."

Constable Knots was used to receiving and following oblique instructions without question. He was a tall, gangly young man with a face that resembled a joint of uncooked meat into which two beady blue eyes had been stamped. He had a crop of unerrupted spots on his forehead and something Fenwick imagined was rather nasty under a plaster on his jaw. His mum was probably proud of him but Fenwick's heart sank at the thought of sharing long hours of investigation with an officer who looked as if he'd only just started wearing long trousers.

"Griffiths admits to growing up somewhere north of Leicester with a woman he called Auntie, after his mum went off with a lorry driver.

"He was five when she left. He never knew who his father was and Auntie didn't have a name. There were a lot of other children in the house so perhaps she was no more than a childminder who was dumped on. Still, we have a geographic area so we can try to find his primary school, assuming he didn't change his name."

Knotty made notes in his book and looked up expectantly for more.

"He went to school for about a year, until one day he came home and Auntie wasn't there. Someone from Social Services was and he ended up in a children's home, again he thinks it was in Leicester. He was there for three years, then he was moved on to a facility between Telford and Shrewsbury. He gave our interviewer an address and the name of the principal: Mr. Custer. They either called him cowardly Custer or the General, depending on their mood.

"This is where things become more interesting. He was fostered when he was about fifteen and the interviewer thinks that the fostering is significant. He revealed so little about it, not even the name of the family or whether there were other children. Whenever the subject came up he became agitated and evasive. It's probably our best chance of finding any teenage companions."

"Is his story to Doctor Batchelor about his foster parents drowning a lie?"

"Parts of it were certainly lies. We need to try and find them. I think he gave us enough information to trace their address. He used to travel to school by bus, a number 69, the number made him laugh. It was a half-hour walk from his home to the bus stop, then a forty-five-minute journey into Telford. He said that he had to walk whatever the weather and if the river flooded he had to make a detour of a mile over a high bridge."

Knotty was scribbling madly now. He pushed the tip of his tongue between his teeth when he concentrated, making him look about sixteen.

"The rest of the report is about his work as a software developer, most of which is already on file."

"Knotty's been on to the personnel department of the company where he worked in Telford. Their Accounts department have found details of the bank they sent his money to but he closed the account shortly after he left the company." MacIntyre passed the report over.

"Why did he leave?"

"He was asked to. A female colleague alleged that he made an unwelcome pass after a group of them went out drinking together. His mates stood up for him, said the girl was drunk and out of order and that Griffiths simply tried to help her find a taxi. But it was enough for someone in HR to call his previous employer. His references were false. Apparently they hadn't bothered to check when he joined."

"Consistent. This is a man who invents his past as he goes along."

"Risky though."

"Not necessarily, he got away with it until the complaint. What did he do after he left?"

"IT contract work as far as we can tell. And we don't know why he ended up in Sussex, without a job or permanent address."

MacIntyre sent Knotty away while he brought Fenwick up to date with developments in Wales and closer to home.

"Although the prints on the knife link to Lucinda's murder we can't prove it beyond reasonable doubt. They were only on a bar stool and tests on her wounds have been inconclusive. Bottom line, we need to build a stronger case. The Home Office pathologist is trying to match bite marks from both girls. If he can, that will be conclusive but right now we're no closer to tracing Killer B.

"We've asked to be alerted on all serious crimes against women anywhere in the country. There have been three serious sexual assaults in the UK in the past ten days but none of the physical descriptions match our man."

"Have you checked the prints from the knife against those we lifted from Nightingale's flat?"

"No . . ." the Superintendent paused and suppressed a sigh, "but I'll get someone onto it."

Fenwick passed the time he spent waiting for Knotty's return by sitting in on MacIntyre's case conference and emerged depressed by the lack of progress. The constable found him at lunchtime, his acne glowing pink in excitement.

"I've found the school and the children's home. Mr. Custer has retired but his successor was very helpful. We know the name of his foster parents and where they lived. We tried ringing but some woman said she'd never heard of them. She's been renting the house for a year, and it had been let before her."

"And the foster family's name?" Fenwick knew he was grinning like an idiot but he didn't care.

"Smith." Knotty winced at his boss's expression.

Fenwick watched Knotty's delight fade. Something in his expression reminded him of his son, Chris, and he said, more positively than he felt.

"But this is progress. We have an address, a family to trace and a school to visit. Did the Smiths have any children?"

"Yes, a son, a bit older than Griffiths called David."

"We need to find out everything we can about Mr. David

Smith and his parents. Get on to it. I think I'd like to interview Custer personally."

MacIntyre was not supportive of the idea.

"It's a long way to go for what will probably be very little. Send Knotty. He's good at digging and you're more use here."

"I'd rather go myself."

Fenwick couldn't explain to MacIntyre the urge he had to visit the place in which Griffiths had spent some of his childhood. It wasn't the sort of thing a chief inspector should do, charge half way across England on a lead ten years old, particularly if that chief inspector was on attachment to the Met, where his actions would be under double scrutiny. In the end, Fenwick's stubbornness wore the Superintendent down but he gave in with bad grace.

Fenwick dismissed MacIntyre's irritation as he raced up the M1 in an unmarked police car with the obedient Knotty at his side. As soon as the Superintendent established a stronger link between the attack in Wales and Lucinda's murder he would become disinterested in the Griffiths connection again. Unless he found something substantive as a result of Claire's work no effort would be spent finding Nightingale and protecting her from Killer B. This trip was his last hope. If David Smith was Killer B he would almost certainly be long gone, but something of him would be there, imprinted in the soil, and Knotty would never find it.

They were shown only average courtesy at Telford Police Station. There was a major case on, to judge by the atmosphere, and visitors from down south were an unwelcome distraction. Knotty returned from the canteen to the tiny office they'd been given with fresh coffee and the latest gossip.

"They had a murder and an attempted murder a week ago. A passenger suddenly went berserk or something and attacked a taxi driver and his girlfriend. Killed the driver but the girl survived. It's caused a helluva stink. Apparently he made an emergency call but it took them ages to find him and by then he was well dead."

"Really." Fenwick gave him one of his "keep your nose out of other people's business" looks and tapped a fax he'd just received. "Concentrate on that and keep your head down, son. It's what little we have on David Smith."

And sketchy it was. David Smith had been born twenty-seven years before in Cressage, ten miles from Telford. His schooldays had been unremarkable although a spell of illness in his early teens had put him over a year behind. Fenwick completed some quick mental arithmetic. He and Griffiths could have been classmates, just. He left school shortly after his eighteenth birthday, without completing his A-levels, though he had done well in his earlier exams and had gained a top grade in computer studies.

Fenwick called the research officer at the Met for the name of the mate who'd stood up for Griffiths when he'd been accused of sexual harassment. Two hours later he had confirmation that the name on file was David Smith and a circle closed.

"Knotty, I want you to trace Mr. and Mrs. Smith. I'm going to interview Custer. Meet me back here afterward and we'll decide what to do next."

His interview with Custer was disappointing. The man remembered Griffiths as an introverted child with few friends. He hadn't been in any real trouble, in fact the only time he could recall him being punished had been as the result of a prank by other boys where he'd been the fall guy.

"So there was nothing strange about him in any way?"

"No. I've told you, Chief Inspector, he was a quiet lad who didn't have many friends. I can't imagine him doing any of the crimes you describe. He blushed if a girl so much as looked at him."

"And educationally?"

"About average but a wizard on computers. We didn't have any in the home but they had a few at his school and he'd stay for computer class. That's really what led to him being fostered out."

"Why?"

"There was another boy in the computer studies group older than Wayne, who befriended him and eventually persuaded his parents to apply to foster him."

"Mr. and Mrs. Smith?"

Custer nodded and another question-mark disappeared from Fenwick's mind.

"Yes. They weren't on any approved list but the father was a local civil servant of some sort and his wife had been a nurse. They were allowed to foster Wayne for a trial period, then it was extended. I was delighted for the boy."

Fenwick called Knotty and told him to find Smith senior's employer but drove back to the station dissatisfied. His assumptions were being confirmed but he'd expected a bigger breakthrough. Knotty was waiting for him with equal disappointment.

"There's no trace of Smith senior or his wife since they moved away from Cressage. According to the land registry they still own a house there but it's rented out. I've been on to the letting agents and they've confirmed that it was put on their books eight years ago."

"By the father?"

"I didn't ask. I assume so."

"Never assume. Call them back and confirm the exact details. What about Smith's employer?"

"He worked in the County Surveyor's department for twenty-three years before resigning ten years ago and I did manage to find out details of the account they paid his salary into. The building society might have an address." He looked up expectantly but Fenwick just nodded as if that was routine. For Knotty it had been close to brilliance.

"Why did he resign?"

"No idea. I mean, I didn't ask, sir. I'll get right onto it." Knotty was beginning to realize that Fenwick didn't believe in loose ends because they were what tripped you up.

"See that you do." Fenwick shook his head at the constable's retreating back and went in search of a map to help him find his way to the Smiths' last known address.

The journey was a fruitless one. Janine Gray, the current tenant, explained that she and her husband knew nothing about the owners and had never met them. Fenwick wasn't invited inside and reference to an investigation into serious crimes failed to win her cooperation. Frustrated, he turned the car around and headed back to Telford, feeling foolish for having made the journey instead of spending his time in meaningful strategy conferences with senior officers in London. It was what MacIntyre would expect and he was out of line. But instead of returning to the station he contacted Knotty on his radio, found out the address of the building society and drove there himself, propelled by a desire for action, not thought. Thinking was getting him nowhere.

The Coalbrook and Watersmere Building Society had resisted demutualization, preferring to remain a service for its members and support to the local community. It had three branches and a very loyal customer base.

Fenwick was learning all this and more as he listened to the

Chief Executive explain, at length, why he wasn't going to reveal any of his customers' private financial information to the police without proper authority. Even the words rape and serial murder failed to have any effect and Fenwick left after a fruitless ten minutes just as the branch was closing for the day.

He stalked off to find the car, oblivious to his surroundings, so he didn't notice a rather breathless woman trotting alongside him for some time. When he did, he stopped abruptly and so did she.

"Can I help you?"

The woman had been serving behind the counter in the Society when he'd entered and announced himself. He hadn't paid her much attention, noting only that she was wearing a twinset like one he'd bought his mother as a Christmas present. She looked over her shoulder furtively then beckoned him a little closer.

"I may be able to help you," she said in a stage whisper, "but not here. There's a tea shop over by the traffic lights, the Black Kettle. I'll see you there." Then she scuttled off, leaving Fenwick to stare after her and wonder whether he'd been mistaken for somebody else.

She was waiting for him at a corner table farthest from the door. A pot of tea for two and a plate of biscuits were being set before her as he walked in.

"Emily," she said thrusting out a bird-like hand. "Emily Spinning."

He took her hand and shook it once.

"I'm D—"

"Ssh, yes, I know who you are. Sit down." She glanced around as if suspecting eavesdroppers but they were on their own. "You came to see Mr. Winkworth about a customer, David Smith."

"How do you know that?"

"The walls are very thin, Chief Inspector. We have few secrets at the Coalbrook and Watersmere. Tea?"

"You said you might be able to help me?"

"Yes, but if Mr. Winkworth finds out I'll be in terrible trouble."

"I see. Well look, I don't wish to encourage you in anything that might . . ."

"Oh shush, it's all right. As soon as I heard you were a policeman, I knew it would be about poor Mr. Smith."

Fenwick sipped his tea and did his best to look calm.

"Go on."

"I've worked at the Society for twenty-four years, ever since I left school, and David Smith senior was one of my customers. His son was named after him. Mr. Smith was always nice to me, even when I was new and used to get into a bit of a fumble. Aren't you going to make notes?"

"Of course." Fenwick pulled out a rarely used notebook and took down details of her name, address and, after much twittering, her age.

"So you knew Mr. Smith. What sort of man was he?"

"Oh quiet, shy. Not given to chatter but he always had a smile and a kind word for me."

"Did you know his son?"

"Young David? Not really. In the early years he used to come in to the branch with his father but that stopped. I think there was a bit of trouble."

"What sort of trouble?"

"He was ill or something and away from home for a long while. I know because Mr. Smith mentioned that it put his schooling back."

"Why did you think my visit had something to do with Mr. Smith?"

"He had his salary paid into our instant access account and he had a savings account too. A very steady man, Mr. Smith. Once a month he'd come in to have his passbooks updated. He didn't need to but he said he liked things regular. Well, one month, it would be roughly fifteen years ago I think, he comes in and withdraws three hundred pounds in cash!"

"I don't see anything unusual about that."

"It was a lot of money, Chief Inspector, and it wasn't just that once. Every month he came in and withdrew three hundred. His deposit account went from several thousands to nothing over the years."

"And what did you conclude from this, Miss Spinning?"

"I worried about it because he'd been such a careful saver up until then. And I thought, perhaps he's started gambling. I sort of hinted at it once when he came in but he made it clear he'd never placed a bet in his life. So then I thought it must be a mistress! But I saw him and Mrs. Smith together and I couldn't believe that either. So in the end I thought, it's blackmail."

She delivered her last word with a verbal flourish and looked expectantly at Fenwick, who tried to hide his disappointment.

"An interesting theory, Miss Spinning."

"Emily, please. What do you think?"

"Do you have any corroborative evidence?"

She looked at him blankly.

"Proof?" he asked, hoping he didn't sound as impatient as he felt.

"Well no, not really but he started to look very worried."

"Money worries?"

"I don't think so. He'd just paid off a twenty-five-year mortgage and had a decent job with the Council."

Fenwick finished his tea and stood to leave.

"Don't go yet. What are you going to do?"

"Try to find Mr. Smith, of course, and his wife."

She looked at him darkly but he didn't have time to worry about her disappointment.

"You don't think he's dead then?"

"What!" He sat down abruptly. "Why should that be the case?"

"I don't know. Just a feeling. If he had been blackmailed then it would make sense if he killed himself when the money ran out."

"But you've just told me that he owned his own house."

"I know but why else would he disappear? He stopped coming in suddenly one summer. There were some letters and phone calls, then nothing."

"Perhaps he and his wife left the area."

"Then he would have closed his account—very particular like that was Mr. Smith."

"I see; well there's certainly a lot of food for thought here, er, Emily."

"Good. I hope he's alive and that you find him. He was a nice man."

"Any idea where I should look?"

"Start with his brother, Frederick. They didn't get on, in fact I heard they wouldn't even speak to each other, but he's kin so it's worth a shot."

"I didn't know he had a brother. Do you know where he lives?"

"Used to have a house in Elm Street. Assisted. Never did a full day's work in his life, that man. Chalk and cheese those brothers were. Poor Mr. Smith."

Fenwick paid for their tea and left but Emily ran out after him.

"If you do find him, will you give him my very best, from Emily, and tell him I still work, you know, at the Society."

"Of course I will."

Fenwick walked the short distance to Elm Street and found Frederick Smith's house. Paint was flaking from the windows and there was an old washing machine on the front lawn keeping company with three cars in various stages of disassembly. He could hear a radio blasting from a shed at the back of the property and followed the noise.

A short, squat man was bent over a car battery on a bench.

"Mr. Smith?"

"Who wants him?" The man didn't bother to turn around.

"Detective Chief Inspector Fenwick, Harlden CID."

The man froze for an instant then carried on working with studied casualness.

"What do you want?"

"To talk to you for a few minutes about David Smith."

That brought him round. Fenwick stared at the blotched face boasting three or four days of stubble and was surprised to see the mouth smile.

"Well, well. At last. What do you need to know?"

"Where to find him."

"Hah!" The man laughed and spat into the greasy dust at his feet. "Buggered if I know. Haven't seen him around here for a couple of years. Good riddance."

"Could you be more precise about when you last saw him?"

Smith scratched an inch of bare flesh between his T-shirt and jeans, leaving a black mark on the skin.

"Must have been . . . around Christmas three years ago. He was with a mate in some shopping center. Can't remember where."

"You saw your brother three years ago?"

"No, I'm talking about his son, David. Haven't seen me brother for longer than that."

"Did you speak with your nephew?"

"What? You must be joking. Soon as the bastard saw me he legged it. He knew what he'd get from me if I caught him."

"And what would that be?"

Smith shut his mouth and it twisted into a bitter grin.

"Never you mind. That's family business."

"You say he was with a mate, male or female?"

"Young lad. The one they took in. Thick as thieves they were."

"Wayne Griffiths?"

"If you say so. Never knew his name."

"You assumed that I wanted to find the son not the father, why?"

But Smith went quiet and refused to say any more no matter how hard Fenwick pushed him. In the end, he decided he was wasting his time.

"If you remember anything at all, please call me on this number. It's important."

"What's he done then?"

"I can't tell you that. We're just anxious to find him. He may have information that would be helpful." Fenwick opened his scruffy notebook again and Smith looked at him with deep suspicion.

"What's that for?"

"Just need to confirm your name and address, sir."

Smith rattled them off quickly, keen to see him go.

"And you live here with . . ."

"My wife, June."

"Any children?"

Smith flushed and looked down at his workbench.

"We live on our own."

"But you do have children?"

"I don't see it's relevant."

"Just a formality." Fenwick watched a vein at the side of the man's head pulse.

"One daughter, Wendy."

"Age?"

Smith rubbed his forehead, leaving a slimy trail of oil.

"Twenty-three, I think. Haven't seen her for a while."

"Did Wendy know her cousin or Wayne Griffiths well?"

"None of your fucking business." Smith took a step forward, his body pumped, his face red. "Now get out of my house and don't come back without a warrant."

Fenwick wrote up his slim reports and wondered what his superiors would think about the flimsy results of a day of chief inspector's time. Not a lot probably, but at least he was starting to frame questions that would take his investigation further. Why had Fred Smith jumped to the conclusion that he was there about David Smith junior? And why had he said "at last"?

He rang Emily Spinning and waited obediently while she put a video in to record *Eastenders*.

"Right, there, I'm all set, Chief Inspector. How can I help?"

"I spoke to Frederick Smith."

"Ah. What did I tell you?"

"He mentioned that he had a daughter."

"Oh yes, Wendy. Nice girl. Looked the image of her mother. Haven't seen her for years. Always wanted to be a nurse."

"Do you recall anything about Wendy's childhood? How well did she know Mr. and Mrs. David Smith?"

"Gosh. You're taking me back now. Let me think . . ." There was a long moment's silence. "I could be wrong but I think her uncle and aunt used to take her on holiday. They had nice summer holidays at a chalet they'd bought years before out in the country. I think Wendy went with them before the two brothers fell out."

That was all she could remember. Fenwick left her to her television and checked his watch. He just had time to call the children before bed. Knotty came in as he was blowing Bess a kiss and did a hasty about turn. Fenwick called him back.

"Before you start I want you to listen to something. Sit down and relax, man."

Knotty folded his long, gangly frame onto a convenient chair. He looked like a stick insect with a weird fungus invading its face. The acne had taken a turn for the worse during the day.

"Here are the facts as we know them about the Smiths: Mr. and Mrs. Smith had a son, David, who is now twenty-seven years old. They fostered Wayne Griffiths ten years ago, when he was fifteen. He and David junior were in the same class at school and were apparently mates. Mr. Smith senior withdrew £300:00 in cash every month for four years up to the point at which he disappeared. He had a major falling out with his brother, Fred, even though previously he'd been generous enough to take his niece, Wendy, on summer holidays with them. Now what does that suggest to you?"

Constable Knots stared at him blankly. Fenwick waited. Intimidated by the silence the poor man eventually forced himself to speak.

"Ah, that we haven't got much to go on, sir?"

Fenwick grimaced wearily.

"Possibly, but we have got the first pieces of a jigsaw, we just don't know what picture to make yet. We need to create a credible hypothesis based on the facts as we know them, which might then lead us to ask further questions in order to test our assumptions and complete the pattern."

Blankness changed to confusion. Fenwick missed Cooper and Nightingale. His sergeants would be ready with equal measures of skepticism and theories of their own. He sighed deeply and confusion morphed into despondency on Knotty's face.

"Go and get me some fresh coffee, black, no sugar. Leave your reports with me."

Knots might not be the brightest penny in the jar but he was quick. Fenwick had only just finished reading the file when he returned with a tray.

"Supper, sir. Thought we might be here for a while. Chicken and ham pie or sausage roll?" Fenwick chose the pie and Knotty's facc brightened.

He ate as he wrote while Knotty chewed as quietly as he could.

"Right, Knotty, this is our work for tomorrow."

Constable Knots swallowed and read the notes with his mouth half open.

Hypothesis: David Smith Jnr met Wayne Griffiths in computer class, became significant influence on him.

Persuades parents to foster Griffiths.

They engage in series of (sexual) minor crimes and/or assault of Wendy Smith.

Frederick Smith finds out and blackmails brother.

QUESTIONS / ACTIONS:

1. Obtain doctor's records for the Smith family.
2. Try for warrant for Frederick and David Smiths' financial records.

3. Interviews re David Smith (snr/jnr)—work, clubs, neighbors, etc.
4. Is there a pattern in minor crime/sexual assaults in the local area at the time they lived here?
5. Find Wendy Smith. We know her parents, age and vocation—nurse.
6. Speak to profiler re background of boys and Wendy.

"Blimey!"

Fenwick knew that he was showing off, and to the least demanding of audiences, but the reaction vindicated his use of the day. Had he sent Knots to do this work on his own they would be no further forward.

"You can start drawing up a list of interviews on question three."

"Where are you going, sir, if you don't mind my asking?"

"To find a WPC and re-visit the Smith's old house. I'll see you back here."

CHAPTER TWENTY-FOUR

For two days he fought the urge to rampage through Telford in revenge for the girl's survival. He'd been unable to rationalize the fact that she'd managed to outwit him by playing dead long enough for the taxi driver to return and act the hero. When the desire for action became too great he paced the hills around the cottage from sunup to sunset, trying to drive the memory from his mind. Twice now he had failed to complete the task that he'd set for himself. It was all Griffiths' fault. He'd jinxed him with his stupid letters and half-arsed ideas.

The police still hadn't linked the girl he'd killed in London to Griffiths' rapes. He'd taken the finger, just like he'd done with the bitch in Wales who had refused to die, so why hadn't they made the connection? Because they were stupid, that's why. He'd have to draw them a fucking map! But he didn't want to resort to sending letters again.

As he ran up one hill and then the next, forcing the blood to flow fast, a new idea began to develop. At the top of the highest rise he paused and drew in long breaths. It was extraordinarily simple. What if he just left Griffiths to rot in jail? He'd been stupid enough to get caught, let him pay for it. Wayne had never been more than an appreciative audience. Why had he saddled himself with such a loser in the first place? Smith couldn't admit to himself that adulation from someone like Griffiths had once mattered. As he walked back to the cottage the limits he felt he'd allowed Griffiths to build around his life dissolved.

He would do what *he* wanted to do in his own way and he would start with a quick visit to Wendy. It usually perked him up and the cottage was starting to drive him mad again, as it always did after a few days. He couldn't bear to be enclosed in one place for long. Constant movement about the country was the only way in which he could ease the tension that was now inside him all the time.

He arrived unannounced and woke Wendy from sleep.

"Any letters?"

He wanted to stop the postal service and destroy all links with Griffiths.

"I haven't been. You know I can't when I'm on nights."

"You don't have to sleep all fucking day do you? Lazy bitch."

"I've not been feeling too good. In fact, I've been quite ill."

"Weak as dishwater you are. No stamina. Look, I want to know if I've got mail. Sort it."

She struggled out of bed to find him a beer and food.

"I'll go tomorrow." There was a pause and she picked at a dry bit of skin on the end of her sharp nose, a habit he hated. He'd kill her for it one of these days. "How long are you here for?"

"Don't know. I'm working on a project. Might take a while."

"What sort of project?"

"None of your business."

"Oh."

That was it. End of conversation. She left a lot to be desired but what little spirit she'd been born with had been beaten out of her by her old man. He considered her greatest assets her lack of imagination and low intellect.

The next morning he woke up with a clear sense of purpose.

Directionless rage had been superseded by excitement for a plan so daring it left him breathless at his own audacity. He exercised for half an hour, feeling strong and powerful again, and tried to balance his desire to hunt down the policewoman with the decision he'd made overnight to go after the taxi girl a second time. Both were compelling but to contemplate killing specific victims was a new experience.

It was ten years since he'd first witnessed death and enjoyed that exquisite feeling of liberation. Despite the impact of seeing life expire close up, it had taken him seven years to cross the line and kill, and then it had been by accident. Only afterward, when he'd pulled away from her and seen the bloodshot eyes and gorged tongue, had he realized what he'd done.

After his first kill the others were easier but infrequent at first. He'd remained cautious, changing location frequently to avoid creating a pattern. The fringes of cities were places that bestowed anonymity and had an acceptance of random violence. This year he'd killed twice within a month, a pace that he found exhilarating. But he'd also failed to kill twice, he reminded himself bitterly.

After Wendy had left he wasted an hour trying to plan the taxi girl's death before giving up as there were too many unknowns. He would tackle it the way he did best, going prepared for every eventuality and then relying on instinct and opportunity. He would succeed despite the high risk.

With renewed confidence he opened up the files he'd extracted from the policewoman's computer. As she had gone online in an Internet café the majority of the stuff was irrelevant. For the rest of the day he trawled through hundreds of electronic files, his mood of elation dying. When Wendy returned from work he slapped her about a bit for making too much noise then bundled the rest of the printouts, his laptop and discs into a bag.

As soon as she'd fed and bedded him he would leave. The thought of another night with her locked up in the flat suddenly nauseated him.

It was late evening when he drove away. During the ride home he thought about the implications of abandoning Griffiths. He might talk. It was unlikely but he had to be prepared. That would mean selling the house and cottage and moving. Abroad would be good. Wendy would have to be disposed of, but that would be at the last minute, in case he needed her beforehand. The idea of wiping out the remnants of his past and starting over was appealing. He'd managed to do so with his parents' lives, so his own should be easy.

The thought triggered an old memory and with it unease. Had he eliminated every trace of them? Nothing was left at the cottage but what about at the old family house? He couldn't be certain that he'd been as thorough back then. The idea grew into an obsessive need to check and be sure. It was important to him that every sign of his existence should be eradicated, otherwise the fresh start he wanted would be tainted. On impulse he decided to visit the house that night, to be sure that all traces of the Smith family had been destroyed.

Janine switched off the TV and put the guard around the fire. Even in the middle of summer the house felt damp. It was isolated and old fashioned but all they could afford. Ever since that policeman had called she'd felt unsettled. Carl had picked up on her mood and grizzled from the time he woke from his nap to when she put him down for the night.

Janine missed her husband with a passion when he was on long haul in Europe. On top of that she was nervous out here on her own. When it grew dark she decided to go to bed early and watch TV. The doors were bolted but the old sash windows were easy to open. All someone needed to do was break the glass and flick the catch. She snuggled down under the covers.

He was hiding outside, excited and too impatient to wait for morning. He'd seen some ugly cows in his time but the bitch in there won the prize. He would be doing the world a service if he put her out of her misery. At least she went to bed at a decent hour. Not long now and it would be safe to go in. He told himself that he was only going to search for anything of his father's, stuff he should have burned long ago. If she stayed asleep, and if he didn't need to go into the bedroom, then he wouldn't do anything. Or so he tried to convince himself as he sucked deeply on his cigarette but his free hand found the new knife lying snug in the pocket of his jeans. He stroked its warm smoothness and thought how different it became with the blade out.

"Come on, Constable, it's gone eight o'clock. I'm pushing my luck calling this late as it is. I thought you said you knew a short cut?"

"I did, I mean I do, sir, but the signpost was down. The river's over there so I just need to take the next right."

Fenwick breathed slowly to calm his irritation. It was always unwise to lose one's temper, more so when on strange territory and particularly with a woman. He also had to remember that *she* was doing *him* a favor. Constable Powell had been about to go off duty when he'd found her in the canteen and told her his problem.

"It's just up there on the right."

She steered the patrol car down a lane and turned the car into the drive. The house was in darkness.

"Great, just what we need. She's gone to bed."

"Maybe she's watching TV without the lights on."

They waited a long time in the porch then rang the doorbell again. Janine opened the door a crack, saw the policewoman's uniform and opened it wide.

"Bill?" she said, her face full of unspoken horror for her husband. Constable Powell calmed her and introduced them, explaining that their visit was urgent.

"Come in then, but for heaven's sake be quiet. Carl's a light sleeper."

She led them into the kitchen.

"What do you want?"

There was defensiveness in her voice that put Fenwick on immediate alert.

"Have you found any papers, anything at all that might have been left behind by the owners?"

"I told you before, nothing. There must've been loads of tenants before us. If there'd been anything they would've passed it to the agents."

"What about the loft?"

"I can't believe there'd be anything up there after all these years."

"Would you mind if we checked? And in the shed and garage. You'd be amazed what people forget."

"Well you can look outside as long as you're quiet but I'm not having you rummaging around upstairs. You'll wake Carl."

Robyn Powell went to search the outbuildings. When they were on their own Fenwick's face hardened.

"Mrs. Gray," she started at his change of tone. "I'm not in the least interested in what your husband is up to."

She was bone white now, staring at him as if he were a mind reader.

"I want to catch a killer, a nasty vicious man who tortures

his victims before he kills them. If there's any trace of him left in this house I want to find it and I won't stop until I've searched. If you deny me now I'll simply return with a warrant and then it'll be all over, won't it?"

"And you promise not to tell?"

"About what?"

The poor woman looked as if she was about to be sick. It was time to try sympathy.

"Look," he said with a sad smile, "you can't undo the fact that I'm here. If you help me I won't personally say anything about what I may see, OK?"

"And your colleague?"

"I can't speak for her. So if we're going to look upstairs we should do it now while she's busy."

Janine rubbed her head in worry, but she went to a kitchen drawer and found a set of keys.

"You'll have to go up there, I hate that ladder. Give me a minute."

On the count of ten he went to find her.

She'd spread a duvet cover and dressing gown over piles of cartons. He could read names of popular brands of cigarettes in the gap between one cover and the next and sighed with relief. Only petty smuggling. He'd been afraid it would be drugs. If it had been, his promise would have meant little.

The attic was almost empty. He took a builder's light from a hook and crawled forward on rough flooring, catching his knee on a raised nail as he did so. His trousers tore and he felt a stab of pain as it broke the skin.

"Bugger! Why is it always this knee?"

Muttering, he crawled forward, feeling a bigger fool by the second. He saw a battered suitcase, a bin liner and a box that said

"A4 paper" on the side. The suitcase held clothes that reeked of mothballs, the bin liner old curtains, but when he opened the box he found a photograph in a frame on top.

"Could you give me a hand? I'm going to wrap something in a curtain and lower it to you. Got it?"

"Yes; you're bleeding, and you've wrecked your trousers. I hope this is worth it."

"So do I. Now I need you to sign a paper and it will say that you gave this to me willingly."

"You're joking!"

"It will be a lot simpler and one good turn deserves another."

She signed grudgingly, hating him with her eyes but he didn't care.

Constable Powell was waiting for them downstairs. On the way to the car she turned to Fenwick.

"There's something funny going on there, Chief Inspector. She was so nervous."

"What do you think it is?"

"While I was outside I had a good poke around and there were dozens of empty cardboard boxes, the sort you see wholesale cigarettes in. Her husband's a lorry driver isn't he?"

"Uh-huh."

"Well then. What do you think?"

"I think that you're smart. Make sure you put all that in your report."

"You don't want to handle it?"

"Not my patch, not my case and you deserve the credit," he smiled into the darkness.

He waited for the lights of the police car to disappear then tried to decide what to do. The man had been carrying something and he'd worked out what it might be. A box had turned up from his dad's office one day and he'd put it to one side to deal with later. He'd burned so much stuff that he could not believe he had forgotten the box.

On impulse he wheeled his bike out into the lane. He wasn't used to being out of control and he needed to find out why the police had been at the house. The car had disappeared by the time he was on the main road but he guessed that it had gone toward Telford and caught up within minutes. They went into the Police Station but the woman was back out again almost immediately. He let her go and waited for the man.

It proved to be a long wait. At eleven o'clock he reappeared carrying an overnight bag. Another man was with him, much younger, with acne. They kept on foot so he left the bike and fell in behind them, used to being discreet when he needed to be.

The street was empty and he could hear stray strands of their conversation.

". . . a walk will do us good, Knotty. It's only half a mile."

"But sir, my blisters!"

"Don't whinge."

They stopped outside a B&B and the young one started up the path.

"This is it?" the older man asked.

"Yes, sir. The hotels were so expensive."

"Very well. Go on."

The door was answered at once by a woman.

"Ah, Chief Inspector Fenwick. We've been expecting you. The police are *always* welcome here. Come in. You'll find us a home away from home. London, wasn't it?"

They went inside and the door closed, leaving him in the dark. A chief inspector from London, and at his old house. It could just be a coincidence but if it was, why had he taken the box away with him? And the name, it rang a bell but from where and when?

During his ride back to the hills he almost convinced himself that his fears were groundless. The police could have no idea of his existence or of what he'd done and planned to do. In his whole life they had rarely come close to him, well except that once all those years ago but since then he'd become much smarter. They had nothing on him. But that man Fenwick had visited the house. It proved that his instinct to make a complete break from the past and start all over again had been right. He was always right.

Constable Powell had revised her opinion of Fenwick. At first she had thought him an arrogant southerner, issuing orders and expecting a driver to be produced for him at the drop of a hat. She still thought he was arrogant but he'd allowed her to take credit for the idea to get a search warrant for the old Smith house. He had a nice smile and attractive eyes, yet he didn't behave as if everything in a skirt should fancy him, which most men did in her experience. So she was pleased when the Duty Sergeant told her that Fenwick had asked for her specifically. She ignored the catcalls and wolf-whistles that greeted this revelation and went to find him. He'd been given a pokey office but didn't seem to mind, and he'd taped up A1 pages from a flip chart all around the walls.

"Ah, Robyn, excellent, they found you. This is Constable Knots, Knotty to his friends. Knotty, this is Robyn Powell. She helped me at the Smith's house last night and is going to work with us. Here's a list of what we found in the box, plus copies of relevant photographs."

"That was quick work, sir." Robyn checked her watch. It was only eight o'clock. They had brought the box in less than twelve hours before and at some stage he must have eaten and slept. Fenwick ignored her remark and read aloud.

"One photograph of three people, presumably Mr. and Mrs. Smith and David. He looks about twelve. I'm having the image aged so that we can compare it with the e-fits in London.

"There's a desk diary but the only entries appear to be work appointments. One bit of luck, his doctor's name and phone number are listed at the back. That's for you, Knotty. Two magazines on coarse fishing and a draft letter of complaint to his son's school. I don't know if it was ever sent but it suggests that the headmistress and teachers might remember him."

"What was he complaining about?"

"His son had been excluded from the school drama society for no good reason. There's a copy for you, Knotty."

"Not a lot for all the trouble we went to." Constable Powell sounded disappointed.

"Possibly," Fenwick masked his irritation at Robyn's lack of enthusiasm, "but the box was covered in prints and my betting is that one of them is David Smith's. I'm sending it to London to be checked.

"Now, today's challenges. Robyn, I want you to go through unsolved sex crimes dating from ten years ago, looking for any that are in a ten-mile radius of where David Smith lived and went to school."

Her face fell.

"I know. There'll be a lot but the search area should help you focus."

"And what am I looking for?"

"Patterns. My theory is based on the profilers' reports that Killer B, possibly Smith, and Griffiths might have engaged in juvenile minor crimes—peeping Tom, indecent exposure, perhaps assault. According to the profiles it's unusual for a serial sex offender to start straight in with rape and murder. And before you ask *why* I need to know, it's for two reasons. First, I'm looking for anything that suggests two perpetrators, and secondly, Smith has disappeared, so we are looking for any clue as to where he might be."

"Do you think there's a connection to our murder here, the taxi driver?" Robyn asked and Knotty tried to hide a smile, unsuccessfully.

"Don't know, but it's a coincidence that I am going to talk to London about. We'll meet back here at six. If you find anything interesting call me."

There was an air of skepticism in the room that Fenwick could sense like a damp fog around him.

"Look, you may think this is daft and I'm sure you think it odd that a chief inspector is up here with you on this sort of background work but we have to start somewhere and I'm more valuable here than in London. Superintendent MacIntyre still has more than thirty officers on the case, not including the local constabulary in Wales. But, and this is important," he paused and looked them both in the eye, "they haven't got a *single* live lead. We have to cover every angle to find this man before he attacks again."

"Why are you so sure he'll do that?" The question from Robyn was respectful rather than doubting and Fenwick relaxed. Officers who felt they were doomed to a wild goose chase were never as committed as those at the center, except for Nightingale of course. She was dedicated even when she went to fetch coffee. Thinking of her brought a hard knot of stress to his throat, and there was increased urgency in his tone when he told them his fears about escalating violence with Nightingale as a target.

"You worked with her. I read about the case. The press made her sound like a hero."

"She's exceptional but she's on leave of absence and we have no idea where so we can't put her into protection. We're doing this for her, and for all the other young women who have had the misfortune to meet Killer B."

He had no desire to share with them his difficult conversation with MacIntyre first thing that morning, nor to admit how far out on a limb he'd had to climb to justify another day away. It was true that MacIntyre had a large team but the Superintendent had asked for him to be seconded to help with the central direction and management of the investigation. That morning when Fenwick had called him, he'd made it very clear that he did not approve of him gallivanting about the country on a whim.

Fenwick put the thought from his mind and he went to find the SIO in charge of the taxi driver murder and assault on Virginia Matthews. The senior officer in charge was Chief Inspector Cave, a stocky man with suspicions of Fenwick and his motives that he did not bother to disguise. Fenwick resorted to charm and persuasion. Eventually Cave accepted that there might be some relevance in Fenwick asking him questions about his case, though when he summed up their conversation it was clear that he thought his time had been wasted.

"So, this Griffiths is in prison for rape and you *think* he had a partner who's carrying on the good work on his own."

"That's right."

"Because of the missing finger in each case."

"That and the subsequent killings and rapes. And we've learned that one of the prison guards who singled out Griffiths for bullying was murdered horribly."

"Coincidence."

Fenwick kept his silence and his temper, just. Cave paused to see if he had provoked a response then continued, a half smile on his face that Fenwick was finding increasingly irritating.

"But Virginia Matthews didn't lose a finger."

"Maybe he was interrupted before he managed to take it."

Cave shook his head in disagreement, then gave another condescending smile.

"Well let's assume for one minute that you're right and Griffiths had a partner, and that it's this man, Smith, who killed Geoffrey Minny and raped the Matthews girl. Why go berserk and kill a man? And why is he stupid enough to come back to Telford?"

"Not stupid, arrogant. He's trying to copy Griffiths and attack outdoors but by nature he's used to charming the girls into taking him home. This crime appears to combine both methods."

"Except that her home was several miles in the other direction."

"His old house was less than a mile away from where the attack took place."

"Another coincidence. It signifies nothing."

"Maybe, but Virginia is in the target age range, slim, pretty, dark haired and confident."

"So are hundreds of thousands of other girls in the country."

"Was there trace evidence at the scene?"

"Masses. Trouble is, the copse was full of debris so it's going to take a long time to sort through."

"What about from the girl?"

"She'd been washed in a stream that runs along the edge of the field but we found a foreign pubic hair, so we've trying for DNA. No semen."

"The washing is consistent with the other crimes. A stream is less thorough, but he must have been familiar enough with the area to know that it was there."

Cave opened his mouth to belittle Fenwick's point but closed it again when nothing occurred to him and tried a different argument.

"The girl was drugged with GHB." Gammahydroxybutyrate had replaced Rohpynol as the date rape drug of choice. "That doesn't fit."

"Far simpler than seduction or assault, and he needed her compliant for the drive. Why risk the taxi ride unless the place was significant to him?"

The same point had occurred to Cave but he didn't see why he should start to discuss his case with this arrogant prick.

"Anything else?"

"The girl's description of her attacker. Did you have a likeness made?"

"It was very vague. She'd been drugged, remember. The waiter in the restaurant added to it but it's not much to go one. Here, you can keep it."

Fenwick studied the e-fit. It showed an attractive man with an unlined face, wide-set green eyes, clean-shaven, wearing an earring. The style of hair was completely different and altered the shape of his face so that there was little similarity with other e-fits.

"Will that be all?" Cave could sense his disappointment.

"For now. Would you have any objection if I interviewed the girl?"

Cave tensed.

"Yes I would. She's completely screwed up by the attack and only came out of hospital yesterday. We have an expert rape officer coaxing information out of her but we're getting precious little."

"Could I speak to the officer, then?"

"If you must."

Fenwick escaped from the office, pleased with his extraordinary, and out of character, self-control.

He parked the car in front of the house, 23 Beech Pass, and waited. The specialist rape officer had arrived to talk to the girl as soon as she woke up and was still inside. She should be due to leave soon. Less than a quarter of an hour later a short red-haired woman left the house and walked down the drive. She stopped when she saw Fenwick step out of his car and glared at him with suspicion.

"I'm not a journalist, don't worry. Chief Inspector Andrew Fenwick, Harlden CID."

She studied his warrant card carefully, comparing his face with that in the photograph.

"Harlden?"

"It's in West Sussex. I'm up here because I think there may be a link between this crime and others that we have under investigation. Chief Inspector Cave has agreed to my asking you some questions."

"OK, we can use my car."

In the privacy of its interior she relaxed a little.

"Fire away."

"Did he say anything when he raped Virginia . . ."

"She's Ginny, or Diamond to her mum and dad. He swore at her. Called her a fucking bitch, a filthy cow. Said women were all the same. It was clear that there was a lot of hatred involved. He despises women."

"And before, in the restaurant?"

"She can't remember but she thinks he was quite normal."

"Confident? Articulate?"

"All I can say is that nothing he said or did made her feel uneasy."

"What injuries did she suffer?"

"He cut and beat her, and her body is covered with bites."

"Bites? Have you sent photos to the Met so that they can check them against those the other girls sustained?"

"No idea, but I'll check with Inspector Cave when I get back. That's all we have from her so far."

After she'd gone he stared up at the house. He was desperate to talk to Ginny and hear her account directly but to do so would put at risk the painstaking work being done by the specialists. After a moment's pause he drove away. Behind him, unnoticed, a motorcyclist quietly slipped his machine into gear and followed.

Ginny watched the man and Siobahn, the nice policewoman, from behind the net curtain at the front window. He looked OK, but she was glad that he hadn't tried to come in. Her face still looked a mess from the bruises, although her mum insisted it was getting better. She had a stinking cold and she had spots like she was thirteen years old. Her hair needed a wash but she couldn't face the thought of doing it herself and had resisted her mum's gentle suggestion that she could do it for her.

She never wanted to look attractive again. Her counselor had explained that she would feel mixed up but none of the woman's words could describe the self-loathing that she felt. Tears of self-pity made her eyes blur.

She went back to the sofa and snuggled down under the blanket. It was comfy and she tried to sleep. Napping during the day was better than sleeping at night, when the nightmares would come and shock her awake into darkness. During the day there were noises of her mum or dad in the background. They were taking it in turns to have time off work so that she wouldn't be on her own. Even her brother was being nice to her. To welcome her home he'd bought her something from the Body Shop with his pocket money. Her little sister had been an angel, drawing her pictures every day. Alex was only ten and didn't know what had happened but she knew that her big sister had been hurt and the knowledge made her eyes grow huge with misery.

She missed them. Dad had driven them over to Grandma's, away from the police visits and the journalists' phone calls. It was better that they'd gone, she told herself, but regretted that she had said no to the opportunity herself. At the time, the idea of stepping outside the house had been too awful. She hadn't worn anything but pajamas and a dressing gown since . . . for a long time.

Sometimes she thought she would go mad. Life would never, ever be the same again and the realization made her weep for her loss. In one session with the counselor in hospital, she had been asked to choose just one word to describe how she felt. To her own surprise she had said bereaved, and had known at once that it was true. She was in mourning for herself, for the Ginny who wasn't afraid of the dark, who could sleep for ten hours and wake with a smile, who had been looking forward to growing up and everything that it would bring.

The old Ginny was gone forever. She'd been killed as surely as if she had died that night. There were tears on her face again. She dragged out one of Dad's big white linen hankies from her dressing gown pocket and dabbed at her face, then pulled the blanket up about her ears and curled into a fetal position with her back to the world.

CHAPTER TWENTY-FIVE

Constable Knots was waiting for him at the station.

"What have you found out?"

"I've spoken with the headmistress and teachers who were at the school when Smith and Griffiths were there. They remembered them, Smith more than Griffiths. Said he was bright, cocky, inclined to bully the younger boys."

He put his notebook away.

"That's it?"

"Yes, sir."

"And were they friends?"

"The computer science teacher thinks they might have been. They sat together in class."

"What about the drama teacher. Why was Smith barred?"

Knotty raised his hand in a plea for sympathy.

"I haven't found her yet. It's the school holidays and she wasn't in when I rang."

"The doctor?"

"Next on my list."

"Then what are you doing here? Get on with it."

Fenwick watched him go, shoulders slumped, feet heavy. Perhaps he shouldn't have been so sharp with him. Knotty was doing his best and he'd only had two hours. Next time he saw him he'd be more understanding.

Chief Inspector Cave was about to leave when Fenwick found him in his office. He let his impatience show as Fenwick detained him.

"What now?"

"Thanks for your help this morning. I spoke with Siobahn."

"So you'll be leaving now."

"Yes."

Cave turned to go.

"There's just one thing."

"If it's about the bites, that's sorted."

"Great. But I thought you'd want to know that there was no police presence at the Matthews' house."

"So? It was probably a shift change."

"Well . . ." Fenwick felt a war inside between the wise diplomat he was trying hard to become and the direct, outspoken know-it-all that he really was. The smart alec won. "Don't you think there should be someone there constantly. She's unfinished business."

"A five- or ten-minute gap won't do anyone any harm. Most of the journos are keeping away—she's already old news."

"Killer B failed to kill the girl in Wales. I don't think he'll be prepared to leave another murder unfinished."

"*If* it is the same man, he's already shown the opposite. You're wasting my time." Cave made to push by him but Fenwick stepped in front of him, close enough to smell stale coffee on Cave's breath.

"*Please*. I know I'm way off my patch, but give me the benefit of the doubt. One extra officer doesn't cost much and it would serve as a deterrent. I'm getting to know Smith and how he thinks . . ."

"You're becoming obsessed you mean."

There was no point getting into an argument.

"Possibly but I don't think so and . . ."

"No, Fenwick. This is my case and there's absolutely no proof that Killer B and/or Smith is the man. Her mum or dad are always there, we have a car outside except for the shift change and there are regular patrols. Nothing you can say will convince me that she's still at risk."

With that he was gone, leaving Fenwick the subject of long looks from officers passing by. In his cramped office he called Robyn but she'd barely started to analyze the old cases and had nothing to tell him. If he hurried he could catch the next inter-city train to London and be back by early afternoon.

While the train was waiting for a signal to change outside Euston, his mobile phone rang. It was Knotty. Fenwick was conscious of the crowded compartment and tried to speak in a whisper but it didn't work.

"Ah . . . yes."

"Is that the Chief Inspector?"

"Indeed it is."

"Are you all right, sir?"

"Oh, yes."

"Except that you sound, you know, odd."

"No, I'm on a train."

"Still? Blimey, that's hours late, that is."

"Quite. What's the matter?"

"Oh nothing. It's just that you said to call you with *anything* that came up."

"Yes." The inflection in Knotty's voice hardly raised his hopes.

"Through Griffiths' headmistress I've managed to trace some of the people who were at school with him."

"And the drama teacher?"

"Still away but these people . . ."

"She's important." The woman across the aisle raised her eyebrows and glanced at him sideways. He ignored her. "Go on."

"Well, these people, one of them, Daphne Middleton, was in the same class and remembers Griffiths quite clearly. She said that he was always hanging around the girls' changing rooms and that he had a habit of following her home from school. It went on for some time."

"How old?"

"About fourteen or so."

"I see. Anything else?"

"Not at present, no."

The disappointment was clear in Knotty's tone and Fenwick remembered that he'd meant to be more encouraging the next time they spoke. A stuffy railway carriage was hardly the time and place to begin so he made another mental note.

"Very well, er, keep at it and call me later."

It was late afternoon when Fenwick finally arrived back in London so he decided to go straight home. MacIntyre didn't expect him and he hadn't seen the children for three days.

His spirits rose at the greeting he was given. Even the housekeeper seemed pleased to see him. After tea, games and a bedside story, Fenwick sank back into an armchair and sipped his single malt. His good mood evaporated as he thought about his difficult week and then inevitably about his career.

He was spinning his wheels and not just on this case, trading off his image as a tough, hard-working and successful detective. Look at him, attached to some task force at the Met that didn't have enough for him to do; jaunting off to the North West on a quest that had turned into a wild goose chase; and apparently not even missed in Harlden. He wondered when people would start to see through him and felt an unusual stab of insecurity.

He poured himself another drink. Nightingale's continued absence caused him great unease. He was failing her and that worried him even more than his drifting career. He was draining his second glass when the phone rang, shattering the silence.

"Yes?"

"Oh dear! Perhaps I'll call back later when you're in a better mood."

He recognized Claire's voice. It only served to remind him that his love life was a complete void as well and he grunted an answer.

"Andrew. Come on. I recognize that tone. You've been spending too much time in your own company and that's enough to make anybody miserable."

"Ha, ha. Very funny. Why are you so cheerful anyway?"

"There's a new man in my life."

"I'm glad, really."

"No, you're relieved. Look, that's not why I called. Are you busy tonight?"

"Not particularly."

"Do you mind if I come round? There's something I should have said to you and it needs to be done face-to-face."

"Sounds ominous."

"Just important. Can I?"

"Come round—sure. I'm here all evening."

Claire arrived within the hour. There was a glow in her face that Fenwick hadn't seen before. She noticed the empty whiskey glass and raised an eyebrow.

"Solitary drinking?"

"When you live alone, it's the only kind."

"Sit down, Andrew, I don't want you charging out of the room because you can't face what I'm telling you." She sounded like the elder sister he'd never had.

He perched on the edge of his chair as if poised for flight. She closed the door and then sat on the floor beside his feet. It was a deliberately nonthreatening pose and he admired her manipulative skill. Even though he knew it was contrived, he immediately felt more relaxed.

"It's about Louise Nightingale."

"You know where she is?" The hope in his tone was painful.

"No I'm sorry, I don't. But I do know one of the reasons she went away."

"She was screwed up about work—she had to get away."

"It wasn't just about work, Andrew," Claire looked at him sadly, her eyes full of sympathy, "it was also about you."

"Me? I was never anything but supportive. I had . . . have nothing but the utmost respect for her."

"That's the problem."

He shook his head in confusion.

"You really don't get it, do you? My God, Andrew, for a man renowned for his insight you can be incredibly dense when it comes to people close to you. Louise Nightingale was hopelessly in love with you. It's why she had to go away. She knew that you only saw her as a police officer, never a woman. It finally got so bad she couldn't cope."

"No way, I'd have realized." He shook his head in denial but as he spoke, images of Nightingale replayed in his mind: finding her distraught in the forest, going to her flat, working cases together when he'd felt an unusual meeting of minds. He forced himself to argue with Claire but even as he did so he realized that she might be right.

"How did you know?"

"I had a fair suspicion of it just by looking at her with you, then after I saw her following us once I went round to her flat." Claire had the grace to blush.

"You confronted her?" There was a trace of anger in his voice and Claire looked away.

"Not exactly, but I needed to know. I thought that I was in love with you. I realize now there was a lot of infatuation mixed up with it—and lust." She looked at him sideways and blushed again. "I was desperate for you to love me back yet you wouldn't. That's when I began to suspect that there was something going on between the two of you."

"That's ridiculous. I'd never get involved with a junior officer."

"I know that now and so did Nightingale, poor thing, but she's a woman and you're a single man . . . most men would do a lot to have a relationship with Louise Nightingale, I can assure you."

"Did she admit it to you?"

"Not in so many words but it was obvious from what she didn't say."

"Why didn't you tell me?"

"In part because she asked me not to, at least that's the reason I gave myself at the time, but to be honest I was scared in case you loved her back. Don't look like that."

"How could you think that? I . . ." Fenwick stumbled over his words.

He'd been going to say that he had no feelings for her beyond professional respect but even as he thought the words, he knew them to be a lie. He cared more for her than that, but what he felt couldn't be love. There was amusement at her outspoken ways, enormous respect for her courage and intellect, perhaps even grudging affection, and he did worry about her a lot. But that wasn't love, was it? It bore no resemblance to the all-consuming fire that he had felt for his wife from the moment he first saw her until the day she died.

He became aware of his silence. Claire was looking at him with a knowing expression, as if she could see beyond his defensive walls. She stood up and kissed the top of his head.

"I've told you now. How you feel, what you do with the knowledge is entirely up to you. I'm not going to give you any advice except to say use the information wisely. Don't squander it. Be honest with yourself. You must—you owe it to her. A woman's love is a rare gift so don't ignore it, even if you do decide, as you did with me, that you can't reciprocate."

She let herself out, leaving Fenwick to stare at the carpet where she had been sitting.

He couldn't sleep. Images of the last time he had seen her kept running through his mind. Her eyes, lips, her dark hair so shiny it looked wet. What should he do? The sensible thing would be to leave well alone. She was too dangerous. He would risk everything if he went after her. And yet . . .

And yet, she compelled him. He couldn't ignore her, not now. If he was lucky enough to find her, and have time with her uninterrupted, would he be able to get away with it?

Her face was beginning to haunt him. There were plenty of photographs around, shots from the newspaper coverage that emphasized her looks, and those eyes. He had seen them fill with tears, had watched while they grew huge with pain and fear. They were wonderful eyes.

There was warmth in his groin and his hand slipped beneath the covers. Thinking of her was arousing, more exciting than anything that had broken the recent ambiguity of his life.

He began to fantasize about what he would do to her when they met, the excitement building inside him. When he climaxed, he cried out and bit the heel of his hand until it hurt. There could be no doubt that he had to have her. She was unfinished business. He needed to prove to himself that he could do to her exactly as he wanted, not because he had any doubts but because it was what a real man would do.

Unable to sleep, he washed and poured himself a large tumbler of gin with a splash of tonic. He needed to quit this place and soon he would have no need of a base. Even the cottage made him feel trapped now. Leaving would be as easy as it had been vacating his parents' house.

When the neighbors had started to ask about their return from the surprise round-the-world trip that he had fabricated to explain their disappearance, it had been time to go. He'd cleaned the traces of their lives from the house and written to a letting agency in Telford, using addressed notepaper and his father's much-copied signature. When a representative visited he explained that his parents were away and sent them the signed agreement and bank details by post.

They called up, of course, as he had expected them to, but Wayne answered the phone, well rehearsed to sound exactly as his father would have done. Afterward they'd moved to this cottage together. That first winter had been quiet. They built fires against the bitter cold and lived simply, using cash they took from his father's account. All the standing orders had been canceled, even the rates were paid by the agents. He had thought of everything.

When they started to need money, Wayne found a temporary job in the computer department at a local firm. He was good and they offered to make him permanent. It was dull work but well paid and he took evening classes to gain more qualifications. After a year he moved on and started to earn them proper money.

For a while he'd simply let Wayne feed them. Apart from videos his amusements were free, after all, but then he'd discovered recreational drugs, simple stuff but it increased the highs and stopped the black spells. Money became a problem. Stealing was easy but carried a risk he didn't want so he'd made a copy of Wayne's NVQ certificate and found himself a job. Anyone with half-decent programming skills was able to get a job back then.

With the advantage of falsely improved CVs they joined a computer games company in Telford. He started to specialize in computer security and Wayne in development. That had been the best time. All the while he and Wayne had indulged their shared interest, becoming better with each experiment. Life could have gone on like that forever if Wayne hadn't got them fired. He identified the start of Wayne's decline to when he lost his job.

That's when the testing started, to give them both a new purpose in life. He would set Wayne a challenge: a location, a woman wearing a certain color, a time of day, and Wayne would have to deliver. Occasionally it worked in reverse and Wayne would test him but the trials were always too easy. He had been superior in every way: technique, daring and intellect.

The thought returned his mind to his unfinished business in Telford. It had been a stroke of genius to follow that policeman. True, he knew the taxi girl's address already from the telephone directory but there was sweet irony in being led to it by a pig.

He started to clear the house, working from the top down. It would be sold; he could do with the money and he had the deeds. He would find a solicitor to handle the whole thing before he left. It was past two in the morning but he wasn't tired. Sleep was a luxury rather than a necessity. With the help of a few pills he could make do with three or four hours a night for weeks on end and still feel sharp in the mornings. By four o'clock he'd selected items to take with him and packed them into the panniers on his motorbike. Everything else was burning in the grate or tied up in a rubbish sack by the back door.

His laptop was still connected to the dial-up phone line. He was about to pack it away when he thought of the policewoman. She had to be found, tedious as it was. Once he'd killed her he could leave the country on top again. She'd seriously inconvenienced him and had to die in order for him to feel free.

He forced himself to concentrate and logged onto the PC as daylight found the edge of the lake. Perhaps it was the early morning clarity or the freshness of his brain but he realized almost at once that he'd been wasting his time going through the data. He didn't need it. The Internet café that she'd used must have been owned by an enthusiast. It had its own server, an extraordinary idea, which meant that there was a registered location and individual IP address he would be able to trace. The two years that he'd spent in IT security were not to be wasted after all. It had been over a year since he'd done any searching but it wasn't something you forgot how to do.

He flexed his fingers, cracking the knuckles, then hovered over the keyboard. The hunt was on. He would trace the location, finish his business in Telford and then go and find her. A ray of sunshine found his open window and he knew then that it was going to be an exceptional day.

CHAPTER TWENTY-SIX

Nightingale woke late and lay in bed staring at the shadows cast by the sunlight on her bedroom walls. Physically she felt fantastic but her mood was restless. She took a mug of black coffee into the garden and noticed fresh weeds growing among her runner beans. Over two dozen slugs had died in a drunken haze in the beer traps she had set and birds had pecked at the salvias. She went to explore the farm outbuildings, like a beachcomber hoping to find distraction in the flotsam. In the old cheese-store ancient apples had rotted to a dried brown skin. Hundreds of swallow tail butterflies, attracted by the sweet cider smell, had died, littering the desiccated fruit in a brightly patterned carpet. Beside the butterflies Nightingale found an old trunk that she dragged outside.

It was a traveling chest that had been used to store her aunt's cast-off clothes. She opened it and sorted the contents onto an old blanket. In the bottom drawer, underneath faded silk petticoats, she found a leather writing box stuffed full of photographs and bundles of letters tied with ribbon. Curiosity triumphed over scruples and she spread out the contents on the blanket.

The first photo was of three people at a picnic—her aunt, father and Lulu. The next was labeled "Christmas" and showed her aunt and father, his mouth wide in laughter. She sniffed and blinked hard before covering the picture quickly with another that stopped any suspicion of tears.

Her father was captured in black and white kissing Lulu firmly on the mouth. The date on the back was the same year that her parents had married. In another photograph, Lulu was leaning back against him, her head resting easily below his chin, looking serious but not sad. Her father's hands rested on Lulu's swollen stomach. There could be no doubt that she was pregnant.

Nightingale stared into her father's eyes and experienced an unexpected burst of anger. She'd seen her parent's relationship as one of contractual acceptance, dry and accommodating, punctuated by episodes of verbal aggression. Humiliated, she realized that she'd had no idea what caused the rot in her parents' partnership.

She ripped the ribbon from the letters. The period of writing was contemporaneous with the photographs. There was a letter from her aunt to her brother, on which he had scribbled a hasty reply.

Dear Henry,

Hope you're well, we missed you at the weekend—that is to say Mother missed you. It was her birthday and you said you'd be here. But enough of that. I don't want to become the latest in a long line of nags. Horror—it might be hereditary!

How's Mary, still suffering from morning sickness? Mother thinks it's going to be twins—be warned—she seems to know these things.

Lulu was asking after you. I know you don't like me mentioning her but she's my friend and you owe her an explanation about the marriage. I know she hurt you going off like that but she's back now and I think she still cares for you despite how she's behaved. She's not been well and her work is suffering. You could at least send a letter asking how she is.

Her father's lazy scrawl filled the space at the end of the letter: *Message received and understood.*

She searched the remaining correspondence impatiently and found a note dated three months later.

Dear Ruth,

I'm coming to stay for a few weeks. Mary's having a touch of the vapors and is going to her parents—too ghastly to contemplate and I could do with a break quite honestly. Marriage is hard work and we don't even have kids yet. Lord help us. What am I going to do with two? One's enough. It's a nightmare.

Nightingale's eyes blurred again. Second born, second child, a girl. She had never felt wanted and her father's callous words cut deep. She blinked and read on, finding a reference to Lulu in the last lines.

Lulu called me at work. Don't get angry but I said I'd see her. Just to talk, try and sort things out. She told me that she's staying the summer with you. You are kind.

I know I have handled this badly. I was too soft, that's the problem but I really am contrite this time. I've caused so much pain—to her yes, but to you too and that hurts most of all. Somehow, I want to put it right but I just don't know what to do. You'll help me won't you? You're a good friend to her and I depend on you so. I can't wait to see you again—I'll be down next Tuesday.

Nightingale tried to suppress her rising anger toward her father. He had put the load of sorting things out, including managing his pregnant ex-lover, onto his younger sister's shoulders without apology. The emotional blackmail in the letter was palpable.

And what had become of her own mother, pregnant with twins? Nightingale felt sorry for her for the first time in her life. The ribbon on the third and final bundle of letters had been drawn tight into a knot and it took her several minutes to unpick it. She saw at once that the first note was dated three days before she'd been born.

Ruth, I need you. Mary only has two weeks to go but she won't budge from the farm. Come back and be with us. I'm sorry to break into your holiday but please?

There was no further correspondence from her father. A yellowed newspaper cutting announced the births of Simon John and Diana Nightingale on the 3rd of September. Finally, she found three letters, still in their envelopes, all written on soft lilac paper. Nightingale checked the postmarks. They were from London and had been sent in the autumn following her birth.

Dear Ruth,

Thank you for your letter. I'm all right, really and I'm glad everyone is well. No, I don't have any message for Henry and I certainly don't want you to give him my address. I'm applying for a job at one of the private galleries. It's nothing much but the proprietor seems decent . . .

Lulu sounded in control. What had happened to her baby? Perhaps it had been given up for adoption. Some of her sympathy for Lulu disappeared as she opened the remaining letters.

Dear Ruth,

Great news. Roger—he's the prop—has expressed an interest in my work! He's very kind . . .

There was a lot more about Roger, and Nightingale skimmed it, interested only in how Lulu was adjusting to life with or without her baby, but of that there was no mention at all.

Dear Ruth,

You don't need to keep giving me the updates you know. I think it's better in fact if you didn't.

I have an exhibition planned for the week before Christmas. Will you come?

The only item left in the bundle was a clipping from a society magazine dated the following year. It was a professional photograph of Miss Lulu Bullock on the occasion of her engagement to Mr. Roger Appleby, son of Colonel and Mrs. A. Appleby of Windsor. Lulu looked lovely and the engagement ring was so large it seemed to weigh down her hand.

No regrets then.

Nightingale bundled the correspondence together, curiously disappointed. The sense of adventure with which she had embarked on her exploration had evaporated, leaving her tired and with a threatening headache. That night, it took a long time for sleep to come and when it did it was full of dreams of abandoned children crying and of her father's laughter behind a succession of closed doors. At one o'clock she fetched a fresh glass of water and lay awake listening to the grandfather clock chime the hour. Some time after three she drifted down into another fitful sleep haunted by dreams of her childhood from which she struggled awake as the birds were singing.

After breakfast Nightingale went for a long run along the cliff top before collapsing onto the sharp sea grass to stare at the sky. She was physically fitter than she had been for years. The painful thinness had gone, to be replaced by sleek tanned muscle. Her face was years younger and had lost lines of tension that she'd thought would be permanent. She refused to become a nervous wreck again.

Back in the house she drank a pint of orange juice and lemonade and started gardening, her mind full of bitter childhood memories. She had been a strong child but her brother had been sickly. Simon had been treated as precious and delicate while she had been the tough one, expected to get on with life without any fuss.

At first she'd tried to earn her parents' affection by being the most amazingly brilliant child. School prizes, Brownie badges, swimming cups, netball trophies, she had delivered them all. Nothing changed. Drops of moisture splattered the leaves of the sunflowers she was staking. She told herself it was sweat and sniffed loudly.

When being the best daughter in the world hadn't worked, she had become the worst. A rebel, rude, untidy, difficult. She was expelled from school twice before fourteen and her mother gave up on her. Her father had used detached humor to cajole her when what she'd really wanted was a hug. That's all it would have taken, a few cuddles from him and her mother, Mary, the ice queen.

A memory of a family picnic came back to her. She'd been stung by a wasp and her aunt and father had scurried around, sucking out the sting, putting cream on it, soothing her with promises of ice cream. Her aunt had enveloped her in a huge cuddle, kissing the swollen hand to make it better but her mother had pulled her away. "For heavens sake, don't mollycoddle her. She's too spoiled already!" She had been eight.

Nightingale sniffed again and went to deal with the dead slugs until a strong westerly wind brought in a front of rain that enveloped the farm in a solid curtain of water. She had a compelling urge to leave the house and put on her waterproof before pulling the front door tight closed. At once she was surrounded and deafened by the rain. It had the force and density of a power shower and she abandoned her original plan to walk up to the top of the cliff and watch the storm in the bay. Instead, she turned downhill, toward the tiny hamlet and the church.

Amelia was arranging flowers on the altar. As she closed the heavy oak door it creaked and Amelia spun around in surprise. Nightingale threw back her hood and waved in reassurance. Her dark hair was plastered close to her skull, longer and more unkempt than ever. Amelia opened her mouth in shock. Her hand flew to her chest as if to ward off a blow, then her face cleared.

"You startled me, Louise." She tried to smile but her eyes remained wide and staring.

"Sorry." Nightingale walked down the checkered aisle, automatically stepping over the worn brass tombstone. "I needed to get out of the house." Amelia was still staring at her, flowers forgotten as water trickled over the alter cloth and dripped onto the tiles below. "Can I give you a hand?"

Amelia turned with a start and mopped at the spreading stain with her apron.

"I've only two more arrangements to see to, thank you." She kept her back toward Nightingale as she spoke but her body radiated defensiveness, as if she had been caught out in some indiscretion.

Nightingale shook her head in puzzlement and retreated toward the font and its vibrant pantheistic carving. She traced the relief with the tips of her fingers. There was something essential about the font. Despite Lulu's strange lifestyle and beliefs she could believe that it had been sculpted with faith to hold this most holy water. Behind her Amelia bustled. Perhaps it was the moodiness of the day, or a bad reaction to the weather, but Nightingale found herself irritated. She was reminded of the story of Mary and Martha. Amelia was Martha, hardworking and earnest, relied upon but fundamentally missing the point.

"There!" Amelia placed an arrangement at the base of the font and stood back with satisfaction. "Pointless putting delphiniums in at this time of year. They never last. I told Lily that when she brought the flowers in but she wouldn't have it. These crysanths are far more practical."

Nightingale glanced at the clump of determined maroon flowers and quickly looked away. She resumed her tracing of the sculpture.

"I like this piece. Somehow, it calls out to me."

Nightingale's simple statement provoked a nervous twitter from Amelia.

"Yes, very nice," she said, head bowed. She was tweaking the flowers, fussing at them unnecessarily with her podgy fingers. Nightingale had no doubt that she was seeking to avoid her eye and her detective's curiosity brought her to full alert.

"What was Lulu like?"

Amelia reached over to pick up her coat from a pew, her back to Nightingale.

"Why do you ask?"

Something, an instinct or a thought so buried in her subconscious that it had as yet no shape, prompted Nightingale to answer as if she knew far more than she did.

"Why do you think I ask? Don't I have a right to know?"

The anger and hurt in her voice surprised them both. Amelia turned around but kept her eyes on her handbag as she fiddled with its clasp.

"It was a long time ago, Louise. You may be upset but I think it best for the past to be left undisturbed."

"But it's *my* past, and I have a right to be told everything, don't I? They're both dead now, what harm can it do? You're a Christian. You're supposed to believe in truth and compassion. If you have nothing more to tell me, swear so now, in this church."

Amelia looked at her at last and Nightingale was ashamed to see tears in her eyes.

"I can't do that; it's not my place to tell you. I made a promise and even if the person I made it to has gone, I still can't break it."

"Can't or won't?" Any sympathy she had been feeling toward the older woman vanished in a flash of frustration that brought fire to her eyes. Amelia stepped back, her bag held defensively in front of her. Nightingale sensed that she was weakening and pressed on, mixing lies with half-formed thoughts.

"Do you think I don't know already? I'm not stupid! Why can't you confirm the truth for me? All these weeks, you've been pretending to be my friend yet you've been keeping things from me, very important things that I deserve to know. You've left me to investigate and guess. That's hardly kind, is it? I can't believe that you could have been so cruel."

As she spoke, Nightingale was horrified to find that her pretended emotions became real. She had been scared by Amelia's reaction. Perhaps there were even more secrets to be uncovered beyond her father's infidelity and the half-sister she'd become determined to find. Her vision blurred with tears she was too angry to want to shed.

"How could you?" She threw the words back over her shoulder toward Amelia's ashen face and fled the church.

The rain soaked her head at once, chilling her. She pulled up her hood and ran on, glad that her tears would be washed away.

By the time she reached Mill Farm she was exhausted and bitterly regretting her outburst in the church. What had she been thinking? She'd engaged in manipulative interviewing techniques, only to be trapped by them into an emotional display it would be hard to forget. Amelia must think her dangerously unstable. Their friendship was probably finished. She didn't regret that quite as much as she knew that she should, given the woman's kindness toward her, but she still felt guilty.

Evening fell with the steady rain and she went to bed ridiculously early. An alien noise woke her. By the light of the torch by her bed she checked the time: ten to ten. She'd been in bed either one or thirteen hours and was too disorientated to work out which it was.

There was another noise outside. Nightingale struggled into jeans and shoes and went to investigate. Perhaps a violent gust of wind had woken her but she knew that she'd be unable to sleep until she had made sure that she was on her own.

She'd reached the top of the stairs when she heard a loud clang. It was the distinctive sound of an old milking pail being knocked over and she knew exactly where she had left it, by the back door. She switched off her torch and waited for her eyes to readjust to the dark.

The drumming of the blood in her ears mimicked the sound of the rain outside as she made her way silently downstairs, remembering to step over the rotten corner treads that would barely take her weight. Outside faint light trickled around into the yard from the front of the house. Inside the dark was impenetrable. She shuffled forward, using her left hand to find the kitchen table and chairs while she grasped the torch firmly in her right.

A sudden banging at the back door almost made her cry out in fear.

"Louise? Louise are you there?" It was a woman's voice. Amelia.

With a curse softened by relief Nightingale switched on her torch and opened the door. Alcohol fumes hit her.

"Oh thank God! I saw the house in darkness and I thought . . . Oh never mind what I thought. You're all right, thank God. Hang on a sec while I go round to the front and turn my car lights off before they flatten the battery."

She clattered off with the torch. Nightingale lit the lamps and was encouraging the Aga back to full heat when her visitor returned.

"You're soaked through, Amelia. Sit here and get warm. Tea or hot toddy?"

"Hot toddy please."

Why was she not surprised?

Amelia stretched her hands and feet toward the stove and sighed deeply.

"That's better."

"What on earth are you doing here?"

"I was worried about you. I kept thinking about what you'd said, about how I should have shown compassion. And you were in such a state. The more I thought about you the more concerned I became. In the end I just had to come and make sure you were all right." She shook her head. "I feel a fool now of course, and it seems I got you out of bed."

"Don't worry. Here, take this." The water wasn't quite boiling but it was warm enough.

Amelia took such a long drink that Nightingale felt obliged to refresh her glass at once. She felt a little guilty that her outburst had caused a sixty-something lady to drive on unmade roads through darkness on a filthy night. But she didn't feel guilty enough to avoid trying to take advantage of the other woman's concerns.

"Have you come to tell me?"

"But you already know."

"I need to hear it out loud to believe it."

"I've said nothing for so very long, not even to Ruth, although I'm sure your father told her. How did you find out?"

"By reading my aunt's papers, finding photographs, matching the dates I know with entries in her diaries."

Amelia took another long drink then rested her forehead against the warm glass.

"I should have realized. You're so bright, just like your mother. Of course you were going to find out. Well at least I won't be breaking my promise if you already know. Your father made me swear on the Bible in the church a few days after you were born. He kept coming to see me quite often for a while," she smiled wistfully then grew sad, "but his visits tailed off and soon stopped altogether."

Amelia took another drink and looked surprised that there had been so little left. Nightingale made them both fresh toddies, hers weak, Amelia's full-bodied, and brought cheese and biscuits to the table.

"Go on."

"He was upset for weeks, torn apart with grief. I can't describe it. We would often hold each other and cry together. When he came to my house that night, George was away, of course, as he always bloody was, I thought he was looking for Lulu but it was me he'd come to see." She smiled, triumphant. "I just hugged him until he could speak."

Nightingale leaned back from the circle of lamplight so that her face was in shadow and her look of confusion hidden. She was baffled by Amelia's words but held her silence, afraid that a question would stop the flow. Amelia drank more of the toddy, her eyes bright with the memories she was reliving.

"You know, it's such a relief to be able to talk at last. Ever since you arrived I've thought of nothing else. The memories bang around inside my head. When you walked into the church that first Sunday I thought I should have a heart attack."

"You knew who I was?"

"Of course. Father Patrick had told us that Henry's daughter might be coming and when you walked in it was obvious. You look exactly like her. It's quite extraordinary. Oh there's a trace of your father in the set of your jaw and you have his eyes, but there was no doubting who you were even though you're tall, whereas Lulu was a petite little thing . . ."

She couldn't breathe suddenly. The sense of panic was so strong that she found she was panting in breaths that failed to deliver sufficient oxygen. Amelia was oblivious. Her cheeks were rosy, her eyes shone as she wittered on. Nightingale brought her breathing under control and made her face expressionless.

"Louise?"

Nightingale reached out to add whiskey to her weak toddy and was alarmed at the uncontrollable tremor in her hands.

"Louise, are you all right? You're shaking all over."

She managed a nod that she hoped was convincing but the

look on Amelia's face told her it was not. A long drink of the toddy didn't help.

"I'm fine." Except that her voice now made it obvious that she wasn't.

"You didn't know." Amelia was horrified. "You tricked me!"

The accusation stung some sense into Nightingale.

"That's not true. I'd found out that my father's affair had continued right up to and after his marriage and that I . . . that he'd . . . but not that I was . . . that . . ." Her voice trailed away and she shook her head in denial. "I don't understand. I have my birth certificate. It can't be true."

The older woman's anger disappeared in the face of Nightingale's obvious misery. She reached out a work-reddened hand and patted Nightingale's, still gripped about the toddy glass.

"Did you never suspect? Were there no doubts?"

Nightingale recalled her sense of displacement, constant arguments with her parents, her mother's icy exactness and denial of love. She nodded.

"When I became a teenager—but I put their treatment of me down to disappointment." She lowered her head on to the rough wood of the table. "Oh God! I even accused my mother once of pretending that I was her daughter when I wasn't." The memory chilled her and she shivered. "That was when she thrust the birth certificate in my face."

The vision of her mother's fury and the fragile piece of paper waved like a flag of victory reappeared in her mind. She had snatched it from her mother—but she was going to have to stop thinking of her like that—from Mary, and read every word. There was no mention of her middle, preferred name, Louise. The real reason for the apparent omission was obvious now. She wasn't Diane Nightingale.

"What happened to the other baby, to Diane?"

"She died, aged one day. Your mother, sorry Mary, had the twins at Mill Farm. They were a little premature but well and a good weight so the midwife said they were fine to stay at home. The doctor sorted your mother out and that was that. Diane was the smaller of the two but she was healthy enough when she was born. Neither of them gave any cause for concern."

"And when she died, they decided to adopt me."

Amelia shifted uncomfortably but kept her free hand on Nightingale's wrist as she sipped her own drink.

"It didn't work out quite like that. You were born the night after the twins, a full term baby. Lulu had come back to the village to live with your aunt but she hadn't registered with a doctor. She was a wild child, back to nature, all of that. She wanted a natural birth and persuaded Ruth to be her 'birthing partner,' I think she called it. Your aunt was nervous but she was so besotted with Lulu that she went along with it."

The contempt in Amelia's voice made Nightingale draw her hands away under the pretense of taking another drink.

"Then your father and m . . . Mary arrived unannounced in August and Lulu had to leave the farm. I put her up at my house. George was away on a trip to the Middle East, otherwise I would have said no but Ruth was a decent friend and . . ."

"My father begged you?"

"How did you guess that?" It was so clear to Nightingale that Amelia would have done anything for her father that she didn't bother to answer. "I didn't want her upsetting Mary."

"You mean upsetting my father, don't you? You still loved him. He knew that and of course he would turn to you if there was a problem."

It was clear from the expression on Amelia's face that she'd taken the comment as a compliment.

"Please go on, for my father's sake. You were such a true friend to him, don't fail his daughter now. He would want me to know the whole truth."

"I'm not sure." Amelia drained her drink and looked hopefully at the bottle. Nightingale made another toddy, willing the alcohol to relax Amelia's inhibitions.

"Whatever you did, I'm sure it was for love of my father." Nightingale forced a smile although she felt an emotion close to hatred inside.

"Oh it was, it was. Trust me. And of course, it was better for you too, my dear. Just promise me you won't be angry. It was all done for the best."

Nightingale's mind had become ruthlessly sharp despite the feebleness of her physical reaction. She had always been logical and this was something she could cling to as the foundations of her world crumbled. Why did her true mother give her up? How could she have borne to part with her own baby? And why on earth had her father's wife accepted his lover's child? She shrugged and the other woman seemed to take it for acceptance.

Amelia settled into the chair and continued her story.

"Diane died suddenly. Your father put her in her cot at eight o'clock in the evening, next to Simon. Mary had kept to her bed after the birth, although it was an easy one. She was exhausted and tearful. Nowadays they'd call it postnatal depression but we just thought that she had a fit of the blues and that it would pass.

"At ten o'clock Simon started crying for his next feed and your father took him through to the kitchen. They were both on bottles. I don't know why your mother couldn't or wouldn't breast-feed. Anyway, your father fed and changed Simon then went back for Diane. He thought she was fast asleep so he carried her downstairs . . . he was still carrying her in her little sleep suit when he arrived at my door. He'd run through the woods in his nightclothes . . . hadn't even stopped to put on a coat." Amelia paused to take another drink.

"Lulu had gone to bed hours before but I was still up. He was almost hysterical by the time he arrived. I took him into the kitchen and he put the baby on the table. I unwrapped the blanket from around her and could tell at once that she was dead. I felt for a pulse to please him but it was clear she'd gone.

"We drank some whiskey and he cried in my arms for a long time. He didn't know what to do. Mary was so depressed already and he thought this would push her over the edge. He fantasized that perhaps she hadn't realized she'd had twins but I put him straight on that, of course a mother would know.

"In the end, he left the dead baby with me and went back to the farm. He was going to tell Mary when she woke in the morning, not before."

"And I was born that night." It was a statement, not a question. Amelia nodded and blinked tears away from her eyes. "Did you persuade my mother to give me up?"

She was amazed at the coolness of her voice when she was having to breathe deeply to prevent nausea from overwhelming her. Amelia shook her head.

"That's not quite what happened."

When Amelia looked up into her shadowed face she flinched and turned away.

"You must tell me. Father would expect it."

"I know." Amelia nodded. "You have to understand, your father was distraught, not just with grief but with fear for your mother's, sorry, Mary's state of mind. And Lulu, well she was a lovely girl in a superficial sort of way, but flighty and high-spirited. She was an artist. Who knows what sort of mother she'd have made. She led a bohemian life, never staying with a man for long."

Nightingale pressed her lips together to prevent an outburst that would only alienate this woman but inside she was burning with indignation for her mother—impregnated then left by her father to fend for herself and to be maligned by his friends.

"Lulu went into labor about two in the morning, after your father had left. It all happened incredibly quickly. I'd been a nurse not a trained midwife, but I had no chance to call a doctor. Her waters broke and within an hour she was in the final stages.

"When you were born you didn't cry straight away and I thought you might be dead too. I wrapped you in a hand towel and I brought you downstairs. Something, perhaps the change of temperature, made you hiccough and your eyes opened but you still didn't cry, you just made a little mewing sound."

Amelia had to stop. Tears soaked her cheeks and she sobbed for some time. Nightingale said nothing. She had guessed what happened next but it was part of Amelia's penance to admit it. The older woman blew her nose and sniffed loudly.

"I found another towel, a clean one, and swapped it for the one you'd been wrapped in. Then I put you in a blanket. Lulu was crying out to me. I didn't even think. It was as if some voice outside me was giving me instructions. I undressed the dead baby girl. My hands and apron were still covered with dried blood. I damped her tufts of hair down and wrapped her in the bloody towel. She was only a day old and still looked almost newborn. I wetted my hands and put some of the blood on her face. Then I took her back upstairs and stood in the doorway.

"I just stood there and Lulu looked at me with this awful fear in her eyes. I didn't say anything, neither did she. She just stared at the bloody bundle in my arms, then she let out a terrible wail. It was awful, like an animal howling. I handed her the baby and she held her to her chest. All the time these terrible sobs just kept coming. She was rocking to and fro. I've never, to this day, seen someone abandon themselves to so much grief.

"But I kept quiet even then. I was certain that I was doing things for the best, you see. I tried to take the baby away from her. It was already starting to stiffen and I didn't want her to notice but she just clung on to it. So I had to sort out the afterbirth, tidy her up, do all the necessaries to the sound of that terrible caterwauling."

Nightingale couldn't keep quiet anymore.

"She was grieving for her child! Don't you think she was entitled to cry?"

It was so apparent to Nightingale that Amelia had hated Lulu, even when she'd pretended to befriend her. Amelia's jealousy, fueled by her father's affection for Lulu, had twisted her thinking until she was able to camouflage the most hateful and spiteful of acts beneath a layer of self-appointed do-gooding. By switching the babies she had exacted a brilliant revenge on all those whom she most resented: Lulu was deprived of her love child and Mary was duped into taking an imposter into her home. Nightingale's anger kept her own grief at bay but only her determination to hear out the final chapter in Amelia's story kept her from screaming.

"As soon as Lulu fell asleep, still clutching the baby, I wrapped you in the blanket your father had used to bring Diane to the house and set off for Mill Farm. I had to reach there before breakfast so that you could be washed, reclothed and laid next to Simon. You were so quiet and docile it was if you were colluding with me . . ."

Amelia ignored Nightingale's sharp intake of breath and carried on talking.

". . . I'd expected your father to be awake, given his terrible experience only hours before, but I had to knock loudly to wake him. When he saw the baby he was furious, thinking I'd brought Diane back, but then you cried for the first time and he nearly collapsed.

"I explained what had happened, about what I'd done. At first he thought it was an impossible idea. He said that his wife would be bound to spot the difference, but you kept on crying and he looked at you properly for the first time. I knew then that he would never let you go. The love on his face . . . I could tell at once that I was right."

Nightingale swallowed the stone in her throat and blinked back tears. She was not about to break down in front of this monster who had played God with so many people's lives while masquerading as their friend.

"He fed, bathed and dressed you while I watched. I'd never felt closer to him and I could tell he felt the same. We formed an eternal bond."

Nightingale snorted and Amelia bristled.

"He never forgot what I'd done for him, how much I'd risked for his sake!"

"And my real mother, what about her? Did she ever find out?"

"No, of course not. Who was going to tell her? Very few people even knew that she'd been pregnant—your father, aunt, me, one or two friends—so there was never any curiosity."

"What happened to her?"

"When I got back to the house she was awake and crying again. She wanted to tell your father about his dead child but I persuaded her that I would make the call. I had to watch her constantly that day. She would have been quite capable of trying to reach the farm on her own, even in the state she was, and there would have been a risk of scandal if someone from the village saw her.

"In the end, your father came down in the afternoon to see her. He looked terrible of course. When he saw Lulu and the baby he broke down completely. For a moment I thought he was going to tell her the truth but he saw me shaking my head and he said nothing. I left them alone. When he came out almost an hour later he kissed my cheek and left without a word.

"Somehow he managed to persuade Lulu not to have the baby buried in the churchyard. She was into some sort of Buddhist hippie cult or other, so it was probably an easy thing to do. The birth was never registered and neither was Diane's death, that way he was able to keep the whole affair secret.

"He and Lulu went out together later with the baby's body and they buried her somewhere. I have no idea where and I never wanted to know. Lulu went back to London and saw a personal friend who was a doctor. Mary and your father returned home days later with their babies and that was that."

"That was that." The anger in Nightingale's voice made Amelia's eyes open wide. "A tricky little problem solved, and in a way that made sure that my father was bound to you forever by the secret you shared. While you had neatly revenged yourself on the two women who had stolen him from you in the first place, his wife and mistress!"

"That's not how it was at all." Amelia stood up abruptly, knocking her chair so that it fell with a clatter on the flags. "I acted in the very best interests of all concerned. Really, Louise, try to understand. It was in your interests too. I admit that I resented Lulu but I'm not being unfair. She would have made a terrible mother."

"She never had a chance to try, you took it away from her! Don't you realize that what you did was twisted and destructive? You almost destroyed my life. God knows what you did to my mother's. And you dare to presume to dress it up as well intended!

What about my mother's right to her child and mine to a true mother who would have loved me?"

"Loved you! What sort of life do you think you'd have had with that woman? She got over her grief quickly enough to be engaged within six months! You have to listen. I knew then that she wouldn't have kept you, and I still believe so now. You would have been given up for adoption and at least this way you grew up with your natural father and half-brother. And I saved your mother the grief over Diane."

"I didn't replace poor dead Diane. My father didn't want me to be her, and I fought against the shadow of that lie my whole life without ever being conscious of what I was doing. I'm *Louise* Nightingale and I know, without you even having to tell me, that that was my real mother's chosen name for me, the one that my father whispered over my cot, then my bed when he thought I was asleep.

"And you failed, don't you realize? As I grew up, looking more like my true mother every day, I was a constant reminder to my father of the woman he had loved and then betrayed. Far from destroying her hold over him, you placed a constant memory in his home. Take that thought to your cold, empty bed each night! Now go, please, before I do something I might regret."

Amelia turned without another word and stumbled out into the storm, her head bent low, perhaps against the wind. When the car disappeared beneath the trees Nightingale turned inside and closed the heavy oak door. There were no bolts left to ram home so she wedged the upturned chair beneath its handle then did the same with the back door.

She made herself a strong cup of tea. Despite the revelations of the past half hour she felt remarkably calm and in control, as if she had fought her way through an exhausting battle and had emerged triumphant. She was filled with new respect for Mary, who must have known but who said nothing to her, even when taunted. More important, for the first time in her life she knew who she really was. With that knowledge came renewed confidence and a sense of responsibility.

There were decisions to be taken but she would make them carefully and with consideration for others. Should she tell Simon and his wife? Should she try and find her real mother? To do so might achieve personal closure but what would it do to her? By now Lulu would have finished grieving for her daughter and have rebuilt her life.

Her poor "mother" Mary. At what stage had she started to suspect the truth about the troublesome daughter she found so difficult to love? When had she finally looked at her and seen that she had a cuckoo in the nest, an interloper who had grown daily more like the woman her husband had taken as a lover right up to and beyond their wedding day? It was a terrible thought.

But there was one decision that was easily made. She was going to find her half-sister's grave and ensure that it was consecrated after all these years. It was the least she could do and she wasn't going to leave Mill Farm with her new responsibility unfulfilled.

CHAPTER TWENTY-SEVEN

Only eight o'clock but London was hot already, exhaust fumes coated commuter throats with an invisible greasy film. Fenwick carried his jacket. There'd been no calls from Robyn or Knotty overnight and he wasn't looking forward to his meeting with MacIntyre at nine. He bought an iced coffee and found a bench in the shade of a tree where he could sit while he called them. Knotty answered quickly.

"I was just about to phone. I spoke to the Smith family doctor last night. He was at home and he'd had a drink or two before I arrived so I think he was a bit more open than if I'd seen him at the surgery."

"Good thinking. What did he say?"

"Physically they were fit as fleas but the father suffered from depression that became worse as he grew older. The wife had anxiety attacks."

"And the son?"

A woman with a baby in a pushchair came and sat on the other end of the bench. Fenwick cursed under his breath and angled away from her.

"He was a bit less specific there but I got the impression that the illness that kept him away from school for so long *wasn't* a physical one. The doctor gave me the name of a sanatorium nearby. They specialize in helping adolescents with problems: drug addiction, anti-social behavior, phobias, you name it. And he also said that David Smith junior went there voluntarily."

"You're going there today?"

"I'm on my way now. Then I've an appointment with the drama teacher at ten. I should just make it."

"Any trace of Wendy?"

"Not yet. Have a heart, I'm on my own up here."

"Yes, right, good. I mean, well done. Call me as soon as you have anything. Oh, and the box from the loft, have forensics found any prints?"

The girl with the baby was staring at him now.

"They've been sent; should be waiting for you, sir."

"OK, I'll speak to you later."

He arrived at the Met early. It wasn't what he'd wanted to do, in case MacIntyre saw him before he'd had a chance to call Robyn. His fears proved justified. When he walked in MacIntyre was leaving him a message on his desk.

"Andrew, good. We can start right away. I have to brief the Commander at nine-fifteen. The Home Office has been on again. Lucinda's father is complaining about our lack of progress. Come along. We'll use my office."

"Any developments while I've been away?"

"Nothing since the breakthrough with the print on the knife . . . and before you ask, no I haven't had them tested against those from the prison letters or the flat break-in, it's been bloody intense here. Unlike Telford, I imagine. What's your news?"

Fenwick experienced an all-too-familiar sinking feeling.

"At the moment, little more than I told you on the phone yesterday. We found out where Griffiths was fostered but there's no trace of the Smith family. I still think there's a strong possibility that David Smith junior is Killer B but at the moment that's just an hypothesis."

"Smart words for pure conjecture." MacIntyre's tone was sharp. "Not my comment, your ACC's."

"Harper-Brown has spoken to you?"

"He called yesterday, curious to know how you were getting on."

Fenwick's heart sank even further. The ACC never missed an opportunity to put the knife in.

"I see." They were noncommittal words but they didn't fool MacIntyre.

"I'm sorry, Andrew, but I just told him straight. I didn't make a value judgment but he drew his own conclusions." Fenwick said nothing as he sat down in MacIntyre's office. "I'm not going to repeat what I said on the phone. You know my opinion of your visit north."

"Yes. You made it very clear. If it all comes to nothing I can't say anything that will make you feel differently but . . ."

"And I've had a call this morning from a Chief Inspector Cave." He waited expectantly for Fenwick to say something.

"Ah," was all he could think of.

"I *told* you not to go in heavy-handed."

"I didn't. I was diplomacy itself. It's just that I'm really concerned about this poor girl, Ginny."

"It's not your case though, is it? And there's no proven link to Killer B though I've sent the bite marks off for comparison anyway. You weren't on your patch. For heaven's sake, grow up."

Fenwick didn't try to excuse himself. If Robyn and Knotty couldn't make a clearer link between Smith and the murders, the whole visit would have been a career-damaging waste of time.

"I'll let you have my report later this morning. Good luck with the Commander."

He refused to become depressed. He'd taken a calculated risk in going to Telford. If nothing more came of it than confirming where Griffiths lived as a teenager then so be it but there were leads still to be checked out and he hadn't given up hope.

The fingerprints from the box and its contents were waiting for him as Knotty had promised. He sent them off for analysis with those from the prison and flat, abusing MacIntyre's name to secure priority treatment. Robyn called him as he was finishing his report at ten.

"Sir, I think I've found something." He could hear the excitement in her voice. "There are hundreds of cases, so I thought of what you said about looking for patterns. I chose two years when Smith and Griffiths were at school together then looked for crimes committed during lunch break or in the two hours after school broke up, and within walking distance of the school.

"I found thirty-two similar crimes that took place during term time, never in school holidays."

"What sort?"

"I'll come to that in a minute." Her directness reminded him of Nightingale and he smiled despite his mood. "I went back over the other years that they were both at school to when Griffiths would have been thirteen. There's a definite pattern.

"At first, it was minor acts of vandalism or theft, a brick through a window, plants pulled up in a back garden, clothing stolen from the line, always women's clothing. But then the incidents became more serious. There were twelve complaints about a peeping tom or prowler, sixteen reports of indecent assault and one for attempted rape. There was a full investigation of the assaults and attempted rape and I haven't had a chance to go through all the files but the attackers are described as teenagers in every case. The attempted rape was reported on July 3rd, the year the boys left school."

"That's fantastic! Write it up and send your report here as quick as you can. This matches the profilers' descriptions of A and B. You've got a copy of the photograph from Smith senior's desk, and I'll send you an e-fit, show them to the victims. There's an officer there who might be able to help you, Siobahn . . ."

"Yes, sir, I know." There was a smile in her voice. "I work here, remember? The report's almost finished and I have the addresses of the women ready."

"You must have worked through the night to do this."

"Almost but it doesn't matter. This is too important."

She rang off leaving the ripple of her excitement in the air. He amended his report, feeling more positive. Knotty called him at ten twenty-five.

"I couldn't find out anything at the clinic David Smith went to, it'll take a warrant, but I've just left Miss Wallace, the drama teacher. You won't believe this . . ."

"Try me."

"The reason she banned David Smith was that she noticed him following her home from school. She didn't like it and asked to see him. They were alone in the rehearsal room. When she confronted him she said that he became abusive and threatening. He denied that he had followed her and she told him he was lying. Smith tried to slap her. She says she was so shocked that she just stood there. Then he said that if she made a complaint he would say that she had seduced him and get her struck off. He knew exactly what her bedroom looked like and even described some of her underwear."

"What did she do?"

"She told him he was excluded from drama club but that was it. His threats were too real for her to dare going to the headmistress, who didn't much like her anyway."

"So Smith told his father he'd been banned but not why, and the father wrote to Miss Wallace complaining."

"Better than that, he went to see her."

"And she told him all about it."

"Everything. He was furious, but not with her, with his son. He told Miss Wallace that this wasn't the first time he'd had trouble with him. There had been an earlier incident with a cousin and other things that he wouldn't specify."

"So there's a confirmed link to Wendy. How was it left?"

"It was toward the end of term. Smith senior told her that they were going on a family holiday and that he'd sort things out 'once and for all.' He asked her to keep it quiet until the new term started."

"But Smith didn't go back to school."

"No."

"Well done, Knotty. Write that up and get back down here. Don't see Fred Smith on your own about Wendy. He's a nasty piece of work and he's not going anywhere."

"Righty-ho. I've a couple of loose ends to tidy up but I should be with you by evening."

Fenwick left his revised report for MacIntyre's attention and went back to studying endless files. As the morning passed he began to experience a sense of disquiet so strong that he rang his housekeeper, who assured him that the children were fine. Next he called Cooper but the Sergeant had no news of Nightingale. By lunchtime he was sweating and could barely concentrate. MacIntyre invited him to join a visit to the Home Office psychologist and he grabbed at the chance. Anything was better than sitting in his office being spooked by feelings of imminent disaster.

• • •

Constable Knots was in high spirits. He'd reported proper progress to the Chief Inspector, much to his own surprise and, he suspected, his superior's. Fenwick was a tough master but he was someone you wanted to please. He felt slightly guilty for holding back in his phone call. Was saying that there were a few loose ends a white lie? Not really, surely, and it might all come to nothing. He didn't want to look stupid now that he'd started to make a good impression.

It had been a pure fluke that he'd asked Miss Wallace whether she had any idea where the Smiths went on holiday, but he knew that Fenwick didn't like loose ends. Miss Wallace had more than known, she'd seen the Smith family on holiday together two weeks later walking in the hills. She had talked to Smith senior and he told her about the holiday cottage, bought with the proceeds of a Premium Bond win. She had been thinking of renting something in the area herself so paid particular attention to what he said.

Miss Wallace had described the location and given him rough directions. Knotty couldn't believe his luck. He glanced at his watch, five to eleven. There was just enough time to get there, explore a bit and, if he was unlucky, be back for the two o'clock train. But if he did find Smith's cottage he would be a hero. As he drove, he could imagine himself calling out SOCO and surprising them with a request for a search. He was smiling as he went.

Finding the address of the café where the policewoman had accessed the Internet took him longer than expected but he had all the information he needed well before eleven. That left him an hour to prepare his gift for Griffiths. Overnight he'd decided that his one-time companion had to die in order to stop any risk of him blabbing to the police. Finding a method had been difficult but he recalled that prisoners were allowed to receive food, provided it concealed no drugs. He would send him a cake!

A special cake to his own recipe. There was an untouched fruit sponge in the cupboard and he knew where a yew grew in the margins of the forest. He gathered quantities of off-cuts to make an infusion. As it cooled he added sugar and pricked the cake all over so that the sponge would soak up his mixture. He repeated the process until the cake was saturated and then cleared his preparations away.

After the cake had drained, he rewrapped it and attached a note from Agnes. He packaged the sponge in a box and addressed it to Wayne at the prison then washed his hands carefully before eating an early lunch. He would need his strength for the afternoon as he intended to walk to Telford and back again. It was likely that the police would discover the Matthews girl's body quickly and set up roadblocks, so he was going to hike across country in order to avoid them.

He checked the contents of his rucksack again to make sure that everything was there, though he had done the same only half an hour before. Preparation was all. This was going to be the most dangerous thing he had ever done and the thought forced adrenaline through his body.

His mouth was too dry to swallow the sandwich so he opened a beer to help it down. As he ate, he added the last elements of his disguise. It was a superficial one: a baseball cap over untidy hair; a rambler's outfit, assembled from clothes he'd worn for years; a plastic map holder strung around his neck, complete with OS map and a rucksack. The glasses he wore were his father's, a mild prescription for short sight that he could tolerate. He looked in the mirror and scrutinized the image of a nerdy walker that stared back at him. Few people would look at him twice and if they did they would forget him quickly.

His penknife was in his trouser pocket. He pulled it out and tested the short blade that he had honed to razor sharpness. If you were good you didn't always need a prop and why run the risk of carrying a weapon that might arouse suspicion?

He left the house by the back door and started up the hill that would take him through the woods and on to a footpath that led to the outskirts of Telford. Eight miles, no problem at all.

He was in good condition and the weather was perfect for walking. As he entered the first fringe of trees a car drove along the private road below him. He froze in the shadows and watched. A man stepped out, foreshortened by the perspective. His face was obscured but something about his figure was familiar. Smith waited, barely breathing. The man went up to the front door and knocked twice. There was unmistakable authority in that rapping and Smith tensed. Silently, he removed his pack and set it down in the bushes. When the man walked around to the side of the house, peering into the windows, Smith crouched down to see his face. He recognized the officer who had been with Fenwick.

The police from down south had found his retreat! What should he do? Choices cascaded through his mind; lie low and let the man go, but there were signs of his lunch on the table. He could run, but his motorbike was parked at the back of the house and that idiot was going to stumble on it at any moment. There was still too much in the house and traces that would need to be destroyed if he were to retain his anonymity. If he couldn't run or hide, he had to eliminate the threat.

The fact that the man was here alone was confusing. He could either be part of an advance search or acting on his own initiative, following up a stray lead. There was no option but to find out. When the policeman moved around the house and out of sight Smith slithered half way down the hill then stood up and crept the final distance. He reached the shade of the eaves in less than half a minute and paused to control his breathing. He could hear footsteps on the shingle path, then the sound of rattling at the locked back door. The policeman was moving casually, not on alert as his shadow detached itself from that of the house and started to turn the corner.

Smith was on him fast, knocking him to the ground with a quick double punch to the jaw and gut. While the man was still struggling to get up Smith grabbed his right arm and twisted it up high behind him until he heard the shoulder creak in protest. He pressed the open knife under the man's jaw with his left hand, close enough to prick the skin.

"Who are you?"

"Knots," the man said and swallowed hard so that his Adam's apple was scratched by the blade.

"Police?"

The man nodded. Beads of sweat were trickling down the copper's face onto his hand.

"Are you alone?"

"Yes." As if realizing his error the man added quickly, "but there'll be others along any moment."

Smith thought he was lying.

"Who knows that you're here?"

"They all do. They're expecting me to call in and report."

The man stank of fear as sweat soaked his body.

"Really." This bumbler of a policeman was thinking quicker now. He'd realized his peril and was improvising rapidly. Smith didn't believe him but he couldn't be absolutely sure.

"I think we'll wait for them, shall we," he said pleasantly, and held the man tighter, causing him to moan with pain from his arm.

Minutes passed. The stench from the man was gross. He could feel sweat soaking his own clothing, making him unclean. He stared at the acne along the man's hairline and dandruff on his collar. Disgusting.

"I don't think they're coming, do you, Knots?" He kept his tone light, playful, and in truth this was a game. He was starting to have fun. "How much longer shall we give them?"

Knot's eyes were huge, the whites completely surrounded his pupils as he stared desperately for help.

"Five minutes should be enough. Then I think we shall have to give up on them."

Knots looked at the watch on his wrist. As the seconds ticked away Smith chatted to him in a conversational tone.

"In the movies, of course, this is the point when the hero comes to the rescue with mere seconds to spare. Do you think that's what's going to happen, Mr. Knots?"

Knotty sobbed.

"Now, now, don't despair. You have, let me see, lift your watch, thank you. Yes, over two minutes left. But in case they don't arrive, you might just want to pray. Best to be sure, don't you think?" He could feel the man start to tremble and he smiled.

"One minute left. Shall we count down? Fifty-nine, fifty-eight, fifty-seven, go on, you do it." There was the stink of urine and Smith snorted in disgust. "Dear dear, come on, you're the good guy. You should either defeat me or die bravely while trying."

His laugh was interrupted abruptly. The man reached back with his free hand and tried to grab Smith by the elbow. The blade shot upward, slicing Knot's cheek open as he swung away. His right arm was held tight but he ignored the pain and threw his whole body weight forward, trying to break Smith's grip. He managed to fall to his knees in a crawl, his right arm bent behind him like a broken wing, with Smith hanging on to it in an unshakeable grip. Blood coated Knotty's jacket but he ignored it and picked up a handful of gravel from the path. He threw it wildly at his assailant but most of it missed. With a cry of rage Smith leaped on his back, forcing him onto his chest. No matter how much Knots bucked in an attempt to shake him off Smith clung on tight.

Knotty crawled toward the back door steps where he might find shelter but Smith moved with him. In desperation the policeman lurched backward and rolled on top, finally breaking Smith's hold. They lay spread-eagled together, arms and legs outflung. Knotty started to rise but Smith was faster. He pulled him back down in a chest-crushing embrace, pinning both his arms to his side.

Terror forced a surge of power into Knotty's limbs. He burst out of Smith's bear hug and rolled away, stumbling across the rough grass toward his car. Smith roared like an animal and ran after him. Halfway there, a rugby tackle brought Knotty down to the ground with a thud that drove the air from his body.

Smith lifted the man's head by his hair and pulled it back to expose the neck. He sliced once, a neat 180° arc that severed carotid and jugular. There was a strange gargling sound and he realized that he had cut the windpipe as well. His sharpened little knife was more practical than he had realized! He sat still, enjoying the shudders between his legs. When they stopped he stood up and took a deep breath.

"What a fucking mess," he said to himself. There was blood everywhere and a dead body to dispose of. He checked his watch, twelve o'clock. He was behind schedule but he couldn't leave this lot out in the open, no matter how secluded the cottage.

The dead man was heavy but he managed to drag him onto a tarpaulin that he normally used to cover his bike. He added rocks and secured the wrapping with agricultural twine then paused to consider what to do next.

His shirt and trousers were soaked. He went inside and washed and changed quickly, drank a beer because all that work had made him thirsty, and made his decision.

The body would go in the lake along with his other secrets. No one ever looked there, at least they hadn't in the last ten years, so he couldn't see why they should start now. Then he would use the man's car and drive into Telford. With luck, he'd be at her house before two, almost on schedule. His only uncertainty was whether the police, other than the bungling idiot at his feet, knew of this address. He kicked the bundle hard.

"Did you tell them, or was it your little secret? Nobody's that stupid but perhaps you," he kicked again, "were dumb enough to play a hunch."

He emptied the dregs of his beer over the wrapped body.

"I think you *were* that stupid. Not like your boss, he'd never have done something so brainless."

To be on the safe side he took the parcel of cake and the packages he had prepared earlier and put them in the panniers of his bike. Then he wheeled it up the hill, well into the wood, and covered it with bracken and fallen branches. On the way back to the house he scuffed grit and grass to cover his tracks. He put on gloves and loaded the body into the car. If the police found the house, he had all he needed hidden away; if they didn't he could come back and scrub the place out.

The drive to the lake was uneventful. He passed a family picnicking, who were too absorbed in an argument to notice him, and drove to an isolated spot where the shore shelved deeply to the water. There were windsurfers far away on the horizon but no one closer. With a final look around he reversed the car back as far as caution would allow and dragged the body out into the shallows.

He had forgotten to bring waders so he was soaked to his waist before he let the package go. Bubbles escaped from the wrapping as the body submerged. He watched to make sure it didn't surface then went back to the car and drove away. The family was still there as he passed. They did not look up.

The radio in the car squawked and crackled, distracting him. He had forgotten that this was a police vehicle and decided to turn into the first car park he came across. Driving the car had become increasingly difficult anyway. Adrenaline had carried him through the disposal of the body and the first miles into Telford but he was starting to shake. It always happened. He was fine on the bike, where he wasn't enclosed. In a car it was different. He daren't buckle the seat belt so he wore it loosely over one shoulder, but even so shutting the door brought with it the claustrophobia of a tomb.

Cars were unsafe places. People died in cars, trapped in burning pools of petrol, crushed beneath articulated lorries, drowned in dirty water. He was sweating as he locked the door and resumed the last part of his journey on foot. The steady pounding of his footsteps, the feel of his muscles bunching and relaxing, gradually calmed him. After a hundred counted paces he paused to gain his bearings. Road layouts changed all the time but he thought he recognized a junction ahead. He took off his gloves, conspicuous anyway on a muggy day and unfolded his map from its waterproof container.

Although he was sure that he was being ignored by the passing traffic, he felt conspicuous on the highway and decided to cut across country. In driving part way he had made good time so he could afford to walk the rest.

A quarter of a mile further on there was a turning onto a bridleway that quickly became a footpath. It passed through allotments, then a nursery denuded of bedding plants, before returning to countryside. He walked on through small stands of trees, pausing at stiles he remembered from childhood.

A cough from behind him made him start. An elderly couple was walking their dog and he was blocking their way. How long had he been standing there, lost in the past? He patted their dog and smiled at them, his eyes crinkling in a friendly way that made them smile back. It was fun doing that, tricking smiles out of people. If they only knew what he had done, and what he was capable of doing to them right now, they would probably die of twin heart attacks before he could reach them. The thought made him chuckle and they looked back. The old man touched his cap and walked on. He let them shuffle out of sight then followed along the path.

They kept to the footpath ahead of him, forcing him to a slower pace. From time to time he would pause and consult his map. With his hat, rucksack and mud-splattered boots he looked a typical rambler. At last they turned aside and he was able to move on. Memories of juvenile explorations, watching, prying, eventually touching, came back to him and his stride grew into the lope he could keep up all day. He felt supremely confident on foot, able to outpace and outdistance most ordinary men. And he knew his way around. Even the air smelled familiar: soil, faint traces of exhaust and a whiff from the municipal tip when the wind changed direction. He was almost there. Telford appeared gray on the horizon. Since he had left the area to work in Birmingham, the town had grown outward in irregular loops. It would take him less time to reach his destination than he had thought.

CHAPTER TWENTY-EIGHT

"Diamond?"

Her mother's voice held the mix of concern and frustration that she'd become accustomed to since her "accident," as her parents had decided to call it. Ginny bit down hard and rolled over in bed.

"Diamond?"

She was tapping on the door now. Ginny burrowed deeper and ignored her. The hinge creaked open, a sound as old as she was that had once been associated with comfort and cuddles, but since she'd started to count her age with two digits, had signified intrusion and unwelcome interference.

She sensed her mother stiffen at the sight of her room. Clothes everywhere, curtains drawn against the day, old toys thrown around the floor during her last tantrum. There was a pause. She imagined her mother trying to master her irritation and smiled grimly. Good.

"Oh sweetheart, another bad one?" The concern in her mother's voice brought tears to her eyes. She felt about five.

A creak, the floorboard at the end of the bed, and then another and her mother's weight bowed down the side of the mattress as she sat. A hand found the top of her head and stroked it.

Ginny felt the next tears of the day roll down her right cheek and into the pillow.

"Would you like something to eat, lovely? It's nearly half past two."

Ginny shook her head. She hadn't had any supper and her stomach ached with hunger but the thought of food nauseated her. She hated her body with its curves and bulges that had drawn that man to her. As every day passed and they faded away she became flatter, more like a boy. One day, when she was too ugly for anyone to notice, she hoped to feel safe again.

"How about some coffee then? I promise not to make it too milky and I won't add any sugar."

Her mother knew how she felt without her having told her. It was one of the reasons Ginny could still bear her presence. With everybody else she found it almost impossible to be in the same room, let alone talk. Even her father, whom she knew loved her so much he would do anything for her, even he made her shudder. He was a man—she couldn't bear to be near men, with their animal smell and thick hands. Her poor dad. She sobbed and her mother lifted her up from the bed into her arms.

"There, there, little one. It's all right. Ssh, everything's going to be OK, give it time."

"I can't bear it, Mum. I just can't bear it." Ginny choked back her words. She hadn't meant to speak but with her mother there so close it was impossible to stay silent. "I dream of him every night. He's coming to get me, I know he is. I can feel him out there thinking about me."

It was the same every day. If anything her conviction had grown since the attack. She knew that he wanted her still.

"I spoke to your dad about this last night, Ginny, and he called the police. They say that he won't come back but they're keeping a car outside and increasing the patrols anyway. On Saturday we're going to go away, just the three of us. Auntie May will look after the others. By the time we come back they are bound to have caught him."

Ginny shook her head.

"He's smart, Mum, really smart. Cleverer than the police. I'm not the first one, you know!" Her voice was growing shrill, rising on a tide of hysteria.

"That's enough, Virginia. Calm down. Come on, I'll run you a nice bath—you can have some of my Chanel No. 5 bubbles if you like and afterward I'll dry your hair."

Ginny sniffed her sheets. They were stale, like her skin. She hadn't showered since hospital and she stank, even to her own nose, yet her mum was hugging her as close as if she smelt of roses. Ginny took a deep breath. Mum was right. She should get up and wash this sweat of fear away. Perhaps then she would start to feel more human.

As her mum ran the bath, Ginny found a fresh white T-shirt and khaki jeans. When she pulled back the curtains and saw the drizzle, she added a thin jumper to the pile and walked to the bathroom. It was steamy and warm inside. The smell of her favorite perfume tugged a half smile from her. On the vanity unit her mum had left talc and body lotion in the same fragrance, hoarded since last Christmas and used only on special occasions. Ginny felt tears coming again and blinked them away.

She threw her grubby nightshirt into the laundry bin and stepped into the bath, lowering herself carefully so that the thick layer of foam stayed below the dressing on her shoulder. The deeper bites stung but even so the water was wonderful on her skin, silky and comforting. She sank lower, until the bandage touched the bubbles.

For a long time she just lay there as the water and oils worked their way into her skin, opening and cleansing her pores. As the water started to cool, she scrubbed around her injuries until her skin was pink. Then she washed her hair with great difficulty, shampooing twice and using a conditioner that she actually left on for the full ten minutes.

Feeling shiny and new, she stepped out of the bath and watched the scummy water drain away, leaving a grubby gray coating on the enamel that made her ashamed. With a start of surprise Ginny realized that she felt better than she had done for days. Her cold had gone and the trace of her last nightmare had left her. Her mother, ever the mind-reader, tapped on the door. Ginny wrapped a towel round herself quickly and opened it.

"Here's another coffee. Hungry yet?"

Ginny realized that she was, for the first time in days. She nodded.

"You know what I *really* fancy?"

Her mother smiled, "No, what?"

"Scrambled eggs on toast and bacon."

Mum's face fell. "I can do the toast part but your dad ate me out of eggs and bacon last night."

"Never mind." But Ginny did mind, she felt cheated.

"Don't look like that, love. Tell you what, I'll pop down to the corner shop while you get dressed."

Ginny felt a spurt of fear. That meant she would be alone in the house. She told herself not to be so stupid. Her mother would be gone only a matter of minutes.

"If you don't mind?"

"It's no trouble. I'll be back before you know it, then I'll dry your hair and make us both a late lunch."

Ginny heard her mother pick up her keys and handbag and close the front door firmly. It was only a small house and she had absorbed the sounds of it from the time she was in her cradle.

She unwound the towel and started to rub in the body lotion sparingly, mindful that it was her mother's favorite.

A loud click made her jump. She listened in absolute silence, frozen with the tube of lotion still in her left hand. The house was quiet, the only sounds the hum from the fridge and the ticking of the immersion heater on the landing. Perhaps it had been that that had startled her, except that it sounded different, exactly like the back door closing.

She let out her breath slowly and put down the lotion, all thoughts of indulgence gone. She became acutely aware of her own nakedness. Her underwear was still in the airing cupboard and she wasn't about to go out there and find it but she pulled on her jeans anyway, ears straining to catch the slightest noise. All was still. She zipped them up, hardly making a sound. Her T-shirt was next. She pulled it over her head quickly, hating to have her ears covered, even for a second, then held her breath and listened. Nothing.

Her mum had pulled the bathroom door to without actually closing it. Ginny crept forward and put her fingers on the handle. She pulled it open another inch and peered out. As she did so there was a creak from the bottom stair, absolutely unmistakable. Someone was there! Her mouth went dry. Without taking her eyes from the top of the stairs in front of her, she found the bolt on the door and closed her fingers around it, ready to ram it home as soon as she slammed the door shut. Whoever was on the staircase had paused too, they must have done, otherwise she would have seen their head by now as it rounded the turn of the stair. Seconds passed, feeling like minutes.

Suddenly, horribly, he was there, hurtling up the last three steps toward her, a knife in his hand. She screamed and slammed the door shut, yanking the cord from her father's dressing gown out of the way reflexively as it almost caught in the gap. He slammed his weight into the wood as the bolt went home, yanking the handle in a vain attempt to force it open. He was shouting at her, vile obscene words that filled her mind and made her panic.

Ginny screamed again. How long would the bolt hold? It was a tiny aluminum thing held onto the panel of the door by only two screws. Over the years the missing ones had never been replaced as it had been there for privacy, not security. Until now.

He was ramming the door hard, throwing his weight against it, again and again. The door groaned under the strain and Ginny screamed louder. She looked around, crazy with fear. The window above the sink only opened six inches at the top. She pulled the net curtain to one side and searched for something with which to break the glass. A marbled duck full of pot-pourri stood on the window ledge. Ginny grabbed it and threw it with all her force against the window as the door behind her creaked ominously.

The glass shattered, spraying shards across the small room. She trod on one of them in her bare feet but felt no pain. Grabbing the bath towel she swept the fragments from around the window ledge then wrapped it tightly around her fist to punch out the broken pieces that still held to the frame. Crying now, the sobs flowing into a constant whimper, she climbed up onto the sink, leaving a trail of bright red blood against the white enamel and screamed for help to the street below. It was deserted. The comforting patrol car that had been sitting outside all day was gone and the pavements were empty. There was a loud snapping from the door behind her and the bolt flew off.

He reached her just as she had one leg over the windowsill.

"Help me! Help me, please!" she cried to the empty air. His hand closed around her ankle and she kicked back viciously, fighting for her life.

"No!" Ginny clung on to the window frame, ignoring the edges of glass that cut into her bare palms.

A delivery van turned the corner of the road as she clung

on. She willed it to stop, ignoring the burning pain that had started in her back and along her thighs. He was hitting her now, harder and harder.

"Help me! Mummy, help me!"

The van drove past and she lost her grip, her bloody fingers slipping over the smooth ceramic surface. She fell back into the room below. There was blood everywhere. It must be hers. They hadn't been punches. He'd stabbed her in the back. Terror gripped her and she started to fight, kicking at him as hard as she could, despite the growing weakness in her legs.

She felt light-headed. Her screams seemed to be coming from a long way away. He was above her now, trying to undo her jeans. She wriggled but his weight pinned her down. He was *not* going to have her. If she was going to die, and with an eerie clarity she realized that she was, she would not be violated again by this animal.

Hatred gave her strength and brought clarity to her thinking. Shards of glass from the broken window lay on the floor. She found one and gripped it tight. Her arm felt incredibly heavy as she aimed a slicing cut at his exposed neck as he looked down to guide his fingers inside her jeans.

It was a weak blow but it ripped open a long flap of skin along his cheek. He yelled and swore at her. One hand went to his face and she watched as he stared in horror at the sight of his own blood. She slashed again, a laugh of triumph bubbling up from her mouth, sending him mad.

She felt his hands close around her throat as she stabbed at him with the last of her strength. The makeshift dagger sliced into his exposed neck then her arm fell. The last thing she heard before the dark beating of wings inside her head drowned out all other sounds was his long, anguished cry, and she smiled.

PART FOUR

WENDY AND NIGHTINGALE

The woman who cannot evolve a good lie in defense of the man she loves is unworthy of the name of wife.

—ELBERT HUBBARD

Vengeance is in my heart, death in my hand. Blood and revenge are hammering in my head.

—WILLIAM SHAKESPEARE

CHAPTER TWENTY-NINE

"Did she know we were coming?" Fenwick felt odd. Despite the heat he kept shivering; perhaps it was the flu.

"Yes. I distinctly told her three o'clock." MacIntyre glared at Fenwick, regretting his promise to the Commissioner to see the profiler personally because of the Home Secretary's insistence.

She arrived at five past with a smile that dismissed the Superintendent's glare. In her office, MacIntyre forgot his diplomacy and pushed her hard for opinions on the probability of a relationship between Killers A and B.

"As I said in my report, Superintendent, I consider it a possibility but one can never be certain. It could be coincidence that two perpetrators took a finger from their victims' hands, selected exactly the same type of girl—looks, age, physique—and chose the same towns in which to prey on women. But I don't think that's likely."

MacIntyre looked distinctly put out. Fenwick didn't know whether to be pleased at Professor Ball's conviction or worried that MacIntyre still had so many doubts.

"May I add more data?"

He told Ball everything he had uncovered about Griffiths' childhood and fostering, the little he knew about the Smith family, including their sudden disappearance, and the pattern of crimes that Robyn had discovered, dating from the boys' time at school. MacIntyre stopped pacing and started to take notes.

"Fascinating! This is very suggestive of an adolescent bonding reinforced by petty crime. Tell me more about the cousin, Wendy Smith."

"I know no more, Professor. My theory is that Smith junior assaulted her or she might have been a willing participant overawed into compliance. I think it happened when she was under age and that her father found out. Fred Smith is a loser quite capable of blackmailing his brother. It would explain the regular cash withdrawals. When the father was told about the boy's behavior by the drama teacher, he commented that something similar had happened before."

"And where is Wendy now?"

"We're still trying to find her."

"Be careful when you do. There's a chance that she's still with him."

"Would B be able to sustain a relationship? I mean, if he's a serial rapist and killer, surely a partner would have suspected something and left him." MacIntyre appeared determined to preserve his skepticism about Killer B's identity.

"Sadly the two things don't automatically follow each other. I can list you a dozen of the worst male killers society has known who had a wife or girlfriend. It is not uncommon, particularly with someone as plausible and charming as Killer B. There are none so blind, gentlemen."

Fenwick shook his head in disgust.

"And Griffiths? Would it have been a menage à trois?"

"I doubt it. Killer B, Smith in your theory, is the dominant member of the group. He might have let Griffiths use Wendy as an occasional reward but there would have been no relationship there."

"We should be going." MacIntyre stood up, suddenly impatient to be gone.

"One final question." Fenwick turned to the Professor as MacIntyre started his pacing again.

"Killer B has failed in his last two attacks. One victim survived because he left her to drown and it wasn't a spring tide. The second—and I accept that it's only me who thinks B is the attacker—was saved by a taxi driver who was killed for his bravery. How will B be feeling? And why is he making these mistakes?"

"Let's take your second question first and assume that your theory of a single attacker is correct. He's attacking outside, forced to behave in a manner to which he is not accustomed for motives you are better at assessing than I. That's one of the reasons he's making mistakes. Despite that he is becoming more confident. Killing the taxi driver before escaping was a bold act. If this is the work of one man he has killed three people and attempted to kill two others within the last ten weeks. That is extremely active, even for a serial killer. If it is one man then the pace of his crimes is accelerating. He's becoming increasingly daring. It's possible he may even consider himself invincible by now."

"Is it possible, and I know this sounds crazy, I've already been told that in no uncertain terms, but could he return to kill one of the girls, say, his last victim?"

There was a long silence before Professor Ball spoke.

"It would be very stupid, and I think Killer B has significantly above average intellect even though he is an underachiever. But . . . he'll be angry. He will be unable to accept that he has failed . . . and he certainly won't lack the confidence to do it."

"Well? Could he?"

"It's possible but I've never known of such a case. When was the girl attacked?"

"Over a week ago. She spent the first five days in hospital, now she's back home."

"He's left it a long time. I don't think of him as obsessive . . ." she paused, then looked confused, "unless he needed to prove himself—failure might eat away at him. I'm sorry I can't be more definite."

"We'd better go. Professor Ball, as always, your insights have been most useful."

"Could I have a word with you in private, Superintendent?"

Fenwick waited in the corridor, feeling like a scolded schoolboy. He could hear the murmur of voices through the closed door and occasionally identified his own name. MacIntyre was tight-lipped on the way back to his office but roused himself as they left the car.

"Are you OK, Andrew? You look pale."

"I'm fine. It's just Ginny, I'm worried for her. If it were my case . . ."

"But it's not and for what it's worth I would have reacted in the same way as Cave. Nothing could happen in a few minutes." MacIntyre slapped him on the back and told him to cheer up. "If it'll make you feel better I'll call Cave again, find out how things are." He was laughing as he walked into his office but stopped abruptly when he saw the urgent message on his desk to call Telford.

The men stared at each other, unspoken fear large between them. Fenwick switched on his mobile, desperately hoping that there were no messages but he was disappointed. He went to the window for a better signal and watched MacIntyre dial. Fenwick leaned against the cold glass and listened to his answering service.

"Fenwick, it's Cave. He went back. I need you up here, now."

Fenwick could taste bile in his throat. Behind him he heard

MacIntyre talk to Cave. He was unable to turn around to witness the expression on his face. The message said only that he'd gone back, it hadn't said that Ginny was dead. She could still be alive, but the dread around his heart told him otherwise.

"I see. We'll leave straightaway. I'll call you for directions when we're closer." MacIntyre replaced the receiver and cleared his throat.

Fenwick wiped his face and found it cold with sweat.

"I'm sorry, Andrew. Ginny's dead. She was strangled and knifed to death in the bathroom of her house this afternoon."

He knew that he was going to be sick and ran to the bathroom, just making it to the sink. His stomach heaved and he retched, then again. He ran the cold tap and used a paper towel to clear the mess away, then washed his face with cool water. The door opened behind him but he kept his head low.

"Are you OK?"

He nodded. MacIntyre walked past, urinated, flushed and washed his hands. Fenwick was still staring into the sink when he'd finished.

"We have to go. They need us."

"You go. I can't. How can I face them? It's all my fault."

"Don't be bloody stupid! Do you know how ridiculous and arrogant that is? You did your best. You warned Cave, several times. It is *not* your fault."

"But I knew he was going to do it. I should have stayed up there." Fenwick straightened and winced at the burning pain in his gut.

"Nonsense. What could you have done?"

Anger filled him, a burning fury like vitriol.

"I could have *saved* her," he shouted, his spittle covering MacIntyre's face. "I could have sat outside her fucking *house* day and night until the bastard gave up and went away."

He wanted to hit MacIntyre. The man had dragged him back here with his sarcastic insistence that he'd been wasting his time, but he stopped himself. He couldn't pass on the blame that easily. It was *his* fault. One time he would have followed his instincts whatever the price. He was too concerned about his own career, that was the problem, too busy trying to please people rather than catch killers. He'd been seduced into forgetting that that was what real police officers actually did.

"Jesus." He turned away from MacIntyre in self-disgust and pulled out another towel to wipe his face free of moisture.

"And where would you have sat?"

"In the car."

"At the front of the house. He went in the back, Fenwick. She was dead in minutes. Her mother left to go to the local shop and shortly afterward the officer on duty had an urgent call of nature and had to leave. He swears it was for less than five minutes. When they returned, Ginny was dead."

"I could have saved her." The possible truth of the statement ate into him like acid.

"It wasn't your case, it wasn't your patch. You were up there on an unrelated matter. A highly experienced local SIO was in charge. If there is any blame it's his, not yours. Do you understand me?" He swung Fenwick round to face him and almost shook him.

"I'm going to be ill again. Would you mind going?"

He was, very ill. Eventually, empty and lightheaded, he straightened his tie and walked back to MacIntyre's office.

"I've changed my mind. I will come with you. I need to see it, to be there."

"Don't be such a bloody masochist. You're coming with me because you're going to help me catch this bastard before he kills anyone else. Do you need anything?"

"My overnight case is in my office. And I'll take my files."

"I'll see you in the car park in five minutes."

MacIntyre had arranged for a driver and Fenwick was glad. He didn't think he could handle a car. They were silent for the first part of the journey. Traffic was thin and the flashing blue light cleared a swathe before them.

Fenwick asked the driver to pull over at the first service station and went to buy a sports drink, bar of chocolate, and two coffees.

"You not having one?"

"Don't think my stomach could take it. I'm craving sugar and salts."

"Perhaps you ate something that didn't agree with you. You were looking off-color all afternoon."

"Probably."

MacIntyre stared at him strangely.

"What?"

"You knew this might happen. Why?"

"Didn't you think it possible?"

"No—even Ball didn't. I've spoken with Cave. He's gone over his rationale for the level of protection with me and . . ."

"Perhaps he's rehearsing his lines." The bitterness inside Fenwick made his mouth twist in disgust.

"I'm sure, but the point is that other officers would have done the same."

"Even though she witnessed a murder?"

"She was unconscious, drugged out of her mind for the whole episode. And he didn't care about being recognized. The barman saw him at the Italian they went to. And the taxi driver, if he hadn't gone back, which was a highly unusual thing to do, he would have been a witness. This man doesn't care too much about being seen."

"Whatever. She's dead. Only eighteen and he butchered her. That should never have happened."

"How do you know he butchered her?" There was a sharpness in MacIntyre's face that jolted some sense into Fenwick. He wanted to stay on the case, catch the bastard, revenge Ginny and save Nightingale. He would need all his wits.

"You said so after Cave's call."

"I didn't describe how she died but you're right. The injuries inflicted on her were dreadful. How did you know?"

"It would be in keeping with his MO. Smith detests young pretty women with dark hair."

"Supposing Ginny's killer is Killer B and Killer B is Smith. Do you think that you know this man's mind?"

All Fenwick's instincts screamed at him to be cautious.

"I've simply studied the crime scenes and I know the profilers' reports off by heart. That's given me an insight."

"Hmm. Do you think he'll still be in Telford?"

"No. His business is finished there. He'll have moved on."

"To find Nightingale." He resisted voicing the thought and concentrated instead on working through what Smith would do next. Despite his careful answer to MacIntyre, he felt unusually connected to the killer. He was convinced that if Nightingale hadn't decided to leave Harlden and her past so completely behind her, she would have been dead by now because Smith needed to punish her for catching his partner. He finished his drink and the last chunk of chocolate then closed his eyes for some precious sleep, on the assumption that there would be little in the days ahead.

MacIntyre woke him as they turned onto the M52, shaking him roughly by the shoulder in impatience. The expression on his face, irritation mixed with a hint of respect, brought Fenwick to instant wakefulness.

"The prints on the knife. I've just had a call. Apparently Forensics were asked to look for matches against evidence you gave them, on my urgent instructions?"

Fenwick said nothing. Yes, he'd used MacIntyre's authority, so what, how else was he to get anything done?

"The prints match a set found on the letters sent to Griffiths. You know what that means, we have a confirmed link. Griffiths knows Killer B. They said that you'd given them a box to test as well?"

"From the Smith house, yes."

"Well they lifted some good prints and ran those against the knife as well. One set is a match." MacIntyre soft punched his shoulder. "Congratulations. You were right, Killer B is Smith. You'd better get on the blower to that sergeant of yours in Harlden. The search for Nightingale has more priority now. Even your ACC should devote resources to it. You sort it while I break the news to Telford. Somehow I don't think it's going to make Cave's day."

The moment of victory meant nothing to Fenwick. It had come too late to save Ginny and he shrugged the Superintendent's compliment to one side. He'd been right from the beginning, but all he could think about was a dead eighteen-year-old lying in her own blood in the supposed safety of her own home.

The autopsy on Ginny had been given highest priority and had started by the time MacIntyre and Fenwick arrived. Fenwick's self-imposed penance didn't extend to compulsory attendance at the weighing and measuring of her mortal remains so he filled in time until Cave's return reading reports and studying the bloody scene-of-crime photographs. There was a full-scale manhunt in progress but so far there was no sign of the killer.

"He ran across a rubbish dump and the dogs lost his trail." MacIntyre shook his head in disgust. "They have roadblocks everywhere but there are so many lanes that the best hope is helicopters."

"How did he arrive at the house?"

"No idea. He walked through the back garden and picked the lock on the back door but there was no sighting of a suspicious car or bike."

"Who found her?" Fenwick radiated flat calm but MacIntyre looked at him warily.

"One of our boys. Her mother was walking back from the shops when she noticed the broken bathroom window. Fortunately the patrolman got there first. Thank God she didn't have to see this." MacIntyre gestured to the lurid 8" x 6" photographs in which the predominant color was red.

"So she broke the window and tried to escape. Plucky kid. If someone had been outside . . ."

"Drop it!" It was an order.

"Yes . . . sir." He was in a filthy mood, making it a dangerous time for employee relations.

"We should go and eat. I know looking at that lot isn't an appetizer but it's going to be a long night." MacIntyre was determined to force him to return to common sense.

By the time they returned, Cave was in his office. They shook hands but Cave couldn't meet Fenwick's eye.

"Any sightings?"

"None. And as we don't know what he's driving the search is slow. The key question is, what is he likely to do next?"

MacIntyre looked at Fenwick. "Go on, you probably know him best."

"If it's Smith, I think he will try to leave the area. It's what he did after the crimes in London and Wales."

"Which direction?"

Fenwick shrugged.

"It could be anywhere but Birmingham's a possibility. He went there by train after London and it's where Griffiths has been sending the letters."

Cave nodded.

"That's what I thought. It's where I've focused the roadblocks. Any other ideas?"

"It's a long shot but his father had a holiday home somewhere. We haven't been able to trace it—unless Robyn Powell found it, or Knotty." Mentioning the constable's name brought a frown to his face. "Damn, he'll be back in London now."

"I think she left her report in your old office if you need it. We've also arranged some accommodation for you both at the Armada."

"So what now. How best can we help?" MacIntyre's tone was perfect. Fenwick tried to memorize it for later use.

"A personal briefing to the team. There's nothing you can do in the search. The Chief Constable himself has become involved. We have all the resources we need, now."

The visitors ignored the trace of bitterness in the man's tone.

"You don't need me for that. I'm going to read Robyn's report and try to contact Knotty." Fenwick left them to it.

Robyn had stuck an Ordnance Survey map to the wall. It had developed a rash of red spots worse than Knotty's acne and they formed a pattern of sorts. She had highlighted the location of Griffiths/Smith's school with a circle drawn around it to indicate the distance the boys could have traveled within two hours. Each red pin had a number by it, which corresponded to one on a list on his desk. By referring between the two he could follow the patterns she had discovered of incidents that slowly escalated during the years before they left school.

It was useful corroboration but they had a physical link between Griffiths and Smith now and Fenwick's attention was drawn to an unexplained splattering of pins to the west of Telford. In the hills on the Welsh Borders she had placed three red pins and several black ones. Why and how had she found these crimes? The answer was in her meticulous report. She had looked through all the records for crimes that matched the characteristics of those around the school and then cross-checked them with the physical descriptions of perpetrators that matched Griffiths and Smith. There were none to the east or north. Every one lay between Telford and the boys' home, or in the hills beyond.

He found the relevant notes and read them out loud in the privacy of his office.

"The black pins relate to reported cases of animal mutilation, ranging from rabbits to farming livestock. The smaller animals were flayed and gutted, the larger (a pony, five sheep, one calf, a pet dog) had their genitalia mutilated. The interesting thing to note is the dates. Every incident takes place in the school holidays.

"The red pins relate to minor sexual assaults, again in the holidays.

"Pin number sixty-three: Indecent exposure. Reported by thirteen-year-old girl near Belsize Lake. Description of a young man with brown hair. August 16th, 14:25.

"Sixty-four: Indecent assault on sixteen-year-old girl in hills above lake. Description as for sixty-three but face was covered with a scarf. August 20th, 17:45.

"Seventy: Indecent assault on twenty-year-old hiker in hills above lake. Description of short, heavy-set youth wearing balaclava does not match those in sixty-three and four. September 2nd, 9:10 a.m."

He drew a line around the pins, encircling an area of less than a square mile, through the middle of which ran a single-track road with a scattering of houses on either side. Robyn had found the Smith's holiday home.

At one-fifteen a.m., Fenwick joined MacIntyre and Cave on a deserted road half a mile from Belsize Lake.

"There are six cottages spread out well back from the road. We have teams ready to enter and search each one."

The three men waited without speaking, then Cave's radio broke the silence. He listened and grunted a response.

"Nothing in cottage Charlie, a family from Cheshire are renting."

The scene repeated itself three times in quick succession.

"Only Cottage Echo and Bravo left. Both are empty. We're waiting for clearance to enter."

Ten long minutes passed before the team at Echo reported back.

"Echo has been lived in. The fridge is stocked and there are fresh ashes from a fire in the grate."

They went down the hill together. It was nearly two a.m. but Fenwick felt alert and full of energy. Cave passed out latex gloves and they were given shoe covers at the door. An armed officer came to find Cave as soon as he arrived.

"You need to see this."

The man took them to the bathroom and an open laundry hamper. He pulled out a shirt with the tips of his gloved fingers. The cuffs were soaked with blood and there was heavy splattering on the front.

"It's still damp in folds of the material, and there are dried traces in the sink over there."

"Get a full SOCO team out here right now."

"Done, sir."

Fenwick's hair was standing up from his scalp as if an electric current was running through him. Smith had been here recently, he was no longer a phantom who could come and go without leaving a trace of his passing other than mutilated young women. He needed air and stepped back outside.

The night was clear, the moon almost full. It lit up the landscape in a gray-blue light that cast dense shadows and washed all color and depth from the scene. He tried to imagine Smith driving through country lanes, heading away from his latest crime but the scene wouldn't fix in his mind.

Smith had killed Ginny ten hours before. It would have taken him twenty minutes to drive back here, another twenty to wash and change. He had more than a nine-hour start on them. It was conceivable that he had even left the country by now. His euphoria faded as the realities of the search hit him. With a wry smile he realized that he had already dismissed his successes: discovering that Killer B was Smith, linking him to Griffiths, finding this place because of his insistence on reviewing old crimes. They would mean nothing if he didn't catch Smith before the man found Nightingale, or some other victim.

MacIntyre came to stand beside him and lit a cigarette.

Fenwick waited for an acknowledgment that MacIntyre had been wrong to doubt his visit north but it didn't come. Instead the Superintendent asked a question.

"What will Smith do now? You're our resident expert on the man."

Fenwick resented the responsibility that MacIntyre had shifted effortlessly onto him. He was wearing the monkey on his back again and it made him angry.

"How should I know? I've been focusing on his past, confirming his identity. My only certainty is that he wants to kill Nightingale. Find her and we'll find him."

"Don't you think you're a bit obsessed with this?"

"I was obsessed with finding Smith. That hasn't done us any harm. Humor me."

He walked away before his temper gained the upper hand. There was a track, bone white in the moonlight and he followed it, rehearsing smart remarks in his mind, oblivious to his surroundings. When it reached the margins of the lake he stopped in surprise. The water lay flat and dead. It looked unwholesome and he shivered. He felt very alone out here, as if demons with slimy black tentacles were waiting to drag him down into its depths.

The lights of a helicopter swept a distant hill and he realized that a lone man by the lake might set up an unhelpful search so he started back. Cave and MacIntyre were waiting for him.

"There you are! Where have you been?"

"Thinking." It wasn't true but he thought "sulking" an unnecessary admission.

"And?" Was MacIntyre deliberately goading him?

"OK. Here are our priorities: match the prints on the knife to those here . . ."

"Already in hand." Cave waved a list in his hand.

"Confirm the bite marks on Ginny are the same as on Tasmin and Lucinda."

"The forensic team in London are treating it as top priority, we should hear tomorrow morning."

"Look for tracks around here. What sort of vehicle did he drive?" Cave was nodding but had not yet added anything to his own notes.

"Find Wendy Smith. She could lead us to him. And keep up the watch on the address Griffiths has been writing to."

"Is there much point?" MacIntyre didn't bother to hide his doubts. "Surely Smith's self-directed. The letters from Griffiths mean nothing to him."

"Perhaps, but they were associates and he went to the trouble to establish contact. I think it's worth it. And we should complete the work on the tapes from Griffiths' trial, see if we have a clear shot of him. We can add that to the e-fit that I imagine you've already circulated nationwide." MacIntyre nodded. "One final thing. There's a lake down there, walking distance. It might be worth dredging for the murder weapon."

This time Cave did make a note but Fenwick saw that it went way down a very long list.

It was gone four by the time they reached the smart hotel where they had reservations. Fenwick was still wide awake but he told himself that it made sense to grab a few hours' sleep. He showered and lay in bed naked, trying to ignore the first chirps of the morning chorus beyond his window.

Flashes of the past few days kept appearing like a disjointed slideshow in front of the darkness of his closed eyelids. Ginny's house, Ginny dead, the shattered window. Red drops of blood became the pinheads on Robyn's map. The holiday home, warm and lived in, still smelling of Smith, blood from his last kill discarded to wash later. He thought of Nightingale, the last time he had seen her, pale-faced, stressed out, too thin. And he remembered Claire's bombshell. Guilt for driving Nightingale away added to the remorse he felt for Ginny's death. No matter what MacIntyre or Cave said, he felt responsible. Of the senior officers involved in the case, he was the only one who had *known* that Killer B would return. He should have stayed behind to protect her. If Nightingale died too . . . He stopped the thought, unable to contemplate such failure.

At some point he must have drifted asleep because his alarm woke him at seven. He took another shower, feeling dreadful, and left a message at Harlden for the Superintendent to call him as soon as he arrived. A full English breakfast and coffee went some way to revive him. By the time he met MacIntyre he had stopped feeling like an old man.

In the car on the way to meet Cave, they both checked their messaging services. There was nothing from Knotty so Fenwick left an urgent message for him.

"We're going back at the cottage. Thought you'd want to see it in daylight." MacIntyre gave him another of his weird looks. "Is there something bothering you?"

Fenwick was becoming increasingly irritated by the man's attitude. He shook his head and opened his window to allow fresh air into the car.

At Smith's house SOCO were still at work, able to move more quickly in daylight. A checkbook stub had been found; Cave had already organized a stop on the account and had asked the bank to tell him immediately of any attempted withdrawals.

Fenwick went outside. A team of officers was searching the grounds in an increasingly large circle, some working down toward the lake, others uphill to a thick set of trees that marked the start of a wood. Areas close by the cottage had been taped off and white-coated scene-of-crime technicians were working on them. He flashed his warrant card.

"What have you got?"

"Signs of a scuffle there and over here. It made us look closer and we found this." The man held up an unimpressive cotton bud. One tip was pink.

"Blood?"

"Yes. There's a fair bit of it."

Fenwick went to find Cave.

"They've found traces of blood outside. There's a possibility the blood on the shirt may not be Ginny's."

"We know."

"If it's not hers, why would he risk a kill so close to home?"

"It's probably an animal's. Remember the reports Robyn dug out?"

Fenwick shook his head.

"Why go back to schoolboy stuff when he was already planning to kill Ginny?"

"There's no point speculating. The results will be through later today."

"But . . ."

MacIntyre, who had been sitting quietly observing them, stood up and put a hand on Fenwick's arm.

"Got a minute?"

They went outside.

"Why are you so concerned about the shirt?"

"It may not be Ginny's blood. Supposing someone disturbed him here and he killed them?"

"I can't see him knocking off a stray passer-by."

"What about Wendy or her dad?"

"Fred Smith is alive and well, though very unamused. Cave has brought him in for questioning on suspicion of blackmail. We'll never prove that now but we might just rattle Wendy's address out of him."

"Then who . . . ?"

"Or what. Leave it, Andrew. Cave has it covered. He has all the resources he needs and we must go. I'm better placed to coordinate a nationwide search in London."

He went back inside and Fenwick called Quinlan again. When he couldn't be found he asked for Cooper and was kept waiting for longer than he appreciated. He couldn't keep the impatience from his voice when the Sergeant eventually picked up the receiver.

"Sorry to keep you waiting. I was in a briefing and . . ."

"Listen, we know who Griffiths' partner was." He explained

the basics to Cooper quickly, not giving him a chance to ask questions. "The point is that he'll be after Nightingale next. How has the work gone in tracing her?"

There was an embarrassed silence.

"Cooper?" His tone rose in warning.

"It's Inspector Blite, sir. The Superintendent gave it to him and he says it's a low priority, that it's one of your obsessions."

"*One* of my obsessions?"

"I mean . . . well, the point is I started work on it but I haven't had a moment to get back to it. There's been thefts and vandalism up at the golf club and the Mayor's car was stolen . . ."

"We're talking about a woman's life here! Put me through to Quinlan. I insist on speaking to him right now."

"No! It'll cause a terrible stink. Leave it with me. I promise I'll do something today. Blite's away all morning so I'll have a chance."

Fenwick paused. He was so angry that he was burning to have a go about Blite to Superintendent Quinlan but Cooper was right. He was far away, out of mind, and Blite would simply say that the investigation was progressing.

"Very well. I'll call again later but for God's sake, don't let me down."

As they drove south, clouds appeared to greet them. The heat turned muggy and he wound the widow down, turning his face to the air like a dog. They stopped after two hours for something to eat. Despite his fifth coffee of the day, Fenwick started to feel groggy as soon as he'd eaten but MacIntyre was wide-awake and curious.

He quizzed Fenwick in detail, asking why he had been so insistent about digging into every aspect of Smith's past. Why had he visited the old family home? Why had he set Robyn to work on old cases and why those cases? Fenwick found it exhausting. To stop MacIntyre talking he said with more exasperation than he would have liked:

"Look I don't *know* why I was keen to find his home, nor why I think his parents are more likely to be dead than to have done a runner. It's logical, isn't it, to want to find out everything you can about a suspect? I just go back farther and in deeper, that's all."

When they stopped to allow the driver a comfort break, he rounded on MacIntyre, too tired to hide his irritation.

"I don't mind scrutiny, curiosity is fine, but I get the sense there's something about me that makes you uncomfortable. Why don't you just come out with it. The cross-examination and deep looks are getting on my nerves."

If he had thought MacIntyre would be angry, he was wrong. The Superintendent just laughed.

"My, aren't we a sensitive soul! The truth is that you are a seriously weird detective. No wonder Harper-Brown can't stand you."

Fenwick opened his mouth, in protest or in shock that the detail of his relationship with the ACC was common gossip, he wasn't sure.

"Don't get on your high horse. You've got to watch that pomposity, Andrew, it's your least appealing feature. Listen, I've worked with all sorts in London and in Scotland before I came down here but you're like no one I've worked with before.

"You're logical, irritatingly so, yet on the other hand, you are intuitive. You keep a complex investigative strategy in your head as if it was a game of cards, but you insist on the most detailed investigations of tangential aspects of a case. And Professor Ball described you as a 'rare empathetic conduit'—don't frown, they're her words, not mine. Whether you like it or not, you *are* different. You combine intellect and intuition. That's unusual, and it's also disconcerting, particularly when you don't even bother to hide it. Most smart people know enough not to appear too clever. You don't even bother to try."

Fenwick did what he always did when he was lost for words, shrugged noncommitally. He made a show of looking for a bottle of water then concentrated on opening the complicated, sportsman-friendly top. MacIntyre wasn't fooled.

"Ask yourself: why are you still a chief inspector? I'm your age and I'm a superintendent, and it's not necessarily because I'm better than you are. Why has it never happened for you?"

Another shrug.

"It just never came along."

He looked around, keen for the driver to return.

"I don't buy it. That suggests a lack of ambition that isn't credible."

Fenwick took a deep breath and tried to control his tone.

"At the time I should have been thinking about my career, other things stood in the way."

"You mean your wife's illness. Yes, I read about that in your file. Reason enough at the time perhaps, but not now. There's got to be more to it."

Fenwick could feel a vein pulse in his jaw. Perhaps the man was being deliberately provocative but he wasn't in the mood to be goaded. Yes, he had a temper. Yes, he had made it clear on more than one occasion that the ACC was an idiot, but those days were behind him. He told himself that he had learned discretion. The last thing he was going to do was prove himself wrong to this nosy prick.

MacIntyre's phone rang, allowing Fenwick to avoid further conversation. The driver returned and no more was said as they drove on. He slept.

In his dream he watched as Ginny ran her bath and slid

beneath the bubbles. He was trapped outside the bathroom window but he could see everything. The scene changed. He was behind Smith as he crept up the stairs. Fenwick tried to hold him back but Smith shrugged him off as if he were of no more substance than a ghost.

Ginny was toweling herself dry. He could see her even though the door was almost closed. When she turned and saw Smith her mouth opened in a silent scream but she didn't try to escape. Instead she picked up something that he couldn't see and advanced toward him. *She* was the predator, smiling now. Smith turned to run. Ginny threw herself on top of him. Her hand with its invisible weapon rose and fell, inflicting terrible wounds on the man beneath her. An arc of warm blood spurted out, splattering a thick, cherry-red spray over Fenwick's face and neck. He swiped at it in a sudden panic and woke up.

Another summer shower was sweeping across the sky. Raindrops from the open window dripped onto his face. He closed it, feeling shaken and disorientated. MacIntyre was still on the phone. The dream had disturbed him. As he stared at the water droplets on the glass he tried to sort through the images for meaning but it alluded him.

He pulled the scene-of-crime photographs from his briefcase, feeling nauseous at the lurch and roll of the car. There were so many images. He sifted through them until a close-up of Ginny's hand gripped tight around a shard of glass held his attention. The broken edges had cut into her palm and along the inside of her knuckles but she held it tight despite the agony of the grip.

Blood had run down beyond her wrist. The shard was thick with it. Fenwick looked at the picture again and his head cleared. Unexpected tears filled his eyes and he blinked them away. She had fought back, this tough little eighteen-year-old. She had kicked and scratched and screamed. And she had stabbed him.

That wasn't her blood staining the glass she had used as a dagger. It was his. She had wounded him! The thought filled him with primeval glee, sending a jolt through his exhausted body. He looked up. MacIntyre was staring at him, phone forgotten. His habitual look of amused curiosity had been replaced with something else. Was it concern? No. It was expectation.

"You've found something in those pictures." It wasn't a question.

"Look at this." He handed him the photograph of Ginny's right hand. "That's his blood, not hers. It was her weapon. She stabbed him with it. Why else is the blood so thick on the edges away from her hand?"

MacIntyre took the picture from him again.

"There was so much blood in that room. It could have come from anywhere."

"I don't think so. In the wider shots you can see clearly that a pattern of blood goes up and away from her hand."

MacIntyre nodded slowly.

"It's possible. Why are you so convinced?"

Fenwick was not about to share his dream with him.

"It's easily tested. SOCO will have kept the fragments numbered and bagged. See if all the blood matches hers."

MacIntyre called in the new information. They were at Watford when the phone rang. A motorbike had been found hidden in the woods. In the panniers were clothes, a laptop, hair dye, other toiletries and a pair of shoes. The fingerprints matched Smith's. The theory was that he had been planning to return to collect it but the rapid discovery of the girl's body and the manhunt that followed had forced him to change his plans.

"Oh, and Cave says could you ask Knotty where he parked the car he borrowed yesterday. They can't find it and need it back."

The first tremor of unease for Knotty ran through Fenwick.

He rang every number he could think of without success. The Constable hadn't been seen in London, his mobile didn't answer and his home number went through to an answering machine. Robyn had no idea where he'd gone but gave him the telephone numbers of people he'd seen before setting off back to London.

"Problem?" MacIntyre raised a quizzical eyebrow.

"Constable Knots has disappeared."

"Lazy bugger!"

"But he's not, is he? If he was ill he'd call in."

"When did you last speak to him?"

"Over twenty-four hours ago."

MacIntyre frowned.

"That is odd, and Cave's complaining about the car. I wonder if he's had an accident somewhere. I'll call Telford and ask them to have a look around, not that they'll have any manpower to spare."

Fenwick started to chew the skin at the side of his thumb, a nervous habit from childhood that he thought he'd broken a long time before.

"What's up?"

"I keep thinking about the patch of blood SOCO found outside the cottage. It may signify nothing, but if Smith didn't take his bike into Telford, how did he get there? He wouldn't have walked all the way, surely?"

"The missing car." MacIntyre called Cave. Without sounding too sensational, and with laughs Fenwick could tell were forced, he explained their worries. "It's far-fetched, I know, but it might be as well to give the car details to patrol, just in case."

"How would Knotty have found out the address for Smith's cottage?" Fenwick found it hard to believe that a junior constable had beaten him to the knowledge by a day.

"Someone told him."

"But he only spoke with Miss Wallace and he said nothing to me about it afterward."

Just the same, he rang her.

"Really, Chief Inspector, you've disturbed my lunch and I have guests."

"This is important. Did you tell Constable Knots anything about where the Smiths used to go on holiday?"

There was a startled pause.

"Why, *yes*, Chief Inspector, how very clever of you. It was only a casual remark but I remember he wrote it down in his notebook." She repeated the information.

Fenwick rang off and covered his face with his hand. "You idiot, Knotty! Why did you go off on your own like that? Why didn't you *tell* me?" He stared at MacIntyre, sick to his stomach. "He went out to the cottage. The teacher told him she'd seen the Smiths by the lake and Smith senior had told her about his holiday home."

"So Knotty found him."

"It has to be. Why else has he disappeared? Dear God," Fenwick swallowed to keep the sickness from his mouth, "we have to find him."

"Smith or Knotty?"

Fenwick looked MacIntyre hard in the face.

"Both."

CHAPTER THIRTY

Wendy Smith swallowed two paracetamol with the last of her coffee and winced as the second pill stuck in her throat. She had been off work for three days with the flu and still felt rough. The last thing she wanted to do was drive over to Shropshire but Dave had been insistent. He had called her in one of those moods that told her the only way out without a beating was blind obedience.

The instructions had been precise and succinct: check the letter drop, pick up some cash and drive over to meet him. Even the sound of the destination made her shudder. In a house nearby, her childhood had ended. She'd been eleven years old when Cousin Dave had started her "education," he fourteen and her idol. She had followed him everywhere, his willing slave; covering for him, lying for him and loving him.

So when he had started making her do *that* for him too, she had taken it as a compliment. It was the most private part of him and he allowed her to touch him there. His reaction the first time had almost scared her away but he had been so kind afterward, washing her hands and sponging her shirt clean that it had been worth it.

She had grown used to touching him, to the reaction of his body. The fact that it was their secret made her special somehow. Then her periods started, her chest went from flat to embarrassing almost over night and his needs changed. She still woke in a sweat at night from dreaming about the first time that he really explored her. He had hurt her so much that she had squealed with pain for him to stop but he'd carried on and she had almost blacked out.

Afterward there was new excitement in his eyes. Looking back through years of exploitation, she recognized it as the first time that he had discovered that hurting her made the sex even more exciting. She should have left then, run away, but instead, slowly, he had conditioned her to enjoy his brand of sex and punishment. Sometimes afterward he would surprise her with a gift, stolen perhaps, but she didn't care, and he would kiss and pet her. She would be happy and hope that next time would be different, but the violence the next time would be worse, the degradation absolute. Still Wendy had waited, hoping that in time he would change if only she could love him enough.

As Wendy dressed and found her car keys she tried hard not to think about her life. The only time she was happy was when she was at work, caring for people, doing her best to stop them hurting. She could sympathize with their pain and loss of dignity and it made her a good nurse. There was only one ward she avoided, which made her the odd one out among her colleagues. For her, the maternity ward was purgatory. She had been fourteen when she'd had her first abortion. Dave organized it and she had been too terrified to do anything but follow his commands.

The "doctor" had worked out of an address in a rundown part of Birmingham in a terraced house that reeked of bleach and something organic and disgusting beneath. His breath had smelled of onions but his hands had been clean and he had tried his best not to hurt her. She went home, aching and sore, with a giant sanitary towel between her legs. When she cried off school, her mum had said, "suit yourself." For three days she'd stayed at home, until the bleeding and the pain became manageable.

Wendy picked up her bags and locked the flat. She didn't know why she'd been thinking about the past so much recently. Normally it was locked away behind a secure wall of denial but during her flu, scenes from her adolescence had played in her mind continuously.

It was a short drive to pick up the letters, and a branch of their bank was two hundred yards away. There were two letters from Wayne waiting. When she tried to withdraw the maximum allowance the machine ate her card so she had to go into the bank and cash a check. There was a good-as-new clothes shop next door and she paused to look in the window. The bright summer sunshine threw her reflection back and she had to peer to make out the dresses.

As she stood back again she noticed the reflection of a woman standing on the opposite side of the road. There was nothing distinguishing about her but something in her attitude made Wendy cautious. Under the pretense of being interested in the window display she studied the woman's reflection, memorizing her face and clothes. She walked a few paces down the road slowly, looking in other shop windows. The woman crossed the road and started walking behind her. When Wendy stopped, so did she, bending to tie the shoelace of trainers that were already done up.

Wendy's instincts, refined over years of abuse and survival, were screaming a warning. She'd done nothing wrong but that didn't make her unconcerned. Memory of the Crimewatch program the previous week about the murder of a girl in London and the e-fit of the man the police were looking for came back to her. If this woman was following her then there had to be a reason and if it wasn't for anything she'd done . . . she stopped the thought and concentrated on the immediate problem of how to get rid of her.

There was a minimarket on the street close to where she had

parked her car. Wendy quickened her pace, glancing at her watch as if she was in a hurry, and made for the store. Inside she walked to the refrigerator at the back and started examining packs of bacon. The woman didn't follow her in but waited on the pavement outside. When she turned away Wendy made her way to the rear exit.

No one stopped her. There was a yard outside with gates leading to the road. She pushed one open and found herself in a street of terraced houses she didn't recognize. Her heart was racing. She was close to panic so forced herself to take deep breaths and concentrate. In her mind, she visualized the shop front, the roads she knew and the location of her car. She should turn right, and then right again.

Her car was where she'd left it, a pale blue, three-door Peugeot that was long past its best. Her hands were trembling so much she had difficulty inserting the key into the ignition. On the third attempt, it slid in and the engine started at once. Aging but reliable, like its owner.

She looked in the rear-view mirror and pulled away. It was only when she had reached the M55 that she realized she could simply have given herself up. It wasn't an expected thought but it was a strangely comforting one. If she'd only gone over to the woman the uncertainty would have soon been over. They would tell her; she would know one way or another whether her fears were the product of an overactive imagination as she kept telling herself, or not. She had written down the telephone number from Crimewatch but all the officers on the program had looked stern and unforgiving. If a woman had been there maybe she would have used it. Even now, all it would take was one phone call; she could still turn around.

Wendy missed the last exit for Birmingham, not on purpose but it flashed by while she was overtaking a lorry. At the next service station she pulled over and turned on the radio, a local music station. She needed the distraction to keep her thoughts from spinning. The tunes meant nothing to her. She never bought the latest hits because she had no one to share them with.

She was sipping a takeaway coffee when the news came on at the top of the hour. The main item was the murder of a young girl in Telford. Wendy felt the acidity of the coffee jolt her stomach even before she heard his name.

"Police are asking the public to be on the lookout for David Smith, a white male, age twenty-seven, six feet tall, slim with blue eyes. He may have scratches to his hands and face. If anyone does see him, they are to call Chief Inspector Cave, at Telford Division . . ."

The voice droned on but Wendy didn't hear it. She was bent double over a wastepaper bin vomiting up bile and drips of coffee.

"You all right, love?"

A kindly-looking man in his fifties was bending over her.

"Yes." She drew a shaking hand over her damp face.

"Only you don't look right. Are you sure you should be driving? I can give you a lift."

"No, really. I'm OK."

Wendy went back to her car, shaking the man's unwelcome attentions away. He was probably well-meaning but she didn't trust him. In fact, she trusted no one. She tried to think. Dave had called her in the middle of the night and told her where to meet him. He had said it was urgent but nothing in his voice had given her reason to think anything was wrong. Now this. The police wanted him in connection with the murder of a young girl. She started to cry, fat tears dropping from her cheeks onto her jeans, but she made no noise. Crying silently was something she had learned as a child. The last time she had howled was after the second abortion, the one that had gone so horribly wrong.

Her father had given her the strapping of her life when she

was finally well enough to return from hospital, scarred and sterile. He had beaten the truth out of her, no mistake, and there had been a terrible row with Dave and his parents. Dad was all for going to the police. She'd been underage and he wanted his revenge. Her mother had simply poured the drinks. Somehow, Dave's dad had persuaded him not to go. They'd gone into another room and spoken there for ages and when they'd come out there was no more talk of the police. She had gone off to nursing college a year later and hadn't been home since.

Stop it! She beat her closed fists against the sides of her head to prevent her mind from being ambushed by the past. There, she was calm again, almost in control. When she locked the car her hands barely trembled. There were phones banked against the outside wall of the service station. She told herself that if no one was using them it would be a sign that she should call the police. Nobody was there so she dialed the number for Telford that had just been broadcast. Perhaps local police would be more friendly. The man at the end sounded bored but when she said she might have information about David Smith his tone changed to one of excitement. Hearing it made her scared all over again and she insisted on speaking to a woman.

"The detectives on the case are all out, love, won't I do?"

"No!"

"OK, calm down; hang on a minute." She heard him put the receiver down and call out in the background. "*Robyn, have you got a sec? A lass on the phone says she has something on Smith but will only talk to a woman.*" Footsteps.

"Hello? This is Constable Robyn Powell; who's that?"

"My name's not important." But Wendy had forgotten to disguise her accent that hadn't changed despite the years away.

"Wendy? Is that you, love?" The woman knew her name! "We've been hoping to speak to you. Don't worry, you'll be quite safe talking to us; there's nothing to concern you. We want to help you."

Wendy pulled the receiver away from her ear as if it had become red hot and stared at it in horror. There was no way she could provide information if it wasn't anonymous. Robyn was still talking, throwing out meaningless soothing words, offering reassurance and protection. Wendy ignored her and put the receiver back gently. Tears threatened but she sniffed them away angrily. There was no turning back now. No matter what the police said about protection she couldn't trust them. They didn't know Dave. If she betrayed him he would find a way to destroy her.

She walked back to the car and drove away. The radio blared on; some ballad or other and she remembered that she loved Dave as much as she feared him. What had she been thinking of to doubt him? Guilt flooded her. She had to keep faith; the police were crazy to suspect Dave. They were always getting things wrong. Heaven knows how they had linked his name to that poor girl but it meant nothing.

Nobody appreciated him except her. She was the one special person in his life and some day he would realize that and their life together would get better. She tried to smile but the thin voice that she relegated to the farthest corner of her mind nagged at her. It was a smart alec voice. When something went wrong with Dave it was the voice that told her to leave him. Like when he had "given" her to his horrible friend, it was the voice that called her a whore. It was the voice that told her now to get away but she decided once again to ignore it. No love came for free. Everything was going to be fine as long as she didn't mess it up.

Smith lay under blankets that scratched the sensitive skin on his face and neck. Outside the sky was a flat blue-gray, the traffic heavy. She had picked him up early that morning after he had dared to leave his hastily assembled cave in the refuse. He had spent much of his long wait for her lying within two extra large garbage sacks, breathing rancid air through a tiny join. He had learned the trick first at fifteen, during his early years of testing his own boundaries of behavior.

Apart from his father's prying, he had rarely been questioned, let alone caught, but on one occasion the police had been waiting. His knowledge of the alleys and gardens in Telford had saved him and he had then hidden himself in a pile of rubbish sacks behind a block of flats. That day there had been a twist to the usual taunts at school. They had called him "stink bomb" but he hadn't cared. He'd proved himself smarter than the police and everyone else at that pathetic school, let them call him what they would. Afterward he had started to carry extra large refuse sacks with him, the black ones, preferably, because they were less conspicuous. He had practiced using them in his bedroom until he'd perfected how to fold them ready for use so that they could be opened with a flick of the wrist and he could be hidden in less than a minute.

When he had run from that house yesterday, concealing bloody wounds to his chin and throat with a thick white towel beneath a clean hooded sweatshirt, he had automatically run back to his old haunts. But in the eight years since he had left, the town refuse disposal had been improved. There were wheelie-bins where there had been mounds of sacks and as police sirens gathered in the distance he'd begun to panic.

Then he remembered the municipal waste facility he had seen on the outskirts. He ran through a large estate, ignoring the burning pain from his wounds, cut across a bypass, along a footpath he thought he remembered and out of an underpass by a stout chain-link fence that bordered the site. He had been in agony but fear was stronger than pain and he cut through the fence with his wire cutters, commanding his shaking hands to obey. Tracker dogs barked in the far distance, sending a shock through him, but he told himself that he still had time to do things properly.

His brain worked quickly. If he just cut one opening in the perimeter fence they would search the site until it was cleared. It was huge but that wouldn't stop them. He needed to make them think that he had left the site and throw the dogs off his scent.

The stench in the site was gross. He pushed his way back outside the fence, ran along it for a hundred meters then cut into it again. This time he pulled the flaps of wire outward, making it look as if he forced his way through. He pulled the towel from around his neck and smeared blood on the wire. Then he ran into the scrub that bordered the site and rubbed more blood on the ground before stepping in his footprints back the way he had come. He ran along the inside of the fence, rubbing the towel on the wire as he went before throwing it far into the scrub on the other side. Opposite the second hole he jumped as far as he could into the mound of rubbish. He landed on a refuse bag that burst open and spilled rancid milk and what looked horribly like the contents of a baby's nappy onto his trainers. Ordinarily he would have been disgusted but today he saw it as a blessing.

He jumped forward again but fell awkwardly. A flash of pain went through his ankle and up his leg. Ignoring it, he ripped open the rubbish bag next to him and spread the contents over the place where he had landed. It wasn't quite as malodorous as the first one but the rotten food should stink enough to confuse the dogs. He straightened up to try one more leap but his ankle was too sore so he hopped forward instead for a distance of about one hundred yards, covering up after himself each time, until the sounds of pursuit became too loud for comfort.

Smith rolled into his own rubbish bags quickly before burrowing into a soft, stinking pile of garbage, as the baying of the dogs reached a peak and they came through the foot tunnel. He heard their noise through the concealing layers of rubbish and the muffled shouts from their handlers as they scanned the area. With luck they wouldn't even bother to search the site. He waited, all his senses muffled by his concealment. After what seemed an age he heard the rustling of sacks close by him and the unmistakable sound of a dog, sniffing.

He pinched the edges of his two sacks close together. The sound of his blood pumping in his ears was so loud that he was sure it would be audible to the dog's sensitive hearing. He willed it to slow down and suppressed his breathing so that it was silent.

There was a sudden rustling next to him and he froze. It was close enough for the pile of rubbish above him to tremble. The noise grew louder and there was a sense of weight close to him. He could hardly breathe. The air in his sacks was almost gone, his chest constricted and his nose pressed against the plastic, damp with condensation. The claustrophobia that had terrified him since childhood threatened to overwhelm him and he had to fight the urge to rear up and out into the open.

There was a distant cry and the presence above him moved away. They must have found the towel or baseball cap he'd thrown into the undergrowth. He counted to thirty then cracked the sack open so that he could breathe. His face was suddenly wet and he couldn't tell whether it was from blood, sweat or tears. He licked the salty taste from his lips and stifled a sob of relief.

He lay there a long time, exhausted and bruised from inside out. At some point he must have slept because he awoke disoriented and terrified from a dream in which he had been buried alive. Fear was a new sensation for him and its power to enfeeble was an unwelcome shock. In the stinking darkness of the dump he felt for his rucksack and the bottle of water it contained. In swinging it from his shoulders a strap rubbed his neck, causing him to cry out in pain. He reached up and touched his injured skin delicately. It felt hot and scabby in some places, still sticky in others. When he sniffed his fingers there was a taint that worried him. He had never been injured before.

The water and sleep revived him and his survival instincts started to reassert themselves. He needed to get away from here. When they failed to find him in a wider search they would return to his trail again. There was silence in the dump so he risked pushing upward until he could see the sky. He checked his watch, almost nine o'clock; barely five hours since he'd killed her. It wasn't yet fully dark but he couldn't wait in case they came back.

Cautiously he opened the sacks, paused, listened and stepped out in a crouch. In the distance against the perimeter fence, two people in white suits were searching the ground on hands and knees. They were completely preoccupied. It amused him to see bright police tape marking the lines of his false trail. His decoy had worked on more than the dogs. Never once taking his eyes from the suited figures he backed away to the far side of the dump. There was an entrance with a pole across and gates, deserted now that the site was closed. His cutters made short work of the flimsy padlock and he was out on the road. From memory he had less than a mile to travel in the open until he came to a footpath that would take him across country.

He tried to jog but the pain in his ankle and the jarring along his neck were too painful and he had to slow to a hobbling walk. Two cars passed him but neither slowed. His rucksack and sensible shoes still made him look like a rambler in the dusk. The hooded sweatshirt that he'd put on to cover the worst of his injuries looked warm for a summer's evening but apart from that there was nothing to distinguish him from any other walker.

A plan began to form in his mind. He would make his way

back to the cottage, clean himself up then take the bike and go down to Devon where he would kill the bitch policewoman and leave the country. He had an escape route worked out; fly to the Channel Islands, which wouldn't require a passport, then take a day trip across to France and a train to northern Spain. He remembered reading at school that the mountains on the border between France and Spain were wild and untamed. Hiding would be easy.

Thoughts of the life waiting the other side of his next killing kept him going despite pain and hunger but he moved slowly. It was well past midnight when he reached the forest bordering the hills where the cottage lay. The night was dark except when the cloud was blown away by the increasing wind to reveal a full moon. As he trudged through the trees he heard the sound of a motor in the distance. He paused, trying to identify the engine. Whatever it was, it was traveling fast and in his direction. He froze in the shadow of a leafy birch. The regular whump whump of rotor blades slicing the air could only mean one thing.

An intense spotlight illuminated the valley he had just left and flickered through the trees. He waited for it to pass then ran for the next dense patch of cover, forgetting his pains as adrenaline anesthetized him. The helicopter swept back and he pressed himself up against the trunk of a larch, hoping that he would blend in.

The sweep finished and he ran on. For half an hour the pattern repeated itself as the helicopter searched the area in a tight grid. Eventually it moved on but the encounter had been another blow to his confidence. His cottage was less than a mile away but it was no longer a place of refuge; if they were hunting he needed to keep on the move. As he limped on he saw a sweep of headlights down the unmade road that led to the cluster of cottages by the lake. He crept to the edge of the woodland and looked back up the road. He could see two other cars blocking access, one of them with a distinctive blue and white pattern down the side. The sight rocked him back on his heels and he sat down, head in hands.

How could they have found him? His first thought was to blame Wendy but the idea was too far-fetched. Wayne then. The little snake had grassed after all, despite his promise of undying loyalty. Until he'd been locked up because of that bitch, his control of him had been absolute. She was the cause of all his problems; this was all her fault. Thinking of the policewoman reminded him that he needed the information he had hidden in the bike.

He trod silently on leaf mold, aware of the stillness around him and the searchers so close by. The bike was where he had left it, the panniers full and ready for his departure. He contemplated wheeling it through the woods but it would be impossible without making noise so he decided he had no choice but to leave it behind and trust his legs for a few more miles. He unlocked the panniers and pulled out one of the bags.

The air was cool on his bare skin as he stripped off his stinking clothes and changed. He folded a couple of clean shirts, underwear and some jogging pants into his rucksack, then put his razor and the computer printouts on top. There wasn't room for anything else.

He walked back down the rise away from the cottage. When he was far enough from the police, he called her number from his mobile phone. It was past two in the morning and he could tell that he'd woken her. Her voice was thick with a cold and he shuddered with distaste. He hated snot, hers in particular, but he set that thought to one side and issued instructions in a low voice.

Call made, he calculated how long he would have to wait and where to hide. He decided to make his way straight to the pickup point he had given her. There was a stream on the way he could drink from and his hunger could wait a few more hours. Ignoring his fatigue, the fire at his neck and the sharp ache in his ankle, he settled his rucksack more comfortably between his shoulder blades and turned south.

The birds were just starting to sing and there was a line of colorless light along the eastern horizon when he neared the rendezvous. The sound of male voices brought him up with a start and he crawled forward until he could pick out words above the sound of splattering as someone relieved themselves.

". . . one hour then home and bed."

"You don't want the overtime?"

"The wife'll kill me. If I have a choice I'm saying no but I've got money on it that they'll cancel all leave and make the extra time compulsory."

"That's crazy. He'll be miles away by now. Let some other division have the pleasure of finding him."

"Maybe, but you know Cave. He's a belt 'n' braces man. He'll have roadblocks up for at least another twenty-four hours. You got any of that coffee left?"

"Half a cup. You're welcome to it. Any more caffeine and I'll be awake 'til Sunday."

As the two men went back to their car, Smith inched forward until he had the height of the hedge between himself and their eyeline then crept on soundlessly. Two fields away he pulled out his map, pleased with himself for keeping it. There was no way that the police would be able to cover all the back roads in this part of the county. He selected an unnamed single-track road and called her again with the change of pickup location, plus a demand for blankets, her medical kit, food and drink.

She wouldn't be able to check for letters until eight-thirty, which meant she should be with him by ten-fifteen at the latest.

When he reached the track he'd chosen, he was pleased to see it was clear of police and he settled down to wait. At ten-thirty he'd rung her to find out that she was still ten miles away. He started to curse her slowness then remembered that she was his only lifeline for now. The sense of dependency was unwelcome and he decided that as soon as she'd done what was needed, she'd have to go. As he waited he worked through his ideas of how to rid himself of her. It was an amusing diversion and he was smiling when she arrived.

There was a new look of fear on her face that he put down at first to her guilt for being late but when she couldn't look him in the eye he'd begun to suspect another reason. As he traveled concealed in the tiny boot of the Peugeot his phobia of cars warred with a terror that she was going to turn him in. By the time they'd stopped somewhere near Hay, away from the motorway, he had been sick with nerves.

He swapped his hiding place for the floor in the rear of the car and arranged blankets over himself. It was still an awful place to be if one had a fear of being trapped inside a small place but it was better than the boot. They stopped in a deserted National Trust car park and he allowed her to wash his wounds with fresh water from a drinking fountain before dressing them.

"How bad?"

"The one on your cheek is a scratch but the gash along your jaw is nasty, you'll have a scar. And you were lucky with the one to your throat. It missed a major artery by less than half an inch but it's deep."

He noticed that she didn't ask him what had happened and was pleased at the control he had established over her.

"A stupid accident. I'll be more careful next time," he explained.

She nodded, keeping her eyes averted but the fact that he had volunteered information made her bold.

"Where are we going?"

"North Devon."

"For how long?"

"As long as it takes. What did you tell the hospital?"

"That I was still sick. I've been off for days."

Her illness was of no relevance.

"So they won't be expecting you back for a while. Good."

Later in the afternoon he kept out of sight while she went to find bed-and-breakfast accommodations in a seaside village. She was gone a long time and he started to fret. When she returned he smacked her head hard enough to turn her ear pink.

"It's summer. Everywhere is full but I eventually found a small B and B on the outskirts of town that had a cancelation. I explained to the landlady that you were recuperating from a car accident. She's given us a room on the ground floor at the back. It's small but it will do, won't it?"

"It'll have to."

"I bought you this." She passed him a walking stick with a carved horn handle.

"I don't need it."

"It will help with the . . ."

"The what?" He was amused by her frightened discomfort.

"It will make it more convincing, about the accident. And if I add some more gauze to your chin, and put the other arm in a sling . . ."

"Don't be stupid." But he submitted to more gauze and consented to carry the stick.

Normally he didn't listen to the news because he had never considered himself vulnerable to police inquiry but with their arrival at the cottage all that had changed. Knowing what they knew about him had become important. He switched on the car radio. When the news came around and he was the main item, he looked at her from the corner of his eye. She kept her face straight ahead, her expression frozen. Her lack of reaction told him that she wasn't surprised and he wondered whether she thought it was true. Best to continue their charade.

"It's a mistake. It wasn't me." He said the words to enable her to agree with him.

"Of course. I know that." Her voice was a dull monotone.

In that moment she fascinated him. He started at her mousy blond hair, escaping from the inevitable ponytail, at the freckles and weak blue eyes. Despite her skinny body and blunt features she wasn't ugly. She could have found herself a man. Why had she chosen to commit herself to him and why, even now, could she pretend to believe in him? It was a brand of loyalty that suggested stupidity not courage, but whatever lies she told herself were fine by him. He didn't care. A couple more days at most and she would cease to be useful. The thought made him smile.

"What?"

"What what?"

"What were you thinking?"

He was sitting next to her in the front seat; the view out of the windscreen helped his claustrophobia and his window was fully open, making him feel less trapped.

"What do you want to know?" His voice held a hint of warning.

She frowned, obviously worried about how she could continue without upsetting him.

"It was a strange look, that's all."

He laughed and bent over to kiss her with a lust that took them both by surprise. It was many years since her body had held any attraction for him but the thought of killing her had an aphrodisiac quality. He thrust his hand between her thighs and she clamped her legs tight on it. This behavior was not like him. It almost amounted to foreplay, something he never bothered with.

Without saying anything she pulled into the curb and switched off the engine.

"We're here."

He withdrew his hand, gave her his sexiest "I fancy you" smile, which he doubted she had ever seen before, and picked up his stick. Because he was smart he remembered to limp, favoring the ankle he had injured the previous day, although it hurt far less now.

Inside their bedroom at the B&B he put the television on and fucked her before she had time to unpack. It was surprisingly satisfying. Afterward she stroked the unbandaged side of his face.

"It's been years since you treated me like that." But instead of being grateful she asked a dumbassed question. "Why?"

He could hardly say, "because I was fantasizing about killing you, you stupid bitch," so he just smiled mysteriously.

"Go and tell that landlady woman I'll have my dinner in here on a tray. You can go and join the others but make sure you're back in here by nine o'clock."

When she left the room he burned Griffiths' letters unread and flushed the ash away. As the black flecks disappeared he experienced a rush of exhilaration. He had killed the girl and escaped against incredible odds. His optimism returned; they wouldn't find him now, not with his ability to change his appearance and blend in. He was within days of closing this chapter of his life and starting over again. With his intelligence, good looks and charm, it would be a piece of cake.

CHAPTER THIRTY-ONE

The unpredictability of the weather prevented Nightingale's days from sliding into complete tedium. If it hadn't been for the promise she had made her dead half-sister she would have left the farm, but she was now committed to finding the grave. She had started the search in a mood of confidence that gave way to determination within a day as she worked methodically, scythe in hand, leaving behind a trail of chopped vegetation that was slowly turning to hay.

Lulu might have denied the baby she thought was hers a Christian burial for whatever reasons held sway in her New Age mind but she didn't believe that her mother would have left the burial unmarked. In twenty-seven years, that marker might have rotted or weathered to anonymity but she had to believe that something would remain.

At the pace she was searching, Nightingale calculated that it would take her at least thirty days to cover the area. On the ninth morning of her search she woke early, ate an enormous breakfast and stepped outdoors into the steaming kitchen garden. It was only seven o'clock but the sun was warm and the humidity high. She was wearing shorts but her shirt was long-sleeved to protect her arms from the briars and nettles that would fight back even as she cut them down.

She decided to try a different strategy today and focus on likely areas. "Likely" meant places that might have appealed to her mother. She studied the background in pictures her aunt had taken of Lulu and identified a distinctive stand of rowan trees where she would start that morning. If that proved unproductive there was a stream with curious flat boulders that she should be able to find again.

Sometime around noon—she no longer bothered to wear a watch, but the shadows were at their shortest—Nightingale flopped down in the shade of an aging rowan. The morning had been as unproductive as the previous eight but at least she'd had the advantage of working in shade. She ate her lunch slowly, savoring the sharp saltiness of the cheese and the sweetness of the tomatoes. Her liter bottle of water was empty so she sucked moisture from some red fruits gratefully, her back resting against the warm tree trunk.

She must have dozed. The shadows were longer than they should have been when she moved and her shoulder muscles were stiff. With a small groan she stood up and decided to clear the area around the stream next. It took her a while to find where the rivulet rose in the hills behind the farm but as soon as she reached the area her hopes rose. There was a feeling of tranquility in this place, a sense that the world stopped outside the circle of mixed holly, rowan and alder that guarded the river's rising. A stone slab, ancient and covered with moss lay to one side of the water, resting level on supporting rocks. She imagined ancient Britons performing rites on it before casting offerings of food to the river goddess. The water was cold and clean-tasting and she drank deeply.

Rather than slash at the ferns and grasses she pushed them back, reluctant to spoil the lush greenness with ugly scars. It didn't take long to find the marker of black granite, polished smooth. Into it had been carved, with exquisite tenderness, a doe and faun. The baby deer was standing in the shelter of its mother's legs, resting its weight against their protecting warmth. Its big eyes stared out as if fear of the world would keep it forever in the protection of its dam. But it was the mother's face that brought a lump to Nightingale's throat. The eyes, more human than animal, the mouth down-turned, the face dark with grief.

She cleared the grasses away from the stone carefully and then picked off the moss that had grown in the carvings. When it was clean, she sat back and noticed lettering beneath the animals: *For my dear Louise, with love forever.* Seeing her own name brought back the shock of discovery. Nightingale hadn't been able to hold on to her hatred of Amelia, although she had tried, because it had taken two to prosecute this deception. Seeing the grave she acknowledged for the first time the enormity of her father's actions. He had robbed a woman he had supposedly loved of her child, inflicting terrible grief on her in order to ease his own loss.

Nightingale wanted to be able to cry for her dead sister and to say a prayer for her but neither the tears nor the words would come. It was as if she were staring at her own grave while an impostor lived within her skin. Would her true mother ever be able to love this daughter of deception or had that opportunity gone forever?

A long time later she made her way back to the farm where, to her shame, she ate an enormous tea and fell straight asleep when she went to bed.

Noise of heavy rain woke her, a determined shower she sensed would stop before long. Wide awake, she decided to get up and plod down the kitchen stairs to make tea, avoiding the rotten treads in the flight to the hall that she still hadn't repaired.

They were dangerous but that was one of many jobs she would leave behind undone when she left the farm.

Now that she had found her half-sister's grave her world had changed. For the first time her life was beginning to make sense. She knew who she was and the reason for her previous sense of dislocation from the real world. Now it was time to decide what she should become. The only certainty was that she couldn't live here forever. She wasn't a recluse like her aunt, nor did she want to become one.

The farm would always be her retreat, a safe place in a treacherous world, but it could never be her home. She had to be *doing* something, that was her nature; she couldn't just *be.* So that meant . . . what?

She sipped her tea and prized the scab off her most painful memory. There was always Harlden. She could go back, to her flat, to her job and her friends. If she was to stay with the police—and that was the only job for which she had any sense of vocation—then it would be in a place of her choosing. Until the Griffiths case she had been making good progress toward her inspector's exams and her operational track record was excellent.

It would mean seeing Andrew Fenwick, of course. The thought brought with it the usual sinking feeling of sadness. Although relationships developed all the time between people in the Force she knew it wasn't his way. The blurring of private and public lives would repel him even if there had been mutual attraction in the first place. She wondered, for perhaps the thousandth time, whether she should tell him of her feelings just in case he was harboring his own but the thought of their mutual embarrassment deterred her. They were of a type, she and Andrew: private, self-contained respecters of personal space. To confront him would be a gross invasion of privacy from which their relationship could never recover. It was a Victorian-era thought, in keeping with the decor of the kitchen, but it was also the truth.

She finished her tea and rinsed the mug, aware that she had come to a decision in the time it had taken her to drink it. As the newly reborn Louise Nightingale there were many open questions in her mind but only one certainty: she wanted her old life back.

It was time to go into Clovelly and brave that awful man in the Internet café, check and send emails; find a path back. Then she would go to the church, take some holy water to consecrate her baby sister's grave before starting the laborious process of packing up the house.

Nightingale arrived at the harbor in time to see some of the fishing boats return, ready to swap their piscine catch for a human load, children of all ages keen to snare mackerel on spinning metal lures.

The sun lit up the sea in slow motion as it rose above the surrounding hills. For a magical half hour, Nightingale imagined the village as it had been when first built in the sixteenth century, the product of one man's vision and thousands of days of manual labor. The perfect safe harbor on the dangerous north coast of Devon, it had prospered accordingly. It was peaceful this early in the morning, the silence broken only by hungry cries of the gulls and occasional shouts from the fishermen, timeless noises that emphasized the essence of the setting.

The newsagent opened first, then a harbor-front café, ready to provide breakfast for those unwilling to make their own. She had eaten before setting out but was hungry again, so she bought *The Times* and went into the café for a bacon sandwich and cup of tea. It was the first newspaper she had bothered reading since her flight from Harlden.

On the front page there was the usual blend of non-news typical of August reporting. A record rainfall in the west of Scotland warranted a picture of a man in a canoe navigating a sign that pointed to the town center. Criticism of the Foreign Secretary's lack of reaction to a rebellion in central Africa while he holidayed in Portugal dominated the center pages, and speculation about Prince William's love life added variety.

Page three focused on home news, the murder three days before of an eighteen-year-old girl in her own home and the search for her suspected killer. It was depressing but it had a curious effect on Nightingale. Instead of reading the story and passing on, she viewed the reporting as so much evidence, to be filtered and assessed. It was a daring crime that reeked of obsession; the word psychopath formed in her mind.

With a muttered "I'll be back" she went out and bought a *Telegraph* and *Daily Mail.* Ignoring the rest of the news she focused on the murder story in both papers. The *Telegraph* quoted extensively from the senior officer in charge and also from a superintendent from the Met who said that there could be links between this and attacks in Wales and London.

He mentioned a man that the police were keen to question, David Smith (27); the public were advised that he could be dangerous and not to approach him under any circumstances. There was an e-fit that she studied carefully, automatically committing the face to memory. From the way in which the police briefing had been reported, she could tell that they had strong evidence to connect Smith to the attack but were only sharing some of it publicly.

The café was starting to fill up so she ordered more tea in order to buy her right to the table while she read the reporting in the *Mail.* As she had expected, there was considerably more human interest. She read the description of Ginny's brief life with sadness and blinked away tears at the quotes from her grief-stricken parents. There was more coverage of the press conference, including a picture.

She recognized Fenwick's face at once and almost choked on her tea. He wasn't quoted in the piece and she couldn't work out why he was associated with the case. Had he moved to the Met in her absence? Nightingale stared at his image for a long time. Seeing his face wasn't as difficult as she had anticipated it would be. He looked stern, just as she remembered him at work. It reminded her that he was a police officer first and a man second. No, she corrected herself, he was a father first.

She left the newspapers in the café, a gift for future patrons, and climbed the hill to the cyber café, leaning into the incline, gripping the cobbles hard through her trainers. The café was empty apart from the thin, hungry-looking man behind the counter whom she ignored.

The sight of her in-box brought a familiar tug of concern. In addition to a new email from her brother, there were more messages from Harlden and one from Fenwick. Ignoring the others, she opened his first.

DEAR NIGHTINGALE (SORRY BUT THE NAME SUITS YOU),

WE ARE ALL TRYING TO FIND YOU. WE (I) HAVE VERY SERIOUS CONCERNS FOR YOUR SAFETY. I CAN'T GO INTO DETAILS IN AN EMAIL BUT TRUST ME WHEN I SAY THAT IT IS REALLY **REALLY** URGENT YOU CALL US. I THINK WG'S ACCOMPLICE HAS TAKEN UP WHERE WG LEFT OFF.

THERE IS A REAL POSSIBILITY THAT YOU COULD BE A TARGET. **PLEASE TAKE THIS RISK SERIOUSLY AND CALL ME.**

SINCERELY, ANDREW FENWICK.

"Bad news?" The man behind the counter had been watching her.

"I'm sorry, what?"

"You looked upset."

"I'm fine, thank you."

But she was far from fine. She thought of the morning's papers, with speculation of links between the girl's murder and other crimes, and of Fenwick's presence at the press conference. If David Smith was linked to Griffiths it could explain why.

"Is there a phone I can use?"

"Not here, but there's a call box on the harbor."

Nightingale logged off, other emails forgotten, cursing the fact that her phone battery was dead and that she lived in a fourteenth century ruin without electricity. She found the phone box, dialed the number for Harlden from memory and asked to be put through to DCI Fenwick. Anne's voice was instantly recognizable.

"I'm sorry. The Chief Inspector is away from Harlden. Can anyone else help you?"

"It's Louise Nightingale. I believe he's been trying to reach me?"

"Oh Louise! What a relief. We've been worried sick about you. Are you all right, dear?"

Nightingale tensed. The prying was starting already.

"I'm fine. Never better. I'll try his mobile."

"Are you sure I can't transfer you to anyone else here?"

"No. Don't bother. If you could just give me his mobile number, please?"

She broke the connection and took a deep breath before dialing. The call went straight through to an answering service, so she left a brief message, including her mobile number. Now all she had to do was find somewhere to re-charge her phone. There was an old coaching inn toward the top of the hill. If she ordered another coffee, they might just let her re-charge her phone while she drank it. The waitress was happy to oblige. Nightingale sipped her coffee and tried to think through the implications of the message she had received; *an accomplice . . . continuing where Griffiths left off . . . you may be a target.*

On the final point at least, Fenwick had to be wrong. She was hidden away where nobody could find her. If anything, this news meant that she should delay her return to Harlden, though she was perversely reluctant to do so, having made up her mind that it was time to leave the farm.

On her way back she stopped at the church to collect water from the font. It felt sacrilegious, this unauthorized taking of something so holy, but she hoped God would understand and forgive her. She took the water to the spring, where she found she could pray at last and did so before sprinkling the water over the stone. She watched in silence as the drops pooled and then evaporated. When the last one had dried she sighed and rose to her feet.

"Good-bye, Sis," she whispered, suddenly tearful. "I won't forget you. Someday, I'll tell your brother all about you but you'll need to let me choose how and when."

She blew a kiss to the stone and walked up to the cliff top. The montbretia, wild and rough on this part of the coast, were starting to bloom, a preview of the color that would soon flood the rowan groves. She picked a few to take home and paused to watch the butterflies darting for nectar in the heat of the afternoon.

At the highest point she turned on her phone and waited expectantly for a signal. There wasn't one. If there was no signal here the chances were there wouldn't be one anywhere. To contact Fenwick she would have to go back to Clovelly and use the phone box again but she'd had enough of crowds for one day.

Tomorrow would be soon enough. It had taken this long for the message to reach her; one more day wouldn't make any difference.

He sent her out first thing in the morning to buy a large-scale map of the area. As soon as she had gone he took two of the antibiotics she'd brought with her and examined his injuries before re-dressing them carefully with smaller bandages. The swelling in his ankle had almost gone so he started some gentle exercises. He needed strength in his legs and hated the idea of incapacity. The muscles ached abominably but he worked through the pain, sweating it away with typical determination. At nine o'clock he went along to the shared bathroom and had a shower.

He could smell toast and bacon. Wendy should have returned by now and his impatience with her increased. He was beginning to feel that he couldn't trust her, which diminished her usefulness considerably. At nine-thirty he decided to breakfast on his own.

Every twinge in a muscle or pain from the cuts as he walked the short distance to the dining room made him more angry. The little bitch he had killed had seen to him well and truly and the knowledge made him want to kill her all over again. The desire to hurt was strong. He'd noticed that on some days now he woke with it already there, which never used to happen. If Wendy had been here he would have given her a beating for being so annoyingly placid. As it was, he bottled up his rage and put on an injured face in keeping with his disguise.

He opened the door and found the small front room was packed. Only one table was left unused, right in the middle. He limped over to it, leaning heavily on the stick that was no longer necessary. A large woman came in carrying an enormous tray filled with plates of hot, aromatic English breakfast. She smiled at him sympathetically and came over as soon as she had served her other guests.

"Mr. Wilmslow. So glad you were able to join us. Your wife said you might have to have all your meals in your room. What can I get you?"

He ordered the full breakfast, toast, tea and orange juice.

"My word! You've a good appetite for an invalid."

"Fortunately my stomach was unhurt."

He had meant it to sound light-hearted, a joke, but it didn't work. Her smile faded and she backed away.

When his meal arrived he ate slowly, his eyes moving constantly from his plate to the front gate, visible through the bay window. She still hadn't returned by the time he had drained the teapot and wiped the last piece of toast around his plate. A brass clock in the hall chimed ten as he walked back to his room. Once inside he started to pack. It wouldn't be safe here if she'd turned from him. He cursed the fact that he hadn't killed her the day before. What if the police already had her, or the house was surrounded?

Their room overlooked a side street. The postman drove past, then a few cars. People were walking up and down normally. It didn't feel like a trap. He turned on the television. A police spokesman was being interviewed, a stocky sandy-haired Scot was doing all the talking but he recognized the dark-haired man behind him as the one who had followed him from his old house in Telford. He was stern, eyes fixed on the camera in a glare, as if daring Smith to materialize. Fat chance. He decided to give Wendy until half past ten then leave without her.

Wendy reparked the car in a spot as close to their original parking space as possible. She had almost made it but when she reached the main road her nerve had failed her. If she ran away he would find her wherever she was and if she went to the police . . . she banished the thought. That would be impossible. She'd been compliant and willingly ignorant for too long. There might be daydreams of rebellion but they remained just that. Her existence since childhood had been based on willing capitulation within a fabric of routines that created a rudimentary structure for her life.

As she had driven away she had searched for a foundation on which to build her rebellion. Instead she found only shifting sands blown into the shape he expected. And so she had turned the car round and driven back, her face wet with tears, her left foot shaking so much she could barely change gear. After she had parked she sat in the car for a long time trying to control her breathing. She was terrified. He would be furious and only the paper-thin walls at the boarding house would prevent him from beating her unconscious, as he had done before. Eventually, she forced herself out, carrying her paper bag of purchases as a pathetic shield.

He was staring through the glass window when he heard the bedroom door open.

"Close the door." His voice was expressionless. "Where the fuck have you been?"

"I . . . I couldn't find the map. Had to look all over the place."

She was lying.

"Come here." Barely a whisper but the venom made her shake her head in protest. "Come here." He turned up the volume on the television and she started to tremble with fear.

"No. Dave, please. I'm sorry I was late."

"Here." He pointed to the bed, directing her like a dog, his fury trickling out around the edges of his control.

She came toward him, so hesitant that his anger made him gasp. Her fear was pathetic. It elated and infuriated him in equal measure.

The first blow caught the side of her face with enough force to knock her glasses flying. She let out a moan of surprise and tried to back away but he punched her hard in the stomach, doubling her over. He knocked her sideways onto the bed, where she curled into a fetal ball in defense, face tucked between her knees. It was no use. He grabbed a handful of hair and yanked her head back viciously so that he could see her eyes.

"Don't you ever do that to me again, do you hear?"

He punctuated his last words with a tug that brought tears to her eyes. The long white length of her neck was exposed and he was filled with an urge to bite and stab at it.

"Go and lock the door."

"No, Dave please, no, I said I'm sorry." Pale liquid tinged with blood trickled from her nose, disgusting him.

"Lock it." They were both talking in whispers, aware of other people in the house around them.

He watched as she obeyed, unconsciously flexing his fists. Before she could turn round, he pulled her backward, spinning her face down onto the bed so that her cries were muffled. She was wearing faded jeans that he undid with the facility of practice and stripped her naked to the waist. He pushed straight into her, her faint squeal of pain sending a wave of pleasure through him. He leaned his hands on her shoulders to take his weight and smother her cries. Gradually they moved forward to circle her neck.

It took him a long time to climax but when he did it was exquisite, so good that he let out a harsh cry of triumph. When his sight was clear again he pulled away and washed carefully in the sink. She lay there unmoving. He waited a while then nudged her with his foot. She didn't stir so he rolled her over.

"Come on you . . ." The words died. She was staring up at him sightlessly, her eyes bloodshot, her tongue gorged and extended. She was dead.

"Shit!"

His first reaction was one of impatience. It was inconvenient of her to die on him like this. What was he supposed to do with the body? Then came worry. He was in a strange house full of people, including a busybody proprietress who probably watched the front door when she wasn't prying into her guest's belongings. He would have to hide her in here.

The room was small with space only for the wash basin, double bed, wardrobe and television. He checked under the bed. Fluff balls and accumulated dust told him that the space wasn't cleaned regularly. He rolled the body off the bed and stuffed it beneath the mattress. Once he'd forced the head under the rest went in quite easily. He pulled the poly-cotton valance back down and made the bed. Then he put her bag under the sink and left with his rucksack. With luck it would be at least a day before she started to smell. He was accosted by the landlady on his way out and explained that he was going to meet his wife and that they would be touring all day. He dismissed her look of puzzlement with one of his disarming smiles and walked on calmly, remembering as he neared the gate to limp a little.

The car keys weighed heavy in his pocket. Once, a long time ago, he had learned to drive a car and he had managed it only two days before when he needed to dispose of the policeman's body. Now it was necessary again; he had no choice.

Her car was parked under a tree further down than he remembered. Opening the door was fine; sitting behind the wheel wasn't too difficult; he even managed to start the engine with only a mild tremor. The problem came when he tried to shut the driver's door. His fingers froze on the handle, his arm muscles locked, unable to pull the door closed. Sweat beaded his forehead and made his hands clammy. He tried revving the engine for encouragement, but the psychology wouldn't work.

Inside his head he was already trapped inside the car, strapped in by a seat belt, unable to breathe properly. He screwed his eyes tight and it was his mother's face that appeared before him. She was screaming, terrified, as the car slowly filled with water. His father was sitting calmly beside her, wrists resting loosely on the steering wheel, impervious to her cries. Inside his head, he could hear him repeating, over and over again.

"It's for the best. It's for the best. This way the world is free of him and neither of us can ever create another one."

The water was up to the front windows by now, and the car started to sink, tipped at an angle. It settled slowly in the silt and carried on down into the lake.

His father had fixed the seat belts somehow so that they wouldn't undo. His feet were getting wet, his new trainers letting in the water. But his father had forgotten to take his rucksack away and Dave was a boy who liked to travel prepared. His penknife was in the outer pocket and he started to cut at the reinforced webbing. The material was tougher than it looked. As his mother screamed and the car gently pitched forward a little more, he sawed away, breathing deep to remain calm. After all, he had been born to dare, escape, and dare again. Since the dawning of his adolescence a sense of invincibility had given him limitless courage.

The blade grew blunt. Water lapped his knees. In front, it was already above his mother's waist because of the angle of the car. She was beating at his father, drawing blood, pleading but he just kept saying, "Trust me. We should never have had him. Even his birth nearly killed you."

Dave prized out the sharp awl that everyone joked was for removing stones from horse's hooves and started to puncture holes across the remainder of the strap. He punched hard, so hard that he pierced his thigh—something he didn't notice until much later. Once he had made a series of holes, he went back and tried to slice between them. Sometimes it worked, sometimes it didn't, the fabric bending before the blade. He was working with his fingers under water now. His mother was holding her head and neck up above the muddy ripples. There was another slow-motion slippery lurch as the car pushed past another lake-bed obstacle on its inexorable slide into the deep dark center of the lake. His father was so stupid to choose to drive in at a point where the incline at the side of the lake was shallow. Even with the brakes off, and how his mother had clawed at the handbrake until her husband had broken her grip, the descent was almost gentle. Had he believed in God, or any almighty presence, he would have offered up a prayer of thanks. As it was he smiled in a wry acknowledgment of fate, which seemed to enjoy testing him to the limit.

The blade finally bent and he resorted to the scissors. They looked too small and for a moment he wavered. Then he rallied and closed the stainless steel blades around one of the holes. To his amazement, after a couple of tries, it snipped through. The next piece of fabric parted quickly. The third was stubborn but he pressed on.

There was silence in the car. His mother had had to keep her mouth closed since the last slide forward. His father, taller, straight-backed stared forward. Dave became aware of the awful stillness of a tomb and looked up briefly from his work. At that very moment, as if sensing his gaze, his father turned to look back over his shoulder. It shocked Dave to see tears in his eyes and an expression not of anger, but pity. His father turned to his wife, struggling silently for life and smiled such a sweet, sad smile.

"It's for the best, my darling," he said then turned forward and lowered his face into the water.

Years later Dave had read an article by some learned professor who insisted that it was impossible for someone to commit suicide by drowning. In eloquent prose he had explained how most deaths by leaping from cliffs or bridges arose because the subject was rendered unconscious on hitting the water. He had demonstrated to his own satisfaction that the survival instinct was inherent in motor functions so that even someone wanting to die would fight to hold their breath when their head was submerged, the lungs screaming for oxygen, the throat closed against water, muscles aching in a fight for air.

The article was praised. It was credible, convincing. Dave knew it to be a lie. His father had lowered his head into the water without a ripple. There had been shudders which he remained convinced were deliberate intakes of water, some involuntary movement of the hands but hardly any threshing; then a new silence. He had watched, fascinated, but then the car moved again and he bent his eyes to cutting the remains of the belt. At some point his father died but Dave had been oblivious to the moment, intent on his own survival.

When the belt finally parted, he and his mother were breathing the last foot of air in the car. The roof had become a very physical presence. His body floated up, away from the seat, as he wriggled free and he tried to open the door. It was closed fast.

At first he had panicked but then he remembered his physics lessons and the rules of atmosphere and pressure. There was too much weight of water against the door. To escape he needed to saturate his body with air, open the window and flood the remainder of the car, then he could float free. Of course his mother would drown. He looked over at her, saw the helpless panic in her eyes and despised her for her weakness. She was always the same, the willing victim. Even when his father slapped her, which wasn't that often or that hard, she'd turn those long-suffering eyes on them both and then carry on making the supper. She had never shown him enough love, even as a baby, as if blaming him for the injuries they both suffered during his birth. He realized with a sense of liberation that he hated her.

Now she was staring at him, pleading with him to help her. The sensation was extraordinary. He could grant life or death to the most powerful woman in his life, the focus of his phobias and fantasies. She was begging him for life with her eyes. He remembered her spurning his touch and her looks of mistrust. A small, reptile portion of his mind, ancient and without sophistication, calculated the chances of cutting through her seatbelt before the car filled with water. Nil. The same cells in his brain assessed his own chances of survival—possible, probably.

He looked at her one last time, momentarily fixated by her thick black hair floating on the water around her. Then he shook his head, grabbed his rucksack and cranked down the window, bracing himself against the fresh cold water that flooded in. As soon as it was open wide enough he wriggled through, the most extraordinary sense of life propelling him upward. Behind him, although he knew that it was physically impossible, he heard his mother scream.

"You all right mate?"

Smith looked up, his face shiny with sweat. A man about his own age had bent down to peer in the car, his beer belly capitulating to gravity.

"Yes, lost in thought, that's all." He remembered to say thanks and to attempt a smile.

"Only you looked proper poorly. You was stuck there like that for ages, and what with the bandages I thought your head might be done in."

The smile was better this time and he saw a look of relief in the man's face.

"I'll be fine. Thanks again."

"Rightyoh, you take care now, OK?" He banged the car roof twice and walked off.

Smith managed to close the door and moved off jerkily. He stuck to the speed limit and drove as if he were taking his driving test. By the time he reached the town with the cyber café he was drenched in sweat. It was almost midday and it was hot. He climbed out of the car gratefully and leaned on the roof with his eyes closed waiting for his shirt to dry. It was the last one he had.

No visitors' cars were allowed into old Clovelly, a feature that preserved the quaintness of the town and the old-fashioned quality of its steep cobbled streets. Donkeys were still available to take tourists down to the tiny harbor, or a less romantic taxi.

Smith chose to walk. He settled the rucksack containing his worldly goods on his back. The streets were busy. August was the peak of the tourist season and Clovelly one of the "must see" places in Devon. People stared at his bandages even though he had reduced the amount of gauze about this face but they provided a good disguise. His picture was front-page news but they'd used a bad likeness. It made him look like a weasel, eyes too close together, pointed sharp nose and receding chin; no similarity at all. He smiled and put on his sunglasses.

When he saw the photo of Wendy on the front page of the *Sun* he stopped dead and someone behind cannoned into him with a curse. He went into the newsagents and bought the paper. The full story was on page five. The public was asked to be on the lookout for Wendy Smith (24), missing from her home in Birmingham since the previous day. The piece mentioned that she might be traveling with her cousin, a man of twenty-seven, six feet tall, and that they might be using assumed names.

Smith felt faint. His head buzzed. He told himself that the reaction was the result of his injuries, not wishing to admit that this feeling was panic. How had the police found out about Wendy? It had to be Griffiths. He must be singing like a canary in exchange for a reduced sentence. Bastard! Well his plan to kill him might have failed when he'd had to leave the poisoned cake behind but he'd make sure he rotted in prison. When he killed the policewoman he would write on the walls in her blood that her execution was on the order of one Wayne Griffiths, currently detained at Her Majesty's pleasure, so he'd never be released.

The thought of revenge calmed him but he remained sensitive to any strange looks he attracted. In the next souvenir shop he bought a baseball cap. When he pulled the brim down the shadow concealed most of his face. More comfortable, he ambled down the hill and slid into the café.

Instead of going straight to a PC he stayed at the zinc counter watching the man serving. Smith prided himself on being a good judge of sexual character, it was one of the reasons he was such a competent seducer. The man's eyes darted across his customers like a lizard watching for flies, constant rapid flicks of acute attention. He caught Smith staring at him and smiled in a way that was instantly recognizable.

"I'm looking for a girl," he said, pretending not to see the flash of disappointment in the other man's face. "Maybe you've seen her? She's my sister and my parents are worried sick about her."

He slid an old newspaper cutting out of his wallet and smiled at the server in a way that was more than friendly. Sure enough the man sat down and extended a hand.

"I'm Frank."

Smith took the offered palm and shook it, squeezing the fingers slightly, just once.

"Danny. Have you seen her?"

Frank took the picture and unfolded it. It was obvious that he recognized her.

"She's been in here a few times. You close?"

"No! She's my half-sister and I wouldn't be here if my mum wasn't worried. We never got along. She borrowed money from me, never repaid it, that sort of thing. Typical woman. You can't trust them, can you?"

"Tell me about it. Your sister's a class act: stuck-up, superior—wouldn't give me the time of day. She was in here earlier this morning, as a matter of fact."

"Any idea where she's staying?" He tried to sound calm.

"Nah. I didn't talk to her. No offense but she's not my type."

Smith looked at him and smiled.

"Really? Men are usually all over her."

"Not this man, Danny." Frank held his eyes for too long and they smiled at each other.

"Pleased to hear it. Do you think she's staying in the town?"

"Check in the pub. She might be more talkative with a drink inside her. Are you thinking of waiting around for her? She doesn't come in every day. You might be here some time."

"Oh, I'm a patient man. And I'm sure there must be something interesting to do around here. I'd best be on my way, Frank, but I might stop by later if that's all right with you." He pursed his lips and Frank smiled back.

The pub was packed with lunching tourists so he decided to try it later. He pulled out the Ordnance Survey map of the area that Wendy had bought that morning and decided to find a quiet place in the country to snooze and regain more of his strength.

He woke automatically at six o'clock and walked back into the village, his legs moving easily as the blood flowed through them. But the motion sent a burning sensation along his jaw, which was ominous. He bought ointment and fresh dressings and ducked into the Gents at the pub to unwrap his wound and inspect the damage. As he'd feared, the long jagged lines were inflamed and weeping pus. He dabbed the ointment along the cuts and pressed fresh lint against them before sticking plasters over the top. Someone came in as he was finishing and gave him a strange look but he ignored them.

He had become more relaxed about being a wanted man during the day. Despite his likeness being in millions of newspapers and on TV, no one had accosted him and he remained a free man. The more hours that passed the more confident he became that it would be easy to complete his plan. If necessary he would stay with Frank overnight and wait for the woman to show up again in the village. Then he would kill her, leave the country and start over again.

In the public bar he ordered a pint of best and a cheese plowmans. He swallowed two more antibiotics and then sipped the rest of the beer slowly, watching the customers in the pub for any signs of interest. He was ignored and he relaxed a little, staying at the bar, half hidden by an upright oak beam. It was almost seven o'clock and the evening rush was starting. When the barman paused to wash and wipe glasses he looked up at Smith eating his crusty bread and cheese with care.

"On holiday?"

"No, more's the pity; probably here on a fool's errand."

"Oh?"

"I'm looking for someone. A woman who, let's say, borrowed from me and inadvertently forgot to pay me back."

"Oh, aye. You can get 'em like that. Bad luck." He went back to polishing, his eyes intent on the glass not Smith's face.

"Maybe you've seen her. Tall, dark haired, some would call her striking. Not from around here."

"We get dozens like that, mister. If you've got a picture it might help."

"Sure." He pulled out his wallet and unfolded the press cutting.

The barman took it and stiffened. Smith tried to maintain his look of mild irritation but it was hard swallowing the mouthful of pulp he found he was chewing.

"Know her?"

"Could be. Hair's longer now but there's not mistaking the face. She came in here once, about a month or so ago."

"And you remember her."

The barman was slow to reply. Smith wanted to shout and scream at him but he took a small sip of beer instead.

"Who wouldn't around here?"

"What's she done?"

"Not her, the Nightingales. Fine name, pity about the family."

The barman paused, obviously feeling that he had said enough. Smith shrugged, hoping that his apparent indifference would be sufficient encouragement. It worked; eventually the publican was compelled to add.

"The Nightingales have been around here for generations. Owned land, ran the mill but they went downhill. In the seventies there were tales of all sorts happening, sort of stuff you wouldn't want your mother to hear."

Smith thought about his dead mother and smiled in agreement.

"Anyroad, when Mr. and Mrs. Nightingale senior left, their son and daughter lived on at the farm, afore he married. Right goings on. They attracted the wrong sort."

Smith couldn't wait any longer.

"And this woman?"

"Daughter of one of Nightingale's liaisons. S'obvious. She

uses his name but she's the spit of that wanton of a mother of hers. Alike as two peas save for she's tall and 'er mum was a tiny thing."

Smith discarded this news; all he needed was an address.

"And you say they lived at a farm. Nearby?"

"Six–eight miles or so from here. Was flourishing once but the old woman let it go, afore she killed herself." He bent forward conspiratorially. "Though they persuaded the priest that it was an accident." He paused and would have spat if he hadn't been in his own bar. "Bollocks."

Over a second pint, Smith extracted details of the location of Mill Farm. He drank slowly, conscious of the need to remain alert. He decided to wait until dark and then walk there. From the directions he'd been given, a car would take almost as long and anyway he didn't think he could face driving again. It would take him a couple of hours, maybe three. And then she would die.

CHAPTER THIRTY-TWO

Mrs. Ironstrong ran an orderly house and that included guests arriving on time for their meals. She had been prepared to make allowances for the young couple because he'd been in an accident but by the evening some of her patience had run out. He might be an invalid as his "wife" had said and his face was messy enough to believe it but he'd been spry this morning when he left the house. Even the limp had looked forced.

It was half past seven. Dinner ran from six-thirty to eight but as the dining room closed at eight-thirty sharp there was a tacit understanding among her guests that "last orders" were best made before eight o'clock. All the others were sitting at their gingham-covered tables, obedient and appreciative. Except for "Mr. and Mrs." Wilmslow. She drew a deep breath, puffed out her ample chest and stalked along the corridor to the back bedroom. Her short rap on the door drew no response, not even the second time.

The master key opened every lock and she used it to peer inside. The room was the same as it had been that morning when she had double-checked the housemaid's cleaning. If it hadn't been for a case under the sink and the coat hanging on the back of the door, she would have suspected them of having skipped without paying. The room was stuffy with late afternoon heat. A solitary fly was buzzing around frantically. She hesitated, then went over to the sash window and opened it a crack to let in some fresh evening air. With a shrug, she left the room and relocked the door.

Well after nine o'clock she closed the front door in a huff, leaving all her guests in the TV room, apart from the two unaccounted for, and joined her husband in their private sitting room. Sensing her mood, he shrank down in his armchair and edged the volume up a notch on the television. It was always soft anyway as he wasn't allowed to have it loud in case it disturbed their guests. He was watching the news.

"They're not back. I think they've gone."

"Oh dear."

It happened once in a while. At least this time their few remaining items of silver were untouched.

"It makes me mad, Courtney."

"Yes dear, of course it does."

"What is the world coming to? I mean, look at that there," she pointed to a photograph of a young girl that had flashed onto the screen. Ginny's smiling face held their gaze for a moment before Mrs. Ironstrong gathered her wind. "I mean, who knows who's out there. We could be murdered in our beds one day. And what would you do about that! A helpless woman like me."

Mr. Ironstrong winced at this but fortunately it went unnoticed.

"Helpless. I could be raped! What would you do?"

"Defend you of course, dear."

"Oh really!" She flounced away, heading for the globe cocktail cabinet. She concentrated on mixing a stiff G&T and didn't see her husband suddenly sit upright in his chair and punch the volume higher.

"Ah, Irene, I think you need to see this."

"Not safe anywhere."

"Could you just look, Irene, I mean I think that's . . ."

"What are you going on about?" She spun round, taking a long swallow of her drink.

"Damn, the picture's gone. I was trying to tell you. They had a photograph that looked like Mrs. Wilmslow. It was taken from one of those video cameras so it wasn't clear but I'm fairly sure it was her."

"Why didn't you say so sooner? What's she done?"

"I don't know. The police want to talk to her."

"What about?" There was a touch of hysteria in her tone.

"I don't know, you were talking too much. I couldn't hear."

Such rebellion was bound to cause an argument but Mrs. Ironstrong was silenced immediately by a photograph of a man on the screen. She took charge of the control and turned the volume up full.

". . . is extremely dangerous and not to be approached by members of the public under any circumstances."

"He was bandaged. It might not have been him . . ."

"Ssh!" Most unusually she shut up at once.

"Police advise that Smith may show signs of a recent injury, which they believe was sustained during his latest crime."

"What's he done?"

As if answering her, the newscaster moved into the recap of his main story.

"So if anyone sees either Wendy Smith of Birmingham [photograph] or David Smith [photograph], they are to alert the police immediately. They are wanted for questioning in connection with the murder on Monday of Virginia Matthews, the eighteen-year-old killed in her own home in Telford. Under no circumstances should they be approached."

A telephone number flashed up on the screen and Mr. Ironstrong reached for the receiver.

"Wait. We need to be sure. If we were wrong the embarrassment would be terrible. Her bag's in the room—lets check that first."

"But supposing they come back?" His voice had dropped to a whisper.

She replied in kind.

"I've bolted the front door. Come on. We have to be sure."

They crept out of their room and along to the rear of the house. Above them their guests were happily watching TV. Mrs. Ironstrong removed her master key and opened the bedroom door again.

"It stinks in here!" Her husband wrinkled his nose. "Have they left a takeaway in the sun somewhere. I thought you didn't allow food in the rooms."

"Never mind that, Courtney. Go and look in her bag."

As his wife hovered by the door, her diminutive husband circumnavigated the double bed that dominated the room and picked through the vanity case with the tips of his fingers.

"Nothing," he whispered and came back to her.

"They must have another bag, try under the bed."

Shaking his head he bent down on his knees and lifted the valance. A woman's white hand was curled delicately on top of the fur balls.

"Oh my God."

"What is it, Courtney? What have you found?" Irene eased her large body around the bed and crouched down beside him, knees creaking. "Move over. You're in my way."

"I don't think you should, Irene."

"Nonsense." She angled her ample chest toward the floor.

"I've seen enough goings on this house over the years. What sort of mess have they left this time?"

Courtney held his hand protectively over the floral sprigged valance but she brushed it away. He moved to one side with a muttered "very well," giving his wife more room.

"I can't see anything. Oh hang on, yes I can, it's a . . ." she jerked back, stared him blankly in the face, and rose to her feet ". . . body."

The remaining rebellious streak in Courtney's ego noted with satisfaction the protest of the mattress springs as she fell heavily onto the bed in a faint, and then he went to call the police.

The helicopter ride was a short one. By the time Fenwick arrived at the boarding house, drawn there by the reported sighting of Smith and the discovery of a young woman's body, he knew that it wasn't Nightingale. But for sixty agonizing minutes, from the first phone call to the rendezvous with MacIntyre, he had feared the worst. The horror he had felt then returned momentarily as he entered the cramped bedroom.

The bed had been turned on its side to expose the body, which at MacIntyre's request, had been left in situ. In the warm night the odor of death permeated the room despite the open window. Local detectives allowed the two men from London scrutiny of the corpse and waited to brief them. As MacIntyre and Fenwick moved to the front room and sat at the table already laid for breakfast Wendy's body was at last bagged and removed.

MacIntyre read out loud from a summary the locals had prepared for them.

"The pathologist estimates time of death at not more than twenty-four and not less than fifteen hours ago but we have witness statements that can pinpoint it more accurately than that, assuming Smith's the killer.

"She was last seen alive just after ten o'clock as breakfast was finishing and the bandaged man calling himself her husband left before eleven."

"Have we had confirmation of matching prints from the room and his cottage yet?"

"Why the urgency?"

"Because if it's him he's here for a reason. It must be Nightingale."

MacIntyre opened his mouth to disagree but then contented himself with a shake of his head. Fenwick had been more right than wrong so far but nothing they'd found at Smith's cottage backed up his concern for his former colleague.

John Oldham, the local SIO, joined them and sat opposite MacIntyre, smoothing the red checked cloth straight.

"Any idea where he might have gone, John?"

"No. We have a witness statement that says he was driving a blue Peugeot but that's all. We think it was Wendy Smith's car and I'm expecting the registration number any moment. I couldn't help overhearing some of your earlier conversation. Do you think he had a plan in coming here?" Oldham directed the question to Fenwick.

"Yes. I don't think this area is a random choice. Did you find anything in his room that might help us?"

"I'll have it bought in."

It was a meager collection, printed and bagged: there was a cheap plastic vanity case with a lipstick, nightdress and an empty purse, with not even a penny in to keep the Devil out, as Fenwick's mother would have said; the contents of the wastepaper bin including a used Kleenex, part of the wrapping from a tube of mints, an empty paper bag and a till receipt dated the previous day and timed at 9:03 a.m.

"What did she buy?"

"Pardon?"

"The receipt. What was it for? It's from a local shop, the name's here."

"The mints, perhaps a newspaper that Smith took with him for cover."

"It's for three items, none of them now in the room. She went out, bought something and was then killed. What had Smith asked her to get? We need to find out now."

John Oldham laughed pleasantly at Fenwick's terse instruction and looked at MacIntyre who shrugged and then nodded. After the local detective had gone the Superintendent said quietly, "Don't push it, Andrew. They're bending over backward to be helpful."

"We need to find him. I'm calling Harlden again to see if they have any news."

He took his mobile into the relative privacy of the hall and dialed Cooper's home number.

"Bob, it's me. Sorry to trouble you at home at this hour. No, it's not Nightingale but we're only hours behind the man I think is after her. I'm in Devon. Is there anything you've found out from your search that might help me?"

There was a brief pause in which MacIntyre stared at Fenwick trying to work out whether to be amused, indifferent or annoyed.

"A supermarket where?" Fenwick called out to Oldham. "Barnstable. Is that near here?"

Oldham nodded, suddenly attentive.

"And she bought groceries there five days ago; you're sure . . . ? And she's called the station today. Thanks, Bob. Call me if you hear anything else at all."

Fenwick rang his messaging service immediately, his face tightening as he listened.

"She left me a message, this afternoon, with a contact number." His mouth was dry as he dialed, then he shook his head in disappointment and mouthed "answer service" before speaking into his phone.

"Nightingale, ah, Louise. It's Andrew Fenwick. Please call me on my mobile urgently, any time day or night. I'm in Devon. The time is eleven-forty p.m. If you're in the area and pick up this message, get in your car, lock the doors and make your way to the nearest police station. Stop for no one."

Oldham sat down opposite Fenwick.

"I've someone calling at the local shop now to find out what Wendy Smith bought."

"I'm missing something." Fenwick shook his head. "I'm sure there's more I could be doing." He paced the small room, circling the breakfast tables. "Her brother."

"But you've spoken to him," MacIntrye argued reasonably. "He had no idea where she is."

"I know but we have an identified area now."

Oldham's officer returned from the shop and reported to his boss while Fenwick waited to be put through to Simon's home.

"The shopkeeper remembers her well. He says that she was in a right state. She bought a map, took her a while to find the right one and he had to help her. She said that it had to be of the area around Clovelly and be to the largest scale they had. I borrowed one just like it."

Fenwick watched them spread it out on the table as he reached Simon Nightingale. He explained where he was and asked whether there was any reason that his sister might be nearby. The color drained from his face as he listened to the response. Oldham and MacIntyre sensed his intensity and waited for him to finish his call in silence.

"Her aunt had a farm in these parts. Her brother didn't think she'd be there because it's a semi-ruin now. He hardly ever went there and his directions are really vague but he said that it's somewhere near Clovelly."

"Wendy Smith bought a map of the area at nine this morning," MacIntyre said, not meeting Fenwick's eye.

"How did Smith know where to find her?" Fenwick answered his own question with a brusque shake of the head. "That's irrelevant. We need to find him before he finds her."

Oldham looked worried.

"We're not a big force out here. I'll get on to Operations right away but if she's in the wilds somewhere up a private road, we'd have better odds finding the proverbial needle tonight."

MacIntryre, in contrast, had a determined grin on his face.

"You get your team moving as quickly as you can, John, and leave the rest to me. You could say that this is one of my specialities."

He was humming the theme tune from *Mission Impossible* as he picked up the phone.

Twelve-fifteen and the cliff-top car park held more cars than Fenwick would have expected until a local bobby explained that tourists were not allowed to drive down the precipitous slope into the village. The blue Peugeot was badly parked beneath a rowan tree, heavy with berries. It was empty, with not even a sweet wrapper in the ash tray.

Fenwick looked around in case Nightingale's car was nearby but there was no sign of it.

"That means she's not staying in the village," he said to MacIntyre.

"Smith might be. We should wait here until we have more

resources. If we alert him with a halfhearted house-to-house he could disappear into the night without our even knowing he's gone."

Fenwick shook his head, frustrated at the delay.

"It's more important that we find Mill Farm but we need better directions. Her brother's are next to useless. Who would know how to find Mill Farm? What are the best sources of local knowledge?"

"Local post office, the church, pub, general store . . . they're good places to start," Oldham suggested.

"Why don't we ask them while we wait for additional support?"

"You can't go knocking up the village. Our top priority is to catch Smith, not find Nightingale. If he's here you'll alert him."

Fenwick resisted the urge to punch MacIntyre, reasoning that it probably wouldn't win his cooperation.

"Tell you what, here's the deal," he said, his voice tight, "you let me go down there. If there's any sign of life, I'll question whoever's still awake, quietly."

"If you scare him off . . ." MacIntyre didn't need to finish the threat.

"I won't. I want him as much as you do."

He followed the signs for the harbor down a cobbled street so steep it was stepped in places. On either side, pretty cottages were dark and closed against the night, their climbing roses and hedges black in the moonlight. Shops and cafés soon outnumbered the houses but they too were dark. He was just about to give up when he saw a circle of yellow light on the cobbles coming from a pub. The publican must still be up. Conscious of his unspoken promise to MacIntyre, Fenwick resisted the temptation to hammer on the door and demand entry. Instead, he found a few coins in his pocket and threw them against the glass of the lighted window. After several tries a man stuck his head out and said, none too quietly, "Whatdaya want?"

"Police. It's an emergency. Open up."

"How do I know you're police?"

Fenwick stretched up as far as he could to show his warrant card. With a grunt the man slammed the window shut. After several minutes there was the sound of bolts being drawn and the door opened, momentarily blinding Fenwick as light fell into the street. He could see a man silhouetted against the glare and flashed his warrant card again, introducing himself.

"I'm looking for two people, not necessarily together. A man, David Smith. Late twenties, six foot, slim build, could have cuts or signs of injury."

He passed over an e-fit of Smith and paused for the man to say something and was rewarded with a shrug. Stepping closer he was able to see his eyes. Generations of smugglers' genes had shaped the expression of distrust he saw there.

"I get hundreds in here every day. Can't help you." He made to close the door but Fenwick blocked it with his foot in a movement so quick it surprised the burly publican.

"And a woman, perhaps you've seen *her.*" Fenwick thrust Nightingale's photograph at him, forcing him to take it.

"Can't see."

The man turned toward the wall light, keeping his back toward Fenwick. His shoulders stiffened.

"No, seen neither."

But the tension in the man's body said otherwise.

"Think again, sir." Fenwick's eyes went flat with anger. "What's your name?"

"What business is it of yours?"

Fenwick looked up at the words inscribed in fading gilt above the door.

"Are you Tremayne, the publican?"

The man weighed even this question before answering, then nodded.

"Well now, Mr. Tremayne, you'll oblige me by answering my question. Have you seen this woman?" It was clear to Fenwick that he had but that either his habitual distrust of law enforcement or a desire to avoid becoming involved was keeping him dumb. "I say that you have."

A flicker of calculation crossed the man's face but he held his silence.

"Did you hear me? That man is a murderer, and that woman," he took a step forward for emphasis and Tremayne retreated in his path, "is his next victim."

He shouldn't have said any of that but he was desperate. Tremayne just stared at him. Fenwick's temper was almost past the point of control.

"If he gets to her and I find out that you knew *anything* at all, I'll have you as an accessory. Right now you're just heading for a charge at wasting police time." Tremayne made to turn away. "Think again before you do that."

The publican walked through to the saloon bar and put the e-fit of Smith and photograph of Nightingale on the green baize of the snooker table before turning on the overhead lamp.

"That's better. Yes," he tapped Smith's face, "he was in here this evening. Left before closing time."

"And the woman?"

Tremayne was looking less sure of himself now.

"He was asking about a girlfriend who owed him money. This photo doesn't do her justice."

Fenwick felt panic flutter at the base of his throat.

"You've seen her?"

"She came in a month or so back. Haven't seen her since."

"Do you know where she's staying?"

The landlord scratched his scalp through thinning hair. It was all Fenwick could do to keep his hands off him.

"Come on! This is life and death, for God's sake."

"Maybe. Her family's been down here forever."

"I know, at Mill Farm. How do I get there?"

"Up in the hills somewhere westerly way. Backs onto the cliffs. A good eight miles from here. Never been there." From the way he spoke it was clear he'd said all he was going to and nothing Fenwick could do was going to persuade him otherwise.

He left feeling he'd been deceived somehow. The bottom line was that he was no closer to finding Nightingale. Above him at the top of the hill he could see a long line of officers deployed along the street. Reinforcements had arrived, organized effortlessly by MacIntyre. At least now they could start waking people up. He went straight to the post office and knocked on the door. A worried-looking man in his thirties opened up.

"Police. We're conducting a murder investigation and need to find a young woman before she becomes the next victim."

The man's eyes widened in alarm and he beckoned Fenwick inside.

"DCI Fenwick. We need to reach Mill Farm, owned by the Nightingales. We know it's near here but we need exact directions."

"The wife might know, she's local. Hang on."

They came back together.

"I know of the Nightingales, of course I do, quite notorious they were back in my dad's day."

"And the location of the Farm?"

"That I don't know but I know a man who does, Pete Trewellin. He was postman here for over thirty years. I'll have his number somewhere. He and my dad were mates." She rummaged in a bureau while Fenwick tried to keep his breathing under control.

"Here. He's still local." She scribbled something down then handed him a number and pointed to the phone. "Feel free."

It took a while for the call to be answered and when it was Fenwick was greeted with an earful of blasphemy. As soon as there was a pause he introduced himself and explained the information he needed. He had to repeat himself several times before Pete Trewellin understood him and gave him detailed directions filled with a local man's guidance. "Turn right just before you get to the hornbeam that was struck by lightning three years ago"—was a classic explanation. Eventually he thought he had enough to find the farm.

It was about nine miles away, not eight, and he couldn't believe that Smith would have set off to find it on foot. Perhaps he was still in the village after all, but he couldn't rely on that. He marched uphill and found MacIntyre directing local operations from the car park.

"I know where to go."

He was given a two men and a patrol car and set off into the dark.

CHAPTER THIRTY-THREE

Nightingale woke to the sounds of the house at night: the clatter of loose guttering, scratchings of mice in the attic, the flutter of a bat around the ceiling, confused and searching for the open window. They were customary noises so what had woken her? There was a shrill bark of a vixen outside and she had her answer.

Moonlight from her uncurtained window made it bright enough for her to read the time on her watch: almost one o'clock, an unwholesome time to wake. She lay in bed, willing sleep to return, enjoying the faint ache in her calves from her run that afternoon. Minutes passed but sleep eluded her. She decided that she needed to go to the bathroom. Perhaps that would settle her. As she walked barefoot along the landing, up and down the steps that negotiated the various parts of the house, she heard a rustling that did not belong, as if something was walking in the long grass outside. She wasn't frightened, more curious. Badgers and foxes prowled her garden at night looking for food.

The noise stopped. When she looked outside the silver-black bars of moonlight and shadow through the surrounding trees cut the familiar view into a visual puzzle of distorted shapes. It was impossible to tell whether anything unusual was out there as everything looked strange.

She went to the bathroom without bothering to close the door, waited for the noise of the flush to die then padded over to the casement window on the landing above the front door. From here she could see straight down the lane. All was quiet and still in the warm night. When she returned to her bed she fell asleep straightaway and did not dream.

The vixen pulled the baby rabbit squealing from its hole, shook it by the neck until the noise stopped, and loped off to find her young. They would have fresh meat tonight. The hunting was good in this place, the scavenging even better. She lifted her head, raising the rabbit so that it did not drag, and quickened her pace. The kill would not be hers until she had returned to her earth and litter. She sniffed the air. Her path through the woods and down the hill was empty, her territory clearly marked but something tonight was not right. There was a disturbance in the air.

The she-fox quickened her pace, concern for her cubs even greater than her hunger. Halfway down the hill a shift in the breeze brought a familiar scent with it, one that did not belong to the night. She recognized the smell and fear for her cubs grew. There was another predator down there, heavy and dangerous. Dropping the warm carcass she stopped and let out a series of shrill warning barks before lifting the dead weight again and running off.

Whoever would have thought that moonlight could be this bright and yet still be so confusing? The rising woodland was floodlit, as clear as day but with color replaced by impenetrable blocks of shadow. Lying in wait, rabbit holes, roots and old tree stumps were ready to trip the unwary. He sucked at recent scratches on the side of his hand and kicked the bramble away viciously.

Smith had started his journey confidently. Despite his

sojourn in the pub he had emerged into the street with a clear head. The path that had been described to him—old tarmac overgrown with weeds—had been easy to find, though further away from the village than he had been led to expect. He had walked onto the thin ribbon of clear asphalt at half past twelve, feeling as fresh as when he had left the village. Only his neck and jaw troubled him. For the rest, he was as fit as he had ever been.

The first easy miles had lulled him into complacency. When the moon hid briefly behind a stray cloud, he had paused, looked about him and realized that he must be lost. Instead of seeing a wooded hillside ahead of him there was a smell of gorse, with the sound of water running far below. *"If you reach the vale, you've gone too far. And no point trying to follow the river back to its source, that's impossible."*

So he had retraced his steps until he found the footpath leading from the track that he'd missed first time. It was late now. He'd been told that Mill Farm lay in a fold on the far side of this hill, beside a river that had once been powerful enough to turn the heavy wooden wheel. He would have to go over the hill, keeping the sound of the sea to his right as he came to the summit. *"Avoid the cliff top,"* the man had said, *"it's treacherous, particularly at night. That's where her aunt topped herself."*

There was a stump by the path so he sat for a moment and opened his rucksack. Smith pulled out a heavy black felt roll from the pack, enjoying the familiar weight of it in his hands. There was a faint clink as one piece fell against another. He spread it open on his knees, then lifted each blade from its wrapping and stroked it. Since Wales, he had kept his tools safe in the rucksack until right at the last minute. Losing his penknife still hurt.

It had amused him how a penknife was considered innocent. Sharpened and shaped it could slide between ribs and slip straight into heart muscle. It could flay, cut and slice as well as any weapon. Of course, he had added to his collection for tonight's very special killing. He had a Stanley knife, the sharpest blade he possessed and good for carving; a sheath knife with a serrated edge; and a scalpel with a remarkably fine replaceable razor blade that he had bought in an art shop. But the penknife was his favorite.

Running his fingers along the cool steel calmed him. The momentary sense of disorientation shrank back and his thinking regained perspective. He reminded himself that this was the night that he'd been waiting for a long time. But he needed energy. The tin of emergency rations was at the bottom of the rucksack. He ate a bar of chocolate, swallowed some pain-killers and more pills, and washed it all down with a high-energy sports drink. Some of his vigor returned; it couldn't be far now. In the distance he heard a fox bark a warning and the wood fell silent.

He wrapped and packed his knives and stood easily, the pain from his wounds fading. His thinking, never logical to a sane person, had a graphic simplicity. The bitch had trapped Wayne, broken their partnership and threatened his own freedom. She'd walked free when Griffiths had been condemned to the cells, so she had to die in order to restore his sense of world order. Not once did he consider the advice he had given Griffiths, the advice his sometime companion had ignored to his cost: *never become fixated; remain detached.* That he could, himself, have become obsessed never occurred to him.

As he walked, his mind turned to the imminent killing itself. At first the variety of options was overwhelming but then, as always happened, he started to match his method to what he thought was the personality of the victim. The perfect assault found the woman's weaknesses and played on them for as long as possible. Usually it was vanity and the threat, then reality, of disfigurement could sometimes cause more agony than simple torture. But occasionally there were other fears. The girl at the caravan park had been scared of water, more petrified of drowning when he'd washed her than of his fists. Her fear had excited him and in the shelter of rocks as he held her face under, he'd taken her again.

But with this bitch there was a problem. He'd watched her for two days in court, automatically searching for weaknesses. She wasn't vain and she was strong, physically and mentally; hard to scare. Her mock faint hadn't fooled him. The only possible source of weakness he could identify was her independence. His intuition, never more sensitive than when he was focused on his victims, told him that having her own space and living on her own terms would be essential to her.

Ideas began to blossom, fed by the knowledge that he would have plenty of time. He would disable her first, crippling her and then smash her fingers. He imagined her trying to crawl away from him on her stomach. When she was whimpering in a corner, he would tell her what he was going to do next, each injury removing mobility and control, every one more destructive than the last. Of course, he would have her too, for as long as it took to rip away her pride and superiority. And all the time his little knives would be working away, busy, busy.

He would let her think that she was going to live, otherwise the idea of being crippled would lose its impact. "*No more jogging, Miss Nightingale,*" he'd say as he sliced and hammered away. Then he would take her again, his hands sticky with her blood, touching her all over.

Afterward he might pause, have breakfast perhaps, or forty winks. Revived and ready again he would string her up and return to his work. Images of what he could do to that perfect skin consumed him, making him stumble as his vision blurred. Perhaps by then she would be so weakened that she would cry out as pain ripped through her.

His breathing was harder now and he forced himself to take a few, calming breaths. Images of her naked and defiled filled his mind. He would hold her, eye to eye, body to body. Little Miss-Fucking-Independent would die in terror, as slowly as he could make it.

He reached the top of the hill and looked down at last into the valley that had cradled Mill Farm for half a millenium. His hands were trembling. The biggest challenge would be to remain in control long enough to complete everything he had planned. He forced himself to stand still and hold out both hands until they were steady. When he was sure that his thoughts were under control he started to climb down to the farm.

"There must be a better way of handling this."

Fenwick looked haggard in the light from the headlamps as he spoke to MacIntyre over the radio.

"I can't spare more men yet, Andrew. We need to cover the town. His car was there and the chances are that it's where we're going to find him. Your tracing Nightingale is only a precaution."

"He's a walker, remember? We heard only yesterday that he was seen disguised as a rambler miles from Ginny's house."

"He'd be crazy to go out all that way on foot. How would he escape?" MacIntyre's voice crackled over the radio.

"Escape from what? He doesn't know we're here. He probably thinks that we're still searching around Telford."

"I disagree. Wendy's body would lead us to him."

"He doesn't think we're smart enough to have found it yet, let alone to make the connection to Nightingale."

"Sorry, Andrew, I'm expecting more men within the hour and as soon as they arrive I'll send some over."

"If we don't get lost, we should be there in fifteen to twenty minutes and I'll need back up. Will the helicopter be here soon?"

"No! I won't put her up in case it alerts him to our search. He escaped from under Cave's nose, remember; the helicopter did no good at all."

"But using one will help us find her more quickly."

"Forget it. You'll have more officers soon and with luck we might have him in custody before you even reach the farm."

Fenwick shook his head. It was no good arguing. He wasn't SIO and he had no control of the way the operation was being conducted. It galled him but if he alienated MacIntyre he gained nothing.

"I'll call in fifteen," he said, biting the skin at the side of his thumbnail in frustration, and then urged the driver on.

The moon was too bright, that was the problem. Nightingale lay in bed cursing her decision to do without curtains. Twice she'd forced herself back to sleep but this time none of her well-tested techniques would work and she decided to make a cup of camomile tea.

She swung her bare legs out of bed and found her trainers with her feet. The old T-shirt she wore was because of the chill of the house not for modesty and it hardly covered her buttocks. As she sat at the table waiting for the kettle to boil she almost nodded off. Feeling certain that she would fall asleep as soon as she was back in bed, Nightingale soaked the teabag and left it in the mug to brew as she padded up the back stairs, yawning.

As she sipped her tea in bed, Nightingale had to struggle to keep her eyes open. She'd barely finished drinking before the camomile flowers did their work and she was asleep.

The wood was completely silent, unnaturally so. In the clearing in front of the farm moonlight burned the earth ash gray. There was no wind and the shadows of the trees pooled in the margin of the forest to create utter darkness, still and expectant. Part of the shadow stirred, detached itself and became a man. He stared up at the rambling house, its empty windows unreflecting holes in the stone. It looked derelict, with no signs of life.

Smith felt a hot bubble of rage swell beneath his ribs. He'd come so far and had been so sure of success that the blank face of the farm was an insult. Then he smelt smoke, soft on the air, and saw it drift up in a column from the chimney. Life. He crept to the door and it opened to his touch.

The air inside was fragrant with soap and herbs. His hope soared. He needed patience and caution now and waited for his eyes to adjust to the deeper darkness. A current of warmer air came from a doorway ahead of him. He followed it into a kitchen, the Aga still warm. He touched the kettle experimentally and pulled his fingers back in shock at the heat.

Someone lived here and had boiled this kettle not long ago. He retreated into the hall and checked the rooms that opened from it. Discovering nothing he paused to orientate himself and decide what to do next.

She would be upstairs asleep. It was time to get ready. He locked the downstairs door and took the key then retreated to the kitchen and placed his rucksack on the table. The knives didn't make a sound as he pulled them out, then the rope and tape, which he put in one of the pockets of his cargo pants. The sheath knife went into a holder on his belt, ready to hand; the Stanley knife in the right pocket of his cargo pants, the tiny scalpel with its protective cover he slipped into the side of his heavy walking boots. He saved the penknife until last and put it in his other trouser pocket. With the familiar weights lying against his skin he was properly dressed again.

Although his eyes were now fully adjusted to the night, he

took a torch anyway before returning to the hall. He studied the stairs. As he reached the first step there was a mechanical whirring from behind him and he spun round, sheath knife in hand. A harsh metallic chime rang out. One . . . two . . . It was a grandfather clock, standing in the shadows. The noise snapped through the hall and ricocheted up the stairs. When it finished he held his breath, straining to catch any sound from above. He counted to one hundred as the house settled back into silence.

He eased his weight onto the edge of the first step and waited for the creak. It remained quiet. The next step moaned a little but it was a whisper of sound, soon lost in the blackness. He started to feel more confident and eased his weight forward.

Nightingale groaned softly into her pillow as the clock woke her from the doze she had managed to drift into. Normally she would sleep right through but this wasn't a regular night. She peered hard at her watch and saw it was two-ten. The old clock was running slow, as always. Stifling a yawn, she stretched beneath the bedclothes, willing sleep to return and tried to ignore the fact that the clock would chime again on the hour for the rest of the night.

There was a click from downstairs, faint but distinct, not one of the customary house noises. It must have been the kettle cooling, or the claws of a heavy mouse. Nightingale listened for the noise to come again so that she could identify the source more accurately and dismiss it. Silence. She breathed in deeply. As she exhaled there was a sharp creak that brought her sitting upright in bed. That was a sound she could place exactly. The third step of the hall stairs protested like that when weight depressed it. If she were right, there would be a softer noise as the boards were released.

There it was, unmistakable. Someone was climbing the

stairs. She waited. Although the fourth step was silent, the fifth was as good as a burglar alarm.

The image of Griffiths floated in the grayness before her but she dismissed it. He was locked up. Could it be his partner, the man called Smith that Fenwick had been trying to warn her about? That was impossible. He would never find her here. It had to be a random intruder. But there was no reason why a casual thief would bother with a house like this. Unless it wasn't a thief but someone who had heard of a stupid woman living on her own and had decided to have some fun.

Despite her attempts to remain logical and keep calm, the hairs were standing up at the back of her neck as she lifted her feet carefully out of bed and into her trainers. The gardening shorts she had worn earlier were on a chair. To reach them she had to cross the old floorboards—impossible to do silently. Her mind was divided in two, hearing focused on the stairs, every other brain cell on trying to remember where she had left her car keys. She remembered and shook her head at her stupidity. They were downstairs in the drawer of the dresser where she always left them.

There was another creak, the fifth step. The intruder was almost at the corner of the stairs. She had to decide quickly: run, fight or hide. Nightingale discounted the last two. She was unarmed and he could have a knife, even a gun. And as for hiding—where? The room was almost bare.

To run. Jump from the window? It was a sheer drop onto a stone path. If she hurt herself it would be over. So she had to dare the landing, which meant she needed a weapon. There was an oil lamp by the bed with a heavy metal base; it would have to do. She picked it up and moved toward the door at a crouch to peer through the crack between wood and frame into the relative darkness of the landing. It was empty but the night pooled dark shadows in the corners, large enough to hide a man waiting to jump on her as she passed.

Nightingale was terrified. The courage she had always relied on deserted her and she realized that in the past it had been fueled by a reckless indifference to her fate that had been replaced with a determination to live a life of her own choosing. She started to shake. The tremor was so violent that it rattled the glass in the lamp and she had to still it with her hand. She felt helpless, a victim, but anger at her weakness forced her to confront her fear. She would *not* become another incident to be reported and pitied. The thought of her body on the slab waiting for a "Y" incision filled her with disgust. If she stayed where she was she would probably be raped or die, so she had to move. She decided to count to three as she had done as a child then run. With the taste of salt on her lips she began.

Smith held his breath and finished counting to twenty. The last shriek from the old wood was so loud that he was sure it must have disturbed her. On the final count he listened but apart from the faintest rattle of glass the house was quiet.

The fantasy he had had, of finding her naked in bed, asleep and vulnerable, made him careful but he had never felt so strong or invincible. There was a smile on his face as he took his next step, cautious as ever. No sound. He took the next one and there was the barest creak. There was a turn in the stair two steps ahead, then a shorter flight up the landing. He was so close. The weight of the penknife in his pocket was like an erection against his thigh. A trace of light caught the blade of the sheath knife in his hand.

There was a rush of air and a white blur above him. A shape darted along the landing, pale as moonlight. Smith let out a cry of rage and sprang forward to catch at the ankle only inches from his hand. His left foot descended heavily on the corner stair, breaking the weakened wood with an audible snap. He fell forward, his leg dangling in the air below. Shouting in frustration he pulled his leg up, wincing in pain as the splinters tore through his trousers. His foot wedged itself in the gap and he twisted it, scraping the bare flesh of his calf but it was stuck fast. He stabbed the rotten wood with his sheath knife until the gap was large enough for him to jerk his leg free.

He climbed the remaining steps and ran after the woman who had disappeared into the darkness. The landing wasn't level and he tripped headlong down a short drop, banging his head on the skirting board at the bottom. After that he used the torch and was more careful. The way before him was empty. To his left was a bathroom smelling of her soap; to the right an old bedroom with mold in the corners. There was a noise, coming from behind one of the doors. He swung it open and found stairs spiraling down. He launched himself at them and saw the glimmer of white below. With a yell he ran forward—to find an empty pillowcase, lying flat against a half-open door. He pushed through it and was in the kitchen, alone.

Nightingale crouched behind the stud wall in the little bedroom and watched for the torchlight to return. When she'd looked out of its window the sight of ripped wires trailing from the bonnet of her car had made her want to weep. Whoever was in her house wasn't a stray burglar, of that she was now certain. It had to be Smith, though she hadn't dared to look down the stairs as she'd made her escape. As he'd pulled his foot free she had acted quickly to drop her pillow into the kitchen in the hope that he would think she had escaped that way. Now she waited to see whether her deception had worked. The idea of running half-naked through the woods in the dark was ridiculous. She would tear her legs to shreds, probably break an ankle. She had acted quickly to set up her diversion as he pulled his foot free. Now she waited to see whether her deception had worked.

She was cowering in her childhood hiding place, a space between wall and eaves that ran the length of the old house. She had to balance carefully on the crossbeams to avoid falling through the plaster ceiling. The room the other side of the wall remained silent. There was a faint crack around the plasterboard that plugged the hole through which she would see any torchlight should he return.

As the minutes passed she began to relax and think about how long she should hide to be sure he was gone. At the count of one hundred and fifty-three a beam of light flicked across the join, bright through the gap. She closed her eyes instinctively and a red line crossed her vision, warning her that some of her night sight had gone. The passage in which she was hiding was low, less than half height. She froze in her crouch and waited for him to leave the bedroom. It was crazy that he was even searching for her. He should be outside and the fact that he wasn't meant that she wasn't out-thinking him. The light went away and she started to breathe again. Surely he would give up soon.

But Nightingale couldn't know Smith's cunning. It had taken him some time to be sure that she had not slipped through the windows, which were swollen shut with age or closed. Then he had checked the rooms downstairs meticulously before closing and securing the doors as he moved on. He grew certain that she was in the house. Even if she had made it to the kitchen in the time it had taken to free himself the locked door would have blocked her escape.

Despite the anti-climax he was starting to enjoy this game of cat and mouse. He had everything he needed, she nothing, perhaps not even clothes. The image of her running had been brief but he could recall long arms and bare legs punching the air. At the top of the stairs he found a chest of drawers which he dragged over to prevent her running downstairs behind him. If she tried the kitchen stairs she would find the door wedged shut from the other side with a chair. Slowly he was closing in.

The upstairs of the house was confusing. It was larger than the space below. He realized that some rooms must have been built over the farm outbuildings. That would complicate matters but he had all night and he could work methodically when he needed to.

She hadn't returned to her bedroom. He sniffed her bedclothes, smiling, before securing the door. Very carefully, he searched each room, finding nothing. He started over again and it was then that he saw the faint scuff marks in the dust in the older part of the house. He followed them down steps and along to a small bedroom, tucked under the eaves. The room was empty, the windowpane cracked but closed fast. He tried to find further traces of her beyond the room but there were none so he went back inside, sat down on the floor and switched off his torch. He was always at his best in the homes of his victims and his instincts told him she was close by. She wouldn't be able to wait long, no woman had that stamina, and when she moved he would hear her.

Nightingale had no idea how long she had been crouching in the pitch black of the eave's passageway. At one point she thought she heard the clock strike but it was so muffled she couldn't be sure. Had one hour gone by, two? It had to be longer since she'd woken to hear him creeping up the stairs. She decided to count to three thousand, and then move.

At four hundred and twenty she heard a noise in the room. She pushed her eye to the tiny crack but could see nothing so she put her nose there and sniffed silently. There was the overwhelming odor of dust and plasterboard but beyond that she could detect the unmistakeable taint of alien sweat.

She was hunched forward, face pressed to the wall when the tapping started right by her ear, forcing her to bite her knuckles to prevent a scream. The tapping moved away and along the wall. He was here and he suspected her hiding place. There was no option now but to move. She would have to crawl from beam to beam, her muscles were too tight to manage a crouching shuffle and she would need to leave her only weapon, the oil lamp, behind. She shuffled forward, her arms trembling with fear, praying that he wouldn't find the gap that revealed the removable access panel behind the bed.

Smith knocked and listened. In some places the plaster was so rotten that his knuckles raised clouds of dust like phantoms in the moonlight. He worked his way around the room, testing the wall at shoulder and knee height at every pace. When he had completed a full circuit he paused and checked the footprints on the floor again, concerned that he had been mistaken.

No. She had run in here and not run out again. He crouched down and shone his torch along the floor to take a closer look. A line of tracks clear in the torchlight ran to the side of the sagging single bed. He inched forward, tapping the walls gently. By the side of the bed he noticed a faint shadow in the peeling wallpaper. The space behind the bed was too small for him to crawl into though she could have managed it. He dragged the old iron frame back with a screech. When he tested the wall behind it the hollow echo was obvious. With his penknife blade he traced the line of shadow, pressing through into a space behind. He levered the panel free. After several attempts he managed to push his muscled upper torso through and the rest of his body followed easily.

On the other side he paused for breath and to orientate himself. He was in a narrow void formed by the angle of the roof meeting lathe and plaster inner walls. There was barely room for him to crouch. When he tried to ease his body into a more comfortable position his head knocked tiles and dislodged dead spiders and dust onto his face.

He flashed his torch to the left toward the front of the house and saw the gap finish at a brick wall. He crawled along, suspicious that there might be a hiding place there but it was a dead end. That left only one direction. He twisted around and dropped into a low crouch, his torch gripped between his teeth, stretching his jaw. Before him the thick dust on the beams had recently been disturbed, leaving black smears of bare wood. With a low grunt of satisfaction he started to inch forward.

CHAPTER THIRTY-FOUR

A quarter of a mile beyond the end of the tarmac the police car came to a crossroads where an unmade track intersected their own. The driver changed down to a lower gear as the hill rose steeply ahead of them and Fenwick raised MacIntyre on the radio.

"We'll be there within fifteen minutes. Can you send us the helicopter now? We need back up."

"We're almost done here, then the boys are all yours. Why don't you wait?"

Fenwick closed the call without bothering to reply and looked at the driver and his colleague. Smith was only one man but he was a psychotic killer and he felt at a distinct disadvantage.

The driver had a gentle Devon accent. He looked about sixteen, and excited in a way that did nothing to inspire Fenwick's confidence.

"What's your name?" He stopped himself saying son.

"Constable Penders, sir, Cal."

"When did you join the force, Cal?"

"Eighteen months ago, same time as Pete here." He thumped his partner's shoulder enthusiastically and was rewarded with a return punch. "Are we on our own, sir?"

"For now. Lights off; we must be getting close."

Pushing his doubts to one side, he started to consider his options as they crawled forward through the darkness.

Nightingale smothered a cough in the crook of her arm and tried to blink her eyes clear of dust. Up here above the old mill wheel, hundreds of years of corn husks coated every surface and she had to pause to catch her breath and avoid choking on the fine powder she raised every time she moved. It was pitch black in the roof void and she was lost. Somehow in the maze of passages she had missed the hatch above the stairs down to the dairy and instead she had crawled to the end of the extension that had been built out over the millstream. There was nowhere left to go and a murderer behind her. She knew that he was there. Less than a minute before she had seen an arc of torchlight on the ceiling before turning a corner into darkness, moving faster in a desperate attempt to outpace her pursuer.

She had to accept that there must be a deeper purpose to the break-in than simple theft. It wasn't random. The man pursuing her had to be Smith, determined to find her. The thought filled her with terror for it meant that he had motive and wouldn't simply go away. Nightingale had read of the hinted brutality of his crimes and knew that he would persist until he caught her. She backed up and turned into a tiny passage, comforted that it would be too narrow for him to enter. Near panic, she increased her speed despite the absolute dark in the void.

Without warning she slammed into a wall that reared up across her path. Stunned, she lowered her head and waited for the stars to clear from her eyes. She felt around for the next turning. There were brick walls on three sides and the roof above was solid. She had nowhere left to run. Behind her she thought she could hear a heavy shuffle and stifled a sob. With dread she turned and began to crawl backward in case she had missed a way out. She caught her knee on a large splinter of wood but ignored the pain and moved on

To her right and left her fingers touched rough bricks and roofing slates as she retraced her route. Her feet stirred up eddies of thick chaff that caught in her eyes and throat, making her choke and forcing her to pause for breath. Her muscles spasmed as she lay on her side and tried to breathe but the air was as thick and foul near the beams as it was beneath the tiles. She was suffocating.

Nightingale struggled for breath in the pitch blackness. Above her the roof pressed down like the lid of a tomb but she could just make out a thin line of light and inched toward it, one hand across her nose and mouth as a mask, the other bearing her weight on the beams. Below the light she could see that the roof lining had come away and there were stars visible in the gaps between the tiles. She used her elbow to punch a slate free from its rotting pins so that it hung at an angle. A draft of air blew in and she sucked at the freshness greedily until her head cleared. Outside she could see Orion low in the sky. The sound of running water was clear in the night. Perhaps she could break through the roof and escape. She felt confident of her strength after months of good food and physical activity and broke more tiles away easily. But the rafters were too close together to allow her body through.

To her left, the roofing came down across the passage but there was a gap, perhaps less than two feet from the floor, where some of the bricks had tumbled away. It was her only chance of escape. She was still trapped with nowhere to go but back, and he was behind her, closing the gap even as she wasted time in this coffin-shaped void. He would search every inch of the house and, if he didn't find her, she was certain that he would burn it down.

The image of being trapped in the roof while fire consumed the dried-out wood and ignited the corn dust was more horrifying than confronting Smith. There was no option but to go back into the main passage she'd just left so hopefully and continue from there. She forced herself away from the moonlight into the menacing darkness, her eyes straining ahead for any sign of escape.

Just before she reached the junction with the main roof space she saw an object looming up on her right, black against the gray shadows. Her outstretched fingers touched wood, a thick slab, set at an angle. Reaching up, she found another, then another. It was the top of the mill wheel, huge, powerful, thrusting up into the roof space to reach the full height of the building. She must have passed it before in the darkness but the filter of moonlight was enough for her to see its outline.

There was a gap in the floor around the wheel, not big but maybe just enough for her to slide through. She tested the space with her hands. It was barely a foot wide but she was so desperate that she pushed her feet down into it without a second thought. Her hips and buttocks wedged tight but she forced them through, reaching out with her trainers to find purchase on one of the wooden slats below. Her waist glided down easily, then her breasts. She was trying to angle her head through sideways when light swung in from the entrance to the main eaves and blinded her. The torch swung up and around searching as she tried to push through, her chin pressed tight against the wood, the back of her skull wedged painfully into the hole in the floor. She waited helplessly as the torchlight came round in a lazy arc until its beam dazzled her straight in the face.

"Ah, there you are." His tone was conversational, almost polite. "My, but what a mess you're in. Stuck with nowhere to run to. This is a little narrow for me but I'll be right with you. Don't go away now."

Nightingale heard herself scream. It was a strange sound,

distorted by the pressure on her jaw but it was a scream she couldn't control and he laughed in delight. Then his face disappeared and the torchlight vanished, leaving her night-blind and in darkness. He had gone to find another way through to her, while she was pinioned here, trapped by her skull.

"Big head!" she shouted, tears streaming down her face. "Stupid woman. *Do* something!" She twisted and turned. At one acute angle her face moved through until the wood caught on her cheekbone. Her ears were compressed tight against her skull. It was agony but she pulled down against them, first one side then the other, feeling the blood start to trickle down her neck as she scraped the skin raw. The right ear suddenly slipped below the floorboards. A moment later, the left one was through. Blood stained her T-shirt but she was finally free, clinging to the old mill wheel like a huge spider in a monstrous web.

Nightingale was crying now. He was coming for her. Her only hope was that he would get lost, as she had done, in the warren of roof space. Using the wooden struts she clambered down the wheel, passing through the second and first floors until she could jump onto the flagstones of the mill room. She paused to ease the cramp from her thighs and to cough up the contaminating dust from her lungs.

For the first time since he'd followed her into the eaves she allowed herself to believe that she might escape. She was at the very edge of the farm. All she needed to do was leave this building, cross the brook and then run into the woods, where she would have a chance to outpace him.

Nightingale ran across the mossy floor and pulled open the door. As she sprinted across the yard, a dark shadow left the side of one of the outbuildings and sprang at her. He had been waiting for her! He hit her head hard enough to send her sprawling onto the cobbles and leaped down on her, his right arm raised to hit her again but she jerked upward, ramming her knee into his groin and butting him under the chin with her head. He howled in surprise as she punched him hard on the side of his head but he kept hold of her, using his weight to pin her down.

The pain galvanized her. She couldn't understand why he wasn't using a knife or gun. It was as if he wanted to knock her unconscious rather than kill her outright. The thought of what this might mean terrified her and she pushed up against his weight. He had an arm across her throat now, choking her, while the other held one of her arms useless to her side. He was like a wild animal, his eyes wide, pupils surrounded by blood-stained whites, his mouth drawn into a snarl. Despite the injuries she could see along his jaw and neck he was agile and aggressive, fueled by his hatred of her and, perhaps, some sort of chemical stimulant that was dulling the pain and boosting his strength. He was the stuff of nightmares.

Black spots started to break in front of her eyes as he choked her; blood drummed in her ears. Her right arm was trapped beneath the weight of his body, the left was held tight in his grip. She was going to black out. A desperate will to live surged through her. She pulled her legs up, braced her feet against the cobbles and thrust her hips upward with every atom of strength she still possessed.

He rocked sideways but held her fast. She thrust again, in a sick mockery of the sex act, and he pressed back against her. Something hard pushed into her hip and she took it for his erection. Then he shifted and the way it moved was wrong. It slid down, across her hip, away from his groin. She realized that it was something in his pocket.

Her arm was still trapped by her side. With what remained of her wits she pretended she was unconscious. Her head lolled to one side, eyes closed. In the blackness, with her lungs compressed and a fire in her throat, she knew how close her masquerade was to truth.

He held her still for a long moment. Her tongue filled her mouth and she started to fall down within herself. Then he leaned back and she could breathe again. She could sense him watching her, ready to squeeze again, so she drew in breaths slowly, despite the protest of her body, and kept her eyes shut. Satisfied that she really was out cold, she felt him start to rise. In her mind she visualized his body, that pocket with the hard shape inside. Whatever it was, it was her only chance to seize an advantage.

As he rose she took a deep breath and launched upward, her head catching his chin hard enough to make him weave to the side. Her hand slipped into his pocket and clasped the smooth plastic she found there. From the feel of it she had his cigarette lighter. She could burn him.

He thrust his weight back down on her, trapping both her arms between their bodies. She wriggled and managed to bring a leg free but his hands were around her throat now, squeezing her back toward oblivion. On the cobbles beside them she could see his knife ready for use. She tried to remember her self-defense classes. Eyes and groin; go for them. With her arms trapped like this she couldn't reach his face but her hands had to be mere inches from his crotch.

He had angled up slightly, the better to choke her. She thrust a hand down, found his balls and squeezed hard. Smith let out a yelp and his grip loosened. She brought her arms up and pushed them wide, breaking his hold. Then she kneed him again for good measure and rolled away, choking for breath.

He was on his feet faster than she expected and he went straight for his knife.

"Have it your own way, you fucking bitch. You die right here and now."

He aimed a kick at her side but she swayed away, keeping her eyes on him and the blade in his hand. It was a sheath knife about five inches long.

"Try it, you sick bastard." She staggered to her knees and raised one leg to leverage herself up but her head started to spin so she lowered it again, like a bull baited but not beaten.

He was smiling now, circling around her, swinging his knife from side to side.

"Don't try to fool me. You're shit scared and you know it."

The laugh she let out didn't sound right but it made her feel better. This man wanted to see her terrified and begging for her life before he killed her. Well, he was going to be disappointed. Now that the worst was happening she was filled with renewed courage rooted in the desire to live.

"You're pathetic." She wanted to goad him closer so that she could flash the flame of the lighter in his face but he kept his distance. He was describing what he was going to do to her alive and dead. She let him, ignoring the words because they were giving time for her head to clear. Without drawing attention to what she was doing, she felt over the surface of the object in her hand, searching for the flint wheel and switch. When she encountered nothing but smooth plastic and a metal trim, she risked a glimpse down.

It wasn't a lighter but a penknife. At first she was disappointed. The plan to raise the flame and burn him was so clear in her mind. But then she realized what she had and new hope filled her. She had a blade to fight a blade. It didn't make them even but she felt her confidence grow. Her lack of fear would be a major advantage, as she doubted he had ever encountered a victim more angry or determined.

Without warning he made a lunge for her. She rolled easily, rising into a crouch when she stopped. He came again, knife thrust forward to strike her. She waited until he was close, then twisted and sliced down with her own blade. There was a yelp of surprise and she saw blood on her arm. He had cut her but there was blood on her knife too and she turned to see him sucking his wrist and searching his pocket.

"That's my fucking knife!" The outrage in his voice was disproportionate to the size of the puny blade.

"Come and get it then." She was on her feet, weaving as if she were drunk but with a wildness in her she had never felt before.

Holding his eyes, she raised her bloody arm to her mouth and tasted her blood. This wasn't a healing suck, or a ladylike lick of a wound, this gesture left smears on her chin and cheeks, and painted her teeth red. The taste of the iron and salt awoke in her a primitive desire to inflict pain on the person who had hurt her. Something of this must have shown in her face as the man took a step back and paused in his circling, appraising her.

He came at her again in a sudden rush. She sidestepped but her mind was moving faster than her injured body and the edge of his blade nicked the skin under her arm, inches from her heart. The pain shocked her but was then forgotten as she was forced to jump to one side when he returned, lightening fast, to the attack. He was closing on her now, confident and practiced with his knife. Her feet felt heavy and she forced herself to think through the fog of her bloodlust. Confidence did not guarantee success. Her opponent was fitter and stronger, fueled by his hatred toward her despite his injuries. If she couldn't out-think him, she would die as surely as when she had lain trapped on the ground.

When he charged again she stood her ground. At the last second, she aimed a sharp kick at his knee and swung the penknife down in an arc. He stumbled, missed his mark and blood appeared along his cheekbone where her knife had opened an old wound. Half an inch higher and she would have blinded him.

He cried out and turned on her at close quarters. His knife sliced the air by her neck and locks of black hair fell to the ground. They both dropped into a crouch, circling each other, snarling, oblivious to pain, equals in the desire to destroy and maim. She saw him feint right but his eyes gave him away and she held her ground. When he rushed her she dropped into a ball at the last minute and rolled into his legs, bringing him down. It wasn't an orthodox move but it floored him.

She leaped onto him, slicing at his neck, while holding his right hand away with her left. He was stronger but she had the advantage of surprise as he hadn't expected her attack. Avoiding his empty free hand, she slashed at the arm holding the knife, opening a gouge from the wrist across his palm. She tried to slice again but he caught her arm and rolled her over onto her back so that he lay on top of her, a knife in both their right hands. His left hand squeezed her wrist until tears flowed from her eyes. Her left hand found his injury and tore at the broken skin on his palm until he pulled it away, moaning in pain, and dropped his knife.

It lay on the cobbles. Before he could pick it up with his good hand she kicked it away into the shadows by the house wall, where it clanged against a bucket. She rolled out from under him.

There was silence. He held his injured arm to his chest and stared at her. She rose to her feet, feeling no pain. Blood soaked her T-shirt and ran down her naked legs onto the cobbles but it was irrelevant. He looked weak, defeated, but then he pulled a little blade from his boot and took a coil of twine from a pocket and she realized he'd been faking his weakness. So be it; she closed in.

As she lunged he grabbed her wrist and twisted so that her fingers dropped the knife.

"No," she screamed, and head-butted him sideways. "Get away from me you fucking pervert." She aimed a kick at his stomach but he grabbed her foot and pulled her forward, unbalancing her. She landed heavily on her side but the momentum of her fall pulled him over. He was focused entirely on slipping a noose of rope over her head. The idea of being tethered like an animal for slaughter made her fight with even greater desperation.

"No you don't!"

She jerked her head back suddenly, accidentally striking the point of his chin hard. The sound of his teeth snapping shut made her grin like a savage as she sprang to her feet and stamped on his injured hand so that he released the scalpel. She picked it up.

He was on all fours, stunned by her blow, shaking his head in an attempt to clear it. The desire to finish him was extraordinary: step forward, yank his head back and slice. It would be over in a matter of seconds and she would be free of the evil crouching on the cobbles before her. She'd be doing the world a favor. Almost without thinking she touched the tiny blade, marveling at its fine edge. She took a step forward.

The man looked up, glancing from the knife to the expression on her face, and his eyes widened in terror. The sight thrilled her.

"No, please." He tried to stand but the blow to his chin had stunned his nervous system and he only managed to rise on one knee in a parody of a romantic proposal. "I'm begging you. For God's sake, don't."

To see this man so helpless, looking up at her and pleading for mercy, brought a rush of pleasure to her body. Her face flushed and her mouth opened wider in delight. He must have recognized the look on her face; perhaps he'd seen it before in his mirror, because he shrank away from her.

She took another step toward him, in no hurry now that he was incapacitated.

"Don't!"

"And why shouldn't I, you sick bastard? It's what you deserve. A life for a life."

The knife came up between their eyes.

"You can't. You're police, you can't kill me. You're not allowed to."

She laughed, a horrible sound, and he struggled into a crouch.

"Get back down on your knees and beg." She spat the words at him and after a split second of hesitation he obeyed.

"Now tell me why you deserve to live."

"I have my rights. You can't do this."

"You just tried to kill me. I'm defending myself—kill or be killed. Everyone will believe it was self-defense."

"It's a lie, look, I'm surrendering, see!" He raised bloody wrists as if to be handcuffed.

She sneered at the gesture.

"See, see, I surrender. You can't kill me. I'm your prisoner."

He was sobbing now, a line of snot trickling from his nose. It was pathetic.

The hatred drained away from Nightingale, leaving her clear-headed and appalled. She'd been ready to kill a man as he begged for mercy and the realization made her feel sick.

As the bloodlust faded, so did her sense of omnipotence. She was a half-naked woman, injured more than she realized, confronting a serial killer with one of his own knives at an isolated farmhouse. What on earth had she been thinking of, taunting him and ignoring his earlier surrender?

Nightingale shook her head. The man was still kneeling before her, his arms raised. She couldn't tell whether he had sensed her change of mood but he was looking at her quizzically now, not in fear. If he suspected her weakness, she had no doubt that he would spring back to the attack.

She made her eyes hard and set her jaw but behind the mask her mind struggled to work out what to do next. Part of her still wanted to kill him because of the menace he was but she had no hatred to fuel her actions, just deep distaste. The thought of touching him revolted her.

"Tie your ankles together. Go on, do it." The tone of her voice shocked her. It seemed to come from another person, violent and ruthless. He was hesitating. "Fucking do it or I'll cut your throat and be done with it."

He rolled onto his backside and brought his knees up as if to obey her but something in his attitude had changed. Nightingale crouched slightly, balancing her weight, ready to spring forward, then realized that he wasn't looking at her. He was staring over her shoulder, up into the sky.

"*Old trick*," she thought, and ignored the implied suggestion to turn around.

"Go on, tie your . . ." She stopped.

She could hear something now. At first she thought it was a car laboring up the hill but the note and rhythm were wrong. Smith recognized it though. A look of panic crossed his face and his eyes darted around the clearing, suspecting a trap. It was a helicopter.

Even as she started to smile the man leaped up. She braced herself for his attack but it never came. He was gone, running toward the trees. Nightingale watched him go with relief that quickly turned to anxiety. Under the leafy canopy he could avoid the helicopter and run for miles, concealed from sight. He would escape and she would never be able to live without fear while he was free. She wept with frustration. It wasn't fair.

"No!" she cried, feeling the weight of choice fall on her. Keeping her eyes on the point at which he had entered the woods she ran, her long legs closing the gap to the trees, her feet squelching in blood inside her trainers.

Once in the wood she stopped to listen, heard his crashing run and turned to follow. Ferns and brambles caught at her legs, fresh blood started to ooze from the cut to her side but she still felt no pain. She gripped the scalpel hard like a talisman. The noises he made grew closer. He was running, not hiding, and she was outpacing him.

She found the rope discarded on the ground. When she picked it up she noticed it was covered with blood where he'd held it. She looped it bandoleer fashion from one shoulder and increased her pace.

The sounds of him thrashing through the undergrowth were loud in the night. Beyond them she could hear the faint echoes of the sea. He was heading toward the cliffs through the thickest part of the woods. If she could find the footpath she would stand a chance of cutting him off while taking a safer route. She slowed and circled out. After a few minutes of zigzagged running she found the track and began to run faster toward the cliffs.

"No! Where did she go?"

"Into the woods, sir. We'll never catch them."

Fenwick had arrived with his small band of rescuers just in time to see a figure he thought was Nightingale run into the woods.

"We have to try and follow them. Spread out either side of where she went in. Keep in radio contact."

He looked up at the helicopter, virtually useless for a search of woodland at night, and cursed MacIntyre for releasing so few men. He called and was told that more officers had already been released from Clovelly.

He and his two helpers set out in an expanding search pattern, each with a powerful torch. Every few minutes Fenwick used his radio to call for silence so that they wouldn't end up chasing each other through the trees. There were noises a long way off to his right but nothing else. He directed the officers toward them and followed.

Shortly after he'd halted them for the sixth time he spotted a clear swathe of broken ferns ahead of him with traces of fresh blood at waist height. He called the others closer and they followed the trail more quickly, even as the noises ahead of them died away.

The sound of a broken twig snapped through the night and Nightingale froze. He was very close. She crouched down trying to control her breathing and to hear beyond the blood in her ears. Not far away she could make out heavy surf breaking against rocks a hundred feet below. They must be near the headland where an ancient path used by smugglers twisted down to a bay concealed beneath the overhang. There was another faint sound, impossible to position, then silence.

She waited in the darkness. Did he know that she was following him? Was he circling behind her even now? Her skin crawled. She twisted her shoulder blades in an attempt to ease the pricking she could feel between them and risked a glance back. Nothing. Just tree trunks and darkness. She swallowed and it sounded too loud. Gradually her breathing slowed. Perhaps she was on her own and he had slipped away after all. She waited. There was another snap, clearly discernable over to her left. She lowered her body to the ground and started to crawl forward, keeping her head below the top of the bracken. She was near the edge of the wood. A faint glow cast shadows back toward her and she could see gray grass beyond. The helicopter was coming back again, the noise of its rotors faint but growing louder.

The shape of a crouching man crossed between her and the moonlight, less than ten meters away. Another few moments and she would have crawled on top of him. As he ran toward the cliff top, Nightingale slipped through the wood after him. He was looking not toward her but into the sky. He ducked back into the margin of the wood, only three tree trunks from where she lay. The noise from the helicopter was loud, then a spotlight swung onto the cliff top, arced over it and away, its search continuing.

The man barely waited once the light was gone. He ran onto the grass but this time Nightingale was right behind him. In her left hand she held the knife; in the right, a fallen branch that she wielded as a club. She let out a terrible yell as she sprang on him, hitting out as she leaped forward. He half turned and the blow, heavy and full of hate, fell on his neck and shoulder. Something cracked and he yelped with pain. A dressing fell from his face and blood spurted from his cheek. His left arm hung limp at his side.

"You fucking bitch!"

Despite his injuries, he sprang toward her, eager to fight. In his right hand he held a Stanley knife. The vicious blade glinted in the moonlight. He swung it at her, narrowly missing her cheek. She parried with the branch, ducking back out of his reach but he came at her again, with an energy that was unnatural given the damage she had inflicted.

"*Never confront a wounded animal*," her father had always said, but that's exactly what she had done. She should have knifed him when she had the chance. Now she had no doubt that he was determined to kill her, even if he died in the process.

She swung at his arm again but missed and he used her moment of unbalance to leap forward, knife lunging like a bayonet.

It caught her lower arm, just a small nick but enough to draw blood and jar her knife to the ground. He laughed in triumph and came at her again, slashing wildly. He knocked the branch out of her hand, and then threw his weight against her. She held his wrist, pushing the knife away from her face and tried to knee him but the angle was wrong. Gradually his weight brought the blade closer to her eyes. In desperation she angled her head to the side and bit down on his chin so hard her that teeth almost met. He howled. Blood filled her mouth and she spat it in his eyes then twisted his badly injured wrist so sharply that he dropped his own knife in shock; she kicked it over the cliff.

He brought his head down and tried to bite her back but she twisted away and punched him in the gut so that he fell into a crouch. He stared at her, grinning crazily through his bloody mask. In the woods behind them they could hear sounds of pursuit and she cried out.

"Over here! This way."

The noises grew louder and, coincidentally, the helicopter turned back from the far headland toward them.

"All right, game over. So I'm going to have to die." He said it in a voice that was too flat and calm. "Not quite what I planned but anything's better than prison." He shuddered. Even saying the word had made him shake.

She stood back and watched him walk the few meters to the edge. He stared down and she willed him to leap, relieved that it would end this way, but without warning he jumped back and caught her around the waist.

"But sod it, you little bitch, you're coming with me. We die together, trapped forever in eternity. I'm almost looking forward to it."

He held her tight. It was almost as if they were dancing. Nightingale pushed against him, struggling to be free, as he pulled her back toward the cliff top. She put her hands under his injured chin, trying to force his head up, putting so much pressure in his neck that it had to break but he carried on in a crazy lopsided waltz, his one good arm locked so tight around her that she couldn't breathe properly.

She could see the edge of the cliff behind him no more than a couple of paces away. With her left foot she kicked his shin then his knee, causing him to stumble. They landed on the grass together but his grip didn't slacken.

"Perfect," he said, as Nightingale's hands kept his teeth away from her neck. "We can go down together." As he threw the taunt at her he arched his back and rolled them toward the cliff.

It was a stupid mistake. Their combined weight crushed his injured arm and he cried out in pain. His hold on her weakened and she pulled away on hands and knees, almost breaking free before he grabbed her ankle with his good hand. She kicked back, catching his injured shoulder but he held on, powered by a superhuman desire to kill her.

"Now, what shall we do in our eternity?" He panted, barely able to speak, driven by the desire to punish her even as he dragged them toward their destruction.

Nightingale stayed silent, uninterested in his attempts to distract her.

He pulled at her as he spoke and they started a tug of war, with her leg as the rope, less than six feet from the cliff edge. She clutched at the springy grass, tearing handfuls out as he dragged them toward the drop and inevitable death. Nightingale was screaming now, at the end of her resourcefulness and strength. The knives lay beyond her reach. The cliff top was smooth, without even a root or stone to cling to. It was only a matter of time before they fell.

The shouts from the wood were getting closer. Hearing

them gave Nightingale one last surge of strength and she held him to a standstill.

"You should be grateful. I could have killed your sister-in-law; you know I met her . . ."

Her distraction at his words cost a precious twelve inches of ground and she willed herself to remain silent. He turned all his energy into dragging them backward; she in resistance. They were held in a motionless tableau in the moonlight like statues in a bizarre piece of modern art left for nature and time to erode. Nightingale's muscles started to tremble with effort. The pain in her leg and down her injured side was unbearable. She could feel herself weakening and this time she knew that she had nothing left.

"You were beautiful before I marked you," he said, in a clinical way, and she could feel his eyes on her damaged skin, naked below the T-shirt. "Finishing you will be the perfect end to my career."

She had no energy left to speak and had long ago dismissed the embarrassment of her nakedness. It was as nothing, weighed against her will to live. She kept her gaze on the helicopter spotlight as it grew larger and concentrated on holding her ground. He jerked at her leg and her knee slipped. She lost a precious six inches but locked her muscles and squeezed her eyes tight against the pain.

The searchlight swung round in a lazy loop over the cliff top then back, as if staring in disbelief. Nightingale heard its roar as it moved in trying to land and was buffeted by the wind of rotors. Then there was a pounding of feet on the ground and somebody grabbed her arms at the wrist to pull her free.

Smith's hand dropped her ankle. She spun round to look as he stood up and took a half leap to the edge of the cliff. Whoever was holding her let her go and ran to catch him before he jumped, wrestling him to the ground. Within seconds two uniformed police officers had pinioned and cuffed him. Smith let out a terrible scream as he felt his freedom snatched away and pulled desperately against them but it was hopeless. They led him away sobbing and she collapsed to the ground.

Nightingale lay prone on the cliff top, her T-shirt up around her breasts, leaving her long body naked in the moonlight but she didn't care. She lowered her head and sucked in the sweetness of the grass, marveling at its salty coolness. Someone put a jacket over her and helped her to rise. When she couldn't they knelt down and put an arm around her shoulders, careful to avoid the cuts on her side. A gentle hand stroked the hair away from her face and rested lightly on the back of her neck, warm and comforting.

"It's all right now. You're safe. Come on, Nightingale, let's get you away from here."

The sound of Fenwick's voice drew a bone-shaking cry from her heart as she leaned her head against his chest and allowed him to carry her away.

CHAPTER THIRTY-FIVE

"Are you sure you want to do this?"

"Positive. Don't fuss."

Nightingale walked up through the wood, marveling at the heavy rowan berries glowing scarlet in the setting sun. There would be a full moon tonight but she carried one of her aunt's outdoor lamps as well as an old travel rug.

"I still don't think it's a good idea."

"This is what I want to do. If you don't want to come . . ."

"You can't go on your own."

They walked on in silence. For weeks she had been cosseted and counseled as the inquiry into the handling of the Smith investigation circled around her, interrupted only by the solemn funeral of Constable Knots. From what she could gather, Fenwick emerged from the internal investigation extremely well. MacIntyre escaped with his reputation intact, just, and only because Fenwick had refused to say anything negative against him. DCI Cave had been less well treated. His criticism of other officers had not protected him from the fallout from Ginny's murder.

She had read the whole file on Smith. Her counselor had supported her request, recognizing in Nightingale the need to confront fear in order to overcome it. But there had been nothing in there to explain or excuse his compulsive attacks on women.

"Do you think he killed his parents?"

She had been asking him questions about Smith constantly since he had picked her up from Cooper's, where she had been staying after leaving hospital.

"We'll never know. When the lake was dragged to find Knotty's body the divers discovered the Smiths' car and two human skeletons. There's no way of knowing whether they were alive or dead when they entered the water as there's no soft tissue left."

"How can someone with decent, loving parents turn out like Smith?"

"It just happens. You've said it to me before, some people are evil."

She turned to him and laughed.

"I can't believe that you're so incurious, Andrew."

He shrugged. "I don't torment myself with puzzles I will never be able to answer. I leave that to the likes of Doctor Batchelor."

"Is he psychoanalyzing Smith for the trial?"

"No, Smith's being held at another prison, in solitary. But some shrink will. The only defense will be insanity."

"Will he succeed in the plea?"

"I hope not. When he went inside there was no doubt that he was sane but I hear that imprisonment is utter torment to him. It may well drive him mad in the end. I keep praying that his sanity will last until the trial."

"I would have liked him to die." It was a simple statement of fact. She would tell no one, not even Fenwick, how close she had come to killing him.

"I know."

They walked to the top of the cliffs with only the sound of the birds and the sea for company. The sun had set by the time they emerged from the wood and Nightingale put a mauve cardigan around her shoulders. As the sky darkened it took on the color of the wool and the sea turned to liquid pewter. It was he who broke the silence.

"Do you really need to wait until dark?"

She nodded.

"Why?"

"It's the best time to lay ghosts to rest."

"Does he still haunt you?"

"I dream of him sometimes."

He stepped closer, not touching but she could feel the warmth of his body at her back. His hand dropped to her shoulder. They stood, inches apart, the closest they had been physically since he had rescued her five weeks before.

Claire's words had stayed in his mind yet he had done nothing about them. He had told himself that it was because Nightingale was recovering and too fragile for him to risk the consequences of a clumsy overture. But when she had asked him to go with her to visit Mill Farm he had said yes immediately and hadn't bothered to question his motives. He didn't know what he felt for her but it wasn't indifference. Almost every night he dreamed of her, and he could recall every line of the purity of her nakedness in the moonlight when he had run from the woods to drag her from Smith's grasp.

"Penny for them?"

He blushed and turned away, leaving her to follow. Unlike Claire, she did not probe but changed the subject.

"Are you hungry? I have some pâté, fresh bread—oh, and some wine."

"I'll take some wine, thanks."

She spread out the blanket on the short grass and sat down with the elegance of a ballet dancer, her long legs folded beneath her. He sat opposite her.

"What aren't you telling me, Andrew?"

He hid his true secret behind another revelation.

"Smith tried to kill Griffiths, with a poison cake, would you believe it? The man's superiority complex knew no bounds. As if the prison would let a prisoner receive food like that. It shook Wayne though. He's going to be a valuable witness."

She sat up straighter and took a drink of wine.

"I wish we still had the death penalty." The hatred in her voice shook him and he distracted himself with a tub of olives.

"Want one?"

She shrugged and took one, biting into it, her teeth white in the deepening twilight. The moon rose over the woods. Nightingale stood up and walked to the cliff top.

"It was just here." She sounded amazed. "How could anything so terrible happen here?"

"No, you're in the wrong place. It happened further along to your left, at least a hundred meters. I remember it exactly."

"I wasn't talking about Smith. This is where my aunt fell. She died down there."

"I'm sorry."

"So am I. In the village they say she threw herself off. I don't think that's what happened." She inched toward the edge until her toes were level with it, then peered over. "I think she just didn't save herself."

For a moment she wavered as if she had lost her balance.

"Nightingale!"

Fenwick leaped up and pulled her back from the cliff. She spun slightly and fell against him. Her body felt loose in his arms, weightless. Instinctively he gathered her in tight against his chest, holding her so close that he could feel the tremor that ran through her, like a wire under impossible tension.

"For God's sake," he whispered, his mouth close to her ear, "don't even think it."

He found that he was stroking her hair gently, smoothing it against the warmth of her scalp. She looked up, almost tall enough to meet him eye to eye.

"Would you care?"

He felt the heat of her, the firm long length of her thighs against his own, the subtle rise and fall of her breasts, and pulled away. Her face was pale in the moonlight, her eyes wide and her expression impossible to read.

"Yes, I'd care very much, but it's not as simple as that." He touched the tips of his fingers against her lips as she spoke against them.

"I know, not for either of us. I'm not sure that I could learn to trust any man and you . . ."

"What about me?" He pulled back.

"It's time you accepted that you don't trust women either."

He was stunned by the simple truth of her words. Eventually her silence compelled him to speak despite his reluctance to reveal his feelings, even to her.

"I'm sorry . . . It's not your fault. Part of me wants you so much . . ."

"But?" Her voice was husky and she wouldn't look him in the eye.

"No buts about you, you're perfect. It's me."

It was her turn to pull away. She went back to the blanket and drank some wine, staring out at the darkening sea.

"I'm sorry, Nightingale . . ."

"My name's Louise, unless you're about to give me an order of course . . . sir." The words were sharp.

"Stop it! Nightingale suits you; it's a beautiful name. It wasn't meant as an insult . . . And we're not on duty."

She looked up at him, not caring if he saw the tears on her face.

"What are you afraid of? What's so frightening about me? You managed an affair with Claire Keating. Why do I repel you?"

"You don't, quite the opposite."

"So what's stopping you?"

"My feelings for you, that's what."

He watched her struggle to remain composed and was impressed when she said simply, "Go on."

He took a deep breath and looked up at the sky.

"Monique, my late wife, was the only woman I've truly loved. Before her, I'd known plenty of women, never at work, that's a line I wouldn't cross, but ever since university I'd been able to enjoy relationships with women without becoming too involved. I liked them all, some I was very fond of, but I'd never loved anyone before."

She was looking at him now with a lopsided smile on her face.

"Does that sound arrogant?"

"Very."

They were sitting cross-legged facing each other. Nightingale took a sip of wine and he followed her example, draining his glass while he watched her in silence. Eventually she said, "Go on, you were a stud who had women falling for you at the raising of an eyebrow and then you met Monique. How was she different?"

"I don't know." He hated this probing into his feelings but he was trapped and knew that he couldn't escape without giving some sort of explanation. "When we met I just, well, that was it. Love at first sight—Bang! I'd have done anything for her. We were married within six weeks, parents nine months later. We had four years together, that's all, before her coma. That lasted another five. While she was alive I always hoped that she might get better but of course that was stupid. She simply faded, then . . . died." His voice faltered.

"I heard what happened and I'm truly sorry." She waited for him to continue but he sat there, head bowed. "So you weren't interested in other women in all those years—that's a long, long time."

"But it's true, honestly. I had the children and my work. I sort of shut down on everything else."

"Including me." It was an unusually self-centered thing for her to say but he forgave her.

"Particularly you. In some ways you're so similar to Monique, not in looks, but your intensity and intelligence." He answered the question he knew she was too proud to ask. "I didn't love Claire, you know. She reminded me of what being with a woman could be like; fun, satisfying, uncomplicated."

"But she loved you. It was obvious when you were together."

There was silence and she could sense his guilt. She sipped her wine carefully but poured him his fourth glass. He was drinking more than he realized.

"Where does that leave us?" She resisted reaching over to touch him as she asked the question that had really brought her to the cliff top.

"I don't know. We work together and there'd be no such thing as a casual affair with you. I wouldn't want to hurt you . . ."

"Or be hurt by me."

He nodded, unable to meet her eyes. She remembered Amelia's words, about the choice between brief love and none at all, and her arguments back. She could hardly criticize him for a concern she had so recently shared. But she had overcome her fears; they had vanished in that sweet moment when she had smelled the grass and known what it meant to be alive.

Selfishly she had hoped that bringing him here would remind him of how close she had come to death and make him realize his feelings for her. She had succeeded in part, but it hadn't been enough. A chill wind rose up over the cliff and across them. A cloud passed over the moon, followed by others crowding in from the west.

"You mustn't leave the Force."

"You're changing the subject, Andrew."

Where had he heard that before?

"You think you have all the answers?" His tone was accusing.

"No, I don't. I have no idea where a relationship with you might lead. The idea of it frightens me. You're not the only one who's used to being in control, you know." She poured the last of the wine into their glasses and took another sip of her own.

"All I know is that what I feel for you is the most honest and natural feeling I have ever had in my life. I'm prepared to take the risks. The question is, are you?"

She took his hand loosely but remained silent. He needed to make his own decision. If she tricked or badgered him into submission whatever grew between them would be based on a false foundation.

"Perhaps I don't have your courage after all."

He said nothing else for a long time, staring out to sea where the milky phosphorescence of the waves was darkening as the moonlight faded. A spot of rain fell on their joined hands then another.

"We'll get soaked if we stay here." He rose to his feet and started to pack the uneaten picnic away. For a long moment she sat still on the blanket but when he lifted his side she stood and helped him to fold it. When their hands touched he gripped hers tightly.

"Do you know what you'd be getting into, the rumor, the potential impact on our careers, let alone putting up with me and the children? I'm a widower, it might not work."

So he could still feel Monique's shadow.

"I'm prepared to take the risk."

The shower turned into a full West Country downpour as they stared at each other. He was swaying slightly.

"I think I've had a bit too much wine. How much did you drink?"

"About a glass."

"And the bottle's empty." He looked her full in the face. "I'm not going to be able to drive."

"I know," she smiled at him, "but fortunately there's a very nice place nearby that will be able to put you up for the night . . ." He frowned in protest. "And it has several serviceable bedrooms."

At least he had the grace to laugh. They turned and walked together away from the precipice and back through the woods to Mill Farm.

COUNTY LIBRARY
TILLAMOOK, ORE.